# When Stars Align

Carole Eglash-Kosoff

authorHOUSE®

AuthorHouse™
1663 Liberty Drive
Bloomington, IN 47403
www.authorhouse.com
Phone: 1-800-839-8640

First published by AuthorHouse 2/18/2011

ISBN: 978-1-4567-3889-1 (e)
ISBN: 978-1-4567-3888-4 (dj)
ISBN: 978-1-4567-3890-7 (sc)

Library of Congress Control Number: 2011901538

Printed in the United States of America

Cover design by Barbara Kosoff.

This book is printed on acid-free paper.

*This book is dedicated to my grandchildren, and all of their generation, in the hope that they will leave our planet a more equitable and healthier place than we are leaving them.*

## Critiques from early readers:

*I am emailing to tell you how much I enjoyed your book, Moss Grove (When Stars Align). Somehow the book landed on my desk and I decided it was fate telling me that I should read it. I'm glad I did. The characters were so well developed, the story compelling, and your writing style had me turning page after page. Congratulations on a fabulous book.*

*Lonnie Quinn, CBS Television, New York*

*WHEN STARS ALIGN is beautiful. I felt like I was right there with the people—the rich characters. I could see them, feel the depths of their feelings and appreciate their circumstances. The story flowed and carried my spirit with it, often shaking me to the core. I loved the narrative and voice of the author. The historical references were educational and put everything into context. Addressing such unfortunate hatred, bigotry and man's inhumanity-to-man is courageous. Balancing those atrocities with stories of kindness, humanity, love, unity, family, cooperation, beauty, and mutual respect is genius. I hope there will be a sequel.*

*Victoria Dahan, Spain & California*

*More on the Web Site: www.whenstarsalign-thebook.com*

*Moss Grove*

# Prologue

The setting sun drifted across the rutted dirt road grooved from repeated attacks of rain, hooves and wagon wheels. Small huts lined one side erratically, grey plumes of smoke stretching skyward from them, anxious to leave the noxious odors and poverty that gave birth to their temporal existence. The main house, the Master's home, Moss Grove, was another hundred yards away, concealing itself from the squalor that was so necessary for it to function.

Rose's body ached as the small buggy lurched first one way, then another, seeking purchase from the mud and slurry that slowed its journey. Her strength still wasn't up to the six hour trip so soon after giving birth. She nestled the unfamiliar tiny breathing mass in her arms...a baby boy, blue-eyed, with soft downy mocha skin. She hadn't stopped staring at him since she gave birth four days ago. Born from so much pain and shame it was almost as if God was apologizing for the anguish he'd bestowed on her. She wanted to hate that part of the child she recognized in the father, the long fingers, the arched strong eyebrows, but most of all those electric blue eyes that stared at her in an unnerving fashion from the first moment they opened and looked into her eyes. She would never forget being thrown onto the ground, her legs being pushed apart and staring into the icy blue eyes of Henry Rogers. Only a few years older than her, he was strong and arrogant, as he forced himself into her. He was also white. She tried to scream but he slapped her. Seconds later he let out a gasp, stood, and smiled as he climbed back onto his horse. He left without a glance or a word while she lay there, crying at the pain and frightened by the blood and dirt spotting her thin cotton dress.

Rose had been away from Moss Grove for more than a month. Massa' Rogers, Moss Grove's patriarch, had ordered that she be sent away to have this child that was such an embarrassment. She would have preferred to stay in her small cabin in Moss Grove's slave quarters. She'd be with people she knew but no one asked nor cared about her preferences. She had been put into a wagon and taken to the home of Massa' Rogers's kin near Baton Rouge to bear him a nigger grandchild, for Lord's sake. The servants there had treated her kindly. They set her in a room of her own in the back of the house. It was clean and dry and even had a real glass window. It was more than she'd had her entire life and when it was time for the baby to come out they fussed over her as if she were their own kin.

As the small buggy and its cargo rode closer to the house it pulled to a stop. Two women waited at the side of the path. Rose recognized the slightly taller one. It was Sarah, Moss Grove's house Mammy. The other, a slave woman that Rose had seen but never met, was a little shorter, a little more bent, stood next to her, head and shoulders cloaked in a shabby black wool shawl. Both women looked grim as their sad eyes tracked the buggy's slow approach. The last embers of the day were the only light illuminating the scene.

"Rose! How you feelin'?" Sarah asked gently, moving closer.

"I be fine, I guess. I'm not sure what to do with this little package the Lord Jesus brung me."

"Ain't no need to worry, youngster. Hand him to me," Sarah said, reaching her arms up.

"I don't wanna let go of him. He a part of me. He look at me and he knows I is his mama." Rose's voice began to quake as words and tears mingled in her throat.

"Rose, just give me the baby. You too young to even produce milk for him. He need a strong teat and someone who know how to care for a new born."

"I learn, Miss Sarah. I learn quick. You know 'ah is bright."

"You'll have more. Big, strong 'uns. When you're older and you'll have the baby's daddy to help."

"But I carried this un'. This 'un is mine….mine," Rose pleaded.

"Rose, go back to your cabin and forget this baby. Massa' Jedidiah has other plans for him."

Sarah nodded to the driver. The man stood and with a gentle firmness he took the baby from Rose's grasp and passed him to Sarah. He hated being involved in these women's troubles. All that cryin'. The infant began to wail at the events he shared but would never comprehend. Rose's body shook, every nerve electric, unable to catch her breath. Her new son was being taken from her. She thought she might die giving birth and now she was almost sorry that she hadn't.

Sarah stared back at the young black slave girl. She understood what Rose had gone through to bear this child but she had her instructions. She passed the baby to the woman who watched silently and would act as a mid-wife and surrogate mother and whose breasts would nourish the infant.

The wagon turned and headed back toward the slave's quarters. Rose watched the two women trudge slowly away from her toward the house, holding her son against the evening's chill and muffling the cries that grew more muted each step away from her.

A horned owl left its perch, disturbed by the noise below. As it soared over the trees seeking an evening meal, its mournful sounds blended into a plaintive duet with the infant's sobs.

Soon the wagon stopped and the driver ordered Rose to get down. The young girl was inert, unable to move.

"Get'cha self down, ah has to get up early and head back to Baton Rouge," the driver said.

The young girl obeyed as if in a trance and squatted on the ground where she landed. Her body hung motionless in the black moonless night as her soul screamed with the maternal hunger of eons. She had lost her first born child.

# Chapter One

A mixed child, a tiny colored baby, had come to Moss Grove. He was neither white aristocracy nor was he a nigger. He was colored, the offspring of two different races and two distinct cultures. He was born from a callous violent act and his presence would bring changes to the plantation's serenity equal to those that were cascading across Louisiana and the nation beyond.

All his life Jedidiah Rogers had avoided mixing with his slaves and except for a few nights carousing with friends that became too much liquor and too little sense at Gentlemen's clubs around the French Quarter, he was chaste. He wasn't pure, but he was circumspect! His wife, Ruby, had her own hot Creole blood, and he was certain she wouldn't hesitate to cut off his pecker if she thought he was sharing it with some hot chocolate pickaninny.

He had had to confront the realization that their only surviving offspring, Henry, still in his early teens, with barely enough peach fuzz on his face to shave weekly, had attacked an eleven year old slave girl working in the fields in the middle of the day and gotten her pregnant.

"Rose returned early this evening with the child," Jedidiah said as he readied himself for bed. Ruby, his wife, looked up from the magazine she'd been reading that had come all the way from France. She enjoyed looking at all the newest styles for 1849 even though they were no longer new by the time the news reached Louisiana. She and Jedidiah had been married more than twenty years and Ruby was used to sitting quietly while her husband unburdened himself from the day's travails. Her love for this tall, gangly man with his graying hair and deep tan from years in the sun, still stirred her inside.

"I only saw the baby for an instant. It's clear that Henry is his father. The child has the same deep blue eyes as our son. I was quite prepared to be stoic about his presence in the house but when the little thing looked at me, I was deeply touched. I hadn't expected such feelings.

"Are you listening to me?" he asked.

"I hear you, Jedidiah. We're in the same room and you were affected by seeing your first and only grandson. I can't imagine you not being touched."

"I was furious when I learned Henry had attacked Rose, one of the young black plantation slave girls. He raped her, right out there in the fields, in the middle of the day. As angry as I was, I thought that was the end of the matter. It wasn't. The nigger girl was pregnant.

"Every time I rode through the fields I'd get furious seeing this child-like girl working. It was as if I could see Rose's belly get bigger every day. She'd struggle to bend over the cotton plants and she couldn't drag a bag with that extra load inside her. It certainly gave proof to our boy's stupidity. I even beat Henry with a cane stick for his vile action. Taking liberties with a slave girl, not yet twelve! Can you believe that?"

"And now you have a grandson. Maybe not the one you would have wanted but we now have a young baby in our home. Henry is back at his Prep school in Alexandria, Rose is back in her quarters and Henry may never have to learn that he fathered a child."

"Don't be naïve. We can't keep the knowledge of this pregnancy from Henry. Moss Grove is a small family. We'll try and keep it quiet but don't expect too much. My God, Ruby. I remember when Rose was born right here at Moss Grove. You remember, don't you?"

"Of course I do," she said, setting the magazine down. "New babies here at Moss Grove are always special. We all came down from the main house and joined the celebration in the slave quarters. The house staff fixed extra platters of food and gave out extra blankets. Then the years just sped by. I didn't even know the girl started her monthly bleeding."

"Jesus, Ruby, I can't continue to punish Henry. Another few years and Moss Grove will be his."

"We probably did spoil him. But it's hard not to be lenient with your only growing child when your other children died at so young an age. I'm sure our Henry will grow out of it. He's a tall, handsome teen and I've seen how all the girls drool and stare at him. But I also seem to remember another sexy young buck a few decades back."

"Well, you must have either a great memory or an amazing imagination. Those days are more often distant thoughts now," he said ruefully.

"Jedidiah, blow out the candles. Come here. Let me take your mind off this matter. I assure you I can refresh those memories. You'll feel much better in the morning."

He smiled at her, pressed his fingers around the small candle tapers lighting the room, and joined her in the big bed. He moved under the goose-down covers and reached for the soft skin of this woman who had always possessed a magical ability to banish the daily clouds from his life.

The arrival of their first grandchild, especially being a son, was touching Jedidiah and Ruby deeply. They named Moss Grove's newest addition Thaddeus, after a brother Jedidiah never knew. That boy had died in childbirth and Jedidiah remembered the black covered mirrors throughout the house while his mother's cries filled every room.

He would have much preferred a white grandson that he could parade proudly. But even this colored infant meant something. He had begun to believe he'd die without knowing whether a Rogers would continue to own Moss Grove. He hated to imagine this house he'd spent his life in, and the fields he rode through each day, belonging to someone else. Henry was young but if he didn't eventually marry and have a legitimate heir, everything could be lost.

Jedidiah knew he was breaking a number of cardinal rules and more than a few laws by bringing a mixed colored baby into the house. He didn't care. At this point in his life he felt free to bend the social mores of Louisiana and the south.

Jedidiah and Ruby decided that Sarah and Jacob, who ran the house, and were childless, would be the perfect parents. Ruby knew that they had always wanted a child. She and Ruby would often discuss it in those quiet moments when no men were around. This baby would be a godsend to them and it would allow the boy to be raised in the comfort of Moss Grove where both elder Rogers could surreptitiously enjoy watching the boy grow.

Ruby knew they couldn't appear to be raising Thaddeus themselves. She just wanted to have the boy close where she and Jed could feel connected. She'd stand in the corner of the room and see Sarah cry as she held the tiny milk chocolate boy with blue eyes in her arms. She'd even seen a tear in the corner of Jacob's eyes. God had finally sent them a child they could love.

The rest of the household staff reacted as well, sharing the small accomplishments of young Thaddeus learning to crawl and stand and take his first steps. A new and gentle warmth pervaded the house as all the blacks watched this unlikely emotional bond between the white masters of Moss Grove and an energetic, gurgling colored child.

Ruby, enjoying the presence of a baby in the house, was also pleasantly shocked at the change in her husband's demeanor. Jedidiah had always been strangely color blind. She knew he loved her in a deep, unquestioning way. Now he was doing the same with a colored grandchild that most white men would have rejected as being 'soiled.' He was truly a special man who she had chosen to love. It had been a good life although she hadn't realized how much she'd missed not having a grandchild to spoil.

Thaddeus was beginning to fill so many chasms in so many lives. More than once she'd see her husband, standing in a corner of the room, watching the baby as he slept or played. It made her regret that they'd never had more than one child survive into adulthood. She rarely forgot the two baby girls who had died, the first from yellow fever, the second from malaria. Both before they reached their fourth birthdays.

The schedule of the manor was soon dictated by Thaddeus' naps and meals. And before the child was even old enough to read Jedidiah and Ruby had pulled out books stored away in the attic since Henry's childhood.

"See, Thaddeus, A is for apple," Jedidiah said, sitting in his favorite chair, Thaddeus squirming on his lap. "And this is a dog. Can you say 'dog'?"

"Jedidiah, the child hasn't even learned to say 'mama' yet," Ruby laughed, standing in the doorway.

"Not to worry! Within a year I'll have him saying 'Moss Grove.'"

The presence of a grandchild had given them renewed energy. The laws that prohibited blacks and coloreds from learning to read weren't going to apply to this relationship.

Rupert Rafferty and his son, Abner, were Henry's only confidants at Moss Grove. The boys often spent their spare time together, being the only two white children on the plantation. Abner was two years younger than Henry. He bore a face scarred with pimples from a case of childhood measles that almost killed him.

Henry enjoyed being around both Abner and his father. He found the elder Rafferty far less critical than his own father as he learned to ride and shoot. Henry was afraid of his father…a fear mixed from equal measures of awe and respect more than with love. His sire could teach him about cotton and managing a plantation, but growing up was a lot more than that.

"Can you imagine my father taking a horse whip to me like he did last year?" Henry recalled as he and Abner rested their horses by a creek and lit up stolen Cheroots from the box in Jedidiah's library. It was a warm muggy day and Henry was glad to be back at Moss Grove and away from the rigid days of his Alexandria school.

"What was he so riled about?" he continued. "She was a cute little nigger girl, for God's sake, and I had a hard-on. She was the closest thing available and fucking her was so much better than using my own bedcovers." He paused to let the smoke from the small cigar circle drift away.

"My old man is clearly getting dotty in his old age. Do you know he's even taken the little bastard child into the house to be raised by the kitchen help. Well, it don't mean a plug fuck to me. I'm not even supposed to know he's my bastard."

Abner remained silent. His father had often reminded him that while he and Henry could associate with one another, Henry was in a privileged position. He was not to be criticized nor encouraged. Abner had had his own skirmishes with young black field girls delighted to bed the overseer's son. But these episodes were voluntary and he had no intention of mentioning them to Henry.

Ruby had insisted that she and Jedidiah spend a few days in Natchez. She needed to get away from Moss Grove and refresh herself with the gaiety of a bustling city. New Orleans was too far and Baton Rouge was small town dull. Natchez could be fun. It was the intersection of the river and wagon trains moving goods to the east. Hordes of settlers passed through heading west to new fertile lands in Missouri and Kansas.

They could have taken one of the paddle wheelers north but decided, instead to go by wagon. Jesse and Sarah would travel with them to ensure their comfort.

At the last minute Jedidiah invited Henry to join them. Ruby was glad. She hoped it would ease the tension between father and son that had existed since Thaddeus came to live in the main house.

"So many people," Ruby gaped. "Seems a whole lot bigger than New Orleans."

"I don't think so. It certainly isn't as lovely and I would never have met anyone as beautiful as you in this place," Jedidiah said, as he looked out the window of their hotel while Sarah and Jesse unpacked their things. He was rewarded with a loving smile from this woman he'd loved for so many years.

They spent a quiet evening together, dining in the hotels large dining room.

"I'd like to do some shopping tomorrow if neither of you gentlemen has any objection."

"I have a meeting with a broker to see whether there might be any advantage in shipping our cotton through here rather than New Orleans. There are more and more factories in the north looking for material," he said before turning to his son, sitting taciturn through the entire meal.

"Henry, would you please escort your mother?"

"Father, shopping?" he moaned. "I'd rather sweep out a stable than watch women try on clothes."

"Natchez is an unfamiliar city and I'm not comfortable having her move without an escort," Jedidiah said, his voice rising as his frustration with his teenage son re-emerged.

"I'll be fine," Ruby interrupted, hoping her two men wouldn't argue.

"I'm sure you will be," her husband insisted, "But I've asked our son to show some diligence and respect to his mother even if it means inconveniencing himself with a task he considers unsavory."

"Alright, father, I get it. You find a reason to not accompany your wife, so you've delegated it to me."

"I think we're all tired from the long ride," Ruby stood, knowing this had to end before their chasm deepened.

Henry and Jedidiah were both sullen as they found themselves alone for breakfast the next morning. Ruby was still in her room.

As the nattily attired black waiter approached the table to take their order there was a loud commotion passing just outside the hotel. Henry rushed to the window.

"Father," he shouted, causing everyone in the dining area to turn. "I believe it's a lynching. They've got two niggers in chains and a bunch of surly looking fellows are dragging them along."

"Lynching? You southerners are barbaric," one man stormed, obviously a visitor from another city.

"Justice bein' done swiftly, more than likely," said another.

Breakfast was forgotten as voices rose in defense and against what some viewed as vigilante justice.

"I'm going outside to watch," Henry shouted as he rushed toward the outside doors.

"Don't," Jedidiah said as his rash son disappeared from view. Reluctantly he stood and followed.

Outside a small crowd had gathered near a hastily erected simple scaffold. Two young blacks stood, tied together, bloody, their eyes glazed and terrified by this white jeering crowd. Some swore while others threw stones or sticks and laughed.

Jedidiah found his son standing off to one side, smiling and enjoying the spectacle.

"What these niggers do?" a voice asked.

"Their wagon splashed mud on my wife," a short middle age man retorted, as he pulled on the ropes that held his victims together. The man's eyes were red from heavy drinking, perspiration dripping down his cheeks while the nerves in his forehead throbbed.

"We didn't know," one of the Blacks shouted.

"It was an accident," pleaded the other.

"We said we's sorry when he told us."

"Uppity niggers probably did it on purpose," said the disembodied voice of a white onlooker. But the words had come from Henry, grinning at the splendid excitement, caught up in the moment.

"Henry! Keep quiet! This isn't our concern," the senior Rogers demanded.

The crowd had become a mob and the protestations of the two young blacks were drowned out. A few minutes later nooses were put around their necks, tightened and pulled taut.

For a moment the crowd stilled, watching these two strong, vibrant young men writhe their final seconds. When it stopped, some stayed silent, while others cheered.

The bodies were doused with kerosene and set on fire. As the smell of burning flesh spread through the air some of those watching blanched and puked their morning's meal or their previous night's dinner.

Jedidiah stood. He was too old and too hardened by life to be shocked but he was furious at the pettiness that had cascaded to this wanton killing.

"I'm going back to the hotel," he said to his son. He turned away from the horror, his shoulders bent with sadness.

"I'll come with you. This has given me an enormous appetite."

Rose saw Thaddeus in passing from time to time. At first she'd try to just visit or find an excuse to be near the kitchen but Sarah had been very stern. Forget the child. Rose tried, she truly did, but in the small enclave that was Moss Grove, she would see him often. Each time the emotional hunger welled inside and she'd have to resist the urge to rush over and embrace him. Massa' Jedidiah would sell her right off if she did that, sure enuf'.

She cried when Massa' Jed had him baptized Thaddeus in Moss Grove's small chapel. Only a few people were permitted to attend the festivity and that didn't include any of the field slaves, especially Rose. She stood behind the smoke house, tucked near a hibiscus bush where she wouldn't be seen but she could still hear the Preacher's voice. She had hoped to name the baby, Matthew, after the father Rose had been told of by her mother. He had been sold before Rose was born and she'd never known the comfort of his arms. Now that name would have to wait for another time.

Her young son grew into an energetic toddler. She'd often see him playing with the young white children that visited but mostly she'd see him with the children of the house niggers…never with the scruffy offspring of the field hands. His light colored skin set him apart from the other darkeys and more than once she sensed they shunned him for that difference. Massa' Jed had made it clear that he'd sell any slave, field or house nigger, who spoke to anyone about Thaddeus' birth.

Rose's hatred of Henry Rogers would burn forever in her loins. The memories of him getting off his horse, grabbing her arms and throwing her down on the ground played over and over in her head. Some days she could still feel the cotton thorns pressing into her back as his body pressed down on hers. She remembered struggling and looking for help from one of the field hands but no one came. Henry hadn't smiled or even looked at her. His blue eyes just stared through her. She'd kill him one day…some day. He'd taken her youth and her innocence and he'd given her a son she wasn't permitted to love. And in the years since that fateful day her hatred hadn't ebbed the slightest. She had grown quieter and more withdrawn. Her emotions simmered inside her, unresolved.

She toiled through her daily tasks, mostly in silence, to the discomfort of those around her. Rupert Rafferty, the Germanic overseer, had made it clear that Massa' Jed's rule applied equally to her. She was not to discuss her pregnancy and Thaddeus' birth with anyone. But no one could control what she felt. Her yearning continued. If she could only just walk over to him, wipe his nose, kiss his bottom, or just hold him. Once she got up enough nerve to walk toward him when Sarah called out from the house for him to come inside.

It was unavoidable that he and Rose's path would cross. He'd look at her and smile, never quite understanding the tears in her eyes as she stared back at him, trying to memorize every feature as he developed from infant to toddler to full boyhood.

Now, years later, the events were still scarred pages in her memory. Rose was back in the fields picking cotton, her back sore by the end of each week, her fingers scarred with small cuts from the cotton boll thorns and living her empty toil-filled life.

"Rose, come here," Rupert Rafferty called out in his heavy accent, as he got down from his horse, and wiped his brow. It was a hot, humid day. She could see his shirt sticking to his body from perspiration.

"Sure is a hot day, ain't it?" the girl offered, as she set her bag down and stretched her back muscles.

"Hot and sticky," he replied, as he paused to take a long sip of water from the barrel. "I believe I have some good news for you."

"Good news? You sure I shouldn't be worried," Rose answered, dipping the scoop into the water to wet a rag and cool her forehead.

"Massa' Jed's arranging for you to marry. Now you can have a husband of your own and start a family."

"Who this man I supposed to share a bed with? Ain't anyone on this plantation I'd think was a gift."

"He told me he's been keeping an eye on the slave markets. He wants to find someone special for you. He still feels bad about what you went through. Most of you darkeys are mated at an earlier age but Massa' Jed wanted to give you extra time. That time's comin' soon," Rafferty smiled.

It had become obvious to both Jedidiah and Ruby that it was time for Henry to get a broader education and, hopefully, one which would instill some discipline. Young southern gentlemen were usually enrolled in one of the prestigious military colleges, where they could acquire the knowledge and manners that were so much a part of southern society.

"I received reject letters this week from both West Point and the

Virginia Military Institute," Jedidiah admitted. "I used every ounce of influence I had. I pulled in favors. Nothing! Neither school will accept our Henry. I'm beginning to run out of options. They don't come out and say it but Henry seems to have already acquired a terrible reputation. He's just too much trouble and too poor a student."

Ruby sat quietly, lifting her eyes occasionally from her crocheting, as her husband struggled with the problem. The relationship between father and son had become a testy one.

"The boy seems to have a complete disdain for learning. I've decided to enroll him at the East Tennessee University. It's over in Knoxville, Tennessee. It's a second tier school but given Henry's history, it's the best we can do at this time. It will at least serve the purpose of getting him some additional education and, God-willing, some maturity."

Henry's departure for Knoxville that fall should have been a time of collegial farewell but he left with a simple kiss on his mother's cheek and a formal handshake with his father. He wasn't at all unhappy about leaving Moss Grove. His self-confidence would be seen by most as sheer arrogance. He was eager to see what lay beyond the borders of Louisiana.

At East Tennessee he shared a room near the college with Philip Lunstrum. Philip's family owned a good part of Memphis and built most of the better homes. He was the youngest of four brothers and by reputation, the wildest.

"What's there to do at this farm college?" Henry asked as he unpacked his bags.

"Depends what you like. There's a library and a gym and you can march like a toy soldier if you have the mind to. They even have sabers and guns to shoot."

"Not my style. Anything more exciting?"

Philip stretched on his bed and studied his new roommate. Tall, handsome, right kind of family! But it was clear to his practiced eye that this fellow would rather play than study.

"Well, there are a couple of bawdy houses that we're supposed to stay away from. They water their bourbon a little but not too bad. Sometimes there's a card game in the back but it can get steep and they don't like people who can't support their losses."

Henry stopped and smiled. "Now that's more what I had in mind. How about tonight?"

Philip stood, laughing, as the two new roomies shook hands.

They found Mandy's just beginning to get busy when they arrived. Mandy, herself, was short with long red hair that hung to her waist. She might have been a beauty when she was younger but now each year meant heavier makeup. If she was to continue to play the aging coquette she'd soon need a palette knife. Her bustier showed her two breasts overflowing her low cut dress. No one would ever use the words modesty and Mandy in the same sentence. By the time the two new friends left they had sampled the food, the bourbon, and several of Mandy's girls.

Like many southern colleges, Henry and Philip were able to find like-minded friends who shared their predilection for liquor, gambling and women much more than listening to mundane lectures. Henry found a little time for his classes but he and Philip and their other new friends could be found most evenings at Mandy's either drinking, playing cards or entertaining the girls who were also entertaining them. But the testosterone-laden teen also found pleasure in developing his body and afternoons he worked out conscientiously using the small gymnasium on the campus. He enjoyed admiring himself in the mirror. He would stand, light hairs glistening from the sweat of his workout, flexing his muscles and laughing to himself. He knew he was the envy of his lesser schoolmates. His six foot frame filled and he developed an agility that made him a good athlete. He excelled in fencing, horsemanship and boxing. He let his hair and sideburns grow long and he began sporting a neatly-trimmed goatee in the fashion of the day. It all became blonder from exposure to the sun while his blue eyes continued to flash with an unabated arrogance.

There weren't any women at the school but there were many at nearby plantations. Being the scion of Moss Grove gave him the cachet to be invited to the best homes. He was introduced to several prominent families including some with hot, sumptuous, yearning daughters, their cherries ripe for the picking, provided Henry's visceral lust was accompanied by an appropriate proposal of marriage. It was a contest pitting young feminine charm against a young man's unwillingness to make a commitment. More than once it all coalesced into a brawl over a progressing seduction by an irate brother or cousin. Milder men and respectable families soon learned to avoid this blonde Adonis from Louisiana.

Jedidiah Rogers sat in his study reading the weekly reports from the college headmaster. He shook his head in dismay. He'd repeatedly had to pay off some lad who'd been badly beaten by Henry or some girl debauched beyond reason. His patience with his son was nearing its end.

Jesse toiled quietly in the back brushing off the Massa's clothes and cleaning dirt off his boots. The dropping of a boot startled Jedidiah from his private thoughts.

"Ah's sorry, Massa' Jed," Jesse said apologetically.

"Not a problem, Jesse. Just thinking about Henry and a little about what the future might hold for us all. When I read the papers that come up from New Orleans I find myself getting more and more distressed."

Jedidiah wasn't about to discuss such matters with Jesse but the political compromises of the past two decades were being shredded. Adding states in pairs, one free and one slave, was no longer working. The economies of the North and the South were changing. Attitudes were hardening. The polarized opposites of slavery and abolition were anathema to one another.

Jedidiah Rogers sent Rupert Rafferty all the way to the slave market in New Orleans to verify the truth of what the slave broker had told them about this young buck available at a bargain price. Seems this huge black had nearly killed a man with his bare hands...unsettled the entire plantation. It was impossible for the slave to remain there and he was too valuable to kill. Given his age and his strength, the purchase price of twelve hundred dollars was well below the market, especially if the man could breed offspring in his image.

Rupert and one field hand had traveled nearly one hundred miles to see for themselves and purchase him for Moss Grove if they determined it was safe.

Faris was everything the broker had claimed. He was tall with rippled muscles creased against the dark metal chains that criss-crossed his chest. His eyes stared with a feral serenity that promised calm and violence at the same time. Rupert kept the chains on him as he completed the transaction and settled this huge man into the back of the wagon. Faris hadn't said a word. He just looked at them and through them as if he were somewhere else entirely. They headed slowly north past Lake Pontchartrain, grateful for the small breeze that eased the intensity of the sun overhead. The journey seemed to calm the man as he eyed this new country he'd been moved to.

"We've got a long ride ahead of us, Faris. Care to tell us what happened over in Alabama?" Rupert asked.

Faris stared out at the large body of water they were passing. It was the biggest one he'd ever seen. It took him several minutes to gather his thoughts. He understood that staying where he'd been probably meant hanging and he was glad to forget the events that had propelled him into new unfamiliar circumstances.

"Killed a man," he said.

"We know that," Rupert replied. "What we wondered was why? Are you just a troublesome nigger?"

Faris stayed silent for long minutes. Words didn't come easily to him.

"The man I killed...he was a bad man. Didn't mean for him to die! The man was a bully, stole from everyone, mostly food. He'd beat up some of the other men who were small and weaker. He liked to slap women around. I told him it needed to stop. But it didn't. One night he came up behind me with a knife. If one of the women hadn't screamed, I'd be dead."

The wagon continued on, the squeak of the wheels the only sound breaking the silence. Rupert understood what hadn't been said. Pulling a knife on a man the size of Faris wasn't a smart thing to do. Faris had apparently knocked the weapon away and flung the man across the ground. The man's head met a boulder and that was the end. There would be no more bullying.

Rupert felt the size and strength of the man chained behind him. Faris could do well at Moss Grove. Concentration on growing cotton was what mattered but there was always a need for a strong young buck. Rupert knew this man would be perfect for breeding and Rose would be an ideal mate. She would submit, she might even be pleased. But she was property, after all, and chattel didn't have a say in the matter. Rupert tried to explain that he was not only being brought to Moss Grove to work but also to sire children. The plantation's Massa' had even picked out a woman for him but he got no reaction. The chained slave retreated back into silence.

Faris was the biggest man Rose had ever seen. When she first laid eyes on him she was terrified. There was a quiet but dangerous quality he exuded. He was like some huge wild bear, black, dark and with deep set eyes that looked warily at every stranger.

Rupert set him to work the next day. Faris could clear the largest boulders by himself off a two acre spread in one day, nearly twice what two men could do. The other field hands avoided him if they could. Rumors of his past spread quickly and no one wanted to offend this new addition.

When Rose stood next to Faris for the first time she felt as if she was in the shade of a giant oak. She looked up and sensed gentleness in his sad eyes. Her tiny hand was swallowed in his enormous palm and a soft tenderness pervaded them both. It was as if they were two broken pieces made whole when they were joined together. Neither of them objected when they were told they were to wed. If it wasn't love, it was something that could heal scars. Their vows were short, just enough words to legitimize their union before God.

They were moved to a slave hut near the end of the row and given two extra days to consummate their relationship. Rose was frightened. Except for the rape, she had never been with a man, and that experience had been so ugly she feared that anything comparable had to be equally painful. Faris had been with women often. They were eager to test out the size and stamina of this big, strong, black male. Too often, however, the women found the experience disappointing. Faris would climax, turn over, and fall asleep.

But this wasn't the same thing. Rose and Faris were both wary, unsure of themselves and how their new partner might respond. The first night they laid down, turned their backs to one another and immediately went to sleep, afraid of what might happen if they faced one another. It wasn't until the third evening when their hands touched and their eyes met. Slowly they embraced with no words passing between them. Long minutes passed and the heat between them rose as Faris grew hard and Rose felt her nipples and her entire body react. Without even lying down the physical urge within them both exploded and their embrace took on a new urgency. Later, they lay down on their bed, holding one another so tightly they might even succeed in ousting the ugliness of their world.

Within months it was clear that Rose was pregnant once again. This time, however, it was with a contentment she had never before experienced. Rose was tiny and as she approached full term she knew this birth would be difficult. Her water broke as she was coming back from the field on a hot and humid day. She was carried to their small shack and made comfortable while others went to fetch the midwife and heat lots of water.

Rose recognized the woman who entered her cabin. It was the same short, bent crone who had carried Thaddeus away that unforgettable night three years earlier. Their history was shared in their eyes and rested silently between them. The woman asked everyone to wait outside and pray as the young mother gasped deep breaths and pushed, hour after hour, alternating sleep with unbearable pain. Soft words of encouragement echoed in her ears. Cool cloths were put onto her forehead as she hovered between life and death. Faris stood nearby with some of the other field hands, ready to help, but understanding that this was women's work. He was unaware of his wife's slim grasp on this life.

But Rose wasn't ready to leave this world. She still had a score to settle and she squeezed the hand of the woman next to her, willing the child forward. Long hours later, the baby took its first breath and Rose's pains finally began to ease.

Faris would never be told what had happened to his young wife years earlier. No one wanted to consider what unleashing that tale might engender. When he was allowed to enter, he just stared at his wife and new son, wrapped in a blanket, lying in Rose's arms. Faris cried, openly, for the first time in his life. He now had a family, like other men. He loved this tiny woman who had become his wife. And, together, they had a son. He had a son. This tiny infant had sprung from his seed. God had done a good thing this day.

The child would be named Matthew. No one would be able to object this time. The infant was as black as his daddy, with lung power that announced his arrival with gusto.

The Sunday after his birth, Matthew was baptized in the plantation's small chapel. The baby was a miniature of his father with wide flaring nostrils, black soulful eyes and hands that might take two years to grow into. Most of the family of field slaves had bathed and put on the one outfit they saved for such days. Rose had been given a hand-me-down dress from Miss Ruby's closet. It was a little frayed but she wore it with a dignity far beyond her station in life. Even the house slaves were encouraged to attend.

Rose and Faris and their new infant son were seated in the front row when Jesse and Sarah entered holding young Thaddeus by the hand. Sarah's grip on the boy's hand made it clear she was uncomfortable with the entire ceremony as a murmur swept through the small crowd. Rose turned at the noise and stared. Her eyes reddened and her hands shook at this unexpected coming together of the two so very different half-brothers to which she had given birth.

The service continued as Rose, Faris, holding a swaddled young Matthew stood and allowed the minister to proceed with the Baptism to the gathering's satisfaction. As they returned to their seats, Thaddeus shook loose of Sarah's grip and walked forward to see the new baby. Those assembled stared as this light colored toddler walked past them laughing. He stuck his finger into the infant's outstretched hand. Matthew stared up at this new face smiling at him. He closed his fist and held tight.

"Look," Thaddeus laughed. "He got a strong grip."

"Yes, he does," Rose smiled. "He likes you."

The two looked at one another as Matthew gurgled happily. Thaddeus smiled, Rose and Sarah smiled, and laughter filled the church mingled with silent murmurs of a shared secret.

# Chapter Two

A small crowd of field slaves gathered behind the unfamiliar wagon and followed it as it left the main road and moved toward the main entrance to Moss Grove. Two white men sat in front. In the back a frail black man sat, chained and manacled.

Jedidiah and Jesse heard the noise from their upstairs sitting room. At the window they saw Sarah offer water, first to the two men up front, and then to the man in back who made it clear with his eyes he'd had nothing to drink in a long time.

"You get the hell away from that nigger, woman," one of the drivers shouted as he hit Sarah's arm and knocked the ladle filled with water from her hand. Jesse and Jedidiah hurried from the room and down the stairs.

"Who are you men?" Jedidiah asked as he emerged from the house.

"We track runaways. This nigger been gone from his rightful owner for nearly three weeks. We found him up near the Mississippi border."

"You've got no right to treat him like an animal. Sarah, pick up the ladle and give the man some water," Moss Grove's owner ordered. "Now, if you gentlemen want something to eat before you go, we're happy to feed you. But, understand, if you eat, so does he. Otherwise, you will please take your wagon and get off my property immediately."

The two men hesitated and looked at one another undecided. Finally they mumbled their thanks, and stepped down from the wagon. In a few minutes Thaddeus came out of the kitchen with some bread and meat for each of them. The drovers grabbed their food and devoured it. It wasn't possible for the enchained slave to reach down for his so Thaddeus climbed into the wagon and sat down next to him. The smell of urine wafted up from the floor of the wagon. It was clear that they hadn't let him down to relieve himself. Thaddeus could feel the near terror of this man who had been severely beaten.

"My name is Walter," the slave said. "They going to kill me when they get me back, sure as God is my witness."

"I'll pray for you Walter, all of us will." Thaddeus wished there was something that could be done but he was still too young to fully understand why this man had been beaten.

"Ah thanks you for the food and water."

As the wagon pulled away, those watching stood silently, each with their own thoughts on the evil of what they had witnessed.

The holidays at Moss Grove were a time of relaxation and restoration for the families of whites and blacks. Crops had been harvested. What canning could be done had been completed and the jars had been stored on a shelf in the cool root cellar. Vegetables were stored nearby. Hogs had been slaughtered and smoked to provide meat over the winter months.

Heavy rains pelted the soil with an endless drumbeat. They washed the skies but left muddy pools in their wake. On the rare days when the sun managed to struggle through the grey mist, it was only for brief moments. It was a time of inconvenience and discomfort combined with the belief that good rain would mean good cotton harvests in the summer. It was a time for the land and those who lived from it to re-energize themselves.

Rogers prided himself on being a staunch Democrat. He had gone to the 1851 party convention in Baltimore as a favor to his long time friend, Stephen A. Douglas. Now, four years later there was another convention to attend and he felt the same reluctance to involve himself. The anger in the country had become palpable. The camaraderie and give and take of earlier conventions had given away to threats and vitriol.

Since he would be leaving in the morning, Ruby decided on having a more formal dinner than normal. It was special when the entire family could get together. She even invited the Raffertys to join them. Candles lit the tables as Sarah and the house staff served the meal in a deferential silence.

"You set a lovely table, Mrs. Rogers," Betsy Rafferty offered once Grace had been said. The overseer's wife was a God-fearing Lutheran woman whose entire life centered on her family and her Bible. Her English was still tinged with the harsh German accents of her youth. Social discourse made her uncomfortable, particularly with those she considered her 'betters.'

"Thank you, but the credit goes to Sarah and our house staff," Ruby said, spreading her smile past her dinner guest to include the black woman who had been her confidante for so many years.

"So, father! Heading off again?" Henry asked. He and Abner sat next to one another. Henry had grown a full-head taller than his friend and their lives were pulling them further and further apart.

"Yes, although I only need to travel to Cincinnati this time, much closer," Jedidiah answered, as he put his hand affectionately over his wife's. "Stephen Douglas and I have agreed to support James Buchanan from Pennsylvania. Stephen is more hopeful than I am that we can arrive at a resolution to our differences. Too much talk of war to suit me."

"I hear tell that Kansas is already having its own miniature war," Rupert Rafferty said. "They aren't just killin' blacks but whites are killin' other white folk. It's rather hard to imagine."

"Yes, the slavers are battling the abolitionists. The government is sending troops in to quell the violence."

Once he started talking about politics, Jedidiah had difficulty remembering he was at his own dinner table. Sarah looked askance at Ruby. Should she continue to serve the meal or wait for the Master of Moss Grove to take a breath? Ruby just smiled and cleared her throat subtly. Ruby's look made him realize he was talking far too long and embarrassing himself.

"Enough talk about politics! Sarah, our family and our guests are hungry," Jedidiah said firmly, a boy-like sheepish grin lighting his face.

Three weeks later a dispirited Jedidiah Rogers returned to Moss Grove. The convention had been as unpleasant as he'd feared. Every conversation turned into a rancorous shouting match. There was a great deal of curiosity about some new political party, the Republicans, and their nominee, General John C. Fremont from California. Votes were going to be split between three parties now…the Democrats, a fading Whig party and the new Republicans.

Buchanan might eventually squeak out a victory but Jed was convinced the man would be as ineffective as his predecessor…rather like teats on a boar hog. The man was a bachelor, for damn sakes. People wanted a family man as their leader.

Jedidiah's ride home from Ohio had taken him through most of Tennessee and Kentucky. Each night he'd find lodging. Sitting, trying to enjoy his evening meal, he'd encounter men becoming more and more bellicose.

"What happened to State's Rights? We're God-fearing people here along the Mississippi and we don't need any Massachusetts nigger-lovers telling us how to lead our lives or treat our property."

"The darkeys here in the South have a decent life...two hot meals a day, church on Sunday. It's a sight better than they had in Africa or chained in the hold of a ship."

The elderly patriarch listened but kept silent, anxious to avoid becoming involved and eager to return to the familiar comforts of Moss Grove.

The next few years passed easily. Cotton was king and those who were fortunate enough to own the lush lands along the Mississippi flourished. And as surely as the cotton seeds blossomed each summer and offered their harvest, Moss Grove thrived and Thaddeus grew. His blue eyes sparkled while he seemed to grow out of his clothes monthly. He continued to occupy his peculiar place in the plantation's hierarchy, never sharing its riches but continuing to read and learn. He was a part of Moss Grove's plantation family. Visitors, however, were not always quite as tolerant. Their children were used to running around and playing games but their parents had always admonished them to avoid the nigger kids.

Thaddeus was sitting on a stack of hay in the stable watching Luther, Moss Grove's farrier, rubbing down one of the horses when three older boys wandered in. Their parents were enjoying an afternoon at Moss Grove, sitting in the shade of the veranda. The men were visiting Jedidiah's new smoke house while the women worked at their needlepoint and exchanged thoughts on the latest fashions.

"What you doin', nigger?" the older boy asked Luther. This white boy was tall for ten. His hair was rumpled and his shirt was no longer tucked in his pants. He and his two friends had already raced through Ruby's prize rose bushes and tomato laden vines.

"Jus' rubbin' down this ol' mare," Luther said. "You boys shouldn't be in here. Could make the other horses skittish if there's too much noise."

"Well, who is that little kid sittin' over there?" another asked, pointing toward Thaddeus and walking toward him in a manner that continued to make Luther wary.

"You're funny lookin'. You a dark white kid or a colored boy?"

"Nobody ever tol' me. My name is Thaddeus," he announced, standing nervously.

"Who're your parents?"

"You boys leave 'em be and go play," Luther interjected, sensing trouble.

"Mind your own business, nigger, and get back to rubbin'," the ten year old ordered.

"Jesse and Sarah are my parents," Thaddeus said proudly.

"Then you colored and you ain't worth shit. Here, clean off my shoes."

"I ain't cleanin' your shoes. Clean 'em yourself!"

"You hear that, boys? Nigger colored kid won't do what a decent white person tells him to. I think this uppity boy needs a good lesson," he said as all three boys drew closer around the much smaller Thaddeus.

The oldest boy stood in the center, his young friends forming an arc around him. Their taunting got louder. The boy, feeling brave surrounded by his friends pulled a knife from his pocket and began brandishing it, back and forth, back and forth.

"I think I'll cut my name into your arm," he sneered. "And I've got a long name."

The other boys laughed but it was a nervous laugh. This was more violent than they'd planned. The knife-wielding boy jabbed first and caught Thaddeus on the shoulder as he tried to avoid the blow. Thaddeus flinched but threw a wild swing and caught his attacker on the cheek, sending him to the ground. The knife scattered away as the other two ruffians both joined in the melee. Eight young arms and legs tangled. Luther dropped his brush and rushed over, trying to separate them as Jedidiah, Rupert, and several of the visiting parents came running from the house.

"What's been going on here?" Jedidiah asked in an amazed voice.

"This nigger wouldn't do what we asked," the ten year old said defiantly as he was pulled, struggling, to his feet, tiny drops of blood dripping from his nose.

"Massa' Jed, I been here the whole time. These boys decided they was gonna' do Thaddeus no matter what and even pulled a knife on him," Luther said softly.

"Let's all go back into the house and have something to drink," Ruby said, arriving late, and trying to salvage what had been a pleasant afternoon.

"I think we'd better leave and get our children home where they can play in a safer environment," one of the mothers said, clearly upset that this colored boy wasn't going to be punished.

Shortly before Thanksgiving, Henry returned from Knoxville. In his wake was a coterie of male and female friends. He had ridden in on a huge roan-colored stallion he had won in a poker game, but only after having to defend himself against an accusation of cheating by the horse's previous owner. A short scuffle ensued. Henry ended up with a few scratches but the other man, too inebriated to focus, was forced to sober up with a broken nose.

Henry's horsemanship was apparent. He sat his horse, which he had named Trojan, like a Caesar crossing the Rubicon, with all the arrogance of a conqueror. He was no longer the boy sent off to school. He had matured into a man that would have to be reckoned with.

"Welcome to Moss Grove. We are so happy Henry has brought his friends," Ruby offered, as she and Jedidiah stood at Moss Grove's pillared entrance, each fluted column decorated with boughs of holly for the season.

"Please, come and sit. Have something to drink. It must have been a tedious ride." Ruby was in her element. Her longing for the active social life of New Orleans, in which she had been an enthusiastic participant, had never waned and only these brief holiday times allowed her to simulate those memories. She had worked the house staff long extra hours to ensure that each room was clean. Spiders, rats, and an occasional snake were known to make their way into the dark hidden crevices of seldom used rooms, nearby stables, and outhouses. Three privies were only as close as the prevailing direction of the breezes would permit. There was one for the ladies, one for the gentlemen and a third for the house slaves. Upstairs, however, Jedidiah had recently acquired small toilets which the servants would empty and clean each day. It was certainly a luxury not having to leave the house when nature called.

In the slave quarters it was a time to patch roofs, repair harnesses and mend clothes. Money was an absent commodity. Bartering was the currency of necessity. Women adept at sewing exchanged the shirts, pants and dresses they'd made for pots, tools or just plain chores cutting firewood and kindling.

Faris sat quietly as Rose spread ointment on his back and arms. Matthew slept in his tiny homemade bed in a corner of their single room hovel. Faris' size and strength didn't exclude him from the sore backs, small cuts and bruises that covered the legs and arms of the slaves who worked the fields. When the white bloom of the cotton plant was full and the plants were tall, picking them was easier, despite the weight and drag of the eight-foot sack draped around one's neck and shoulder that grew heavy as it was filled. When the boll was only partly open, however, it gave up its bounty with less enthusiasm. The sharp thorns adorning the plant pricked their adversaries with their own fury. Left untreated, these scratches often became infected and fetid.

"You quit movin'," Rose said. It was cold and damp outside but they had covered all the openings with blankets and she felt as if they were in their own private world.

"You keep rubbin' me like that and I'll be taking you to bed," he chided.

"Big talker," she said, slapping him gently on the back of his head.

Without a word he grabbed her hand and pulled her around, their eyes laughing. He picked her up and set her gently on their thin cotton-filled mattress. She feigned protest but her heart wasn't in it. She spread her legs apart as he lifted her dress and bent down to kiss the dark mound that seemed to him like God's own nectar. Rose's breasts were small and lost in Faris' huge hand. He grew hard quickly and Rose giggled as she felt his huge shaft press against her.

"You got enough down there to service all the women in Moss Grove," she laughed. "But you better not!" she added as Faris just smiled.

They took a long time with one another, enjoying this rare moment while the wind whistled just outside.

From Moss Grove's earliest days its patriarchs set aside one and two acre plots that the field slaves could farm on their own. Some families grew vegetables while others raised a few chickens or pigs. It was calming to be able to make your own decisions without a white boss watching from atop a horse. The field hands had to work the plots on the brief times that were their own. On moonlit evenings and on Sundays when regular chores were completed and one could relax, those who wanted a little more for themselves, kept working.

In the distant lee of the political storm that would determine their future, slaves could often trade their beans and collard greens for books. Rose had made several such exchanges, convinced that Matthew should learn to read and write. It all had to be done surreptitiously. Most plantation owners didn't favor educating blacks. It was a widely held belief that learning was unnecessary and might make slaves too difficult to control. A weekly church service singing the praises of Jesus and the plantation master were more likely to keep blacks focused on having the proper work ethic. It was a pattern Jedidiah's father had followed and there seemed to be no reason to change such things. The few slaves that had been taught to read and do simple numbers were in high demand to teach others. Most kept their skills hidden from their masters.

Moss Grove had been built by the Rogers just after the turn of the last century when Louisiana became a part of these new United States and land was open for development. Jedidiah's grandfather built the first Moss Grove and his father, Samuel, had made it larger and more elegant. Moss Grove was part of the grand south, profitable from cotton and full of the pleasures of the plantation lifestyle it cultivated. Further south, closer to the low lying lands around New Orleans, rice was the crop of choice for the swamp-like terrain. But here in the north central part of the state where the earth was rich, fed from small tributaries and rivulets of the eternally flowing Mississippi River, cotton was king.

Each Rogers, as he became lord of his domain, had been schooled in caring for his property whether it was land, horses or slaves. Blacks were property, bought and paid for with written Bills of Sale to document the transaction. At their owner's whim they could be treated no better or worse than a good hunting dog. Women could be raped, men beaten, families separated. These evils, and more, fueled the slavery argument. A few men, north and south, argued for humane treatment as an alternative to abolition but militant Southerners would brook no interference while the Abolitionists believed that anything less than the instant cessation of slavery was wholly inadequate.

Overseers were hired to be stern but not cruel. Whites and blacks had both heard stories of the cruelty of mean ignorant men given a little power by absent land owners whose only concern was tons of rice or bales of cotton and the profits they produced to support their life style.

The anger that was so bellicose in Georgia and the Carolinas was only an echo by the time it reached Moss Grove. Jedidiah felt a kinship with everyone at Moss Grove. They were property but they were also his family. He hoped he could live out the remainder of his life in the tranquility of the past half century but as one year passed into another even he became ever more dejected.

# Chapter Three

Moss Grove was located midway between Baton Rouge and St. Francisville in the lush land of Louisiana that benefited every few years from the overflow of the Mississippi River and the deposits of rich loam it carried with it. Its thirty-five hundred acres were shaped like a wedge with less than a hundred yards facing the river. Away from the river the land opened like the fan of a seductive Southern belle. Goods could be received or shipped up to Natchez where new fangled rail cars moved sugar, indigo, rice and cotton from the plantations to northern factories or south to New Orleans where strings of ships waited to carry their cargo to England and Europe.

The South had survived the collapse of cotton prices a decade earlier. Now, with war threatening, cotton was King and some of the richest men in America were Jedidiah's neighbors as prices soared and demand flourished.

Jedidiah Rogers sat at the long dining room table, the bright morning sun streaming across the veranda and through the large windows. It was early, but, as was his habit, he was enjoying his breakfast of strong French black coffee, heavily sweetened with sugar and chicory, hot cream and a fresh, warm beignet. Two years earlier he had managed to hire a Creole woman to oversee Moss Grove's kitchen. It had taken his wife's graceful Orleans accent and manners to convince the heavy-set woman to leave her urban comforts.

Celeste Montaigne was well-known in southern Louisiana for her bouillabaisse and etouffee. The woman was convinced she was the direct descendent of European aristocracy and she insisted on being treated with the utmost respect. Her father had been a French naval lieutenant professing aristocratic lineage while her mother had come to New Orleans from Jamaica. Ruby flattered the woman's ego, and her arrival had made Moss Grove's kitchen the envy of all its neighbors. Their previously bland meals now included all manner of highly seasoned sauces, and things with catfish and rice never considered.

The patriarch sat, quietly pondering the weather, its possible effects on next year's crops and whether war was more or less likely. It was difficult to tell Jedidiah's age. He was nearing fifty and in complete denial that he was any less virile than in earlier years. If he couldn't maintain an erection with Ruby, it had to be the brandy or the after effects of a heavy meal. Ruby, adroitly, always agreed with his assessment.

Jedidiah thought of his son, Henry, when, as if on cue, the strapping, blonde blue-eyed man entered.

"Good morning, father," Henry said as he casually scanned the silver dishes on the sideboard before fixing himself a coffee.

"Henry! I trust you slept well," Jedidiah said, eyeing his son in a totally new way. This golden bearded young man was a new person, someone he struggled to understand. He still felt a paternal pride in his son's bearing but intertwined with that pride were concerns about Henry's overt aggressiveness. Similarly Henry's respect for his father was limited more and more by their differing views on almost everything ranging from the possibility of war to the management of Moss Grove. The two men were tentative with one another, circling like fencers ready to thrust or parry as the situation demanded.

"Fine, thank you. Mother looked grand, didn't she? All my friends remarked how young and spritely she seemed."

"Yes, she seems to absorb new energy around the holidays. She relishes in the gaiety of so many young people visiting. Will your friends be staying through the new year?"

"One or two, perhaps. Most will move on to their own families."

"Any of the young ladies who rode in with you 'special'?"

Henry laughed. "Special as in a marriage way, you mean."

"Your mother certainly wouldn't mind hosting an engagement party here at Moss Grove."

"Not yet, father. I'm having entirely too much fun without the entanglements."

"I may need you to alter your pleasures sooner rather than later." His father's tone turned noticeably grave, the lines in his forehead deepening and reminding Henry of the plowed furrows he recalled as a young boy astride the back of his father's horse as they watched seeds disappear into the brown rich loam of the earth.

Henry sat across from his father stirring his coffee, a worried look on his face.

"We should consider an earlier return to Moss Grove for you and having you assume a greater role in its operations. I will be gone more and I prefer that the plantation continue to have a Rogers riding through the fields where he can be seen every day."

"Are you ailing, father?"

"No, I've been asked to add my voice to those in Baton Rouge and Washington who hope to avoid war."

"Father," Henry smiled. "I assure you, there will be no war. The northerners are all bluster. Almost the entire Army's officer corps are Southerners. Most are from Virginia or Georgia. There are even many from Tennessee where I attended school. Who would attack us?"

"They would find men. Much more critical is the reality that we don't have a single factory in the south capable of manufacturing adequate weaponry. What would our officers fight with?"

"My friends and I have discussed this at length, father. Rest easily. The French and Spanish will not forget us. They would prefer a separated, independent South. They will gladly trade our cotton for weapons. Are you growing soft in your advancing years?" he teased.

Jedidiah smiled at the brash young man grinning across the table at him.

"You still can't take me, youngster. Move your chair and I'll give you another try. Advancing age, my arse!"

Both men laughed as Henry moved closer and the bonding ritual of arm wrestling erased the friction of the past years. They were father and son, patriarch and heir apparent of Moss Grove's bountiful acres.

The years had been good to the older man. Many of his peers had already withered from one infirmity or another. But time eventually balances the scales and this morning Henry's youth forced his father's arm down onto the table for the first time. Their faces, beads of sweat evincing the effort they had both expended, didn't signal victory and defeat so much as it signaled an inevitable transition to the next generation. Afterwards, as they rested aching muscles, and Jedidiah rubbed his arm, they sat silently, their eyes linked more strongly than a steel chain, thoughts of the meaning of this small, but significant event, reverberating between them.

"Excuse me, sirs." A soft, deep voice broke the reverie. It was Jacob, the tall, lean, grey-haired house servant who had been a fixture when Jedidiah's father ran the estate. "May I bring you gentlemen more coffee and hot rolls?"

They both smiled, forgetting the recent muscle strain and regaining their composure.

"Yes, Jacob, thank you," Jedidiah said with a small nod.

Henry rose and walked to the window lost in thought. The sun's arc was beginning to bring the day's warmth. He stared at the morning's last drops of dew fading from the rose bushes he had helped his mother plant when he was only four.

Jacob returned, carrying a silver tray, steam wafting from small pitchers of coffee and cream. As Henry walked the few paces back to join his father he noticed another pair of feet trailing in Jacob's wake. It was a young colored boy, attired as a miniature Jacob, carrying a basket of baked goods. It was Thaddeus, tall, thin, walking erect, his blue eyes glued to the basket he carried and the back of his mentor, Jacob. The boy's pants stopped well above his ankles, evidence of the growth spurts that occurred more quickly than clothes could be altered.

It was the first time Henry and the boy had been this close and the cacophony of silent thoughts among the three adults was deafening. Only the boy was ignorant of the events in which he was a central character.

"Father," Henry seethed. "Is this your doing? Is all this paterfamilias talk simply an opportunity to mock me?"

"Rubbish!" Jedidiah fumed, as he stood up. "Jacob, send the boy back to the kitchen."

"Yes, Massa' Jed. Ah is so sorry."

"Wait!" Henry's voice rose, the veins in his forehead pounding like a Cajun drum. "As long as he's here I'd like to speak to him."

"Please, Henry, leave the boy alone. He has no idea…"

"No idea? Don't be naïve, father. Look at Jacob. He knows. He may have even brought the nigger bastard in here to vex me. Did you, Jacob? Is the lad here to torment me in front of my father?"

"No, Massa' Henry. Truly I didn't connect…"

"Henry, leave Jacob alone," Jedidiah rose, the morning's calm shattered, the arm wrestling already forgotten. "I'm sure...."

"Defending a darkey against your son? No wonder Moss Grove needs a new hand. Perhaps your commitments elsewhere will be a good change for everyone. Jacob...leave!" Henry ordered. "The boy stays. Boy, come here and tell me your name."

Thaddeus was nervous from the raised voices and the threatening tone of this blond bearded white man who beckoned him.

The steel blue eyes of the father and young son met. They were as identical and as different as males of the same species can be. Their sameness was in the genes they shared that gave them their temperament, their intelligence, and their survival instincts. They differed in their rearing, their education and the color of their skins. In this year, in this place, that mattered most.

"My name is Thaddeus," the boy said softly, his eyes retreating to the floor. Having to talk to white folks was something in which he had little experience.

"My name is Thaddeus, **SIR**," Henry corrected. "Hasn't Jacob taught you any manners?"

"Thaddeus, **sir**." The boy looked up over his bowed head, speaking with an undertone of bravado that Henry missed but Jedidiah recognized from when Henry had been that age.

"Tell me, Thaddeus, how old are you?"

"I'm ten."

"Ten, **SIR**." Henry corrected.

"Ten, **sir**," Thaddeus added.

"And your Mother. Who is your Mother?"

"Momma Sarah...**SIR!**"

Henry laughed. "Much better, you brazen scamp. Tell me, father, isn't Sarah a little old to have a ten year old?

"Leave it alone, Henry!"

"But father, a snotty nigger child before breakfast...what an entertainment."

"I'm glad you're enjoying yourself, Henry. But before you get too carried away, don't forget who this child's father is."

"Father, I know who the boy is. His presence is a pestilence to me. I don't know why you haven't gotten rid of this nigger brat and his mother all these years."

"I could give you a long explanation but I will just leave it that I choose not to. Leave it for now," Jedidiah said, turning his attention away from his son. "Thaddeus, go back to the kitchen."

Thaddeus stood frozen for an instant, looking from Massa' Henry to Massa' Jed, before bolting from the room.

This time Henry voiced no objection as he dropped into a chair, his eyes following the boy's exit.

"What does the boy know?" Henry asked.

"Nothing! He was taken in and he is being raised by Sarah and Jesse. Everyone was ordered not to say a thing and as near as I know that instruction has been followed to the letter."

"Get rid of him, father. His presence casts a permanent pall over Moss Grove."

"Perhaps you're right, son. And I've often thought about it. Your mother and I have even prayed on it but the fact is he's the closest thing we're likely to get to a grandchild and until you provide us something better we want to stay connected.

"He gives your mother and me great warmth. We lost two beautiful young daughters when they were just toddlers. You would have had two older sisters," he sighed mournfully. "We were extremely fortunate that you survived. There have always been so many diseases to contend with here in Louisiana.

"Thaddeus fills a gap in our lives. You'll just have to ignore him. Or, better still, get married and have children of your own. Sire a son that can inherit Moss Grove as you will inherit it from me. Surely among all your friends there must be someone you fancy and who fancies you."

"I will consider it." Henry said. "I will give it very serious consideration."

Among Henry's friends that had arrived with him at Moss Grove were Elizabeth Williams and her younger sister, Amy. The girls lived in Baton Rouge and only on special occasions were they able to visit their cousins, the Rogers. In past years the girls had accompanied their parents to share several yuletide seasons.

Elizabeth was going to her first debutante ball in February and would be 'turned out' to all of Baton Rouge society, small in number, but each family protective of its place in the local hierarchy. Despite the anticipation of the upcoming event, the flowering teenage girl cast covetous eyes on Henry as she had ever since her first awareness that boys were not an alien species.

No one would claim that Elizabeth was a pretty girl but the gawkiness and dissatisfaction with her appearance had diminished as her breasts developed and she could see her hips beginning to curve in sensuous ways. Her brown hair, however, was stringy, and then suddenly it could turn to a head of Medusa-like curls when the humidity rose. Still, her brown eyes widened with a covetous intensity when Henry entered a room. She practiced endlessly how to walk and sit demurely and how to hold an interesting conversation that a young gentleman might find entertaining. But it was Henry who most occupied her waking moments. She would have given him anything if only he wouldn't continue to ignore her.

At ten Amy still enjoyed being a tomboy and no amount of pestering from her parents or sibling would get her into a dress. Unlike her older sister, it was clear that she would grow into being a beauty if she ever chose to prefer it. Amy had a face full of freckles that rested atop a milky light complexion. Her bright red hair and an ever-present grin always seemed to foreshadow some form of mischief. Her green eyes seemed to be laughing even in the most serious moments. She cared nothing for decorum. Her mother, Sylvia, was constantly on edge, worried that her younger daughter might suddenly appear, covered with mud, or cuddling some stray animal, and create an embarrassment when she was entertaining Baton Rouge's small social cadre over afternoon tea.

Thaddeus had his chores to do every morning. He'd begin by feeding the chickens and collecting the eggs that had hatched. Then he had to bring water in from the well. It was hard work hauling up each bucket filled with water, dragging the bucket to the kitchen or the outside pot being filled, and heated, for the white folk's baths. After that, if it was warm enough, he'd sit along the river underneath a hundred fifty year old magnolia tree, imagining all the places that the river might take him. He'd bring one of the books from Massa' Jed's library. He knew he was supposed to ask before he took one but since the elder man never refused him, he rationalized that it was OK. Some of the books told of pirates and gold and adventure in the open waters beyond New Orleans.

"What're you doin' there, boy?" the soft voice asked, his imaginings dissipating in the breeze.

He looked up to see that it was the white girl he'd seen arriving with Massa' Henry and his noisy friends. Their arrival meant a lot more horses to feed, stalls to lick and hay to spread.

She had the brightest red hair he'd ever seen with bangs that fell onto her forehead and freckles that dotted a cherubic face. Her shirt and overalls had clearly been meant for a boy. Thaddeus had never seen any girl that looked so contrary but there was something about her green eyes that quickened his pulse in an unfamiliar way. The sun was behind her as she stood over him and the reflection made her look even more heavenly.

"Jus' sittin'," Thaddeus said, studying each feature carefully.

"Why ain't you doin' your chores?"

"I did the first batch already, 'sides, you ain't my mammy."

"Pretty sassy for a nigger slave brat, ain'tcha?" Amy teased.

"I'm not botherin' nobody…ain't no reason for you to hassle me," Thaddeus said, upset at the interruption to his privacy but strangely thrilled at the same time.

"I'm sorry. I'm jus' lonely. I'm Amy. We're cousins visitin' from over in Baton Rouge. What's your name?"

"Thaddeus! You should probably go find white kids to play with."

"They're all so dull and prissy. They'd rather play quoits or try on new clothes. Any frogs in this river?"

"Lots, but you've got to sit real quiet to get 'em."

Amy dropped down next to Thaddeus and the two sat there, waiting, next to one another. Amy could feel Thaddeus' eyes stare at her but as she turned her glance toward him, he just smiled at her.

"You sure you should be here?" he asked, nervous about being so close to a white girl. She smelled different. Do all white girls smell so good, he wondered.

Long minutes passed, the initial tense silence they each felt, slowly dissipating with their shared pleasure of finding someone new their own age. Their differences seemed to vanish. Neither the color of their skin nor their social standing separated them. Even their new sexuality was untested.

They watched as the small flies and mosquitoes hovered over the still waters that rippled lightly from the occasional breeze or passing boat. The cicadas sang in the trees overhead, their sounds blending with the lapping of the water against the shore as the river's busy traffic moved in both directions.

"That one's headed for New Orleans," Thaddeus said, pointing to the paddle river boat churning in the middle of the channel, steam pulsing from both its stacks.

"I've been to New Orleans," Amy said. "But only once. Sure is big."

"I'll go there someday when I'm older," Thaddeus said confidently.

"There's a frog," Amy shouted, as she jumped up toward the river, slipping on the muddy bank. "It's a big green one."

"Careful," Thaddeus cautioned, laughing at his new companion's enthusiasm. "You kin end up in that river and float all the way to the ocean."

"Don't you worry 'bout me," she said reaching into the dark water and finding herself sliding down the grassy bank. "Oooohhhhhh," she laughed as her rump and the riverbank collided.

"I'll getcha'," Thaddeus said as he stood and grabbed for Amy's hand.

At that moment, unaware that others had come looking for the young girl, a hand swung wide at Thaddeus' head, knocking him over.

"What the hell do you think you're doing, you black piece of shit?"

"Cousin Henry! Stop! Thaddeus was just trying to grab me from the water," Amy shouted as she grabbed Henry's other hand to pull herself up.

A crowd had gathered including Rose, Faris, Matthew, and Elizabeth, who had been on the veranda when she and Henry had first seen the two children sitting near the river. There was confusion and tension as Amy stood there muddy and dripping, her hair streaked with brambles. Thaddeus stood aside, his hand trying to cool the heat from the cheek that had been slapped with such fury.

"Amy, let me take you to the house and get you some dry clothes," Elizabeth cried. "You've no business playing with niggers."

"Don't be a prig, Lizzie. That was more fun than I've had being with your friends."

"Don't sass me. You're nothing more than a little brat," Elizabeth wailed as she strong-armed her younger sister back toward the house.

"Leave me be," Thaddeus said as he tried to wriggle from Henry's grasp.

"I'll take him," Sarah interceded. "He'll be taught a lesson."

"No", Henry commanded, his face red with anger. "That's the second time this boy has sassed me. He needs more than a lesson."

"There will be no lesson!" It was Rose's soft voice as she came forward and stared at Henry, all the vitriol of her soul fastening on the tall white man before her. He had changed. He was older and bigger. His eyes were still that sapphire blue she remembered as he straddled her in that field more than a decade ago. In other ways he was still the same. He was a white bully who took what he wanted at any time it suited him.

Faris was stunned at his wife's soft declaration and he hurried to stand behind her. But his huge presence was unnecessary. The years vaporized as Henry and most of the other blacks stood aghast at the scene they were witnessing.

Jedidiah and Ruby joined the small throng and hastened to make their presence known.

"Everyone back to work. Sarah, take Thaddeus with you. The rest of you, if you have chores, get to them…if not, go back and find something to occupy yourselves. Henry, let us all go back to the house and check on Amy. I'm sure she'll be fine with Elizabeth helping her."

Henry continued to stare at the black upstart boy and the small black slave girl from his past. Rose's intervention had taken him aback. A pox on them both! He pulled his eyes away uneasily. Then he ran his fingers through his hair, arched his shoulders, and strode off.

"Rose, why you do that?" Faris asked as he walked slowly back to the slave cabins with Rose and Matthew at his side.

"He no right to tar that boy, thas all," she said, not wanting to meet her husband's questioning stare.

"He a funny lookin' nigger, that boy," Matthew said. "He so light and I think he got blue eyes. Not many niggers I've seen that got blue eyes."

"You ain't seen many niggers, young 'un…you too young yourself to know what's common and what's not. I hear there lots like that in New Orleans," Rose added.

Faris looked at this wife he had shared his bed with now for six years and for the first time he wasn't sure he knew this woman.

"Those niggers mostly had white daddies, Rose," he spoke even more quietly than his usual soft tone.

Rose struggled to avoid his gaze. "Ah don't know nothing 'bout that, Faris. Ah got to get back to weedin' 'for that overseer Massa' get angry. You take Matthew." She moved away quickly, not wanting her husband or son to see the tears forming rivulets down her cheeks.

"Father, I've asked you to get rid of that child. He's trouble, real trouble."

"Henry, you're overreacting. The darkies that were there all agreed that Thaddeus was simply trying to keep Amy from falling in the river."

"And you believe them? With all due respect, sir, you are in danger of becoming an old fool. Of course they would tell the most favorable story to you."

Jedidiah fumed as his son's tone. "I'll not brook that tone from any man…not even my son. This is still my plantation and I will run it as I choose and I will believe whom I choose to believe. This matter is closed. I suggest you look to your guests." With that he stormed from the room.

The incident was set aside in the familial warmth of the holidays. The Williams sisters were the last guests remaining and they would be leaving the next day.

"I have a small present for you, Henry," Elizabeth said coyly as she presented him with a small wrapped package, a red bow neatly tied on top.

"I do hope you like it. I knitted it myself, although I'm not sure I'm very talented."

"A scarf! How lovely, Liz. That was very sweet of you," he answered, not sure he actually liked the gift. "And I have something for you."

She took the small box from his hand and opened it nervously. It was a pearl locket.

"Why, Henry, this is so beautiful. Would you help me put it on?" she cooed.

As Henry struggled with the clasp, he silently thanked his mother for providing him with the gift. Getting Liz a gift was something that hadn't even crossed his mind.

Baxter Williams, Liz's father, had sent up a box of cigars for Jedidiah with a note, "These are from Cuba, Jed. They tell me they're the finest tobacco. Enjoy!"

The next morning the servants loaded the wagon. There was a light dusting of frost on the bushes and both Liz and Amy were bundled up.

"One minute, Liz," Amy said. "I'll be right back."

"Where are you going? We need to be on our way,"

She was shouting to her sister's back as Amy scampered toward the stable.

Luther looked at her but said nothing. He tilted his head toward the back where the horses were stabled. Amy smiled and ran down the row between the stalls.

"Thaddeus," she smiled, out of breath, as she found her new friend putting down fresh straw for the horses.

"Miss Amy? What're you doing here?" he said, putting down the wood rake and trying to brush himself off.

"I didn't want to leave without saying goodbye and making sure you were alright. I think the adults all wanted to keep us apart after that river episode."

"Yes, they surely did," he laughed. They had drawn closer to one another. Thaddeus could feel her warmth and scent sending a tingling sensation through him. For a while there were no words but it wasn't an uncomfortable silence.

"I brought you a holiday gift," she said. "T'aint much."

He took the small package nervously. Thaddeus had received small gifts from Jesse and Sarah but it was always clothes. Miss Ruby and Massa' Jed gave him a book of poems.

He opened the gift, stared at the unfamiliar item, and then broke out laughing as he realized what it was.

"We both could have used this," he said as Amy joined him in the laughter. "I'll save it for the next time we decide to catch frogs together but in the meantime I'll put it somewhere special."

Amy's green eyes stared into the deep pool of Thaddeus' blue eyes.

"Friends?" she asked.

"Friends," he answered, as Amy smiled and ran back to the wagon.

# Chapter Four

Jedidiah Rogers sat in his upstairs study, sharing a rare morning coffee with his wife and reflecting on how much things had changed since his childhood.

"We have a good life, don't we, Ruby?" Jedidiah asked, half to himself.

"Jed, listen to you. You're sounding somber again," Ruby smiled. "Yes, it's a good life, a rich and happy life."

"And a prosperous one as long as people around the world need cotton. Rafferty wants to hire two more overseers to help him with the new acreage we'll be planting," he said as he stood to pour himself more coffee.

"I remember my father telling me how he'd bought the first parcel of Moss Grove for less than two dollars an acre. Then a second, much larger parcel became available when his neighbors decided to return to England. They'd lost one child to malaria and a year later, they lost their daughter to influenza. Damn diseases wreak havoc on young children and the doctors with their leeches are useless."

"I know, Jedidiah. I know! We lost two young 'uns as well."

"I haven't forgotten, Ruby. It never stops hurting, does it?"

"No, Jed. It's sort of a hole that never quite gets filled in."

Jed took a breath and continued, "You and I bought the last parcel...800 acres, the year after Henry was born. You were so nervous when I admitted we would have to borrow from a bank to finance the purchase," he laughed. "Ten years later we paid it off and celebrated."

Neither of them had discussed the episode at the riverbank. Ruby knew her husband was still upset with Henry and Henry continued to stomp around the house being curt with the servants and slamming doors unnecessarily. The New Year had come and after a brief Auld Lang Syne, Henry had returned to college. He had kissed his mother but avoided his father.

Jedidiah would be departing soon for another damned useless political convention where men would argue about the same things they'd argued about since he was a boy. They would be nominating someone to represent them in next years' 1860 elections. Jesse moved quietly around the room, selecting clothing to be packed for the upcoming trip.

Jesse had been with Massa' Samuel, Jed's father, and had seen the same changes but he wasn't asked to share his thoughts or opinions. Jesse understood he was almost invisible to white folks. He and Sarah had discussed it many times. It didn't make them angry. That's just the way things were. They were grateful to Massa' Jed for letting them raise Thaddeus. He had brought them such joy and they hoped the boy would have an opportunity for a different kind of a life.

"Jed, I hear rumors that six nigger field hands from over near the Arkansas border ran away with that Underground Railroad group. Is that true?"

"Heard the same thing but it's hard to know what's true these days. They should find that Tubman woman and lynch her from the nearest tree as a sign to any other darkey that thinks he can just up and skedaddle from his God-given responsibilities."

"But those northern lawmen are supposed to send 'em back. That's the law."

"Bein' a law seems to be irrelevant. That Fugitive Slave Law says you're supposed to catch runaways and put 'em in jail until they can be returned but there are so many free blacks in the north they just blend in. It's getting' worse, I tell you. Jesse," he said, turning aside, "Bring an extra coat, please, and an extra blanket. We could still have some cold nights on this trip.

"I tell you, Ruby, things were simpler when I was a young boy and my father was teaching me about the business of cotton. He knew every acre and tree on the property. His father had made him learn it all, including every Latin name. I never knew my grandfather but my father said that he was a dark, somber man whose beard scratched my father's young face in those years when men still found it acceptable to hug their sons. The men of those days were giants, melding divergent colonies into a nation. And most of them owned slaves."

Ruby sat, silently, looking out on her gardens. Jedidiah always got like this when he was getting ready to leave for politicking. She knew enough after so many years together to not interrupt or offer her own opinions.

"There is just too little courtesy these days. Everyone speaks with a strident tone. The north is overflowing with too many Irish and German immigrants fresh off the boat with no appreciation for our history. The Mason-Dixon Line that historically defined our states geographically had become a demarcation point for attitudes."

It was an early spring morning when Jedidiah Rogers climbed his favorite horse, Nellie, threw a last kiss to Ruby, and headed off from the comforts of Moss Grove. Jesse rode quietly behind him. His man-servant's grey hair and well-lined face gave evidence that he and the master of Moss Grove had grown old together. At the last minute, and with no prior discussion, Jedidiah decided that Thaddeus should join them. The young boy sat astride Bessie, a mule, well-packed with their needs for nearly a month. It carried a tent for sleeping as well as some food and the dress clothing the Massa' would need for the political meetings that were such a major part of getting things done.

The three spoke little during the journey. Jesse was not Jedidiah Roger's friend. He was a servant and his job was to make his master as comfortable as possible at all times. Besides, having Thaddeus along made him terribly nervous. The boy might say or do anything. This was his first trip from Moss Grove and over this distance and length of time it was impossible to predict how the youngster might react. None of these were thoughts he could share. It had always been enough that Massa' Jed had arranged it so the boy could be close, but neither man spoke of it. That would be unseemly. Each man had his role to play in this societal melodrama and crossing that invisible line would not be countenanced.

It would take more than a week for them to ride the eight hundred miles to Charleston, South Carolina. Within a day, the aches in Jedidiah's back and legs from being astride a horse all day reinforced his realization that his age was proving to be a limit on his dwindling stamina. It made him realize that he and his generation were becoming more and more ignored by the younger political hotheads who were infused with conviction, but ignorant of the ramifications they would be unleashing. Louisiana would be obligated to join with the other Southern states, whatever damn fool decision they reached.

Jedidiah had planned their first stop to be Mobile, near the center of Alabama. He could rest at the new Mobile Hotel. Jesse would find accommodations in the black section of town or at the stable for him and Thaddeus. Jedidiah intended to order some cast metal parts that his farrier needed to expand the Roger's family mausoleum. Mobile's metal industry was flourishing. Some Jewish manufacturers had come down from up north with a new process for firing the metal. It made the metal stronger and still cost considerably less. He didn't know many Jews. They mostly stayed up north. But if they were God's chosen people, he mused, it would be alright to trade with them.

The two night stay was refreshing. Over dinner the second evening he found two companions to join them who were also heading east. The conversation on the ride was convivial but the men were younger and eager to reach Charleston. They intended to meet some young women and celebrate before the business of the convention began. The two riders stopped only briefly in Columbus, long enough to rest their horses before continuing on. Jedidiah needed a full night's sleep to refresh him and a hotel bed was so much better than the ground.

As they approached Charleston, Jedidiah stopped his horse on a knoll overlooking the city and the three of them stared in awe as the sun reflected against the metal roofs spreading out below. The effect made the city look almost ethereal. Charleston was the Queen of the south and if there were to be a confederacy, this city would surely be its heart. Jedidiah hadn't been to Charleston in nearly twenty years and he was amazed at the transformation. He had traveled here with his father. It was the last trip they'd taken together. Samuel Rogers died a few months later. His now elderly son remembered the respect his father engendered from everyone they met. Jed stood a little taller as he felt himself walking in his father's shadow.

Large homes, hotels and shops abutted the harbour. Nearly 50,000 black, white and mulatto souls lived and worked here. It had grown from a tiny village on the ocean into a cultured city. More than 3,000 of various non-white racial color hues were free, both blacks and mulattos. And the children of these freed blacks continued to swell these numbers. This was something that was rare in upper Louisiana.

Jesse and Thaddeus left Massa' Jed at his hotel with his traveling cases and walked the horses to what looked like a clean stable they'd passed on their way into town. For fifty cents the horses would be fed and stalled. For an extra dime the two of them could sleep in an empty stall. They'd been given money to find themselves lodging but this would be cheaper and they could save or spend the rest. Massa' Jed would never ask.

They left the horses, the mule, and their bedrolls and decided to see the Atlantic Ocean. The sight would be a first for each of them. They watched as the waves crashed onto the sandy beach. The noise was as deafening as a Louisiana thunder storm. White caps ebbed and flowed, changing the sun's reflection every few seconds. The two of them laughed as they took off their shoes and waded in the surf. Jesse watched as Thaddeus raced back toward the shallow water as another wave attacked the shore. On a few occasions he wasn't fast enough and he fell onto the sandy beach, wet from top to bottom, enjoying a new experience with his father. This Atlantic was certainly more powerful than their Ol' Miss.

Jesse had visited New Orleans but Charleston people seemed different. Everyone walked faster and he had never seen so many colored folks wearing suits or running businesses.

"Daddy Jesse," Thaddeus asked. "How come they' is so many folk same colorin' as me when there ain't none like me back at Moss Grove?"

The observation caught the older man off guard. He doubted Massa' Jed had thought of it either.

"Can't say for sure," Jesse hesitated. "Maybe it's somethin' we need to ask Massa' Jed on our way home."

Jesse knew that there were a lot of such coloreds around New Orleans, many well-off, schooled in both French and English. These mulattos and quadroons had evolved a separate culture of their own. Massa' Jed had once remarked that all them mixed folks in New Orleans together 'cause all those Frenchies have such loose morals. He think it a sin for white and black folk to be together. Jesse doubted Massa' Jed connected the fact that Thaddeus was the product of that same moral lapse. This was now an open subject to the boy and the elder slave and surrogate father just wasn't equipped to deal with it.

They stopped at a small bakery where two black women tended the counter.

"How about somethin' sweet, Thaddeus?" Jesse asked as he and the boy eyed the sugared treats and felt the pull of cinnamon and chocolate wafting through the door.

"I'd surely love one of the buns," Thaddeus said excitedly.

"How do, Ma'am," Jesse said as they entered the small shop. "Nice lookin' baked goods."

"Thank you," the older woman answered behind a clean white apron. "You and your boy visitin' Charleston?"

"Yes'm. We're from near Baton Rouge, over in Lou'siana. We come a long way and your rolls look mighty appealing. We'll take two of those with the chocolate, won't we, Thaddeus?" he said, pointing at a stack of sweet buns.

"Where's the white man own this shop?" Thaddeus asked in a loud whisper that made the women smile.

"Shhhh, boy! You don't ask folks questions like that," Jesse's voice turned stern.

"We own the shop. Me and my Clarence! He sleepin' right now. He does all the early mornin' bakin'. My name is Harriet and this is my eldest daughter, Helene," she said, her eyes shiny with a pride rare among the field and house slaves back at Moss Grove.

"How you come to own your own business?" Thaddeus persisted. "Ain't you blacks, same as us?"

"Thaddeus," Jesse scolded, "You bein' pesky. Jus' eat your roll and we be on our way."

"Would you boys like some fresh milk? Helene, go get them some milk," she told her daughter, without waiting for a reply.

"Well, Thaddeus. What a nice name," Harriet continued. "We be born free. Our daddy was freed from his master more'n twenty years ago and that makes us free. We ain't white or colored but we sure is free. Lotsa' blacks here like us. Some is carpenters; some tailors…all kinds of things. Some even work on ships as seamen. They sometimes come back with stories 'bout things they seen 'round the world. Ah, here's Helene with the milk. Enjoy it."

Thaddeus devoured his sweet bun in three bites, sugar all over his face. Jesse just smiled with the pride of a father watching his son. Harriett brought the young boy another bun and refused the few pennies offered to her. By the time they left the sun was beginning to dip behind the buildings. They walked faster trying to see as much of Charleston as they could before the day ended.

Jedidiah Rogers joined his old friend, Stephen A. Douglas, for dinner in the large dining room of the Charleston House, a glittering new establishment replete with chandeliers from France and crisp, white linen table cloths. Black waiters, carefully mannered and exquisitely attired, provided unobtrusive service with well-honed skills. Crystal goblets were never empty of their Bordeaux.

Douglas had aged but he had clearly lost none of his fervor. He was still the "Little Giant" that had helped craft the Missouri Compromise a decade earlier.

"You'll support me for President again, Jedidiah? I need your help if we are to keep this Union together," Douglas asked after dinner as they enjoyed their brandy and cigars on the veranda overlooking the harbour, the American stars and stripes fluttering high on the stanchion atop Fort Sumter framed in front of a full moon.

"I'll try Stephen, but I have little influence outside of Louisiana and less and less even there. It seems that age and experience are irrelevant these days. These young studs want what they want and they want immediate resolution."

"We must try. We must keep our Democratic party united."

"Who is this tall, gawky man from Illinois I hear mentioned?"

Douglas laughed. "Ah, Abe Lincoln! Tallest politician I've ever seen. He can't enter most rooms without having to bend over. Country bumpkin from Springfield. Ran against me for the Senate! We crossed most of Illinois debating. I beat him in the election but he's a spellbinder when it comes to talking to folks. He's part of another new political party. They call themselves Republicans. They're mostly Illinois folks. Except for the fact he's a new face those Eastern wheeler-dealers will have him for lunch."

The Charleston convention was opened with a hearty cheer from all those present. On the first ballot Douglas had a hefty lead against six other nominees. He needed only 57 votes to garner the nomination. Perhaps it would be a short agreeable event after all. But the days wore on. Jedidiah cajoled men from every state. They'd meet over coffee in the morning and brandy in the evening. No one seemed amenable to moderation. The summer heat and humidity plagued and exhausted the delegates.

Sixty more votes spread over two weeks failed to resolve the issue. With tempers festering and unable to reach a consensus, the convention was adjourned until mid-June. It would be held nearly a month after the

Republicans were to meet. The delegates hoped that if they waited, they might better able to assess their future.

Jedidiah, Jesse and Thaddeus returned home weary from their journey. They had been gone just over a month and they could feel both the humidity and the breeze of the great river as another mile passed and Moss Grove neared. Ruby and Sarah ran to the front of the house as the whoops and hollers of their returning champions reached their ears. Jedidiah had told Thaddeus to shout his loudest and the boy's deepening voice scattered the birds in the trees as all three men laughed.

"Jedidiah, this fabric is beautiful," Ruby said, as her fingers played over the silver threads interwoven into the fabric her husband had brought her from the new textile mill in Charleston.

"I can make something really lovely. It is a beautiful choice. I plan on looking positively radiant the next time we entertain. You, on the other hand, look tired and pale. Are you sure you're alright?"

"I'm exhausted," her husband said, as he collapsed into his chair. Jesse had rushed into the room as soon as he'd said his hellos to Sarah. Massa' Jed would need help pulling off his riding boots.

"It was a long and tiring trip," Jedidiah said. "The last two nights were chilly and even with an extra blanket the dampness just seemed to soak into every bone."

"Well, I'll have Sarah heat up extra hot water for a bath and I'll have dinner brought to your room. I don't need you getting sick."

Jedidiah climbed into his bed, tired and sad that it wasn't just an oncoming cold that was frustrating him. It was the realization that none of the troublesome issues they'd spent days discussing had been resolved.

Thaddeus returned to his small room and unpacked his few things. He had seen so much. The world is certainly much larger and grander than just Moss Grove, he thought, lying on his back, staring through his small window at the night sky. Just imagine, looking at water that goes on forever, not just New Orleans. And black people that are free. And people, light-skinned, like he was. He so badly wanted to ask someone about all of these things and more. Maybe Massa' Jed or Miss Ruby could tell him things. Maybe it was in one of those books they gave him to read. Maybe it would explain why he was so much lighter than Papa Jesse or Mama Sarah and why his eyes were such a different color.

Newspapers from Baton Rouge reached Moss Grove weekly. Occasionally Jedidiah might even receive one from New Orleans. The news was disheartening and did nothing to improve his disposition. They reported that, like the Democrats, the Republicans had been unable to settle on any of the likely candidates. Each man had taken positions that alienated one or another faction. They were either too pro-slavery or too abolitionist. In the end they compromised on a dark horse, Abe Lincoln. At least, Jedidiah thought, Douglas assures me the man is a moderate.

A week later, however, another copy of the Baton Rouge Register arrived and, as Jedidiah read, he wept openly for the first time since he was a child. Lincoln's acceptance speech was anything but temperate. Instead, paraphrasing Jesus' message from the New Testament, Lincoln said, 'A house divided against itself cannot stand.'

Ruby came into the room and heard her husband's deep sighs.

"We will have war now, for sure," Jedidiah said softly. "Listen to the man's words, 'I believe this government cannot endure permanently half *slave* and half *free*. I do not expect the Union to be *dissolved* -- I do not expect the house to *fall* -- but I *do* expect it will cease to be divided.'

"His message is clear. Slavery will not be allowed in any future states. A Lincoln victory will mean an end to the south as we've always known it."

The following month the Democrats reconvened in Baltimore but Jedidiah didn't feel strong enough to make another trip. A twelve hundred mile journey was more than he could even consider. He thought of sending Henry in his stead but his son's views were so divergent from his that it would have counter-productive. He would have to sit this one out and hope for the best. He sent letters to everyone he knew, urging them to continue to support Douglas but he was not enthusiastic about the outcome.

Within days of the convention's opening more than a hundred delegates from southern states stormed from the meeting in anger when they were unsuccessful in adopting a single resolution supporting slavery in new states or territories. With these angry militant men gone, the convention proceeded to nominate Stephen Douglas. It was a pyrrhic victory. The nation was divided as never before.

The news reached Moss Grove about a week later when a neighbor, one of Henry's friends from a nearby plantation, rode in shouting and waving his hat joyfully. War was inevitable and the generations viewed it from alien points of view. While Jedidiah understood that Moss Grove and

Louisiana would not be able to remain passive bystanders, the younger men saw only the glamour and excitement of battle as they got drunk from too much brandy and the heady anticipation of victory.

The political campaign was filled with vitriol. Outbreaks of violence were the rule rather than the exception. Stephen Douglas campaigned endlessly from north to south trying to hold the Union together. One mid-October evening in the midst of the campaign, Jedidiah hosted a dinner for his old friend at Moss Grove. Exhausted, the candidate's voice was raspy from too many speeches in too many towns. Douglas had ridden up from New Orleans, where he had spoken to meager crowds more interested in seeing this famous man than supporting his position. These were city folk and rice growers. Their primary concern was keeping goods flowing along the Mississippi and through that gateway into the Gulf of Mexico and the eager markets of Europe that lay across the Atlantic.

Friends and supporters rode in from as far as Baton Rouge. Many would spend the night. Mattresses were placed on floors when all the beds were taken. Tents were strewn across the lawn. It was a festive event. Douglas arrived early. After cleaning up from his long ride he joined Jedidiah and Henry on the veranda. A nattily attired Thaddeus poured from a newly filled decanter of port. Jedidiah smiled at him and nodded approvingly. Henry scowled but kept silent. Thaddeus met the man's glare and stubbornly refused to lower his eyes.

"Stephen, you're looking very hale considering you have been making speeches across the country for nearly three months," Jedidiah smiled, easing the tension he sensed was building between his son and Thaddeus.

"Yes, but I don't know how many people I've convinced," Douglas mused. His friend had aged and the bags under his eyes were testimony to the strain he faced from the long campaign.

"What are you finding out there, sir?" Henry interjected.

"Anger! Fear! You name it. Everyone has become radicalized."

"If Lincoln gets elected, so be it!" Henry proclaimed. "The South will secede and we'll go our own way."

Henry's voice rose with the absolute assurance he expressed in all things.

"Yes, the South may certainly secede. And that may mean war. It will certainly mean an end to this noble union of which we have been so proud. We have built a nation unique in the world. Our people move steadily westward with energy, new families and new industries. How it will all end and what will become of these United States will be an issue for your generation to resolve."

"Don't you worry, Mr. Douglas. It will only mean two countries vying for success sharing adjacent geographies but with very different philosophies."

"You see, Jedidiah. This younger generation is brash. They are self-assured. Perhaps they are right and you and I have become anachronisms."

"I fear you are right, Stephen. But if it is so, let us make this last election battle a good one."

*In the end, however, all of Jedidiah Roger's efforts on Stephen Douglas' behalf were not even enough to give Douglas a victory in Louisiana. He had campaigned with the energy of a younger man but his quixotic efforts were futile. John C. Breckinridge, Buchanan's Vice-President, and the only candidate openly in support of secession, won almost every state that would form the Confederacy.*

*The election confirmed the divisive nature of the country. Despite a huge turnout no candidate would get a majority. Lincoln won the election with a plurality, garnering fewer than 40% of the popular vote but a majority of the electoral votes. The Republicans were in the White House for the first time.*

*Within days of the Electoral College certifying the national vote, South Carolina voted for secession and on December 20th their entire Congressional delegation stormed from the Senate and left Washington. Their State Assembly demanded that Federal troops abandon Ft. Sumter, the large Federal military post established nearly fifty years earlier to protect Charleston harbor.*

*In his final month as President, Buchanan sent a ship loaded with military reinforcements to bolster the fort and add to its garrison, but on January 9th 1861, as the ship approached the entrance to the harbour, southern guns opened fire. With those salvos the Civil War began. Louisiana and the other southern states followed suit. Within weeks the Confederacy had been officially established with Jefferson Davis as its President.*

# Chapter Five

Thaddeus was eleven, nearly twelve, and his voice was beginning to deepen. The boy was disappearing and a confident young man was appearing in his stead. Jesse tried to rein the boy in and teach him the dos and don'ts of what was acceptable for a house nigger but there was something of his daddy in him that emanated rebellion. In Henry it was arrogance. In Thaddeus, even though it was hidden behind a mischievous grin, it possessed a trace of rebellion that could have dangerous consequences.

Until they'd visited Charleston the growing boy never questioned why he was so much lighter in color than the other children he saw and grew up with. If he was aware that his eyes were startlingly different he kept it to himself. He did his chores, said his prayers, and was respectful to his elders. He was careful to avoid white folks but he generally comported himself as a young house slave should, at least on the surface.

When they all returned from their trip to Charleston, Jesse had seen a lifestyle he didn't even know existed and he felt different. It was likely that his son was absorbing similar feelings. For the first time in his life Jesse questioned his docility as a slave and the unquestioning obeisance of nearly fifty years. It was a silent contemplation, more worrisome than a sudden change in the weather. He'd seen black freedom. He'd seen black schools. He didn't understand why some white folks would fight other white folks over black folks, but it was plain as your nose that's what they were getting' ready to do. He liked and respected Massa' Jedidiah and Miss Ruby. They'd always been kind and caring to him, Sarah and the staff. But they was kindly to their pets and livestock also. Free? At his age? Where would they live? How would he earn a living? Would they be permitted to take

Thaddeus with them? And what about Thaddeus? The boy was beginning to ask questions. He would soon be old enough to demand answers.

Jesse and Sarah shared a small room off the pantry where dishes were kept and food was readied for the family meal. Thaddeus' bed was in the corner. The kitchen itself was away from the back of the house where the heat, the smells, and the danger of a fire from the cook stoves was less likely to spread to the main house. A cable-connected bell that allowed Massa' Jed to call at any time to bring a drink or empty a chamber pot, hung near their room.

It had been a quiet life until they had been told they would raise Thaddeus. They would have loved to have had children of their own but Sarah had had a botched miscarriage when she and Jesse had been put together for breeding by Samuel Rogers. They were forced to adjust to the knowledge that it was not to be.

Thaddeus had immediately become an integral part of their life. He had grown into a willful young man, always asking questions, never accepting the simple answer of 'that's how things are.' 'Why?' was his favorite word. The growing boy adored Jesse and Sarah. They were his parents and he never had a reason to question their love.

They had been back for a few days but Jesse hadn't had an opportunity to tell Sarah about his Charleston adventure. Jedidiah's aching chest and cough meant extra care and attention by everyone and that became the priority of the entire house staff. Now that the Massa' was getting better the house staff had a little more time to relax around the kitchen stove. In the midst of summer the stove was kept low, just enough to boil water but it was still a preferred meeting place.

He, Sarah and Thaddeus were joined by several other house blacks and cooks once the food and dishes from dinner had been washed up and returned to the pantry, they began describing some of the amazing things they'd seen in Charleston.

"You should have seen all the colored people walking down the street, side by side with white folks," Thaddeus said.

"This boy didn't stop asking questions the entire time we was there," Jesse smiled. "Why the ocean so big? What's on the other side? He even fell in the first day. Got his'self soaking wet. He's just getting' too big to tar, this 'un!"

"You wouldn't do nuthin' to him, Jess, no matter what he did," Sarah laughed.

"Free blacks," Luther mused. "Imagine me having my own forge." He and Thaddeus had grown even closer since the episode with the visiting boys in the stable. Luther was a first quality farrier and Thaddeus would sit nearby in his spare time, fascinated by the ease the older man had with horses. "I could be a smithy, get paid for my work, and have a family of my choosing."

"We'll tell missy Trudy you don't want to marry her," Sarah laughed. She knew Luther would rather be wed to Trudy than shoe horses and clean stables.

"It ain't that. I do care for Trudy. But I mighta' cared more if I could have made the decision myself instead of Massa' Jed making the decision like I was one of his prize studs."

"Rumor has it, Luther," Jesse added, "That you might just be one of his prize studs."

They all laughed. It was a convivial laugh from men and women who shared the same hardships, difficult lives controlled by others.

"There's gonna be war soon," Jesse continued. "It was all they talked about over in Charleston…war this, war that. Imagine all those white folk worryin' about us blacks. Nuthin' in my life prepare me for this."

The older ones in the kitchen nodded. It was a difficult concept when you were someone's property your entire life and a white master made all the important decisions of how you lived, who you married, and how you spent your time.

"Let's not forget that life here at Moss Grove has been good to us," Sarah said.

"I ain't denyin' that but wouldn't you like to take a boat ride or buy a piece of gingham when you have a mind to with money you earned?" Jesse countered.

"Either way, whatever gonna happen is gonna happen with nobody asking us."

"Working for Massa' Jed has been fine but I'm not likin' the idea of workin' for Massa' Henry," Luther declared. "Sarah, you and Jesse better make certain Massa' Jed gets healthy and stays healthy for a long time.

"Sides, I'm not sure that field nigger girl, Rose, would agree with you that life at Moss Grove has always been good," Luther added with a grunt.

Heads turned nervously toward Thaddeus. Luther's slip had broken an unspoken taboo and his embarrassment was evident. There was no way he would ever want to hurt this young boy who had become a friend and helper.

"You shush up," Sarah said quickly. "That was a long time ago and that bad thing brought great happiness to Jesse and me."

"No matter," Jesse said, "White folk been decidin' these things without asking us what we want, no how."

Thaddeus sat quietly in the corner on an upturned pail. If he understood Luther's remark he kept it to himself. His thoughts, too, were on the possibility of a war.

"I hear some of the white kids talking, father," he said. "They say their folks worried what all the darkeys do if war come. Will we kill all the white Massas or jus' leave and head north."

"Most won't do nothin' of the kind. Moss Grove is our home. We gonna' jus' stay and keep workin'."

Conversations among the field slaves weren't terribly different. Picking up supplies, visiting, and just general travel between the plantations brought news of the world across the south. It wasn't always current and it wasn't always accurate, but there was a new urgency to what was going on now all around them.

"Rose, I want to take you and Matthew up north," Faris said. "I don't want him to grow up as a slave. He bright. Look at how much he know from the little readin' you give him. He already know more than me."

"I'm not goin' nowhere, Faris. I been born at Moss Grove and I 'spec' to lay my head down here when it all over. Anywhere else I just another nigger."

"Girl, you just another nigger here too, and don't you think otherwise. Someday soon Massa' Jed will go to his heavenly due and we'll all have to deal with Massa' Henry. I see how he act and look when he at the river and I's afraid what I might do if he bring that anger down on you, Matthew or me."

Rose grabbed his hand and pulled him close. "I know you protect us no matter what but for now we need to stay put. If there's a war it'll come to the north same as Moss Grove. No point bein' among strangers if'n it do start."

Matthew watched his parents hold one another. He was nearly nine and becoming increasingly aware of everything around him. His early childhood had been marred with pneumonia and tuberculosis from the dampness that pervaded most of the slave cabins. There was too little heat and no way to keep the dirt floors from passing the outside chill into everyone's bones. The sacks that were put on the floor, or the occasional wood slats they could lay down, offered little warmth.

Massa' Jedidiah had noticed Matthew's frail body and instructed Rupert Raffery to give less work to Rose and her son. That extra time in the sun worked wonders for them both. Whether the plantation owner truly cared for the pair's well-being, or whether he wanted to protect his investment, would remain an ever present question.

Matthew was, once again, working the fields. He was given a smaller sack for the cotton when the crop was ready to harvest. Other times he helped feed and milk the cows and slop the pigs. He was as black as his father, nappy-haired, and with the same huge hands. But unlike his father, he shared the delicate features of his mother. He loved them both and he knew he was fortunate to be growing up in the collective warmth of their caring.

"OK if I come in and watch," Matthew said, standing in the entranceway of the barn. He had heard the hammer attacking the anvil and followed the noise.

"Just don't get too close to the furnace," Luther warned. "Sometimes sparks can fly unexpectedly. Thaddeus, stoke it some more. Needs to be real hot to get these tools real sharp and the iron hard."

Thaddeus grabbed the bellows and began opening and closing them, letting the air heat the coals.

"I know you. Your name is Matthew. You're gettin' pretty big. Must be 'cause you got a giant for a daddy," he smiled as he pushed the huge handles down.

"And I hear about you, too. You that house nigger with the funny eyes."

"And you're both bein' lazy," Luther admonished. "If you want to chatter, go somewhere else. I got work to do."

The boys smiled at one another as Thaddeus began pushing the bellows in earnest.

"You want heat, Luther, I gonna give you the most heat ever."

In a few minutes Matthew joined in, and as the two half-brothers jumped up and down to feed air to Luther's forge, their laughter filled the barn.

"My family says we'll be at war within a month," Philip Lunstrum said as he and Henry shared a drink at Mandy's.

They had both returned to Knoxville and school not quite ready to begin another year.

"I don't doubt it," Henry replied. "I don't know why I even bothered to come back here."

"Probably the same reason as me…to have a romp with one of Mandy's girls. Not much opportunity for pussy at home."

"Well then, let's get to it," Henry laughed, standing and adjusting his pants.

A few days later he simply walked out of his classes and returned to Moss Grove. He made several stops en route and by the time he reached home he was fully attired in the grey uniform of a Confederate Captain, a rank he had purchased as befitting his age and bearing. Once again his parents came out to meet him on the front portico but the gaiety that existed at his last return was gone. They smiled at their handsomely attired son but they both feared what the months ahead would do to the life they had so assiduously protected.

Henry was due to report for duty in one week. He had been posted to the staff of Major General Mansfield Lovell, a West Point graduate and veteran of the Mexican-American War. Their unit was to be part of the Confederate River Defense Fleet organized to defend New Orleans and the Mississippi River from Federal forces.


The next morning Henry and his father rode together through the day's early mist along the furrowed fields and through the green, brown and white mature cotton plants that extended in every direction. The recent anger between them was forgotten. They had ridden together often when Henry was younger and both father and son needed to replenish their memories of those happier times.

"The cotton crop looks as if it will big this year," Henry said.

Glistening black bodies, stripped to the waist, rose from their tasks as the two passed, nodding in respect, and witnessing the pride the elder Massa' felt accompanied on the tour by his handsome son.

"Yes. We should do well," his father answered.

"Well? Better than well, I'd think. Cotton futures are the highest they've ever been. I'm told France and England are prepared to buy every bale we can ship them. It may well have more value than Union dollars."

"Yes, we should be fine as long as we can protect New Orleans and the Mississippi. Everything depends on our ability to ship our cotton," Jedidiah said.

"We will, father. That's the task of the River Defense Fleet. I'll be joining them next week. The Union doesn't have the testacles to come this far. They still have to figure out who's going to run their army and get enough recruits to defend Washington.

"Tell me, any trouble with the slaves?" Henry continued, changing the subject. "I hear rumors that many of them are abandoning their homes in droves and heading north?"

"We lost one man…a field hand who hadn't been with us more than two years. Most of the rest of our people have families and history with us. We've treated them well. I don't think they'll leave, but we can only hope. Rafferty tries to stay abreast of what the slaves are thinking. They seem to be spending a lot more time talking to one another in groups but that's all we actually know."

"Perhaps your humane concern for them will benefit us at this time. Time will tell, although I suggest you teach mother how to fire a pistol and hide extra rifles where you can easily get to them."

"Henry, I'm just a cotton grower. I've gotten my hands dirty my entire life. I've pulled weeds with the slaves, planted seed, and fed the hogs. If I need to arm myself against these same folks, my life is over. God will protect us or he won't. It is all in the hands of the Almighty."

"Nicely said, father! But I prefer to believe that, on occasion, the Almighty can use a little help and direction from each of us."

From New Orleans north to the Mississippi border across the breadth of the state, a heightened fear and nervousness gripped white and black alike. Moss Grove and its neighbors harvested their crops early, smoked their pigs and emptied the bee hives. No one was sure what they would face in the months ahead. Word had reached them from Baton Rouge that all plantations had been ordered to gather as much cotton as possible and prepare it for shipment and sale. The proceeds would finance much of the south's war preparations. It had to be shipped before any Union military actions prevented its movement. The North's plan, dubbed 'Anaconda,' was to blockade all major harbors within the south, capture the Mississippi River, and divide the confederacy. It was named for the deadly snake that squeezed rather than poisoned its victims.

"Father, I'll be leaving in the morning," Henry said as he entered his father's study. Jedidiah stopped writing and looked up at his son.

"I will worry about you, Henry, as your mother will, as well."

"Yes, she and I talked for nearly an hour. I'm sure you will both be safe here at Moss Grove."

"That's what families do, I guess. Parents worry about their children and children fret about their parents. It is you that will be in harm's way. We are proud of you. We need you to return and assume your rightful role as master of Moss Grove."

"I will father. I am certain of the righteousness of our cause. We will be victorious and I will return."

The next morning Henry rose early and began his ride toward New Orleans and his new Confederate Army responsibilities. As he neared the outskirts of Baton Rouge, he decided to make a detour and visit his cousins, the Williams. He had not seen Elizabeth since the holidays. He knew she fancied him and he was certain she'd be impressed seeing him in his new uniform.

Tiny, rural, Baton Rouge had become the state's capitol only sixteen years earlier when fear of the growing influence of New Orleans angered the rest of the state's landowners. New Orleans was the fourth largest city in the United States with more than 100,000 souls. Baton Rouge, by comparison, had less than 3,000.

One of the families that made up that small populace was Baxter and Sylvia Williams and their two daughters. The town was quaint and unsophisticated. It was no more than several streets of flowers surrounding a grotesque capitol building newly built to resemble a neo-gothic castle complete with turrets overlooking the Mississippi. The city didn't yet suffer the pompousness of most state capitols that were populated by those interested in spreading largesse on government office holders.

Baxter Williams, tall and willowy, with just a fringe of grey hair, walked with a noticeable limp. He'd taken a musket round in the War of 1812. He would frequently rant that this was an important war. It asserted American naval power against the colonially-minded British Empire, still stinging from their loss of the American colonies. To his friends and the rest of the country, however, that war, now largely forgotten, was a matter of little consequence.

Baxter Williams had come home from the war without financial resources. His family owned a General Store in Western Pennsylvania but that business would be inherited by his two older brothers. He knew he'd have to look elsewhere to make his fortune. Like many others, he headed west. He was riding toward Texas when his horse came up limp. He walked it slowly into the nearest town and found himself in Baton Rouge.

While his horse was being cared for he walked the entire two blocks of the town. He asked a passerby where he might get a meal. That passerby happened to be Sylvia Weatherby, a local, rather provincial, girl. This casual accident kept Baxter in town and soon evolved into a romance and engagement. Her parents' offer of a dowry was an additional enticement. It provided him enough money to open his own small business and finalized his reasons to marry and settle down.

The new business provided supplies and feed for the growing population of farmers and plantation owners in Baton Rouge and the surrounding parishes. The Weatherbys had agreed to the dowry on the condition their daughter would remain in Louisiana and away from the influence of the northern abolitionists. Sylvia's parents had since died but the Williams now had their roots in Louisiana. There was no reason to change.

Elizabeth was more than delighted to see the man she wished to be her beau, lover, husband, and the father of the many children she wanted to bear. Henry was absolutely dashing in his uniform and shiny boots, his saber hanging cavalierly at his side. A red sash at the waist accented his blonde hair, muscled chest, blue eyes, and good looks.

"Why Henry," she blushed. "What on earth are you doing in 'lil ol' Baton Rouge?" she said coquettishly, making every effort to appear cool and mature.

"Miss Elizabeth, you look lovely, as always. I am on my way to my post near New Orleans and I couldn't miss an opportunity to extend my best wishes to you and your family."

The pirouette of social etiquette began. Tea was served in the dining room. Amy was sent to her room to scrub her face and change from her tomboy togs into a dress. The elder Williams', meanwhile, were eager to hear the latest news from Moss Grove, Confederate war preparations, and any news their small coterie had not yet heard. Henry was happy to accept an invitation to stay for dinner.

Henry's decision to alter his journey to visit Elizabeth and her family had been made after considerable thought. He had left Moss Grove with the awareness that his father had a bad cough in his chest. His father's illness and his surprising, first ever, victory at arm wrestling validated both his worries and his aspirations that Moss Grove would be his to own and manage soon enough. He would need a wife to run the manor and even help take care of his mother. You couldn't anticipate how fast a woman faded when she lost her husband and anchor.

Henry had always busied himself with male friends or tarts, no woman he'd want to represent him with the stature into which he saw himself evolving. He needed a woman from a good family who would bear him sons. Elizabeth was one of the few he knew that fit that description. He hated that she was so plain. Not just not pretty…plain and simple, she was plain! What the hell, he thought, when the lights are out you can't tell a pretty bitch from an ugly one. He could always keep a mistress.

Henry wavered even as he displayed the full panoply of southern grace. He would look over at Elizabeth, smile, and renew his conversations with her mother or father. Amy just stared, bored, and continuing to dislike this man who clearly felt himself so superior. She hadn't forgiven him for his overreaction at the river with Thaddeus.

Fuck you, you little bitch, he grinned at her. I don't give a shit what you think about me. It's your sister I'm here for. You aren't even extra baggage. Not you, and not my nigger kid!

That evening, after dinner, Henry and Elizabeth found themselves alone in the small gazebo behind the house. This would never have been permitted in a traditional courtship where parents were always within sight of their daughter and her beau to avoid any chance of an embarrassment to the family. It was a practice the Baxters' chose to ignore in hopes of having this particular relationship move along more rapidly.

Henry had drunk a little more than was socially polite. He breathed deep, desperately needing to reinforce his courage. He sucked in an extra breath and asked Elizabeth if she would consider an eventual marriage if her father agreed. The proposal was so sudden and so unexpected she had difficulty comprehending the question she was being asked from the assembly of his words. When she regained her composure she was still unable to hide the surprise in her voice and she let out a scream that brought out the servants. She waved them away, eyes tearing, and sat, trying to imagine that everything she'd ever fantasized over might come to be. Henry waited and smiled, a knowing smile, a triumphant smile. This will work out just fine, he thought, just fine.

"Well, Baxter, it looks as if you can stop worrying. Elizabeth won't become an old spinster after all," Sylvia Williams said as the two readied themselves for bed later that evening after Henry had departed.

"Frankly, my dear, I was struck dumb when young Henry asked my permission. I almost leapt up to embrace him. Let's be honest, a plain girl in a small town like Baton Rouge has few decent marital prospects and our daughter, as much as I love her, will never send men into an emotional tizzy. The boarding and finishing school in New Orleans we hoped would solve some of the problem, accomplished very little. And, we certainly spent more than we should have."

Sylvia nodded in agreement. "If we wanted to find her a proper husband there was no choice but to choose an exclusive school for girls who came from families with means. All it seemed to do, however, was to help Elizabeth develop a taste for expensive silks and brocades."

"She also developed that inane shrill high pitched giggle, and a lurid taste for any male old enough to shave.

"So, if Henry is such a prize, there is only one question. Why?" Baxter wondered, "Why would a handsome wealthy boy, due to inherit his family's wealth and station choose our daughter? I am so tempted to ask but I'd be afraid of putting doubtful thoughts in the boy's head. I can only assume the boy has his reasons."

Assuming Henry could convince his military superiors, and, assuming the war and the Union forces wouldn't object, the engagement would be formally announced in four months with the wedding to follow. His mother and father would be overjoyed.

Amy, on the other hand, was appalled at having this arrogant distant cousin move closer along the family tree. She understood her older sister's limitations but she loved her and wished her happiness. She just couldn't accept that such happiness would be found hanging onto Henry's arm.

Jedidiah Rogers, much to his personal discomfort, had heeded Henry's advice and set pistols and rifles up in his library and bedroom. One lay openly on the nightstand close to the bed he and his wife had always shared in quiet warmth. The gun made Ruby nervous and she refused the pleas of both her husband and her son to learn how to fire it. Jesse saw the weapon each time he entered the room. It was a nervous addition to the décor and he judiciously avoided any reference to it. The realities of how close the war might come to Moss Grove were becoming all too evident.

Bastions of gray uniformed men passed Moss Grove on their way to one place or another. On each occasion Ruby ordered the kitchen staff to feed them and allow them to rest and refresh themselves and their horses. Officers were invited into the dining room with the graciousness of long absent relatives. Those coming up from the New Orleans area were asked whether they'd met Captain Henry Rogers, assigned to the Fleet command. On a number of occasions the question gave rise to an uncomfortable silence. Captain Rogers' military reputation had already begun to develop and not in a favorable light.

Thaddeus tended the soldier's horses, bringing them water and oats and listening to the gossip of the young men in the fresh grey uniforms. It was exciting for the growing boy. These men were going off to do something important. His thoughts wandered to Amy, her red hair, freckles and her milk white skin. He dreamt of protecting her against horned blue invaders. Somehow each invader in his thoughts looked exactly like Henry, scowling and violent. More than one morning he awoke to find his bedcovers damp and sticky. He was embarrassed but glad his mother simply washed them without a word. Thaddeus understood that colored men weren't supposed to fantasize about white women of any age. It could prove fatal if he ever acted on it. His feelings became his most sacred secret and he tried hard to forget Amy and concentrate on his chores.

One day he built up enough nerve to ask one of the Confederate soldiers who were passing through and whose horse he was rubbing down, if he could hold his rifle.

"Listen, nigger," the man snarled. "You jus' keep rubbin' down my pinto. Guns is for white folks." He turned toward his friend. "This little piss-ant colored boy wants to hold my rifle. He so fuckin' stupid he'd probably blow his own head off."

Thaddeus struggled to retain his calm as the young Reb soldiers all laughed. It was a shock to a young boy not yet steeled against how some white folk felt about anyone with even a drop of black blood in them.

The workday of the field hands lengthened as every available acre of land was cleared and planted. The work grew more difficult. The ground in this part of Moss Grove was strewn with rocks and was further from the water that was needed for irrigation. Overseers demanded more... more hours, more clearing, more planting. Jedidiah's health and these new financial strains kept him in the house. He was no longer able to enjoy his daily rides through the fields and his absence was taken as a bad omen by the slaves tending the young cotton plants and who counted on seeing him as regularly as hearing the morning cock crow.

Eight more field hands from nearby plantations had run off toward the north. One overseer had been bludgeoned to death. Four blacks had been strung up and left along a road known to be frequented by runaway slaves. The Apocalypse was surely coming to their lives earlier than expected.

Jedidiah sat at the small desk in his bedroom. The winter cold penetrated into his bones and Thaddeus began keeping the room's small wood burning stove stoked at all times. Even with the stove going, Jed found himself more comfortable with a blanket covering his shoulders.

The Moss Grove Massa' began taking more of his morning and mid-day meals right there in his room, eschewing the need to dress for anything but an informal dinner. It was an unnerving change of life style that was already undergoing profound changes from the tradition of generations.

"You warm enough, Massa' Jed," Thaddeus asked. "I can get you some of that sweet coffee you like."

"Thank you, Thaddeus. That would be wonderful. Why don't you bring some for yourself as well and keep me company?"

The two sat together enjoying that relationship so unique to grandparents and grandchildren.

"Are you still doing your schooling?" the elder Rogers asked.

"Some. Not as much as I'd like but I can do my numbers and I like to read the newspapers after you're done with them. Papa Jesse saves them for me."

"Then you're aware of the war?"

"Yes, Massa' Jed. I'm almost old enough to enlist. I want to kill them blue-bellies."

Jedidiah laughed. "Well, you might be old enough if the war lasts a few years but Miss Ruby and I hope it won't. War is a terrible thing, Thaddeus. Don't be too much in a hurry."

Financially, Moss Grove would be fine for the next year. Profits from the sale of their cotton crop were substantial and Jedidiah had been careful to spread the money into several banks around the country, including a few in northern cities. He would need to make certain that Henry, as well as his solicitor, knew where everything was. He was old enough to hope for a much longer life but prudent enough to plan for anything sooner than might occur. Ruby would need to be cared for. He wasn't sure whether she'd prefer to return to New Orleans when he died or remain at Moss Grove with Henry. And Thaddeus. What would happen to the boy? It wasn't likely Henry would want the boy to remain at the plantation. He would have to give that some thought.

So much would depend on the war, the slaves, and whether Henry married. It was 1863, the year after next, which worried Jedidiah. If he was unable to plant and tend his acres in the upcoming season there would be nothing to harvest the following year. He could sell off a few slaves, if there were any buyers, but that, too, would presage a dramatic break with the past. Moss Grove had never sold a slave. It was a matter of pride to the Rogers and a comfort to their slave family. It was all just too much uncertainty for a man his age.

> *The first major battle, abutting both the Union and Confederate capitols, Washington D.C. and Richmond, Virginia, became known as the Battle of Bull Run. General George McClellan, head of the Union Army, sent his troops against a smaller Confederate contingent. In the midst of oppressive July heat and humidity, his forces moved south toward Manassas, Virginia. It was little more than a railroad junction but it was a strategic one, with trains departing from there to both cities and the entire Shenandoah Valley.*
>
> *What first seemed an easy victory turned into a complete rout when additional gray uniformed brigades moved up in support. It was here that the Confederate General Jackson received the nickname "Stonewall" for seeming to stand bravely, almost inert, in the face of cannon fire. The Rebs drove the Union forces back toward Washington and the south had gained its first military victory.*

Patriotism energized everyone at Moss Grove. Seeing Henry in his finery made Abner Rafferty impatient to enlist. And in the slave quarters, stories of the Louisiana Native Guards, blacks wanting to fight for the South, spread. The excitement was palpable, and young men, black and white, wanted to participate.

# Chapter Six

The first telegraphs in Louisiana had been put in use just three years earlier. The people of New Orleans and Baton Rouge would now know what was happening elsewhere in the country within hours. No longer would communication depend on teams of riders to spread the word.

Jedidiah began sending servants from Moss Grove every two days the forty miles to Baton Rouge to get the latest news. The South had emerged victorious at Manassas, but that military triumph neither resolved anything nor swayed anyone. The South gained confidence while the North became more determined. Both remained intransigent. There were continuous rumors of reconciliation with the North, of treaties about to be signed with England and France, which way cotton prices would move, but it was all just so much newspaper gossip.

Included in one set of week-old newspapers Jedidiah received, was a brief note from their son.

"Ruby, come here," Jedidiah shouted from his office that was set on one side of their joint bedroom while his wife's sitting room sat on the other side.

"Jed," she said, carrying some needlepoint work she had been working on. "I detest when you shout so."

"Forget that. It seems our son has up and gotten himself engaged to Elizabeth Williams."

"That is wonderful," she said, sitting on the bed. "Wonderful, but quite surprising! I always thought his tastes were toward more…," she paused.

"Yes, girls with bigger bosoms! Flashier young ladies! His note goes on to say that their nuptials might depend on his military obligations but it was his hope that they would be married before the year was out. He wants us to contact the Williams to work out the details."

Jedidiah and Ruby stared at one another and then both broke out laughing. Their initial shock at Henry's actions and choice were quickly overshadowed by the excitement of planning for the happy event and the expectations that their son might be maturing after all.

"Our son is getting married; the Confederate army is doing well and the price of cotton is soaring. Perhaps the war might end quickly and we can return to normal after all," he mused, returning to his newspapers.

*The wintry months of 1862 passed into an unusually wet April east of the Appalachians, drenching the countryside and impeding military action on both sides. The arrival of May, however, brought the sun, and as the foliage burst forth with flowers and fruit, fertility smiled across the landscape. Calves, lambs, and chicks romped noisily on farms. Children read their McGuffey readers and dreamt ahead to summer.*

*Unconcerned with the beauty of the land around them, military commanders on both sides began to implement the battle plans that had lain dormant through the winter.*

*Under pressure from Lincoln and his cabinet the Union army launched an attack on Confederate forces in Virginia. As they moved south, however, their efforts continued to be blunted by southern forces half their size. Various northern generals, in dispute with others on how to conduct the war, refused to send reinforcements to aid beleaguered Union troops. This continual infighting caused a heavy loss of life and a deterioration of morale. Southern confidence was being increasingly buoyed by these multiple victories and farm boys rushed to enlist. The Confederacy was not going to be coerced into rejoining the Union.*

Henry left Elizabeth, his newly betrothed, in a state of planning frenzy and with a perpetual glazed look in her eyes, to join his battalion eighty miles south to New Orleans. He arrived none too soon. A small Union naval group was sighted moving up the mouth of the Mississippi to begin implementing a blockade. The flotilla had assembled at Ship Island, Mississippi and headed north, their American flags billowing arrogantly midst the clouds of steam belching from the small ships' twin stacks.

As soon as they were within range, the boats would begin shelling the Confederate gun emplacements along the riverbanks. It was the task of this Yankee West Gulf Blockading Squadron to stop the shipment of cotton from the Mississippi into the Gulf where it could be transferred to waiting British and French ships and to prevent the shipment of arms and supplies transiting north to the Confederate states that bordered the river. Except for the occasional gun batteries that the South had quickly situated, only two serious fortifications might block the Union's progress. These masonry forts were on opposite sides of the river, seventy miles below New Orleans proper. Captain Henry Rogers was ordered to help defend Fort Jackson on the west side of the river.

Confederate forces had already attempted to impede this small naval armada by blocking the river with chains and scuttled ships. Two Confederate ironclad ships were anchored mid-river to assist in their defense. These efforts might delay the Union ships but by themselves they would be unable to stop their advance. Henry arrived at Fort Jackson and was ordered to command the gun crews operating four cannon pointing down river. These were powerful smooth bore 'Napoleans' capable of firing large 90 lb. shells.

*The art of killing and maiming had come a long way since the muskets of the Revolutionary War that had defeated the British and helped establish a nation. European countries had developed much more effective weaponry for killing during their Napoleonic wars. The American army began importing these new state of the art cannon, nicknamed the Napoleon, in the late 1850's. With solid shot they destroyed fortifications. With 'grape shot' they destroyed troops. Small pellets were packed into a tin can wrapped in cloth and with string like a bunch of grapes, that exploded at the target, disintegrating the cloth and spraying small pieces of metal in every direction, shattering arms or legs with ease.*

Henry's men were young and inexperienced. Few were literate and simply signed their name with an "x". They had come directly from farms, given uniforms that were often ill-fitting, and formed into squads with no training. Most knew how to fire a gun although they had never aimed it at another being. Discipline was non-existent and except for their patriotic fervor and dedication to the young Confederacy, there was little to commend these men.

One man did stand out, but solely because of his brashness and his complete disregard for authority. He was a squat, hairy Irishman named Sean Regan. The man's perpetual rose-colored cheeks sat just below eyes that twinkled with a mischievous glint. Life was a joke and he was going to enjoy every moment of it. Regan was a poor scrub farmer. His few acres were located on the outskirts of Biloxi. He had left his wife and six children to tend their few acres of cotton, milk cows, pigs and chickens. He owned no slaves…never had. He worked the land side by side with his family. He didn't care about blacks…didn't like 'em, didn't hate 'em. He just wanted to be left alone and not be told by any government official what he could and could not do. He had traveled west several years earlier from Georgia when he felt it was getting too crowded. He was like so many of the hordes of settlers who had no hesitation picking up their few belongings when rumors of good farm land and fresh water beckoned.

Sean did like to fight. His body was scarred from scrapes he'd had from the time he was a child in New York's infamous Five Corner slums. Animals, siblings and total strangers were all reasons to exchange blows. He didn't care who he fought. The Reb forces were closer to his Biloxi farm, so he joined them.

Regan laughed at everything around him…his food, his uniform, even his weapons. But his favorite targets were young, arrogant Confederate officers who had spent more money on their fine uniforms than Regan had seen in his life. This lack of respect by an ignorant no-account farmer made Rogers and the other officers furious. They might have punished him severely but the Irishman was better at aiming the cannon and faster at loading it than anyone else in the gun crew, but to him it was all a game. Rogers would shout at him, make him stand at attention for long periods and refuse him his ration of rum, but Regan's bluster never seemed to cease. He'd make some face, or scratch his ass in a provocative way and the rest of the men would laugh. Eventually Rogers and Regan reached a silent truce and the futile attempts to discipline him ceased along with Sean's attacks on the officers.

Henry worked his crews tirelessly to the annoyance of other, less arrogant, officers. In the close quarters of the artillery batteries many of the officers had taken to removing their jackets and sabers. Not Henry. His self-image would not permit sloppiness in himself or his men. His team was made to rise early, down a breakfast of tea and hardtack, and begin the practice of loading, aiming and firing. Sloppy loading could cause the breech of the gun to explode and kill an entire gun crew. His men's abilities improved slowly but no one wanted to venture what they would do when the Union ships coming up the river might begin firing back at them.

The unceasing spring rains made visibility down river more difficult. Word that the Union ships were getting closer to the forts reached them and the gun crews waited, ready at their cannon, rain pelting them in furious staccato outbursts, the river below belching white caps as if angry at this intrusion of their domain. The Union ships plowed slowly north, moving against the current, as thunder and lightning occasionally lit up the night sky to mark their movements.

As the flotilla reached the artillery range of the forts above, the bombardment began. It was mid-April. Cannon from both sides of the river matched each clap of thunder with their own fusillades as the Union ships directed their artillery up toward the forts. For seven days Henry's men and the other batteries sent forth shell after shell. On those nights devoid of the moon's light to direct them, an eerie quiet pervaded the scene and the men on the boats and in the forts gathered for delicious minutes of sleep, still clothed in their soaked wool uniforms, smelling of dirt, sweat and gun smoke, all mingled into an acrid stench.

In the fifth week of the battle as the increased pace of the flotilla's salvos hit the Fort with more frequency, Henry lost three more of his men to the spray of grapeshot exploding nearby. Their bodies were sent below to a small infirmary set aside for the wounded and dead. A day later, Sean Regan was hit. A mortar shell exploded within feet of his gun emplacement. He fell to the ground, grabbing his midsection where a large piece of shrapnel had entered. Henry knelt by his side until two orderlies carried the delirious Irishman below. There were no cots and only the flickering light of candles to mark the way. The smell of seared flesh and dying men blended into a putrid combination.

During a lull in the battle, Henry went to see his Irish fusilier.

"How are you, Sean? You look fine," Henry lied.

"I don't think so, Captain. I think it's God's last and best joke on me." Sean pressed an envelope into Henry's hand as his eyes made a silent request. His eyes closed and his head fell to the side. A huge smile never left his face.

During a heated battle the wounded men lay side by side for hours in that dark, dank room that had been built to store ammunition but now only warehoused bodies, the living crying for something to ease their pain before they expired to join the men lying still next to them, the stench of the decay hanging invisibly from the walls. Death would be a pleasant release from the agony of their untreatable wounds.

Henry didn't remember the envelope he was given until days later when it was clear the Union ships had passed the range of the Confederate guns. It was a letter to Sean's wife. He knew it was personal but he understood, somehow instinctively, that Sean had wanted him to read it before sending it on.

> 'Dear Beth,
>
> If you're reading this letter it means I ain't gonna be comin' home. It's up to you to see to the kids and the farm. I know it ain't what you figured when I got you drunk enough to agree to marry me but you always were a softie for an Irishman with a line of Blarney. I loved you mightily, Beth ma' lass, and the bonnie kids you bore us. It was a good life and I'm sorry to be leavin' it though I figure where I'm goin' there'll be lots of good scraps waitin' for me.'
>
> Sean

Henry had heard that a lot of the men wrote final letters and kept them to be sent in the event they were killed. It never occurred to him that it would now be his responsibility to have it delivered. He put a $100 Confederate bill into the envelope and carefully resealed it. He wiped a tear, careful that no one saw him. He'd miss the cantankerous Irishman.

Eventually the north was able to get thirteen small ships past the forts and continue unimpeded toward their upstream destination of New Orleans. Each force had lost nearly a thousand men but the entrance to the nation's longest river had been breached.

> As early as 1718 the city of New Orleans had been a different sort of a destination. Explorers, fur traders, and those lusting for adventure found themselves enjoying its loose, uncritical life. From Spanish to French to American control, the city evolved its own energy and personality.
>
> Development along the Mississippi meant growth for the city.

*Plantations and towns began to surround the riverfront. Sugar, rice, indigo and cotton moved in increasing tonnage through the city's warehouses despite frequent outbreaks of malaria, cholera and dysentery from the city's sea level terrain, uncertain weather, and unsanitary living conditions.*

*Brothels and gambling establishments prospered. Races mixed as nowhere else in the country. Black mistresses were desirable consorts for the wealthy white planters. Their offspring, mulatto children, became adults, mixed again, and a quadroon population evolved. It wasn't uncommon for the fathers to support these children with housing and education. It was a city that enjoyed the success of the Deep South but it was not of the south. It was its own mistress.*

*At the beginning of May the city surrendered to the small approaching Union forces without a shot being fired. Union rule over the city would be stern but the city would not be razed. The loss of this important port would have a major adverse effect on the ability of the South to sell its cotton, and the survival of the Confederacy.*

The news of the fall of New Orleans reached Moss Grove within hours. Jedidiah came in from one of the few morning rides he'd enjoyed in months. Ruby joined him in his study, tea untouched on the table, as they tried to absorb the news. New Orleans was gone! In the control of the Union army! Here in our own heartland! It was an emotional blow. How could we lose this prize jewel so easily? How did our son fare? Was he one of those killed defending the river? Did he comport himself with honor?

Questions without answers flooded both Jedidiah and Ruby's thoughts as they held one another's hands in disbelief. Jedidiah sent out another rider just to find Henry and bring him back, if necessary. The rider could get no further than the approaches to New Orleans and was forced to return with no information on Henry's health or his whereabouts.

That evening Jedidiah asked Thaddeus to eat with them in the dining room. As Jacob served the meal he stared at this boy he and Sarah had raised, smiling to himself. Thaddeus sat at the big table for the first time, unsettled by the occasion. Ruby understood. It was her husband's concern for Henry. If he had been killed in the battle, Thaddeus might be their only surviving child and possible heir to Moss Grove. He wanted to keep the boy close.

"We've got to do things differently, Rupert," Jedidiah said as he and his overseer watched newly born piglets suckling the huge sow. "We've got to think about how things might change now that New Orleans is in Yankee hands."

"I agree, Mr. Jed. At some point those Union troops will be heading this way," Rupert nodded.

"I will not wait idly for that moment without doing something. These perilous times require action. There could only have been a limited number of troops aboard the Union ships and they will be busy trying to occupy the city. That will give us time. It is unlikely an attack on Baton Rouge or the state's northern parishes can be launched in the next several months. The Union Army will first have to ferry more troops, cannon and supplies. We must be prepared. Let's invite all the other nearby plantation owners for a meeting here at Moss Grove. We will need to work together."

"I'll have riders sent out today and I'll have some of the field hands help Miss Sarah get things ready for a large crowd."

Within days fifty of the most influential land owners in the parish congregated at Moss Grove. Most, but not all, were slave owners. Some had learned they could make more money from the frequent breeding and sale of their slaves than they could from raising cotton. All were independent men, religious, and self-righteous. All were firmly committed to the retention of their lifestyle. These were serious men with serious problems. Jedidiah organized the meeting while Ruby and the house staff kept food and liquor readily available. The discussions and planning were projected to last three days.

"I want to thank you all for coming," Jedidiah said. It was early evening and the men stood in small groups around the patio in the rear of the house. Most had had time to wash and remove the dust from their journey. Others had just arrived.

"We have a serious task ahead of us," he continued. I've worked out an agenda but we want everyone's input."

"We don't need too much yakking," one man shouted, "We'll just kill those blue bastards when they come 'round."

Laughter and cheers made it clear they all agreed.

"I'm sure we all feel the same way," Jed continued. "Unfortunately our plight is a little more complicated. I think we've got four separate problems to deal with. We need to be able to ship our cotton. We need to protect our families. We need to defend our property and we need to think about what to do about our slaves.

"I'd like each of you to focus on one of these problems tomorrow and then we'll reconvene and hear from each of the groups. One committee will work on ways we can continue shipping our products. We're going to need to find some way to circumvent the Union blockade. Another group will focus on the best way to protect our women and children. The third group needs to assume the Yankees get here and consider ways to thwart any Union attack against our homes and our land. And the last group needs to figure out to do with the many slaves we own. What is the likelihood that they would stay and help, or revolt and side with the north? Meanwhile, drink up and relax this evening. We've prepared a good meal to warm your innards."

Moss Grove's house staff served and tarried as unobtrusively as possible within each group. Over the next three days the men filled rooms, sat under trees, and walked along the river as each man shared his thoughts. The lives of these blacks might well depend on what these white folk were talkin' about. When the staff returned to the kitchen they shared what they'd heard, who had said what, and from the fabric of each discussion group they tried to assemble the whole cloth.

Sarah helped the girls fill another tray of chicken and biscuits.

"We should just up and leave," one black commented.

"I don't know how far it is to a free state but it can't be far," said another.

"It's near two hundred miles," Jesse interjected. "And neither of you has ever been further than a mile or two. You'd probably get so turned around you'd climb up your own behind. Now, stop chattering and serve that food before it gets cold."

As the two men grabbed the trays, they continued to voice their thoughts.

"We could just follow the river."

"Too easy to get caught and I ain't ready to be tarred and lynched."

"We'd be OK if we had a compass. I seen Massa' Rupert's but he keeps it close. Ain't no one gonna steal it."

Leave or stay? Northern troops might soon arrive and free them. We have a good life here and we need to defend it. They weighed their options. Framed by their life's experience, their age, their family responsibilities, and the treatment by their masters, convictions swirled in the kitchen and slave quarters. Each man would make his own decision but without any assurance that it was the right one.

Thaddeus was a constant presence among the white guests. He served these men folk with the care and the courtesy he'd been taught, and with a respectful smile. He wanted to go to war. He was a southern boy. The only thing he knew about the north came from Massa' Jed's newspapers and that wasn't very much. He'd overhear Massa' Jedidiah talk about the 'blue bellies' but he was sure he didn't mean that for real. He'd swear a lot when he mentioned some devil named Lincoln. On the other hand, the men who came through Moss Grove wearing the grey uniforms of the Confederacy looked mighty fine. Even the rude ones looked good and he was sure they were rude because he was a kid. It didn't occur to him that the difference in his color was the sole basis for their attitudes. He just knew that he was old enough to have opinions and do more than say 'yessa' to the white folks.

Jedidiah's guests submitted their reports on the third day of their meetings. To assist in the fight against the Yankees, the plantation owners would commit men to the Third Louisiana Cavalry formed to fight alongside Captain James Wingfield's infantry company from St. Helena Parish. These men had already seen action against the Union force at Ship Island and had accounted themselves professionally.

Dealing with the slaves was inexorably more complicated. Young black men who wanted to actively support the Confederacy would be encouraged to join the Native Guards, an all black pseudo-military organization assigned to protect homes and property. They, or their masters, would have to provide them their uniforms, horses, arms, and ammunition. They would serve under white officers. They would join the same groups to which free blacks were already serving.

Thaddeus' eyes lit with excitement when he heard of this group. He would join, either with Daddy Jesse's approval, or he'd run away and simply volunteer. He was nearly a man. It was his duty, he reasoned.

The meeting ended enthusiastically. They would be doing something about their fate. Each man committed himself and his family's resources to do his share to repel these abolitionist heathens.

As Jedidiah and Rupert had foreseen, the only Union attacks on Baton Rouge were from scouting parties. During June and July various squads of Wingfield's Confederate Cavalry harried and ambushed them. Meanwhile Moss Grove's only news these days came from riders passing through, or an occasional copy of the Baton Rouge Gazette. It was no longer feasible to send out regular house slaves to ride that far south. By late July the Gazette reported that Union forces had been bolstered enough to make parallel thrusts on both sides of the Amite River, a nearby fork of the Mississippi.

> *By late September Lee's army had been halted at Sharpsburg, Maryland in the battle of Antietam. Hoping eagerly for a black rebellion that would collapse the Confederacy from within, Lincoln issued his Emancipation Proclamation. Effective the following January all slaves owned within states that had seceded from the Union were to be considered free. He did not free the smaller number of slaves owned within Border States. It was clearly a decree of military expediency rather than moral indignation.*
>
> *As the holidays and the cold of winter approached, the South won another major military victory at Fredericksburg, Maryland. In a single day more than twelve thousand Union soldiers were killed or wounded as they made repeated and unsuccessful frontal assaults against southern troops comfortably ensconced in higher positions well-hidden by heavy foliage. It was a blow to the army, Lincoln and the entire north. How could such a massive loss have happened?*

Henry left Fort Jackson badly depressed. While the fort was still in Confederate hands, it had failed in its task of keeping the Mississippi open and New Orleans safe. It was his first brush with failure and nothing in his life had prepared him for it. He blamed his commanders, his gun crews, his weaponry, and even God, for the adverse weather. The loss wasn't supposed to happen. All officers that had defended both forts were being reassigned to Port Hudson, further north up the river. The Confederate army would amass weapons and troops to make another stand. Their troops would be better trained and they understood the strategic importance of their task. They would be facing resupplied Union forces, whose flotilla was expected to continue to ply its way north up the river.

Henry detoured through Baton Rouge to see Elizabeth and her parents.

The city was in an emotional shambles, unsure of its future after the fall of New Orleans. There was talk of military law being imposed. Those families able to leave the city were packing their wagons and heading north or toward Mississippi. Fear of an impending attack by Union forces was on everyone's mind. Rumors abounded. The attack would come next week, next month, not for awhile. No one knew and everyone knew.

Henry understood he couldn't leave his fiancé and future in-laws there to fend for themselves. Whatever business Mr. Williams owned, he would likely find himself out of merchandise to sell if the blockade was successful. After a dinner that first evening they all agreed that staying was too dangerous. They would assemble whatever wagons they could gather and move their belongings north to Moss Grove where, at least for the foreseeable future, they would all be safer.

Amy didn't want to leave. If Henry wanted them to go, it had to be the wrong decision. She continued to see bad things in his eyes. Baton Rouge, even without her family, would be better than being at Moss Grove with Henry. She would like to see Thaddeus again, but even that wouldn't be worth disrupting her life. No one seemed to care what a tomboy younger sister wanted. The rest of the family continued to be enthralled by Henry Rogers and his decisiveness in this perceived emergency.

Within days of the Moss Grove meeting Henry and the Williams family arrived. There was to be no respite. Henry had been given an additional month before he would need to report and that would leave enough time for the wedding. No one expected a winter attack by Union Forces. He could get married and get to Port Arthur in plenty of time. Perhaps Moss Grove would be able to enjoy one more holiday season with pleasant memories.

# Chapter Seven

The winter that saw the end of 1862 and the arrival of 1863 was cold and cruel. Animals that were generally able to forage for themselves now needed to be fed. Deer that could be hunted had gone far afield seeking warmer environs. Ice had to be broken in the wells and at the river to get to fresh water. Kindling that usually lay close was too buried in snow banks to be visible. Important rooms at Moss Grove had to be heated constantly. Spare bed covers were pulled from storage to fend off the freezing temperatures that blew across the land. Snows continued to lay white blankets everywhere and fears of whether the next cotton crop would yield anything worried whites and blacks alike.

In the slave cabins colds were commonplace. Coughs racked every hut and spread easily among those living together in cramped quarters. Several slaves developed severe cases of chilblains that kept them bedridden and unable to work the fields. Rose's godmother, the woman who cared for her since birth, died, unable to sustain the cold with her frail health. She had been Auntie to everyone. She was one of those ageless, heavily wrinkled, crone-like women who carried the unwritten knowledge of herbs and roots that cured so many different ailments.

Auntie had done everything possible to bring Rose into the world and she had succeeded against all odds. It had been a complicated breech birth. The cord had been wrapped around the baby's neck. Rose's mother never survived long enough to see her daughter. As a slave she'd been mated to so many different men no one of them ever stepped up to claim fatherhood. Auntie was ever present, always there when Rose needed anything. And when Rose returned from giving birth to Thaddeus and then having to give him up, it was she who cuddled and consoled the young girl. Now, she, too, had passed on. And in Rose's heart she was certain that Auntie had gone to a better place. It was a cold, white, uncaring time. There just wasn't enough warmth anywhere.

Rose and Faris cuddled together under their two thin blankets. Stray beams of light from a cold quarter moon wafted through their small cabin as two candles lit their sparse furnishings. They could see vapors rising from their son's breath sleeping close by.

"Rose, ah gets hard just lyin' next to you even after all these years," Faris muttered, spooning closer.

"Shhh, you'll wake the boy. He don't need to hear us."

"You silly girl. The boy would have to be a deaf mute. He sleepin' only a long arm away. Oooh," he said, "you got the softest, tightest, pussy a man would ever want."

"How many pussies you know about? You a expert on 'dem?" she teased back.

"Man got great imagination and I seen enuf' to say you in a class a' your own, dat's fo' sure," he laughed.

Faris turned Rose toward him and his hard staff, pulsating at full strength, throbbed against her. Faris was a big man by any standard and his massive weight almost overwhelmed her tiny body. It frightened her when they first made love, nearly total strangers to one another. As her love for this gentle man grew through the years, so did her comfort with the energy of their love making. She could feel her nerves tense with pleasure and her nipples harden. Even in the dim light they could see enough of one another to smile, a harmony of blended thoughts and feelings.

He entered her slowly and kissed her to block the tiny sounds that came erotically to the surface from deep within her being. In silence they coupled, sharing their bodies as they shared the love that had evolved between them. That love had salvaged Rose in ways she'd never thought possible. She had grown from a frightened damaged child to a woman fulfilled by a wonderful man. Together they had produced a son she loved as much as the other son she could only watch grow into manhood from a distance. Faris, too, had changed. He spoke more and laughed with the other men as they worked. Feelings that had always been locked inside him began to surface. He had a wife and son, just like other men. It was something he never thought he'd have. Matthew, his son...from his seed.

Gentle like his mother but Faris knew that the boy carried his traits as well. He could see it in his boy's eyes and in his smile.

The winter continued to take its toll. Jedidiah recovered from his cough of the previous fall and then fell ill again. Ruby's stomach became distended and her temperature rose to a dangerous level. But it was difficult for doctors to make the trip from Baton Rouge with so much illness and sickness rampant among that precarious population. What little medicine might have been available had been confiscated by the small Confederate force still hoping to defend the city against impending Union attacks.

> *Over the generations the slaves had developed their own pharmacology. They rarely had access to doctors or traditional medicines. The tribal knowledge of a thousand years had come with them from Africa. It was passed on to each successive generation. It evolved in this new country, mixing the knowledge of American Indian shamans with that of blacks and whites. Slaves learned to use the plants that grew around them.*

Sarah mixed an ointment for Miss Ruby that would reduce the swelling that was causing the woman so much pain. Sarah had watched Auntie through the years and she was quick to learn and make notes. She would never have the older woman's instinct and magic fingers but she had slowly gathered her own store of healing roots and herbs. Now she could watch with satisfaction as Miss Ruby's discomfort eased and her mistress could sleep soundly.

The wedding of the future Captain and Mrs. Henry Rogers, nee Elizabeth Williams, was held the first Sunday following the New Year. It had been a quiet Christmas. Friends were reluctant to travel, fearful of being shot by Union scouts moving through the countryside and a winter that was equally unforgiving. In the end the wedding was a small Moss Grove family affair supplemented only by the Raffertys and families from the two nearest plantations. Elizabeth wore the gown her mother had worn a quarter century earlier. The girl certainly wasn't pretty, Sarah thought to herself silently.

"We make you real pretty, Miss Elizabeth. You be the prettiest bride

Moss Grove ever done seen," Sarah said before realizing that Miss Ruby herself had been married at the plantation many years earlier.

"'Cept for Miss Ruby," she added, seeing her mistress' grimace change to a broad, happily reminiscent, smile. Moss Grove's matriarch sat huddled in a chair nearby, clutching the few rays of the sun and the limited warmth they exuded. She felt well enough to sit in a chair. She'd rather be dead than miss her only son's wedding.

Ruby had assigned Sarah to help the girl get herself together. A corset was found and tied so tight the young girl thought she'd pass out from a lack of air. Amy sat on the bed laughing hysterically.

"Looks more like medieval torture than a beauty aid," Amy grinned as Sarah pulled the strings ever tighter.

"A lot you know," her sister gasped. "Someday you may want to be married. That is if you can ever find a man who likes girls with dirty faces and muddy coveralls."

"Don't care none! Ain't never marryin'!"

"Aren't ever marrying," she corrected. "You'd be pretty now if you wanted to. You're going to need a brassiere pretty soon for your little titties."

"Ooooh…I'm leaving." Amy ran from the room and the laughter of Sarah, Ruby and Sylvia Williams.

Flowers were in short supply this icy winter season but the slaves had managed to creatively string branches and tree boughs to add a little beauty to the otherwise stark surroundings.

Standing alone at the altar, Henry waited. He was bedecked in his Confederate grey finery. His boots and saber cast a reflective luster. His bearing left no doubt that this was his day and in the not too distant future he would control all he surveyed.

House and field slaves didn't attend the ceremony in Moss Grove's chapel but everyone was invited to partake in the celebration afterward. Huge fires had been set up to ward off a little of the cold. Two pigs had been slaughtered and spit-roasted along with a hind quarter from one of the small herd of cattle. A small orchestra of field hands played their harmonicas, fiddles and banjos. The music was loud and enthusiastic, spirituals mixed with war songs and tales of Confederate victories.

Guests gathered in small clusters, eating and drinking. House servants, at least those that weren't working, hung close together but instinctively they had separated themselves a fair distance from the field slaves. They had little in common other than the color of their skin in this caste-based society.

Mrs. Rafferty and her son, Abner, stood off to one side. She wore a black dress, plain, with long sleeves and a small ribbon at the neck. Her son, now a young man, wore ill-fitted clothes that had obviously belonged to his father.

Rupert Rafferty, Moss Grove's long time overseer, had died three months earlier from pneumonia. He was a big, tough German who spoke with a heavy accent until the day he died. He, his wife, and son had their own quarters where they lived a quiet contemplative life. They had brought their Lutheran faith from Germany. Mrs. Rafferty stayed to herself as much as possible, uncomfortable with her limited English and her different religious beliefs. She had no interest in socializing with the Catholics or Baptists that dominated Louisiana and the nearby plantations. She was comfortable in this religion of her birth and she had no desire to have other beliefs contaminate her family.

This Teutonic plantation foreman had been especially good with horses and was patient in sharing his knowledge with any of the field slaves interested in caring for the horses. These four-legged animals were often as valuable as any slave and they needed considerable attention. It had been he who had trained Luther as well as his son.

"I hope you're enjoying the festivities, Mrs. Rafferty. How're you feeling," Jedidiah asked as he walked toward the woman and her now, grown son.

"It's a beautiful wedding, Mr. Rogers. Please thank Mrs. Rogers for all the extra food and concern she's shown since Rupert died but it isn't necessary. Abner and I are managing quite well."

"Well, we've both been concerned. Abner, may I speak to you for a few minutes?" The two men walked off toward the river where they could talk without interruption.

"Abner, I need you to reconsider leaving so quickly. Moss Grove needs your skilled hand and I need you."

"You've been kind to my family, Mr. Rogers, but I have to leave. I'm joining up with the 1st Mississippi Battalion in three days. We're heading for Vicksburg. They tell me there'll be a major battle there by late summer and the Confederacy needs every able bodied man."

"Abner, I understand your urge to join the other young men but I need you. Your father ran Moss Grove, even more than I did since I've been ill and Henry is gone. You know almost everything he did and you probably know all of our people by their first name. Give me time to get a suitable replacement."

"I'm not the right man, Mister Jed. I grew up with these niggers. We been tussling and playing together my entire life. I don't feel right bossing them around. Blacks are blacks. They're niggers and that says it all. They don't think like white folk."

"Then don't boss them…just direct them in what needs to be done. You'll have some of the other overseers your father hired to help but they can't do it by themselves. They haven't been at Moss Grove more than a year."

"I'm not sure. I would have gone earlier but my father asked me to stay. Now that he's gone I thought I'd be free to go my own way."

"What about your mother? She's newly widowed and she's still grieving. You'd be asking her to lose a husband and her only son in just a few months. Give her a little time, give me one harvesting season, and then I'll not only wish you well, I'll pay for your uniform and a new rifle."

In the end Abner agreed to stay until mid-August. Whether it was his commitment to his mother or a new rifle, Jedidiah couldn't be sure but at least he'd be sure of someone familiar with Moss Grove to plant and harvest the cotton.

Abner would want to get to his Reb unit in Tennessee. If he rode hard he could be there in four days and he might not be too late for the battle. Early September and his life would change. Killing blue-bellies would be great fun. He never met any but they had no fucking business comin' down here and tellin' us how to run our lives. We need to run 'em off. Then I think I'll head west. Maybe I'll go to California. Might even still be some of that gold out there. Sh-e-e-t…that gold stuff seems to be everywhere. California, then Colorado, now here tell, way up in Alaska! Now that's a place for a feller to go.

There was Faris, Abner thought, standing on the fringe of the crowd amidst the field hands, looking uncomfortable at being directed to eat and enjoy himself.

"Hey, Faris. Quite a shindig, ain't it?"

"Hello, Abner. How's your momma doing with your Daddy gone?" Faris asked.

Even in his near stupor from too much drink, the young man, and now

an overseer, realized Faris never called him 'sir' or 'massa' as was the proper
way to talk to your betters. That's what comes from growin' up together,
he mused. No respect. But it's too cold and too much of a celebration to
hassle anyone any which way. At least he could sleep it off tomorrow.

"Thinkin' of headin' for Alaska to dig for gold next year, soon as we
lick the blue bellies. Wanna think 'bout comin' with me?"

"Don't likely think Massa' Jed favor such a thing. Maybe if 'ah be
freed....some day," he added as an afterthought.

"That ain't likely. South growin' stronger everyday. I goin' to Vicksburg
in the fall. Gonna' kill me some union soldiers."

Rose, Matthew and few of the other field slaves had been ordered to help
the house servants. The large number of visitors as well as the extra chores
necessary because of the unseasonably cold weather had overburdened the
regular staff. Matthew, because of his age was assigned limited tasks. In all
his years he'd never been in Moss Grove's main house. His large black eyes
widened in amazement at things he was seeing for the first time. Imagine,
rugs on the floors to keep your feet warm. Chamber pots at the bedside.
No need to go to the outhouse in the freezing cold. Wash basins, soap,
towels and clothes. So many clothes. Seems like these white folks can wear
a different outfit every day of the year, if'n they choosin'. And so many
shoes and boots, 'nuf to cover the feet of a caterpillar, he imagined.

Thaddeus moved steadily between the crowd and the kitchen, carrying
trays of food and drink. He stopped briefly to watch the ceremony, standing
close to Sarah and Jesse. They put their arms tightly around him, almost as
if they were afraid to have him separated. Massa' Henry looked real nice in
his uniform. I know he don't like me, the boy thought. Well, I don't like
him no way either. Then he noticed Matthew hovering nearby.

"Whatcha' doin, Matthew?" Thaddeus said as he approached the wide-
eyed boy.

"Thaddeus! You sure look nice in your dressy outfit. Mine sure don't
fit me. It must be nice to work in the big house. They got so many things
I ain't never seen before."

"It is nice, but what are you doing here?" Thaddeus persisted.

"They got some of us field hands helpin' out cuz there's so many people
visitin."

"We can talk later. Right now we both need to keep moving and not
staring at the white folks."

"Well, most of 'em look the same. I'm not sure sometimes how to tell 'em apart."

"Want me to tell you a secret?" Thaddeus asked.

"Shee-it, you don't know no good secrets."

"Ah do. Ah gets to listen to all the white folk talkin'. Ah seems to be invisible to them. This war thing has 'em in righteous terror. Did you know they got groups that black folk like us can join and fight the blue-bellies?"

"What're blue-bellies?" Matthew asked.

"Don't you be a ignorant nigger," he teased, wanting to show off to the younger boy. "It's what they call the white soldiers from the north."

"They got blue bellies?"

"Nah, blue uniforms," Thaddeus answered, feeling quite superior.

"Ain't the north fightin' for us? Ain't they gonna make us not be slaves no more?"

"Ah'm not sure. I hear some folk say they goin' to free all the slaves but I hear other folk say they goin' to ship us all back to someplace called Africa," Thaddeus said.

"I don't know no Africa. If it's a long way I ain't gonna go unless my mammy and daddy go. My daddy wants to head north but my mammy, she born here, and she want to stay. So, I reckon we gonna' stay. She da' boss in our place. He da' biggest, but she the most ornery when she sets her mind to it."

"I know your mammy...her name is Rose. I saw her face down Massa' Henry at the river that time. She really somethin'."

Amy wandered through the party, returning the smiles of the few white adult guests that were brave enough to have made the trip, most of whom she had never met. She felt uncomfortable in her crinoline dress but she had to confess to herself that the tiny protrusions on her chest did evoke special feelings. Maybe she'd have titties after all. She took a small piece of crisp burnt pork and moved closer to the fire, enjoying the heat and glowing embers crackling upward into the black sky.

Looking back toward the house she eyed Thaddeus talking to another black boy wearing serving clothes clearly too large for him. She tossed the last of the pork into the fire and scurried over.

"Thaddeus, how good to see you. Land's sake, you've gotten so tall."

"Miss Amy," Thaddeus stuttered, suddenly wondering whether Massa'

Henry might be watching them. "You look real nice in a dress. I didn't recognize you."

"You look nice, too. Different than the coveralls and mud," she laughed. "Don't worry, Thaddeus. Henry and my sister aren't around. I've been staying as far away from them as possible myself. The family made me dress up. I like my other clothes better," she smiled.

"And who is this? Aren't you going to introduce me?" she said, smiling at Matthew, standing there startled and frozen at the interruption by this young white girl.

"Well, if he won't say anything, I will. My name is Amy. I'm Elizabeth's younger sister, and, to my regrets, a new resident of Moss Grove. There!" she said. "And who are you?"

Matthew's eyes widened. No white girl, particularly one not much older than himself, had ever addressed him before.

"My name is Matthew, Miss Amy," he stuttered. "Nice to make your acquaintance." He bowed his head as he had been taught to do when speaking with white folks but his voice came out haltingly. He was confused and uncertain how to act.

Amy turned her attention back to Thaddeus.

"Maybe we can meet by the river and look for frogs," she smiled. "It sure riled a lot of people last time."

"I think if Massa' Henry's around it probably wouldn't be a good idea."

"I was just teasing. I felt really bad the way you were treated."

"Could have been worse, I hear. My mama stood right up to him," Matthew interjected.

"That took some courage," Amy said.

Matthew knew about the altercation at the river. The entire plantation knew some black kid had been hit by Massa' Henry over some white girl a year back. He even knew his mother had intervened but no one would ever tell him the details. Only now did he realize it must have been Thaddeus and Amy. Here he was, with the two of them, afraid of getting into trouble and too proud to just bolt. He realized he was getting really nervous.

"See that, Thaddeus, at least Matthew didn't lose his tongue," the red haired girl teased.

"Maybe not, Miss Amy, but he does look as if he could wet his pants," Thaddeus laughed.

A small wet spot had appeared on the front of Matthew's pants. The younger boy, feeling the dampness and the surprised smiles on Amy and Thaddeus' face across from him were too much. He was so embarrassed. He knew he'd cry if he stayed. He ran toward the slave quarters, ignoring Thaddeus' pleas to come back. Matthew knew he'd be in trouble. There was work to do. He was supposed to be helping, not scurrying away from the house.

Faris had seen his son talking and then running away. He was concerned and followed him. Matthew stood as close as he could stand to the sole fire going in the slave quarters, willing his pants to dry. If he didn't return to the kitchen soon, he'd be tanned for sure.

"Matthew, are you alright?" Faris asked.

Matthew jumped. He wiped the tears from his cheek with the sleeve of his borrowed jacket, ashamed at being such a baby.

"I'm fine. Jus' wanted a break," he lied. He could hear the music and singing coming from the veranda.

"I don't think you're fine. What is it? Why are you standing so close to the fire?"

"I got my pant's wet…that's all. I was jus' talkin' to Thaddeus and a white girl and I got nervous."

Faris smiled. "Wet…from the inside?" he asked softly.

"Yes, sir. I am so embarrassed."

"What happened is normal to boys as they become men. You and I will have a long talk tomorrow. Meanwhile, if your pants are dry you should get back to your duties."

Matthew and Faris hugged and the young boy scurried back, careful to avoid both Thaddeus and Amy, and, except for a scowl or two from Sarah, nothing was said. With all the hubbub he hoped that she wouldn't remember later.

Jedidiah rose, faced his guests, and smiled. Ruby sat close by, a shawl wrapped tightly around her shoulders. Henry and Elizabeth stood to one side, the husband uncharacteristically more handsome than his bride.

"My friends, I want to thank you all for coming. I know traveling these days is not an easy task. I don't know which to dread most, the intrusion of the cold or the northerners. Perhaps one is responsible for the other."

The guests nodded and smiled, all of them too aware of the events whirling around them.

"We are here," he continued, "To celebrate the wedding of our son,

Henry, to his lovely bride, Elizabeth. Her parents have been dear friends and kin of ours for many happy years.

"Given the situation south of here around Baton Rouge, the Williams have kindly agreed to remain at Moss Grove as our guests for as long as necessary. Henry has been posted to Port Hudson and will need to be leaving us quite soon. The year ahead will put a strain on each of us but as long as a breath remains we will strive to protect our homes, our families, our way of life and our best hope for keeping them all...the Confederacy.

"Friends, please join me in raising your glasses to President Jefferson Davis, our beloved General Robert E. Lee and our Southern Union."

"Long live the Confederacy," they shouted in unison.

# Chapter Eight

One of the wedding guests had brought week old copies of the New Orleans Picayune. Jedidiah has been so caught up with all the planning and turmoil he had lost track of what was going on elsewhere in the nation. He awoke early, donned his robe, grabbed the stack of papers and stood quietly by their bed, watching Ruby sleeping, her hair splayed across the satin pillow case. Her breathing was smooth and untroubled. She was as beautiful to him as she had been for so much of his life. She was both the ballast and anchor to the winds of change that were buffeting their lives.

He leaned down and brushed her cheek with his lips. She stirred but didn't waken. It had been a long but happy evening. He smiled and closed the door softly behind him.

Jesse, Sarah, and the rest of the house staff were already awake, tidying up the loose ends from the evening's revelry. Normally Miss Ruby would have been awake as well, distributing food for the day to the slave kitchen staff. But the party had lasted well past midnight. Burnt down candles had been replaced twice and the guests, who had not already left, were still asleep.

"Good mornin', Massa' Jed. You up early," Jesse said.

"Couldn't sleep. I thought the wedding events went well. Please thank the staff for me. Just bring me some coffee. I want to get caught up with these newspapers."

He sat, looking out on what promised to be a slightly warmer day. Perhaps the winter's cold would disappear soon. He smiled and then scowled as he read the headline:

### "Union Forces in Disarray. Stonewall Jackson killed"

The Union Army continued in disarray despite having a two to one military superiority. Lincoln continued to replace generals he deemed ineffective as fast as a coon chases a fox. Burnside replaced McClellan, who, within months, was replaced by Hooker. As April rains ended and the blue skies and floral mists of spring blossomed, Hooker's 130,000 man Army of the Potomac confronted our Louisiana boys fighting with Robert E. Lee's Army of Northern Virginia, with half the troops and artillery, facing them.

The Union force, well-supplied and well-rested from their long-winter hibernation, crossed the fast-running Rappahannock River at several different points. The balance of Hooker's army attacked through the near impenetrable thickets of scrub and copses of pine that surrounded Chancellorsville. The Yankee artillery was useless in this terrain and ineffective against our sharp-shootin' Rebs.

Hooker's plodding and unimaginative tactics allowed Lee to split his forces and attack the Federal forces from both the front and flank inflicting heavy damage. Other units cut the Union telegraph lines making it impossible for the separate northern units to communicate.

Another rebel unit launched a surprise attack on General Howard's 11,000 man corps. Most were killed or taken prisoner in the midst of preparing their meager evening meal. Nearly 4,000 Union soldiers surrendered and were marched away from a battlefield strewn with bodies. Those that survived were sent to our Confederate prison at Andersonville, and good riddance.

Pressing his advantage, our beloved Stonewall Jackson, moved too far ahead of his own troops and was mistakenly shot by his own troops.

On May 3d, as the battle continued in an inconclusive exchange, nearly 18,000 troops from both sides were killed. Many of the Union dead were German and Irish immigrants, not three months off the ships that had brought them to American shores filled with aspirations of hope and freedom from their restrictive lives in Europe. They had arrived with smiles, having completed a most difficult journey. Most arrived without any money. It was easy for those Yankee enlistment scoundrels to convince them to enlist in the Union Army for a pittance. Within days they were given a uniform *and ferried south to fight against us, bearing the south no ill will, but tricked to swell the number of troops attacking our sovereign nation.*

*On May 6th our boys forced the blue coats to retreat back over the river they had so confidently crossed six days earlier. We won an astounding victory that day but at a terrible cost. We lost 25% of the infantry soldiers that had begun the battle. It will be difficult to replace this loss of men and materiel as a result of the ongoing blockade harassing our southern ports. Thanks to some brave privateers and weapons we captured from retreating northern forces, however, we are continuing to wage an aggressive campaign wherever Lincoln's lackeys confront our brave men.*

Good men were being killed, Jedidiah sighed. He sipped his coffee, now cold, and stared out across his veranda at the gardens he had enjoyed so many mornings. This war will be at our door soon enough, he feared.

Upstairs Henry Rogers stirred and was happy that his honeymoon would be brief. His new wife was as ardent as yeast rising. He performed his husbandly duties but it was clear that Elizabeth's limited sexual experience would never quell his lust. Henry didn't mind. There were plenty of whores around who knew how to satisfy a man. His wife would fulfill her familial duties and raise him a family. He would find his sport elsewhere.

"Henry, come back to bed," Elizabeth said, as she stirred and realized she was alone under the heavy comforter.

"Good morning," he responded as he continued to shave, standing at the basin filled with the hot water he'd been brought.

"Go back to sleep. It's still early."

"I feel so different," she sighed. "I'm a wife. You are my husband. Did I do alright last night? I mean…"

Henry turned toward her and laughed. It wasn't a mean laugh. He knew the moment he'd entered her that it was her first time. Hers wasn't the first cherry he'd popped. Eventually the entire house would see or know there'd been blood on the sheets and they'd smile knowingly.

"You were fine. Did you enjoy it?"

She sat up on her elbows. "It was a little scary at first. I knew about men and their erections but then I was sort of lost and carried away. I'll do better when you teach me what I should do. Henry, I want to be a good wife."

"I'm sure we'll do just fine. Meanwhile I have to get ready to leave. Port Hudson is waiting for me!"

Port Hudson lay just forty miles west of Moss Grove. It was the last Confederate stronghold on the Mississippi river. If the Union ships and support troops could get past this turn in the river it would be easy traversing the remaining unfortified 250 miles to Vicksburg.

> The Union army had not been idle since taking New Orleans. They had resupplied their garrison with both men and ordnance. Nearly fifty thousand fresh troops would be able to march north along the river to strengthen the blockade.
>
> As the Union force moved into position a separate force under command of General Ulysses S. Grant formed to launch an attack against Vicksburg, Tennessee. If they could win victories at Port Hudson and Vicksburg the entire west and all of the Mississippi would be under Union control. The Confederate forces would be reduced to defending the Southeast. The city of Vicksburg, however, sat, nestled in the hills overlooking the broad Mississippi River and would prove to be a difficult and deadly adversary. The Confederate army also understood the implications of defending the city and they were prepared to commit enormous human and military resources to succeed.

Other servants had told Sarah of Thaddeus' spending time chattin' with that Miss Amy. The morning after the wedding she and Jesse had a no-nonsense conversation with their son.

"I ain't done nuthin'," the boy averred. "She came over to me and started talkin'."

"I don't care. You got no business laughin' and spending time with a white girl with all those other white folk standin' round. I seen men get lynched for doin' less," Jesse shouted, frustrated with their boy's naiveté.

"She not like that," he insisted.

"You stupid, boy. Massa' Henry or one of them otha' folks coulda' grabbed you right there. You a slave, a nigger boy. No matter how Massa' Jed and Miss Ruby care for you, you still property. I seen 'em take niggers your age and tie their arms and legs to different horses and whip those animals until they pull a person apart. It ain't pretty. You understand me?

You understand what ah's saying?" Jesse's voice rose in a frightened frenzied tone that surprised even Sarah. Tears were in the corner of his eyes.

"You ain't to speak to white folk les' they speak to you first. It always been that way. You hear'n me, boy? You listen'n good or I need to put some listen'n into your backside."

Thaddeus stood there, on the verge of tears. His parents, always soft-spoken, had never shouted at him like this before. It wasn't fair.

"Go do your chores, boy, and mind what we're tellin' you," Sarah added, knowing that she had to separate these two men who were her life.

Thaddeus sulked from the house, shoulders bent, hurt by the sting of his parents anger. He went about his chores but hours later he could not recall a single thing he'd actually done. He was sitting in the stable near the forge, allowing the smoldering fire to warm him, when Luther wandered in.

"What you doin', boy?" Luther asked.

"I've been hollered at for talked to that Miss Amy. 'Tisn't fair! She'd come over to Matthew and me. We just friends."

"Your folks worry about you. They seen a lot in their years. Maybe things are changin' and maybe they ain't. They love you."

"I know, but I'm too old to be treated like a child. I'm thinkin' maybe it's time I should leave Moss Grove for awhile, show'em I'm nearly a man. I could just go with some of the men passing through here on their way to join the Native Guards. I hear the white folk at Massa' Jed's meetin' say that more than three thousand colored and free blacks had already volunteered to fight on behalf of the Confederacy. There were even black folk that were landowners that were fightin'. And some of those blacks even owned their own slaves. Can you Imagine, Luther, one darkey owning another darkey?"

"I guess some blacks have their own reasons for wantin' to continue slavery, Thaddeus, but you think long and hard on just disappearin' from folks who care for you."

Luther left after making sure all the tools were put away but Thaddeus continued to sit...and think.

Sure, there were coloreds and free slaves movin' here and there, Thaddeus thought, but ah ain't seen no one askin' for any papers. And, 'ah is light enuf. That should help some. I'll come back after I've showed 'em what I can do. I'll make 'em proud. Ah've decided!

He hesitated. The older part of him had decided to go but the younger part of him was still nervous about leaving his family and Moss Grove. He would have liked to talk about it to someone he could confide in but who would that be. The younger 'him' could talk to Sarah or Massa' Jed but the older 'him' wanted to talk to Amy. In the end he realized he had to go and there was no one with whom he could share his feelings and uncertainties.

He gathered his few belongings after Sarah and Jesse had gone to bed. He scribbled a note in the letters that Massa' Jed and Miss Ruby had taught him.

> *'Goin' to fite for 'da South. Ah'm a man now.*
> *Love, Thaddeus*

Grabbing some bread and cheese from the larder he struck out, hoping to meet others on the road toward the Mississippi.

Amy joined her teary-eyed sister in her room.

"It was such a short honeymoon," Elizabeth complained as the late morning sun warmed the otherwise cold room.

"It was certainly a noisy one," her younger sister teased.

"You know nothing. That's what married couples do."

"Well, you'd certainly think they could do it more quietly."

"Anyway, Henry is gone and I'm not even in my own home. That isn't fair."

"What isn't fair is that I have to be here too and the only people my own age that I can be friends with are coloreds mother and daddy don't want me to associate with."

"Amy, grow up. Niggers aren't friends, they're slaves."

"Well, maybe the abolitionists are right and they shouldn't be."

"Keep those blasphemous thoughts to yourself. My Henry is off fighting to keep things just as they have always been. God has said that it's the natural order of things. I mean, it is in the Bible, isn't it?"

Sylvia Williams insisted that Amy spend at least two hours each day reading and another two learning how to play the piano and do needlepoint, the talents she would need at some point to be an accomplished southern bride. Reading wasn't a problem. Amy had already read most of the books available at Moss Grove. She had begun to join Jedidiah in the dining room each morning sharing any newspapers that arrived.

"You won't punish Thaddeus when he returns, will you?" she asked him one morning.

"I'm not sure what I'll do," he confessed. "I guess we both miss him, don't we?"

"I do, he's so different from the few boys I've met."

"Yes, he is special and I miss him, too. But, Amy, you can't forget that you're white and he isn't. I'm sure your parents would not want you to have anything to do with him."

"I know coloreds aren't the same as us but Thaddeus is different and I don't see his color."

"I don't either," Jedidiah acknowledged, although he realized he had never admitted that to himself. "But let's keep this between ourselves. You and I will have to think hard on this problem."

*Sixty-eight hundred Confederate soldiers massed to defend Port Hudson. Its defense was critical. A loss would mean the Mississippi was gone. The movement of Confederate arms and supplies would be severely hampered and without cotton to trade, munitions and supplies wouldn't be forthcoming from England. Union troops coming up the river could join Grant's troops attacking Vicksburg without resistance.*

The Rebel forces held the high ground and, once again, Henry Rogers was given the command of adjoining artillery batteries. It was only days after he arrived that the Union forces could be seen mustering to their south and west. No time to improve the training of his crews this time. He thought of Sean Regan and wished he could have that cantankerous Irishman with him again. His good humor and bluster would add energy to any group of soldiers.

He was surprised how many niggers were there along with the Confederate forces. He knew they were just there to support the white soldiers and most were freemen, but still, he hated their cocky *'I'm equal to you'* attitude. They certainly were not equal to me nor any white man and especially not a Confederate officer.

Port Hudson boasted three units of non-whites. The Second and Third Louisiana were composed of free blacks and former slaves. The First Louisiana was all men of color. Some were mulatto while others were Mexican, white, black combinations. They were treated with just slightly more respect.

Thaddeus approached the Port Hudson sentries nervously. He didn't have the uniform he was supposed to provide for himself and he had never shot a gun. If they sent him back he'd be tarred as a runaway for sure by Massa' Jedidiah and Daddy Jesse.

"Who goes there?" the young gray uniformed guard queried as he brought his gun into position, ready to shoot anyone sauntering nearby without a pass. It was nervous being a sentry on a moonless night. Stars flickered overhead and the weather was beginning to be almost balmy but Union soldiers were close by and the young Reb wasn't ready to die.

"Ah'm lookin for my brutha," Thaddeus lied.

"Come closer where I can see you."

"My brutha came to fight with the Native Guards and 'ah come to join'em."

"What unit is he in?" the guard asked, looking at the young boy carrying only a few things in a knotted rag.

"Ah didn't know there was more than one," Thaddeus answered, uncertain as to what he should say.

"Well, if he looks like you he'd rightly be in the First Louisiana. That's where the colored are. Blacks are in the other units."

"Thas' right. Now 'ah recall. He did say somethin' 'bout a colored troop. Where's they at?"

"Down that path, about fifty yards. Hope you find 'em. Things getting nervous with Union forces ready to attack any time now."

"Thanks. 'Ah'l find 'em."

Thaddeus moved quietly along the path, hoping he could avoid any more questions. The lying was getting easier. He began to believe he did have a brother in the First Louisiana. He realized he'd need a last name. Slaves didn't need surnames but free blacks and coloreds all had them. He couldn't use Rogers and the only other name he knew from a white person was Amy. It was nice to think of her. She was special. He'd be Thaddeus Williams.

"Ain't no colored Williams in the First Louisiana, nigger. Now leave… we's got to get ready for the battle," the colored sergeant told him. Thaddeus was impressed with the way the soldier was dressed. He was light skinned, like he, himself was, but with the confidence of any white man.

"Can 'ah stay and fight with you?" Thaddeus asked. "Ah don't want to keep lookin' for him with a battle ready to start."

"Boy, you too young. I'd like to help you but I got troops to get ready. I'll bet you never even shot a gun."

"Ah'll clean your boots and gear and get'cher grub when you hungry. 'Ah needs to stay for the battle," Thaddeus pleaded.

The sergeant, Rufus Carmody, smiled. It was against regulations but he didn't want the boy wandering around in the dark in the middle of a skirmish and all the shooting that would begin at any time now.

"You'd better take any order I give you without complaining," Carmody said sternly, hiding the humor he saw in the situation.

"Yes,suh. I will, yessuh, Massa' sergeant," Thaddeus answered gladly, his heart racing.

"Until you find your brother, we'll just say I'm your uncle. You understand? You aren't to embarrass me."

Rufus Carmody had left his family in Houma, a rural farm village southwest of New Orleans, when Federal troops came in. Staying could have meant jail or worse. Rufus was a known Confederate sympathizer. His father, also colored, had been set free nearly thirty years earlier by the French plantation owner who had sired him. His mother, openly the man's mistress, ran the plantation household. The man's Cajun wife had died of tuberculosis years earlier and despite pleas from his family, the man chose to live openly with a nigger woman. Before he died he signed an order of Manumission, freeing his mistress and her family. Soon after, his mother and father married. This made their son a second generation free-colored, a rarity even in southern Louisiana.

When Rufus was old enough he'd been apprenticed to a blacksmith, caring for horses the white folk brought for shoeing. Later he and the family opened a feed store.

Rufus, his two sisters and a brother, pretty much stayed to themselves growing up. They were tolerated by whites and blacks but they belonged to neither culture. Still, they were successful Louisianans and saw no reason to support Federal aggression. Their choice to support the Confederacy came easily.

Rufus was a stocky, nearly six foot, latte-toned man. A deep scar crossed from his right cheek down to his chin, about four inches long and badly stitched. He had gotten into a fight with a white 'cracker' who thought he didn't need to pay for the feed already loaded onto his wagon, calling Rufus 'a fucking nigger.' Rufus had dragged the man from the seat of his wagon as he was about to ride off and the two had gone at it. The younger white man had pulled a knife and cut Rufus on the face before the stronger colored man was able to dislodge it, grabbing and breaking his opponent's arm in the process.

An attack on a white man by a nigger always unnerved both blacks and whites and with Union troops poised to take over any moment it seemed a wise time to leave. The Native American commanders were glad to have him.

The first salvos came two days later in early morning as the sun broke over the muddy river and the evening's heavy dew still hung in the air. The shells bursting over Port Hudson seemed tentative, meant less to do damage than to ferret out the positions of the Confederate artillery. By mid-morning, however, both sides were exchanging damaging volleys. The land forces had not yet been committed. Union commanders hoped that their artillery might reduce the possibility of the type of infantry slaughter their forces had faced at Fredericksburg.

Henry's batteries kept up a furious barrage, slowing only when the barrels of their Howitzers heated to near self-destruction. Twenty yards across the citadel Captain Andre Cailloux, a prominent free slave from New Orleans, was busy directing Sgt. Rufus Carmody and his gunners. By the end of the third week, however, he and several other officers had been killed, victims of deadly shrapnel wounds. Carmody continued to lead crews of colored and black gunners' busy firing on the blue-coated units facing them below. Thaddeus hung to one side, out of the way, ready to bring them water or wipe their faces from the black smoke that belched from the gun after each discharge.

Days passed with an ugly repetition. Each morning cascades of northern and southern shells passed one another, sometimes within feet, as they arched high in the sky before descending toward their target. Mid-day breaks were followed by further afternoon attacks. Night, gratefully, came with quiet and a few hours welcome sleep.

On and on it went without resolution, the smaller southern forces holding the more advantageous positions against the better equipped northern troops always having to look up. By the time the second month had arrived, exhaustion and limited resupply of food and ammunition began to have an impact on the tired Confederate forces.

More than forty days had passed since that first artillery shell crossed the Mississippi's horizon when three shells in succession cascaded into the

Howitzers stationed between Henry and Rufus. The guns were destroyed and men were lying dead or nearly so, screams everywhere while arms and legs splayed at obtuse unnatural angles on the dirt floors, running red with blood.

Half the men from each adjoining battery came over to see who might still be alive and could be moved to the small infirmary thirty yards deeper into the fort. Thaddeus joined Rufus as the two hurried to move unspent shells away from danger. As the young boy tried to help one of Henry's men who had gotten too close to the explosion, he heard a shout.

"Get away from that man, you fucking nigger. Get away!" Henry was screaming over the noise of the explosions.

"What are you doing here, Thaddeus? How the fuck did you get here? You're a dirty runaway slave. I'll have you hanged for leaving Moss Grove, you black piece of shit. I knew you were trouble."

Henry's face was red with anger and black with soot as he shouted over the artillery shells exploding around them.

Rufus stood astride the wreckage watching this white Captain scream, his face contorted with a fury having nothing to do with either the battle or the Union troops lobbing ordnance on them. Thaddeus stood frozen at the unanticipated sight of Henry Rogers, forehead throbbing with anger. In all the franticness of the battle their paths hadn't crossed.

Henry's blue eyes stared in icy focus at this familiar nigger boy that continued to cross his path in unexpected ways. Thaddeus had completely forgotten that Massa' Rogers had been posted to Port Hudson.

"Captain, I'm sure there will be time to have this boy hung once the battle is over but can we deal with more urgent matters first?" Rufus asked, making certain the Captain recognized another professional.

Henry stopped, caught his breath, and moved his attention toward the colored Sergeant standing before him. He was angry at being addressed by a nigger...colored...they were all the same. But, of course, the man was right. He'd lost his control in front of his men...quite unseemly.

"You're right Sergeant. I'll hold you responsible for this boy's arrest until we've time to deal with it. Please continue to move the survivors to the medical tent. Men," he said, turning away, "back to your guns. We have blue-bellies to do away with."

Rufus, Thaddeus and three other men began to carry the injured survivors away from the gun mounts toward a safer position when more shells exploded close by. Union gunners were apparently satisfied they'd found the range and the target they'd been seeking.

Thaddeus turned at the sound of the explosion to find two of Captain Roger's guns aflame, smoke everywhere. Lying askew, atop two of his men was Massa' Henry, his blonde hair blackened and laced with rapidly caking blood.

Rufus and Thaddeus moved quickly, turning their damaged comrades over to others and hurrying toward the newly wounded men. Rogers was alive, but barely. His eyes were glazed but he was semi-conscious.

"Don't want help from a nigger," he gasped.

"It's us or no one, Captain Rogers," Rufus said angrily.

"I don't want to die," Henry admitted before drifting into unconsciousness.

"C'mon, Thaddeus, let's get this white officer gentleman to the medical tent," he said with obvious sarcasm.

"You've got to save him," Thaddeus said through tears. He had no reason to like this arrogant blond scion of Moss Grove but something he didn't understand coursed through him. Henry Rogers needed to survive.

The doctors, their aprons covered with blood, their hands and arms red with the dry flesh of wounded soldiers and those who had already died from inadequate knowledge, inadequate supplies, and filthy conditions, hurried from man to man. Their demeanor, looking at this newly arrived Confederate Captain, turned grim.

"We'll do the best we can but we have little to work with," the Confederate doctor complained. His white apron was covered with the dried blood of the many men he had attended these past weeks. Most had died of their wounds, some of which had turned gangrenous. Others had lost limbs. The doctor's eyes were red, his face unshaven and his hands shook with a tremor from working with too much carnage and getting too little sleep.

"Can we do anything? Anything at all? He hasta' live, he jus' hasta," the boy blubbered.

Rufus looked at Thaddeus, confused.

"If he lives, he could hang you, you know," he said softly.

"He won't. I knows he won't. We's got the same eyes. We don't like one another but we's got the same eyes."

"Thaddeus, a lot of people have blue eyes."

"Not like mine and not like his. They's different. I ain't smart enuf' to know why. I jus' knows it, inside me. I jus' knows it."

# Chapter Nine

Ruby never fully recovered from her distended midsection. The illness, the continuous cold, and her age, combined to fail her. Moss Grove lost its mistress. One morning she just didn't waken. Sarah had brought her breakfast as she did every morning of every year but this morning was different. Ruby's sleep would now continue peaceful and forever.

Ruby's funeral was a family affair with only the Williams, Sarah and Jesse in attendance. His beautiful Creole wife, mother of his son, and his best friend, was entombed in the family plot under her favorite hundred year old oak tree. Jedidiah's life would never be the same. His anchor was gone.

Jedidiah became morose. His love and his life mate had left him. His son, with whom he had always had a contentious relationship, was off to war. Even Thaddeus had run off. He felt old. The cold soaked through every bone. Aches he had always shrugged off, now nagged unceasingly. He tried to find solace in prayer. He would sit for hours in the small plantation chapel searching for meaning. It was the same chapel that had known joy at his son's wedding only months ago. Only God could give rise to such conflicting emotions in such a short time.

At midday Jesse brought him a small meal and hot tea. Often he put a shawl over his Master's shoulders. In those rare instances when the grieving man spoke to his servant it was to ask if there had been any word from Thaddeus. He had read the boy's note. His grandson, too, had gone off to war. Jesse just shook his head as the two shared the same sadness.

Faris was no longer content to remain at Moss Grove. He had no formal education but he knew what he felt. There had to be more to life than moving boulders at the order of some white boss. Neither Rose nor Matthew would agree to join him. It was the way of plantation life. She was his wife and Matthew was his son but they were all Moss Grove property, a family but not really. Not voluntary like white folks. He loved what Rose had given him these past eight years. He had become calmer. At the same time, though, he had grown hungry for another life. He had no inkling what that might be, but he knew that the ceaseless toiling would kill his soul if he stayed.

"When you leavin', Faris?" Rose asked. They had discussed his plan many times. She wouldn't try to stop him. He was a man who needed to do what his spirit told him. She'd stay at Moss Grove with Matthew and hope that Thaddeus returned safely. She ached for Thaddeus, off fighting somewhere.

"Ah'll wait until after dark. With luck ah'll meet up with some others, might be safer with all these scouting parties ready to shoot anyone they meet up with. Ah's a pretty big target."

Rose laughed. "Yes, my dear Faris, you are definitely a big target. 'Course, if you's growl, they may take you for a bear and run away."

Faris smiled and they hugged. Matthew joined them and they stood together for long moments, understanding that once they let go it might be forever.

"Be safe and try to get word to us," Rose added.

"If it's good, I hope's you'll both join me. Rose, imagine! Matthew could be free. He could choose his own life. Ain't that somethin'?"

"For me it's hard to imagine any life but Moss Grove but for Matthew ah'd try, I surely would."

When the fires that struggled to warm the huts of the field hands burned their last embers and the night's chill set in, Faris left. He and Rose held hands until the last second and the emotion between them reflected in their tears like a silver chain connecting them forever. Then it was broken and he was gone. Rose put her blanket over Matthew and climbed in bed next to her son, sobbing silently, lonely once again.

The battle at Port Hudson continued another week before the Confederate forces succumbed to the constant bombardment from Union artillery. It had been almost two months since those first salvos. Surrender was imminent. The reduced southern forces that were still standing had exhausted all their supplies and energies.

Rufus Carmody stood next to Thaddeus, his arm around the boy's shoulder, at the bedside of Captain Henry Rogers. Since he was a white officer, they'd found him a cot. Most of the enlisted men rested on the cold concrete floors. Rogers was heavily sedated with brandy, the only anesthetic available to dull the pain. His right arm had been amputated just below the shoulder and he had limited sight from one eye only. How much of this he was conscious of could only be imagined. The doctor said he was lucky to be alive. Most men in his condition had perished; their bodies cremated or hauled off to a mass grave.

"Thaddeus," Rufus said carefully, "Could this white man be your daddy?" He had thought a great deal about his young friend's conflicting emotions and the strange, intense blue eye color they shared.

"Yo' crazy. My daddy is Jesse. He and Mama Sarah my parents," the boy, near-man, protested.

"Thaddeus, listen to me. You was right. You got the same blue eyes and skin a color mixed with white and black blood. I seen lots like that in New Orleans. They's called mulattos. 'Ah has that same kinda' mixed blood. It's what makes us coloreds different from blacks. Usually some white daddy and a black woman gettin' careless and havin' a child. Could be where you come from."

"Thas' crazy talkin', Rufus," he spoke this time with less certainty. "What about my folks?"

"They coulda' been tol' to raise you. Someone had to."

"If'n he be my daddy, who's my mother?"

"Don't know. Answer's probably back at your plantation."

"Whatever. All 'ah know is I gots to get Massa' Henry back to Moss Grove. 'Ah can't let him be taken by the blue-bellies."

With Rufus' help they were able to scavenge a small buggy and an old nag. They muffled Henry's groans and forced more brandy through his lips. The jostling wouldn't help his pains and if the stitches holding his wounds closed burst, he'd die.

The battle was over. Union commanders had not yet bothered to send troops to occupy Port Hudson. There was little left to occupy. Meanwhile the confused remnants of the Confederate force spent their time caring for their wounded friends, heading back home, or awaiting orders from the few officers still standing.

Rufus stayed with Thaddeus and Henry until they reached a fork in the road. He needed to head north toward Vicksburg. All able Confederate soldiers were directed to help defend this last western stronghold. Thaddeus said a tearful goodbye and slowly led the horse and his wounded patient south toward Moss Grove and, perhaps, some answers.

The return of Henry Rogers to Moss Grove lifted Jedidiah from his grief. The entire population of the plantation stopped whatever activity they were engaged in whether picking the sparse fields of cotton, chopping kindling, shucking peas or doing laundry. They stared as a bedraggled black young runaway slave led a near dead horse and buggy carrying a white wounded Confederate officer up the same rutted path his mother had traveled, cradling him in her arms, thirteen years earlier.

The shouts grew louder as Thaddeus passed the slave quarters and headed directly toward the main house. The boy was beyond exhaustion. They'd been on the road for nearly a week, hiding from Union scouts and moving only at night. Thaddeus had to remain constantly vigilant. Henry's cries of pain might come at any time and alert anyone in the area. They spent two nights in a barn where the missus was kind enough to feed them and keep them secreted. She didn't ask for any explanation, which was fortunate. Thaddeus was too tired to lie convincingly. Now approaching his destination, he ignored the stares, matching each strained limping step of the horse with one of his own.

Field and house slaves gathered slowly around Moss Grove's front portico, anxious and eager, as Thaddeus dropped the reins and fell to the ground. It took a moment for everyone to translate their confusion into some form of action. Sarah and Jesse wept openly as several men lifted Henry and carried the plantation's scion carefully up the stairs to be cleaned and tended. Elizabeth sobbed at the return of the Adonis who had left her only months earlier, and who had now been returned, wounded and damaged. Sylvia Williams was frenetic, admonishing everyone to bring hot broth and boil more hot water.

Amy stood next to her parents but her tears were for her friend, Thaddeus. She would have loved to rush over and make certain he wasn't seriously injured but she understood that such an open display of emotion might hurt rather than help him. Rose and Matthew stood with the other field slaves in awe. Henry, with so much anger and hatred in his heart, brought home by the son he had never acknowledged.

But the one most affected by this return was Jedidiah. Somehow, in God's mysterious way, his son and his grandson had been drawn together.

"Thaddeus, when there is time, I would like to understand what happened," Jedidiah Rogers said, a tearful smile on his aged face. "Meanwhile, get warm! Get fed. I'm sure Sarah and Jesse are glad you have returned."

The boy ate, bathed, and slept for a day and a night. Sarah could hear him screaming in his restless sleep, throwing off covers, as his dreams took him back to the cacophony of artillery blasts seared in his memory. When he woke he was drenched in sweat and given the luxury of another bath. His blue eyes were puffy but it was clear he was happy to be back among the people who loved him in the only home he'd ever known. When he finally gathered himself he sat on the edge of the bed watching Sarah straighten the bedcovers.

"Ah'm sorry I left. Ah was angry, I guess," he confessed.

"Bygones, son. Glad you is back with us," Sarah said, embracing this boy they had raised and holding him with all her being. She cried openly. Her son was home.

Thaddeus hesitated. He knew what he wanted to ask her but she was the only mother he'd ever known and he wasn't sure he was ready to ask if she was his true mother, the one who had given birth to him.

The entire trip back from Port Hudson he replayed Rufus Carmody's words over and over in his head. Could Massa' Henry be his father? He stared at the loving woman in front of him, searching her face for signs. She and Jesse were black with wide noses and large lips. He had none of those features. Their eyes were both dark brown, his were blue. Neither was as tall as he would grow to be. Already he stretched slightly over them. He had never thought about these things but the signs were there.

"How is Massa' Henry?" the boy asked, trying to clear his mind and confused as to how he could approach this conundrum without hurting these people he loved and who loved him.

"He be weak. Miss Elizabeth and her mother takin' turns bein' with him round the clock and Massa' Jedidiah there every few hours. What you done was special, Thaddeus. Right special! Does you feel strong enough to tell us what happened?"

Slowly, over the next few hours, the boy told of his desire to join the Native Guards and how a colored sergeant had befriended him. He told of the constant artillery barrages and the smoke and the noise. He began to cry as he spoke of all the death and how quickly the smell of the decaying bodies filled his senses. He explained how he was helping the wounded when Massa' Henry saw him and began shouting. Not long after that there were more explosions and he saw Massa' Henry lying unconscious and bloody across bodies and smoking cannon. He never got to explain his need to bring Henry home nor was he able to ask his question about his parentage. Exhaustion overcame him again and he fell asleep sobbing in Sarah's lap.

Henry hadn't awakened in the days since his return. A doctor from Baton Rouge had been well-paid to leave the beleaguered city and travel to Moss Grove.

"A weaker man would not have survived either the wounds or the travel," the doctor said gravely. Each wound was examined, cleaned, and carefully wrapped.

"The Army doctors must have worked hard just to keep him alive. And the trek from Port Hudson here couldn't have been easy. There are few roads and the Union soldiers would have been on the look-out for Reb deserters. Some of his stitches burst. He could have bled to death. He's a very lucky man. They even did a decent job when they amputated his right arm. I fear that they have had more than their share of experience. The removal was well-cauterized but there is always a danger of gangrene setting in. It will require constant cleaning.

"And we won't know the extent of his eye damage for some time. Keep the room dark and both eyes covered to avoid any strain."

"My God, mother," Elizabeth cried, standing over the prostate person sleeping restlessly. It was no longer the handsome man that had stood awaiting her at the altar.

"Just look at him. He is so different than the gorgeous husband that left me a few months ago."

"He's back," Sylvia Williams answered calmly, "And he's alive. Would you rather he not come back at all?"

"Of course not, but it is not the husband I imagined I would be sharing the rest of my life with. This is a stranger, lying near-dead, in that bed."

"Grow up, girl. Whatever you imagined, this is the life that has befallen you. You need to face up to it."

Her mother's admonishment was like an icy wind blowing through her. She'd have a husband with one arm who might not even be able to see. She didn't deserve this. The glamour of being a bride who'd made a successful catch to a handsome man poised to inherit his family's plantation had imploded over her life with damage akin to what Henry might sense of his own future. In that instant her youth vanished.

Amy worried about her sister. She was shocked at what had become of Henry. Her dislike for him now seemed petty. The war, an abstract vision of handsome men on horseback, carrying sabers, and looking ever so valiant, was now real. The reality of the war meant broken men, deprivation and danger. She went looking for Thaddeus. He, too, had to have been damaged. But what bravery he'd exhibited. Her adolescence had also vanished as a result of these tragic events.

As Amy approached Thaddeus, sitting quietly under a tree, she saw that he was not alone. Jedidiah Rogers, looking older and more tired, sat next to him, his attention rapt.

"Honest, Massa' Rogers, I didn't mean to run away from Moss Grove. Truly, I didn't," Thaddeus' voice quivered. He was full of guilt and fear that Sarah or Jesse might face retribution for his act of rebellion.

"Thaddeus, leaving was wrong. Moss Grove has always been your home and you have been given a good, decent life here, haven't you?"

"Yessuh'," the boy said contritely.

"Tell me what happened. Henry left here weeks before you did, yet somehow you found one another and you were there to return him, and yourself, back to us."

For the next hour Thaddeus once again explained the strange events that had led him to Port Hudson, the friendship of Sgt. Carmody, and the artillery battle with the Union forces. He explained the fear he felt at the noise, the dead all around him, and the fear of what might happen if they were made prisoners when the citadel was set to surrender. He didn't relish reliving the events. Somehow telling them first to Sarah and Jesse clarified it all in his own mind and he could now recite them more clearly.

He had to stop, push back the tears, and regain his breath on more than one occasion. When he was finished Jedidiah rose and gathered the boy in his arms. It was an act without precedent for them both, an act of undefined love and gratitude, an act that on such a rare occasion could erase the barrier of color that had always separated owner from slave. Amy, standing at the rear of the house, couldn't hear the conversation but the actions she witnessed brought tears to her eyes as well.

"We are not your birth parents," Jesse explained as he and Sarah sat across from the boy. Thaddeus had finally reached the need to know the truth.

"Massa' Henry is your father but the terrible act he committed that brought you to us to love was an evil act of violence. Your true mother is a field hand named Rose. She was younger than you are now when she became pregnant from his attack. Massa' Jedidiah wanted us to raise you. He knew we had always wanted a child of our own and a good God brung us you. We were told that we were never to say anything." The three held one another in silence, finally able to rid themselves of the cloak of silence that had enveloped them for thirteen years.

"You'll always be my parents," Thaddeus said somberly, his youth finally gone, left in the belly of the Port Hudson citadel. For the first time he understood the compulsive need he had felt within himself to get Henry back to Moss Grove.


"I worried about you," Amy confessed, as she and Thaddeus sat side by side at the riverbank where they'd first met.

"And I missed you, Miss Amy," he answered, tired, still drained by his ordeal and the new revelations of his birth.

"Please drop the 'Miss'. Can't we just be Thaddeus and Amy? You're my friend…my best friend, I guess."

"You need more friends," he smiled. "Miss Amy…Amy, I am so glad to be home. I wanted to talk to you before I left but I didn't know how. Then everything happened so fast."

"I heard about Henry being your birth father. It made my sister furious. Henry doesn't know you've been told. He hasn't recovered enough yet to face more emotions. Are you O.K.?"

"Not sure, but it don't really matter. It is what it is. Does that make us relatives?" he laughed.

"Maybe we can be kissin' cousins or something," she teased but the idea sent unexpected tingling through her body.

"I think we'd better leave it as 'something' before it's too late."


August arrived, bringing the summer's humidity that left everything damp and tempers short. Any crops that hadn't been harvested had already turned brown. The smell of rot hung in the fetid air and weighed heavily on everyone. From the north copse of trees two horsemen approached. Visitors along this stretch were rare and never the bearers of welcome tidings.

As they approached, Abner Rafferty, who had taken over as overseer since his father's departure, rode out to confront them. He intersected them some ways off and an angry exchange of words ensued. The field hands couldn't hear them but the arm waving made it clear that the young Rafferty was furious. The two riders dropped the rope they were toting and rode off waving their arms in an obvious threat.

The overseer turned back and rode quickly past the fields to the main house. Henry was seated in a chair in the yard surrounded by the entire family. Rose watched the coming and going with a sense of involvement she couldn't explain. Her hands began to shake. Within minutes several men followed Rafferty back to where he had argued with the two men. They lifted something heavy between them and slowly carried their burden back toward Moss Grove's slave quarters.

"Rose, take Matthew over to Sarah in the main house and come back," Abner ordered as he rode off.

"Wha' for Massa' R?" she asked, called Rafferty by his nickname.

"Just do it. I'll explain why later."

Rose grabbed Matthew and ran with him to the house where Sarah waited. They stared at one another without exchanging words.

"You stay with Sarah until I return," Rose ordered, much to the boy's confusion.

Rose raced back as Abner and the other men returned from the field. The heavy load they carried between them was a man. It was Faris, dead. He had been tar and feathered. Then he had been strung up and burned. After this wanton and tortuous death they cut him down and dragged his body across fields for nearly twenty miles to Moss Grove, brambles and rocks cutting what remained of his black seared still-warm flesh.

"I'm sorry, Rose," Abner said, dismounting, as the men set the huge black man softly on a sheet someone had kindly provided and closed the two large dark eyes that had stared in terror and anger in those final minutes. "It was those damn militia people. They find runaways and they brutally kill them, not even bothering to bring them back to their lawful owners."

Rose collapsed next to her husband, her lungs opened and her soul burst forth, inconsolable. She began beating on Faris' chest.

"Why did you has to leave? Why couldn't you stay with me and Matthew? Why? Why? I loved you. You was my man. Why wasn't that enough? Why?"

Two of the women lifted her slowly and carried her back to her home, her sobs continuing to pierce the air from the slave cabins to the main house. Two of the other field hands grabbed the sheet under Faris and carried it gently to where it could be prepared for burial.

Matthew had broken away from Sarah as soon as he realized it was his father who had been brought back but who would never again be there for him. He cried as he tried to console his mother.

The next day the entire plantation overflowed the small church. Words of prayer echoed in the rooms of Moss Grove's main house and each slave shack. They brought little solace to any of the mourners. Matthew hadn't been permitted to see his father's body but he had overheard some of the slaves speaking and understood the terrible things that had been done to him. He put his arm around his mother, feeling her entire being convulsing. This will not go unpunished, the boy mused. Slave or not, I will find a way to avenge this ugly and brutal killing of my father.

The white families stood in the back of the church joining in with their slaves in the singing and prayers. They were conflicted. Faris had been a runaway and caught at a time when tolerance and rational action were in short supply. White men, like them, had committed this atrocity that was so out of proportion to the crime of trying to be free.

Thaddeus stood next to Jesse and Sarah. When the service ended he went over to Rose and Matthew.

"My heart goes out to you," he said. "I think everyone shares your grief."

Rose looked at him through her tears and willingly took his hand. She had lost her husband but she would find strength in her two sons.

"Your wound is almost fully healed and the chance of infection is now quite small. It also looks as if your eyesight is slowly improving, Henry," the doctor said as he began to put his instruments away.

"It's a little better, although if I'm looking into direct sunlight I feel totally blind; the same with any reflection off something shiny. It sends waves of pain ricocheting through my head."

"Your father tells me you're still taking heavy doses of laudanum. I'm telling you again that you needed to wean yourself off it. It's an opiate, terribly addictive."

"I only take it when the pain gets bad. Trust me, I can handle it. I can stop anytime I choose," he said, but with little conviction. In truth he wasn't so sure. The pain could be searing. And he still felt the missing arm anytime his shoulder shifted, sending a signal to a hand that was no longer available for use. So much of his body was going to need to be retrained.

And here he was, idle. More weeks had passed. He needed to return to his unit. Could he still mount a horse? He wasn't sure. It was time to try. Rupert Rafferty could have helped him but he'd died. Abner had stayed at Moss Grove as overseer as he'd promised but when the crop was planted and Faris' was laid to rest, he, too, left and there was no way Henry could deny his boyhood friend the privilege of fighting for the Confederacy. Abner said his goodbyes and left. If he was still alive, he'd be defending Vicksburg. Henry would need to find someone else to assist him.

"Good morning, Henry, my dear. Did you have a good night?" Elizabeth stepped out of the sunlight, breaking her husband's concentration.

Henry had neither seen nor heard her approach. When he looked up all he saw was the bright morning rays. It had the same effect as another artillery shell exploding next to him.

"Elizabeth, please do not sneak up on me," he said, holding his head until the throbbing subsided.

"I'm sorry, Henry," she said contritely. "Can I get you something to eat?"

"Not hungry, but have someone bring me some brandy, if you please."

"Henry, you need to eat to regain your strength."

"Dear wife, do not harp at me. It is not becoming. And now that I can see you better, you look terrible. Your skin is blotchy and your hair reminds me of Medusa."

"What a sweet compliment," she answered, pouting and visibly upset. "I'm pregnant and I'm nauseous most days. Have you forgotten?"

"Of course not," he lied. "The pain makes me most intolerant."

Elizabeth moved next to him and held his good left hand. They had had so few moments alone together since Henry had been brought home. He had been semi-conscious most of those first weeks. Jedidiah, Elizabeth's mother and Sarah had been in almost continual attendance, shuttling their son's new wife to one side.

"It is your first pregnancy. You must be careful," they all echoed in one form or another.

"How will I be a decent father to my son?" Henry asked, tears forming in his eyes as his left hand rubbed the wrapped stump of his missing appendage.

Elizabeth met his glazed look with a forced grin. "We will manage, my husband. We will manage. But I cannot promise you a son. That is in God's hands."

The veins in Henry's forehead began to visibly throb and his face turned red.

"It must be a son. This child must be a boy. It must be...it must be. Please don't disappoint me, Elizabeth."

His voice grew louder as he gripped his wife's shoulder.

"Henry, you're hurting me. Please, you must relax. We will have a son. If not this pregnancy, then we will try again."

An evil laugh passed through his closed lips. "Are we so sure I'll be able to perform my husbandly duties? Perhaps I've lost that as I've lost my arm and some of my vision. I tell you now, I cannot and I will not live the balance of my life as a subject of pity. Give me a son, Elizabeth. Give me a reason to live."

Steam rose from the large cast metal pot sitting atop the flames. With a long, heavy stick Rose stirred the laundry, trying to avoid the stench of the lye and soap and boiling water that was necessary to clean the clothing that got so dirty picking the cotton or just working in the fields. When she looked up she saw Thaddeus nearby. He was just standing and staring. She had no idea how long he'd been there. Their eyes met and everything seemed to stop. Rose's tears began to trickle into the vat. She wiped them with her sleeve but her eyes never left her lost son's face.

He approached her slowly.

"Mama Sarah and Daddy Jesse tol' me that you my real mother. That true?"

"Why they say that after all these years?" she asked, the stick in her hands frozen in place. She was shaken by the question and all that it implied.

"Cause I got blue eyes like Massa' Henry and a light skin and things happened and I begun to wonder, thas' why. They tell me Massa' Henry attack you when you 'bout my age and Massa' Jedidiah say you got to give me away. All that stuff true?" he asked.

Rose stopped stirring the laundry and wiped her hands.

"It's true," she said, finally able to release the secrets and emotions that she'd been forced to conceal for a decade. She took her time putting down the laundry stick. She had no idea where to take the conversation. She would have liked to tell him how often she'd wanted to rush over and cuddle him, lavish all the mother's love she felt, but she couldn't. She had never admitted it to Faris and it had been buried so deeply within her all these years it would have to remain locked inside. "You bringin' Massa' Henry home, that was really somethin' alright. You growed into a big brave young man."

"I needed to meet you but I also wanted to know if you're OK. All the house staff, even Massa' Jed, is feelin' real bad for you and wants to know if they' is anything they can do."

"That's mighty sweet. Please thank them for me. I still have Matthew with me and he a God-send."

"I'd like to call you Momma Rose if you lets me."

Rose nodded as tears streaked freely down each cheek. The two drew closer, neither fully understanding what emotions they were meant to feel. Once they touched, the bonds of blood drew them closer and they embraced, each crying for this new long-delayed connection.

"If Matthew your son don't that make him my brother?" Thaddeus asked as he stepped back and looked, once again, at his mother.

"Yo' got different daddies so he a part brother. But I guess a part brother is better than no kin, ain't it?"

"It sho' is," he said softly, a soft grin lighting up his blue eyes at this new family he had discovered. "It sho' is."

# Chapter Ten

Jedidiah Rogers sat pensively alone in the chapel. His wife had died and his son was facing a long uncertain recovery from his wounds. The war had brought a bleak future to Moss Grove and to them all.

"Mr. Rogers, sir. May I speak with you?" a woman asked, both her hair and her shoulders covered in a shawl, her back bowed, her voice weak, almost contrite. "I am truly sorry to bother you while you're praying."

"Oh, it's you, Mrs. Rafferty," he said, shaken from his reverie.

"Please, sit here beside me. I was just thinking about Ruby and your husband. You and I have both lost our loved ones and life has become so lonely even when we are surrounded by others."

"Yes, Mr. Rogers. I am sorry for your loss. Miss Ruby was a lovely God-fearing woman. I miss my husband but he is with God now and that gives me great joy. God giveth and God taketh away, the Bible says, and we have to accept that it is all a part of his divine plan. I still have my faith and it makes my loss easier to bear."

Jedidiah knew of Mrs. Rafferty's religious ferocity. It seemed to work for her now during these forsaken times. He had never been able to find such solace in scripture.

"I have come to tell you that I will be leaving Moss Grove. You were so kind to let me remain after Abner left but I have decided to settle with my sister and her family in Chattanooga. Whatever will happen in these weary days of the war, families should stay close to one another. Her husband is a minister and they can always use another devout Lutheran woman."

"We shall miss you, Mrs. Rafferty. Rafferty men have been overseers at Moss Grove for so long it will be difficult to imagine it being supervised by anyone else. Have you heard from Abner since he left?"

"Yes, that is the other reason I wanted to see you. I received this letter just two days ago and he thought you should know its contents."

Jedidiah took the letter and set his glasses carefully over his ears. Mrs. Rafferty's somber countenance and her decision to leave would certainly mean further instability in his life. He set those thoughts aside as he unfolded the letter and read:

*'My dearest mother,*

*I trust this letter finds you well. I reached Vicksburg and joined the Confederate forces under siege by General Grant's Union forces. The blue coats was well-rested and well-supplied. They had twice as many men as we did and I nearly lost my hearing from their cannon that seemed to never stop firing. Before I got my uniform the Yankee's first assault was turned back by our boys up on Stockade Redan where we had good cover. They said it was great to see the back ends of so many blue bellies high tailing it back down toward the river.*

*But then the Union troops seemed content to just wait us out. Oh, they kept up their artillery barrage but they didn't attack much. Problem was, we was boxed in. There were dead bodies everywhere …boys in both in blue and gray, just lying there, rotting. The smell on a hot day was more than a man could bear. Couldn't get no more ammunition or food. A lot of our men got scurvy. Some got malaria and we all had dysentery. Some of our troops got so hungry they took to eatin' their horses or dogs.*

*I took a piece of shrapnel in my leg but the medics were able to save it. I limp a little but I still got two legs which is more than I can say for a lot of my friends. I just wanted you to know I was still OK. It don't look too good holding 'em out much longer, but we'll try.*

*In God's good name, I love you. Please give my regards to Mister Rogers. He was always a fair man to our family.*

*Your son,*
*Abner'*

Jedidiah folded the letter and handed it back. "You've raised a fine son, Mrs. Rafferty. Let us pray for his survival."

Together the two bowed their heads and prayed, each in their own way, for the salvation of their kin, and the Confederacy.

Weeks later an old copy of the New Orleans Picayune newspaper arrived telling of the fall of Vicksburg:

> *Nearly 3,000 Confederate soldiers died from the unending Union assaults and nearly 30,000 starving and dejected men were captured. This last passage along the Mississippi River lifeline was now closed. Thoughts of sending more Confederate troops into the beleaguered city had come to naught. General Lee hoped that a penetrating attack into the north might force the Union to relocate some of their forces away from Vicksburg. With that hope he moved his Army of Northern Virginia into Pennsylvania toward Gettysburg. His plan failed and the resultant Confederate losses at Gettysburg and Vicksburg were cataclysmic.*

"There is no one to help you learn to ride with one arm, Henry. It may not even be possible."

"Father, there must be one or two of our house slaves or field hands that you can spare. I'm sure I can figure out something," he pleaded uncharacteristically.

"My son, look around. The only slave we had at Moss Grove that was good with horses was a man named Luther. A few weeks ago he stole one of our better horses and ran off. Sarah tells me he went with one of the young house maids, a girl named Trudie. They had spoken of marrying so I suppose they headed north. It's happening all over. Darkeys are just up and scamperin' away in the middle of the night.

"You know that both Rupert and Abner Rafferty are gone. I finally found a new overseer. His name is Simon Hannify but it will take time for him to really understand Moss Grove. Our field slaves are leery of anyone new so that gives them another reason to run. Hannify and I agree that stopping this sort of flight is one of his most important tasks. Unfortunately, he hasn't had much success catching them or convincing them to stay."

"Where did you find this Hannify fellow?" Henry asked.

"We got him from somewhere near Biloxi. The man had some excuse about the Confederates not wanting him but with everything going on there really isn't any way to confirm it. Actually, I think he's some sort of a Quaker that doesn't believe in fighting. He seems decent enough but he doesn't know our people and everyone is nervous about all the Union and

Confederate forces fighting so close to Moss Grove. Anyway, all we have now is the boy Luther was beginning to train who seems to have a knack with the horses. It seems he's the only one we have that knows which end gets fed and which ends shits."

"Then I shall use the boy."

"I don't think that's wise, Henry. The boy is Thaddeus who, I understand, you were ready to hang back at Port Hudson for being a runaway. I've been told, without knowing for certain, that he now knows you are his father and Rose is his mother."

"That was a lifetime ago and since you were always so reluctant to get rid of him it is an issue I will continue to ignore. The boy was a runaway when I saw him at Port Arthur and I would have been quite justified having him hung. Then, somehow he got me back here alive. It's all way too complicated for me at this time. My head isn't clear enough to worry about it. I need to move forward with my life and if he's the only one that knows what he's doing, you leave me no choice."

"And the fact that he knows you're his father and how he was conceived. Does that change your decision?"

"No. The boy is still a snot nose nigger and now he's back as the property of Moss Grove. He'll do what he's told or suffer the consequences. I must be able to get back on a horse and have people stop treating me as a cripple. It's either that or I shall put a bullet to my head."

"Don't be melodramatic. Get off the laudanum. Get your strength back. You will be a father soon and your wife and newborn child do not need an addict to fret over during these harsh days."

"I will do it all, father. Fear not."

Thaddeus pushed down hard on the bellows and expelled the air that fed the fire and sent forth the flames high into the air. The forge was a good place to work when it was cold outside but it was no place for a man, black or white, on a hot, humid day. Luther must've known some secret way to keep cool that he didn't tell me about, Thaddeus thought. He grabbed the heavy mallet and pounded the red heated horseshoe. This was his third try. He had already spoiled two shoes and he didn't want to admit to Massa' Jed or that new overseer, Massa' Simon, that he couldn't do the job.

He felt like a man now that he was able to work as a farrier. He had returned to Moss Grove to discover that much had changed. Some of the slaves he knew were gone, had run off, or were dead. Miss Elizabeth was heavy with child but he and Miss Amy still smiled at one another when their paths crossed. They hadn't been able to be together but he knew it would happen soon. And Matthew wanted to be everywhere Thaddeus was. His new, younger brother needed a role model now that his father was dead.

Thaddeus knew he had grown taller and gotten much stronger. Working the bellows and having to care for all the plantation's horses had built up his chest and arm muscles. His legs hung further down from the bottom of his pants and he had more hair down there in his private parts. Even his face would need shaving soon.

Most of all his relationship with everyone had changed. He was treated with more respect, even by people he hadn't known before. He knew he was still Moss Grove property but bringing Massa' Henry back and learning who his birth mother and father really were, made people look at him differently. If he wasn't mistaken he was finding a little more food on his plate at meals. It was all strange. He liked it alright, but he didn't really feel it was deserved.

"Thaddeus, stop what you're doing and come here," Henry ordered, as he entered the barn and approached the horse stalls.

The young man looked up from setting down clean hay in the stalls and saw Massa' Henry standing unsteadily at the entrance. The sun behind him gave off golden reflections against his blonde hair. He set down the pitchfork and slowly walked over to this always angry white man who had sired him.

"Yessuh, Massa' Henry." It wasn't a question and yet it lacked the subservient tone slaves were expected to maintain.

They met near the barn's entrance, the forge smoldering to one side. Their steel blue eyes locked, reminding each of them that their blood connection would always be present, albeit below the surface. There was so much to say and there was nothing to say. Neither man was of a character to voice his feelings unless provoked. Anger, gratitude and confusion all mixed in profusion but remained unspoken.

"I want you to help me to learn how to mount a horse with one arm. Once in my saddle I believe I can manage," Henry said and the moment passed.

"Yessuh, I'll try but 'ah'm not sure what'll it take," Thaddeus answered, equally glad that at least this angry white Massa' no longer seemed intent on having him hung.

"It will take more effort and less sass from you."

Thaddeus stared and willed himself to stay silent. Instead he turned, ignoring the sarcasm, saddled a work horse, and led it from its stall.

"I want a decent white man's riding horse, not a plow nag," Henry said with his continuing arrogance, feeling a need to demonstrate his dominance over the boy.

"Massa' Henry, I'll saddle whichever horse you want but I thought it would be easier to try with somethin' ol' and tame, **sir**!" Thaddeus answered, no longer willing to be cowed.

Henry stared at the boy. In the past he might have slapped him for being snotty but everything considered, it no longer seemed appropriate. "Alright, we'll try this one first," was all he could muster in response.

For two hours they worked. Henry grabbed the saddle pommel with his left hand, put his left leg into the stirrup and tried to throw his right leg onto the horse. There was just no leverage to do it. It took Thaddeus, standing behind him, to provide the push that got the bigger man up and sitting tall. Dismounting was a lot easier although Henry found it difficult to keep his balance once his feet hit the ground. Twice the big man fell. Thaddeus had come over ready to help him up but was met with anger.

"Leave me be. I'll get up by myself," Henry fumed.

It was a frustrating time and the beads of sweat on Henry's forehead gave evidence that this was going to be a lot more taxing than he had thought.

"More tomorrow! Same time! We're going to keep at this and not a word to anyone, Thaddeus. You understand?"

"Yes, suh. It'll be our secret," Thaddeus answered, a mischievous glint in his eyes.

By the end of the first week Henry had gained enough strength and confidence to ride comfortably but he still needed Thaddeus' help to get mounted. Watching one of the field hands pulling a plow behind a horse, Thaddeus had an idea. He got some old sheet material from Sarah, refusing to give her a reason for the strange request. Tying knots, he fashioned a makeshift shoulder harness. When Henry arrived for his lesson, Thaddeus tried to explain his idea but it was met with anger and resistance. It was demeaning to always need a nigger just to get on a horse. He needed to get this task behind him so reluctantly he relented.

Thaddeus took the harness, put one end over Henry's neck and the other under the missing arm where the big man could use his shoulder muscle as additional leverage. It was loose enough to permit it to also be thrown over the saddle's pommel when mounting. After adjusting it and making several vain attempts Henry was able to mount without any help from Thaddeus.

Henry was beside himself with satisfaction. Perhaps he could still be a man after all. Astride the horse he began to canter toward the front portico, not even turning back to thank the person who'd made it happen. Thaddeus knew he had done well and returned to his forge satisfied he had bested this oft times white adversary.

"Will you teach me to ride?" Amy asked, wandering into the barn in her overalls, white ribbons holding her red hair off her freckled face.

"You know how to ride," Thaddeus said, continuing to pump his bellows.

"Not well."

"You're a girl. You don't need to know how to ride well."

"Don't be that way. I want to be able to ride well and even shoot a gun, if necessary. These are dangerous times."

"All right," her friend smiled. He knew he was being played but the thought of riding off with this girl was like a pleasant shot of adrenalin. He saddled two horses and led them to the front of the barn, helping Amy mount the smaller of the two.

"Just give him a light kick in his flanks and he'll move. Pull the reins to the left to get him to go left and pull them to the right to make him go right."

"You mean like this," she said, giving the horse a kick and galloping away from the stable with the skill of a trained rider as she threw her head back and laughed.

"You scamp," Thaddeus shouted. "You know how to ride. Come back here." He mounted his own horse and set off after her.

It took him several minutes of hard riding to catch her before they slowed their horses and continued on through unplanted fields and into the woods. It was serene until a shot rang out and two Reb soldiers blocked their way.

"Get down," one demanded, holding his rifle in front of him but not pointing it.

"We're from Moss Grove," Amy said, "Just out riding."

"You always go riding with a colored boy?" the other asked.

"Absolutely! He's my friend and he watches out for me. Could be Union troops around here. We're certainly glad it was you and not them," she said coyly.

"Well, they are around here so we suggest you ride back to your plantation. You take care of the little lady, boy. You hear?"

"Yes, sir. Thank you," Thaddeus said, not knowing whether to laugh or be angry.

The two turned and headed back, smiling at one another.

"Somehow being with you always means trouble for me," Thaddeus said.

"But I'm worth it."

"Yes, you are," he acknowledged softly.

They rode slowly back to the stable, dismounted, and walked their horses toward the back of the barn where they could be rubbed down. As they each grabbed a brush, their shoulders, damp from perspiration, touched. Their eyes connected, their brushes dropped to the ground and they stood there, inches apart, not certain what to do next. Amy moved first, her body now touching Thaddeus. She tilted her head and pressed her lips against his. It only took a moment for him to react. He pulled her toward him and they embraced. Their mouths opened and each of their tongues searched wantonly for the other. It was a kiss they had both yearned for. He could feel her breasts pressed against him. She could feel him getting erect. All the air around them seemed to stop. Time froze! Neither of them wanted to release the other.

"Thaddeus? You in there?" a voice called from the front. It was Matthew. "I just wondered if you'd teach me more about shoeing. Thaddeus?"

Thaddeus and Amy eased away from one another slowly as they shared one last kiss planted lightly on their lips.

"I'll be right there, Matthew," Thaddeus said, his eyes still riveted on this freckled face he adored so much. Slowly, discreetly, they walked separately from the stable.

"Oh, Miss Amy! I didn't know you were here," Matthew stumbled. "I can come back later."

"No, need. And please just call me Amy. We were just putting the horses away."

The look on both their faces said it was more than just a strenuous ride, Matthew knew. He wasn't sure what he'd interrupted but Amy's face was flushed and she wouldn't look directly at him. He moved into the stable, away from his brother, giving them time to part without embarrassment.

"More hot water! Get more hot water!" Sylvia Williams cried out. "Sarah, get the mid-wife, now!"

Elizabeth's contractions were coming closer together. The men had all been sent from the room. This was women's work. Amy stood off in the corner, occasionally approaching the bedside to wipe her sister's damp forehead.

"If that's how much hurt it takes to have a baby I don't think I want any," she said.

"Be helpful or leave, Amy. At this point, just don't be a bother," her mother warned.

The mid-wife arrived, quickly washed her hands, and went to Elizabeth's bedside.

"Don't you worry, Missy. I been delivered hundreds of newborns. You be fine," she spoke calmly, her warm hands caressing the arms and stomach of the very stressed young white woman lying before her.

"Give me something for the pain, damn you," Elizabeth shrieked.

"Whatever you take goin' to slow the baby comin' out."

"Do something. I'll die if this pain continues."

The ancient woman pulled some dry roots from her bag and set them in hot water. After a few minutes the ugly twigs settled to the bottom and the water turned brown. The bent black woman put the brew to the prone woman's parched lips.

"Drink this, missy…slow, it's hot. Just take a few sips and you'll feel better."

"What is that wretched smelly stuff you're giving my daughter? I don't cotton with black voodoo," Sylvia Williams said, trying to grab the cup from the slave woman's hand.

"This will put calm in her, nothin' more," the woman promised as she continued to hold the lip of the cup to Elizabeth's parched lips.

"It better be nothing more than that or I'll have Master Jedidiah see that you are properly punished," the matronly woman added as she slowly retreated, knowing how much they all needed the help of this black midwife.

Elizabeth's plaintive cries grew softer and her body slowly relaxed. As it did, the tension in the room began to dissipate. The contractions were now coming closer together.

"Push," the woman urged. "Push! It time for yo' chil' to be born."

Sylvia and Amy joined the chorus, wiping the pregnant woman's forehead, encouraging her.

A few minutes later they could see the baby's head and their encouragement took on a lighter note. They jointly breathed a huge sigh of relief as the baby fully entered the world and the umbilical cord was tied off. Nothing could have brought more elation among the women than hearing the baby's screams as its lungs filled with air.

"It's a fine boy, Missy. A fine boy! You done real well," the mid-wife smiled.

"A boy! You hear, mother, a boy! Henry will be so pleased," Elizabeth said, a smile now on her face as if she'd passed this most crucial challenge her husband had placed before her.

The baby was cleaned, wrapped in a warm blanket, and set into his mother's anxious arms. She cried as she looked down at her new son's steel blue eyes.

"Henry certainly can't ever deny this is his son. He definitely has his father's eyes."

Amy brushed her sister's damp hair. There would be no need to add color to her cheeks, they were still flush and she carried a glow of deserved satisfaction.

The men were allowed in and Henry approached his new son with trepidation. This was a different Henry Rogers. He was devoid of his aura of superiority. He was a one-armed father and he stood there, uncertain of what to do, his nervousness apparent. The midwife took the baby from his mother and tucked the child into the crook of Henry's left arm. He looked at the newborn and a smile spread across his face. His eyes began to tear. From near death only a few months ago, he had survived and had fathered a son, his son, an heir to Moss Grove. No one could deny this young lad was a Rogers in the finest tradition.

"Thank you, Elizabeth. Thank you for my son. The Rogers family name is now secure."

The baby would be named Josiah R. Rogers. Josiah was the name of Jedidiah's paternal grandfather and the initial "R" was chosen out of respect for Ruby. It was a fine name.

# Chapter Eleven

Moss Grove erupted in celebration as the news of the arrival of Henry and Elizabeth's new son spread. Jedidiah brought out the last of the fifty-year old brandy his father had served when he was born. The last time Jedidiah had sipped this liqueur was when Henry was born. A male heir had been born to continue the Rogers name. It was a proud moment.

A Baptism was arranged for the following Sunday. Everyone knew to don their finest. A legitimate heir for one of the parish's oldest families and largest plantations was cause for a celebration. Any and all land owners who could safely be told of the upcoming event were invited to attend. Few came, given the danger surrounding travel, but many who chose to stay close to their homes still arranged to send some gift to Moss Grove and the new parents.

Elizabeth had recovered much of her strength. Her breasts had swollen and she was able to begin breast feeding their new son. Her blotchy skin began to clear and she began to emit a glow that had never been present before. She would still need to lose at least twenty pounds of the weight she'd put on during her pregnancy. The extra weight did nothing but amplify her plainness and had it not been for the almost perpetual grin of satisfaction from having succeeded so profoundly in becoming a mother, there would be no attractiveness on which to comment.

Henry dressed in his well-mended Confederate officer's uniform, the sleeve of the missing right arm neatly folded and pinned upward.

It was an unseasonably warm day and the service was held outdoors on the veranda. The minister had come up from Baton Rouge to conduct the ceremony. He had been stopped by both Union and Confederate troops on three occasions but being a man of the cloth they had allowed him to proceed.

As the baby was presented for his formal Baptism a restless stir went up among the crowd and the minister stopped. Simon Hannify, noticeably out of breath, rode his horse to the front of the small assembly and dismounted, rushing over to Henry and Jedidiah, who had been standing close together, sharing this important ritual.

"Union troops! Looks like a small company! They're at the edge of the road heading straight here," he whispered, removing his ever-present slouched hat.

"We will continue the ceremony. Mr. Hannify, please remain and join us," Jedidiah said, standing more erect and determined.

"I'd prefer to get our men together and dispatch them to their maker," Henry interjected.

"We will continue the Baptism. We will not engage the soldiers in combat. Reverend," the patriarch demanded, turning aside. "Please continue."

The baby screamed as he was tilted backwards toward the small Baptismal water basin but Elizabeth, Jedidiah and the minister seemed to be the only ones in the small throng that were still focused on the rite in front of them as blue clad Yankees, rifles at the ready, walked forward four abreast.

Finally, Jedidiah Rogers moved back from the baby, turned and faced the soldiers.

"My name is Jedidiah Rogers. You have arrived at Moss Grove. This plantation has been in the Rogers family for more than a half century. We are in the midst of my grandson's Baptism and I ask that you respect this moment by putting down your rifles and joining us in our celebration. No one here is armed. You will be safe."

An officer stepped out from the midst of his men and strode forward.

"I'm sorry to intrude, sir. My name is Captain Andrew Lindblade. We are an advance column of General Ulysses S. Grant's Twelfth Brigade, Union Army. We will not put down our arms. I see that man near you with a slouched hat is carrying a pistol and the man standing next to you stands in the uniform of a Confederate officer. I salute you, sir. You have obviously seen action. I am sorry for your disability. What other men I cannot see, may add to the danger of my men. Moss Grove is now under control of Union forces. All of your weapons will be confiscated. My men will collect them. And, as of this moment, all your slaves are now free of their servitude. It is our intention to rest my men and our horses before continuing northward."

The last statement sent a shock wave through the crowd. Both the house slaves and field hands just stared at one another until one let out a whoop that sent them all into fits of laughter and dancing. Jedidiah and his family stood, framed in icy fury. Sarah and Jesse stared at them all, confused as to what they should do next, waiting for Massa' Rogers to tell them they were free or assign them their next duty.

"My men need to be fed. The more quickly you can accommodate us the more quickly we will move on. We have considerable ground to cover. Please show my officers the quarters you will provide them in your home. I assure you they will not steal your silver," Lindblade added, with obvious irony in his voice.

"Jesse, show these men to the spare rooms," Jedidiah ordered, his voice barely above a whisper. "Sarah, have the staff provide food for his men."

With that he turned his back and occupied himself with what remained of the ceremony. He grabbed Henry's shoulder and forced his son's attention and fury away from these blue coats whose cannons had taken his arm.

Turmoil engulfed every corner of each cabin as the field hands gathered, ecstatic at their new status, but unclear as to what it now meant. Everyone seemed to have a different interpretation as to how it would affect them personally.

"Did you hear, mother," Matthew exclaimed. "We is free. What does we do now? Where we go?"

"We ain't goin' nowhere. You get back to your chores," Rose declaimed, confused herself as to what would happen next. If only Faris had been more patient, she mused, her eyes tearing at the hole his absence left in her life.

For the next several hours everyone mingled aimlessly. It was Sunday so chores were minimal. Would they return to the fields tomorrow or pack their few belongings and leave. Leave? Where? How would they eat? Where would they sleep? Would Massa' Jed even allow them to leave?

Rose knew she and Matthew would stay as long as they were wanted. And what would happen to Thaddeus now? There were too many questions…too much uncertainty.

Rose watched as a group of the field hands approached the Union soldiers spread out resting under a tree. She was unable to stop Matthew from joining the field hands moving toward them in a group.

"Massa' soldier! Please, suh! What we do now's we free? Where we go?" several asked.

The white, blue-clad soldiers, mostly young, all of them tired and hungry, grinned. This wasn't the first time they'd been asked this question since heading north from New Orleans and past Baton Rouge.

"You find a job and the man who hires you, he have to pay you," said one soldier with stripes on his arm. "And don't take none of that Reb money, it ain't worth a squat. With the money the man gives you for working, you buy food and you rent a place to live. It's why you is free. No more bullshit from your white 'Massas'. You is all equal. Thas' what Old Abe say. We is all equal. Problem is that some of us is more equal than others. Go talk to your black brothers over there on the hillside. Maybe they can help ya'."

The conversation brought gales of laughter from the Union soldiers and nothing but confusion to the blacks. We was slaves...now we ain't! What that mean today and what that mean tomorrow?

Down a slope and off to one side a small contingent of black and colored soldiers rested. The Moss Grove field hands approached them cautiously. Many of them had never seen a nigger that wasn't a slave. Free blacks had always been something not quite real.

"Samuel? That you?", Lem, one of Moss Grove's long time field hands, said in startled tones as he recognized his cousin, now bedecked in a blue uniform, leaning against a tree.

"Lem? Why you ol' bastard? Never thought I'd see you in the middle of a war," the black Union soldier stood, his arms wide in greeting.

"What're you doin' in those clothes, Samuel? Last I hear of you, you pickin' cotton more'n a hundred miles from here."

"Was 'til the Yankees come in and freed us. 'Magine, Lem, we is free. Too bad our daddys weren't alive to see this day."

"Amen to that," Lem and the others added solemnly.

"But that don't 'splain how you got here and why you wearin' those clothes," Lem continued.

"You all lookin' at Private Samuel Johnson, Union Army, on the way to join General Sherman near Vicksburg. We is now the L'Corps Afrique! We is an all black battalion and it sure is a whole lot better than bendin' over breakin' your back pickin' cotton all day. We is soldiers and God Bless

Mista' Abe Lincoln. Da' pays us ten Yankee dollars each month. We kin gets drunk with it or send some money to our kinfolk."

"And they gives you rifles and everything to fight the Rebs?" Another field hand asked as they all tried to absorb what they could do with ten dollars.

"Yep! Some of us fight, some cook and some bring supplies. Whatever the officers need, they tell our Sergeant and he tells us," Samuel continued.

"Some of our men fought with the Rebs at Port Hudson. They was Native Guards. But when the gray coats lost that battle lots of 'em offered themselves to the Yankees. I'm told the Union Army captured nearly thirty thousand Rebs in that battle and didn't know what to do with 'em. Most of the white soldiers just went home but the black folk had nowhere to go so they just up and decided it was better to change sides than wander around the countryside. Dey jus' took off their gray coats and put on blue ones. Makes more sense anyhow. Yankees doin' away with slavery. We ain't property no more."

The Moss Grove blacks looked at one another trying to absorb so much that was new and strange.

"Samuel, can we join and go with yo'all?" Lem asked, surrounded by the others.

"Don't see why not. Let's ask the Sergeant." Together they walked over to another small group of colored and black Union soldiers smoking and lazing in the warm afternoon sun.

"Sgt. Carmody," they interrupted. "These men want to join our 'L Corps Afrique and shoot Johnny Rebs."

Sgt. Rufus Carmody turned and looked at the group of men arrayed before him. They were mostly field hands, uneducated, wearing torn coveralls and ragged-edged straw hats. Some wore sandals on their feet while others looked as if they'd never worn shoes. They emanated the submissiveness that had been bred into them. It was the same thing at every plantation he passed through. These slaves were eager to leave the life-long back breaking work of picking cotton where they might also face the occasional sting of an overseer's whip. These men were always the first to volunteer.

"Is you Sgt. Rufus Carmody from Port Hudson?" Matthew asked, forcing himself through the throng of bigger men. He had heard Thaddeus' story about this sergeant who had taken him under his wing, trained him, and later helped him get Massa' Henry into the buggy.

"Who are you?" the tall colored Yankee non-com asked.

"My name is Matthew. You the same nigger that help Thaddeus save Massa' Henry?"

"Thaddeus? And Captain Henry Rogers? My lord, is this his place?"

"Yessuh, it rightly is. Wait here." Matthew ran off toward the house, his arms and legs flailing in all directions. Half way there he realized that Thaddeus would more likely be in the barn with the horses. He turned sharply, almost knocking Sarah down as he altered his direction.

"Thaddeus," he said, out of breath. "Sgt. Carmody is here, your Sgt. Carmody."

Thaddeus dropped the rake he was using to spread fresh straw and began running, Matthew following in his wake.

"Rufus," he shouted as he reached the hillock where the Union soldiers stood. Rufus smiled and the two men hugged as Thaddeus embraced this soldier and friend he thought he'd never see again.

"You've certainly grown taller and filled out," Rufus said, smiling at the young man before him and who he remembered being so much smaller and frail when they'd separated just months earlier. Rufus explained how he'd been caught by Union troops and returned to Port Hudson before he could make his way to Vicksburg. With so many captured Confederate soldiers on their hands they told all the blacks and coloreds they could just leave or join the Yankee army. Neither he nor most of his men had any place to go. The entire company had taken a vote and decided to join as a group with him, Sgt. Carmody, still their leader.

Thaddeus led Sgt. Carmody to the main house to see Henry. While they waited for him to join them, Sarah served drinks and cakes on the veranda. She thanked this stranger profusely for returning her son to her. The man was clearly embarrassed at the commotion he was causing. He knew his white commanding officer, Captain Lindblade, wouldn't be pleased at this turn of events.

Jedidiah, Henry, and Elizabeth exited the house together along with Captain Lindblade, who had been given a room upstairs in which to bathe and don a clean uniform.

"Sergeant," Captain Lindblade, the Union commander demanded. "Why are you here and not with your men?"

"Sir," Carmody began to speak before he was interrupted.

"I can explain, Captain," Henry interjected. "This is the man that helped Thaddeus, one of Moss Grove's young slaves, who had run off to join the Confederate Native Guards. During the battle at Port Hudson I lost my arm in an unfortunate confrontation with Yankee artillery shells. Sgt. Carmody had been in charge of two artillery units firing at Union troops the last time I saw him, although, I must say, he was wearing a different color uniform at that time and seeing him this way is most upsetting. I later learned that as the battle was ending the two of them moved me from our small hospital into a buggy they'd found. I never fully awoke until weeks later here at the plantation."

He turned toward the man that had been so vital in his return to Moss Grove.

"Are you a traitor to the Confederacy, Sergeant?"

Before Carmody could speak, the Union Captain interceded, angry at the question.

"It is you who are the traitor, Rogers. You and your damnable kind, share the responsibility for killing thousands of good men. You and your Jefferson Davis buddies just up and leave the best country in the world to protect some imagined right to own other men. You disgust me, and if I see you in that gray uniform after today I shall arrest you and have you taken to a Federal prison that you can share with others of your ilk. Sergeant Carmody, return to your men.

"Mr. Rogers, sir," he spoke softly now, turning to Jedidiah, "I know you are a gentlemen but your son is a personal insult to me. I lost my brother at Bull Run along with many close friends. Please assign one of your men to show me around Moss Grove so that we can make certain you have no weapons stash. We will also require several wagons of food and provisions. Captain Rogers, I have no desire to have an altercation with another officer, especially one who lost an arm in battle. You will do me the kindness of remaining in your rooms until my men are gone."

"Captain Lindblade," Jedidiah said. "If you take our provisions we will have nothing to eat. It is too late in the season to plant another crop."

"I'm sorry, sir. I have my orders and your future is not my concern."

# Chapter Twelve

Three days later Lindblade's small Union force massed at the entrance to Moss Grove preparing to depart. Each of his companies had grown by the addition of several field hands and wagons of various sizes filled with sacks of grain, crates of live chickens, and small casks of salted dried pork. His blue clad troops had also harnessed several of the Moss Grove horses. An army can never have too many quality horses.

Jedidiah, Simon Hannify, and the family stood at the entrance of the main house witnessing the procession. Sylvia Williams, Elizabeth, and Amy cried openly as Captain Lindblade saluted smartly from the back of the same fine black stallion that Henry had ridden only days earlier. The elder patriarch struggled to keep from breaking down as he saw his efforts of a lifetime driven off. How had it all gone so wrong? How would they all survive? Sarah stood nearby, holding Josiah, Jedidiah's new infant grandson. What would the child inherit? What would become of Moss Grove? Most of the field niggers were gone. There was nothing to keep the house slaves from leaving as well. His son was noticeable by his absence. He had remained in his room as ordered. Henry had stopped wearing his uniform but with his ever present smoldering anger and only one arm, how much help would he be?

They stood there, silent, each deep in his own despair, until the last blue uniform disappeared over the knoll. Occasionally their eyes would connect with a slave, like Lem, who had been part of Moss Grove for decades. He, like other Moss Grove slaves who had decided to leave, looked away, not wanting the meet the stares of this family that had owned them, often since birth. It was a strange feeling, just marching away, leaving one life and embarking on another.

Jedidiah slowly climbed the stairs, laid down on his bed and quickly fell asleep. He was thoroughly exhausted from the turbulence and the events that seemed to be coalescing into the ruination of his life. Ruby had died, he had a new grandson, his son was much diminished, and Union troops had invaded his personal sanctuary.

When he awoke he wasn't sure whether it was even the same day. He was wearing the same clothes in which he'd fallen asleep. He pulled the cord to call Jesse but several minutes passed and his man-servant still hadn't appeared. How unlike him, Jedidiah thought. Suddenly he realized it was quite possible that Jesse and Sarah had also left. He hurried downstairs where he found them both, along with Henry, Hannify and the Williams all gathered in the kitchen.

"Father, I'm glad you're here. We have much to discuss," Henry said. "Simon was able to hide some provisions from those marauders. Equally important, we were able to remove and hide all the wrought iron parts from the balconies and a lot of the farm tools. Those Yankee bastards had taken every piece of iron they could steal to melt down for ammunition.

"I also went through the slave cabins. Several of our people have stayed. Not many, but a few, mostly the women and children and a few of the older men who had been at Moss Grove all their lives. We even have three horses Lindblade's men didn't want. They weren't our best ones, of course, but they can be a help in planting," Hannify added.

"Thank you for your ingenuity, Mr. Hannify. Sarah, may I have some tea?" Jedidiah asked, still exhausted and eager to sit down. "Jesse, I rang for you and when you didn't answer I was afraid you and Sarah had left us as well."

"No, Massa' Jed. We is stayin'. This is our home, always has been, and if you wants us to stay, we is too old and stubborn to find a new life somewhere else jus' cause Mista' Lincoln and other folk we don't know, say we can go."

"Thank you, Jesse. You, too, Sarah! That's very kind of you. I know Miss Ruby would be grateful, too, if she were here to say so."

"She still with us, Massa' Jed," Sarah added softly as she put the steaming cup of tea in front of this kind man she'd served her entire adult life.

For more than an hour they exchanged thoughts on how Moss Grove might survive.

"We will need to plant in the next two months to have any chance of even getting a small crop," Jedidiah said, warmed by the tea and the surprising energy of his son. He sat a little more erect, feeling stronger already.

"We can issue bank drafts to pay for what we need if we can replace what the Union troops took"

"I doubt anyone will trade goods for Confederate currency, father." Henry added.

"No, I have a little money deposited in northern banks as well. It is not a great deal but used carefully we should be able to avoid disaster."

"Even if we find livestock, which will be difficult, we will also need people to work the fields," Simon Hannify said , his brow furrowed by the problems of producing a crop under these circumstances.

"Yes, I don't doubt that without slaves to work the fields our problems will be most severe."

Early that evening Rose rushed into the kitchen at the rear of the house, "Sarah, Matthew is gone. I been lookin' all over and no one seen him since the Yankees left. I looked in the stables and Thaddeus ain't there either."

Together with Jesse and Simon Hannify to help them, they scoured the area but the boys were nowhere to be found. Back at the foundry, however, they found a hastily scrawled note on a nail near the horseshoes.

> *Don't nobody worry. We're with Sgt. Carmody. We needs to not be slaves no more. Mammy Rose, I look after Matthew. Please tell Daddy Jesse and Mama Sarah I luv 'em and that Massa' Jed and Miss Ruby got special places in my heart for all they done.*
>
> *Thaddeus*

He left a separate note for Amy and hid it under the saddle she always used. He would have preferred to say his goodbyes in person but it wasn't possible. They had to be creative in finding time alone together and away from prying eyes.

> *Dear Amy,*
> *I'm off with Rufus and Matthew as part of the Union army. I*

*wanted to tell you that I'll miss you. Take care of Massa' Jed. Maybe*
*things will be different when I return.*

*Thaddeus*

The Union soldiers marched north following the Mississippi River
and through plantations not unlike Moss Grove. The new recruits were all
issued uniforms but only a few of the older, more experienced men were
issued rifles and shown how to load and fire them.

Since Thaddeus had learned so much about horses since returning
to Moss Grove from Port Hudson, Rufus Carmody assigned him to the
chief farrier, George Voulez. Voulez was a huge man who seemed to lope
rather than walk. He had a unique ability to calm the horses that always
whinnied nervously at the sound of cannon and gunfire. Sometimes they
would spook and begin kicking their stalls. With the additional horses they
were gathering from the plantations, Voulez was glad to have experienced
help. The man wasn't exactly lazy but he preferred the company of the
horses to that of other men and he would often sleep in one of the stalls
rather than return to his tent.

Voulez had grown up as a free black in New Orleans. He had white
blood in him back somewhere. In all likelihood it had been a drunken
plantation owner or ship's captain passing through that his black mother
had entertained and didn't care to acknowledge. He imagined his mother
had been quite a looker when she was young. She had become a seamstress
sewing gowns for the French and Spanish ladies who dined and shopped in
the French Quarter. These women had money to pay for the best silks and
taffetas, and the ships that docked weekly at New Orleans harbour were
always laden with fabrics and new fashions from Paris and the glamorous
cities of Europe.

Voulez had gone to school all the way through the sixth grade before
he got restless. His café au lait coloring and six foot height was an exciting
combination to every young female in the locale. Girls seemed to follow
him everywhere, breathless for his attentions. He had that look of danger
and excitement so attractive to the other sex during those restless years
surrounding teenage puberty. It mattered not whether the girls were
white, colored, or black. He was maturing into an equal opportunity
rake. By the time the war came he had already deflowered more than
one panting miss and leaving New Orleans quickly seemed logical.
His mother didn't object. George was her eldest and she still had three

younger children to provide for. Getting rid of him would make her life so much simpler. She kissed him, wished him God-speed, and returned to her sewing.

Enlisting in the Native Guards seemed an appropriate destination. The girls loved men in their gray uniforms and the Confederacy needed men. They preferred white men, but colored was the next best thing. At least they weren't actual 'niggers.' He was assigned to a squad responsible for supplies but his natural affinity for horses was quickly recognized. Before he reached Port Hudson, several months and several skirmishes later, he had been promoted to chief farrier of the unit. After the Confederate loss at Vicksburg he switched his uniform to one of blue with the same ease he would change his socks.

Rufus Carmody enjoyed having his protégé, Thaddeus, with him again although having Matthew tag along everywhere made him uncomfortable. The boy was younger and less educated than Thaddeus. Rufus didn't think of himself as being racist but he did prefer the company of coloreds to that of niggers. Somehow, he felt they were smarter. Thaddeus certainly fit that bill. Most of the really black ones he'd encountered even lacked the ability to do their numbers or write their names. They had never risen above the level of field nigger, good for breeding and raising cotton.

He acknowledged that, at least, Matthew knew his a,b,c's. Rose's insistence had born fruit and her boy turned out to be an apt student. Most of the books were tattered but every evening after chores she insisted he read to her. She understood very little of what Matthew read but one or two of the other hands were willing to tutor Matthew in exchange for some extra mending or laundry.

Carmody assigned Matthew to work with the cook and kitchen help. The younger boy worked without complaint. Everything he was asked was part of this new grand adventure. Thaddeus missed his new half-brother and asked George Voulez if he could have Matthew help with the horses. He felt an obligation to keep the boy close to him. With the extra horses in the battalion an additional worker to keep the stalls clean was useful and Carmody and Voulez agreed.

Thaddeus was excited. Being in the Union Army in a blue uniform instead of a gray one didn't bother him at all. It seemed as if the Yankees were winning the war. They certainly ate better than the terrible rations he and the other Confederate soldiers had been reduced to at Port Hudson.

There were two other smithies working with Voulez, both colored. At first they were leery having a new boy thrust into their private preserve but as soon as they recognized Thaddeus' comfort with horses he was allowed to do more than shovel their shit and feed them.

With Matthew close by and helping, Thaddeus' life reached a level of satisfaction he'd never felt before.

*Capt. Lindblade's battalion was integrated into General Sherman's army under overall command of General Ulysses S. Grant. The combined Union armies, now in undisputed control of Vicksburg and the Mississippi River, were readying themselves for their next objectives.*

*One force would move toward the Confederate capitol at Richmond. Another would strike due east across the Shenandoah Valley. A third army, led by General William Tecumseh Sherman, would march east nearly five hundred miles across Tennessee and Alabama to Atlanta and the Atlantic Ocean.*

*Lincoln had concurred that the objective of the war was no longer to simply defeat the Confederate forces. It was to be the complete destruction of the economic base of the South. Homes, farms, and railroads were to be military targets. It was to be a 'scorched earth' policy that would leave nothing in its wake. Its intention was to destroy southern morale and their ability to continue the war.*

*The Union forces were organized to live off the land. They were ordered to leave Vicksburg with no more than twenty days of rations. Small companies were assigned as bummers, or foragers, to seize food anywhere they could find it while other units dismantled or burned farms, shops and mills that might aid the Confederate cause. Railroad rails were heated over fires and twisted. They were nicknamed 'Sherman's neckties.'*

Sgt. Carmody was assigned one company within the battalion to act as bummers once their initial rations were nearly gone. They'd been on the road for two weeks and were approaching Selma, Alabama. In the distance behind them and off to the west the smoke from Union fires burning farms they'd passed twisted upward, giving the sky a bright orange glow. Confederate sharpshooters harassed them constantly. Carmody lost two men, shot dead.

Another man was wounded, hit in the upper leg. They applied a tourniquet to stop the bleeding but it was likely he'd lose the leg.

Decent doctors and a hospital were still at Vicksburg and white field medics had little patience with colored or black wounded soldiers. At one point Sgt. Carmody had mentioned this to Capt. Lindblade. The Captain said he'd forward the concern to his superiors but nothing changed and Rufus was certain that Lindblade immediately and conveniently forgot the entire matter.

Whenever possible the Yankee battalions tried to take horses and mules from the wealthier farms or shop owners while leaving the poor, usually recently freed blacks, with something to maintain themselves. If necessary they'd exchange a tired Union army horse for a rested animal they'd come upon.

Sgt. Carmody assigned his first squad to approach the farm from the back. The men moved stealthily. They hadn't encountered the owners of the farm and if there had been slaves working the land at one time they had all left hastily. The farm looked as if had been well cared for. The soldiers could hear the squeal of the pigs and hens cackling not far away. It was a bucolic setting until one of the Union soldiers went to unlatch the barn door. Then all hell broke loose.

From behind wagons and through the house's windows gun fire burst forth. The soldier opening the barn door fell in a heap as the rest of the squad scurried for cover. It was impossible to know whether the rifle fire was coming from people who lived in the house or from Confederate soldiers, but it made little difference. Bullets from either one could end your life.

The exchange of gun fire lasted close to an hour. Carmody decided to flank the house with the reserves he hadn't yet committed. He wished he had more men but all that remained were his blacksmiths. Reluctantly he ordered Matthew to stay with the horses but he ordered Voulez, Thaddeus and the other two blacksmiths to pick up guns and join the rest of the men approaching from the north side.

Twenty minutes later, having scrambled through the brush, the reserves reached the back of the house and began firing. George Voulez was killed before he'd gotten off a shot. Angrily, Carmody and the rest of his men quickly killed the men shooting from behind the wagons and, after threatening to burn the house, the residents surrendered. All that was there was a father, three boys, a woman and young child. The other men that had been firing from outside were uniformed Confederate soldiers.

"Good job, Sergeant," said Captain Lindblade as he rode up on his black stallion. "Make sure you gather all their arms, and then burn the place. Every stinking shred! We'll take the livestock."

"God damn Yankee bastards," the father shouted. "We'll starve. How am I supposed to feed my children?"

"Mister, I don't give a rat's ass if your entire family dies. You killed three of my men."

"We didn't want to fight," the woman cried. "The Johnny Rebs said if we didn't help them surprise you, they'd kill us. Please leave us something. This place is all we own."

"Burn it!" Lindblade ordered as he rode off.

Sergeant Carmody shouted, "You heard him, men. Start with the barn. Be careful with our dead comrades. They deserve a righteous burial. Thaddeus, come here. I want you to gather one sack of grain, a boar and a sow, and two chickens. Give them to that farmer out of sight of everyone."

"But sergeant, what about what Captain Lindblade said?"

"Never you mind! Just do as I say. You are now in charge of the horses. I will submit your name to be promoted to Corporal."

The Union troops spent the night near the farm, keeping warm from the heat of the barn being burned. Since the Captain had moved on, Carmody was able to avoid burning the house. Both the farmer and his wife cried, full of thanks, surprised that they had been spared, especially by someone who wasn't even white.

"Amy, we did good," Jedidiah smiled. "We will have vegetables and tomatoes for the table. Your mother and Sarah will be so pleased. And even the small cotton crop is doing well."

"You did it Mister Jed," Amy said as they both rode old mules through the fields. It had been a struggle. There was not much seed to be had at any price. It was actually Rose that found some at a nearby plantation. It was expensive but through careful bartering they got enough to plant several rows of turnips, collards and corn.

Henry and Simon Hannify had done most of the work and even Amy had to admit her brother-in-law was less of a bother now that he had to face hard work and fatherhood.

As Amy and Jedidiah neared the far end of the cotton crop, near where they always diverted the river for irrigation, they spied three black men taking the cotton from the bolls with expertise.

"What are you men doing?" Jedidiah shouted. "That is our cotton, you thievin' niggers. Get off my land."

Two men stopped, surprised by the interruption. The third man ignored the order and continued to fill the large sack that hung over his head and shoulder.

Jedidiah pulled the revolver he carried on his saddle, always loaded, and pointed it at the man still hunched over.

"Don't shoot, Massa'," the other two shouted. They raised their hands and dropped the sack of cotton.

"We don' mean no harm. We is hungry. We jus' want 'nuf to sell to buy some food. We ain't put nuthin' our stomachs for nearly a week."

The third man continued to ignore him, pulling the cotton, dragging the sack and moving down the line. Jedidiah fired his pistol and a red welt appeared on the back of the man's head. He stood, put his hand to his head, looked at the man riding toward him and in one movement took the sack off and leapt at Jedidiah. Before anyone could move the two were entangled in the midst of the sharp thorny cotton plants. Amy screamed and the other two black men just shouted, "He's deaf, he's deaf, thas' why he didn't stop. Couldn't hear ya. Oh, my lordy."

By the time they reached the intertwined bodies of Jedidiah and the deaf slave, both men were unconscious and bleeding badly. The deaf man had found enough strength after being shot to attack the elderly plantation owner before collapsing himself.

Henry was riding hard from the house with Hannify running as fast as he could. They had heard the shot and Amy's scream. Both men were armed but Hannify's Quaker beliefs made him reluctant to ever use his weapon. The other two blacks looked up, saw the men coming toward them and immediately began running away toward the river. They didn't get more than a dozen paces before a bullet from Henry's gun dropped one of them. Henry had learned how to shoot from a horse even as he rode with one arm. The other slave made it to the river and scurried across. The dead black was left where he fell. The deaf black, his arm resting limp across the body of Moss Grove's patriarch, never survived.

Hannify lifted Jedidiah carefully and carried him toward the house. He hadn't gotten far when Jesse came to help. The patriarch was still alive, badly bruised. His arm was broken but at least he was still breathing. For two days the elder Rogers hung between life and death, waking occasionally, barely long enough to recognize those around him. He died on the third afternoon, the sun's rays almost ethereal as they passed through the curtains and brightened the room. Elizabeth, Henry and the baby were there, as were Sarah, Jesse, Sylvia and Amy.

"Henry," Jedidiah said weakly, "Moss Grove is now yours. She is like a woman. If you show her love and attention she will return that love many fold. You must respect her and hold her in trust for Josiah. He will come of age soon enough. I miss my Ruby. I'm tired now. I think I shall sleep." His eyes closed, his head turned to one side and the air in the room stopped, each person stunned by the suddenness of with which their lives had turned once again.

Sarah wept softly as Jesse pulled the sheet respectfully over the face of Massa' Jed, a special man who functioned best in a world that no longer existed.

Now both men, the white patriarch of Moss Grove and a deaf black slave, who had lived their lives in such separate worlds, would travel to their eternal heaven on the same wagon.

# Chapter Thirteen

*Sherman's army moved quickly to the east, encountering little rebel military resistance. The city of Atlanta, jewel of the south, fell in September 1864. The Yankee forces had totally destroyed nearly all the farms they passed through in Alabama and Georgia. By December his Army reached Savannah and the Atlantic Ocean. His 'March to the Sea' had laid waste much of the Confederacy. As they marched across the south, thousands of freed slaves followed in their wake, sustaining themselves off the leavings of the Yankee army.*

Thaddeus and Matthew swelled with pride as the field hands and house niggers they encountered each day thanked them with tears in their eyes and a warm clasp of their calloused hands. Most of the slaves wore little more than tattered clothing but eagerly they showered the Union soldiers with gifts of small dolls, boots often removed from dead Confederate soldiers, or whatever paltry possessions they had gathered. The two youths from Moss Grove understood that what they were doing was evolving into a holy mission. What had begun as an adventure was now a crusade. They and the other 'blue-bellies' were bringing an end to slavery, one farm at a time.

The Confederate forces that continued to fight had been vastly diminished by casualties and desertions. The attack near Selma had been the last organized foray against Captain Lindblade's squads that they'd encountered. The Rebs were finding that their munitions and supplies were dwindling and difficult to replace. Morale across the Confederacy continued to sink. No longer did Confederate statesmen speak of state's rights. Most of them now just wanted this grand adventure to end.

Everywhere Robert E. Lee turned he was faced with numerically superior, better rested, and better equipped Union forces.

*In the midst of an ongoing string of northern victories the election of 1864 was held. Lincoln's slogan "Don't change horses in mid-stream" held sway over fractured Democratic hopefuls. In an unanticipated turn Lincoln selected Senator Andrew Johnson from Tennessee as his running mate. The logic was sound. Johnson had been the sole southern senator to remain in the U.S. Senate when the mass exodus by southern states divided the nation four years earlier. Now he was Military Governor of that state. Naming a southerner as a running mate was a conciliatory gesture toward the states that had seceded. The north, as well as the south, was eager to end the hostilities.*

*On April 9, 1865 Robert E. Lee quietly surrendered what remained of his Army of Northern Virginia to Ulysses S. Grant at Appomattox Court House. Confederate soldiers standing in formation, openly cried as their vanquished leader rode among them. The remnants of the Confederate army would surrender piecemeal all the way into June.*

*Buoyed by the imminent end to the war, President Lincoln and his wife attended an evening performance at Washington, D.C.'s Ford Theatre. It was only five days since Lee had surrendered. The beloved President that had brought them successfully through this bloody internecine conflict was shot by a crazed assassin and died within hours. The nation was stunned.*

"Mr. Rogers," Simon Hannify said respectfully, addressing Henry, now master of what remained of Moss Grove. "I intend to leave at the end of the month. I've decided to head west, maybe California. They say there's lots of good land there and plenty of water just for the taking."

"But Simon, you've become part of the Moss Grove family. We depend on you. Is it money? I'd be happy to discuss increasing your wages," Henry said, not used to bargaining with those he deemed clearly inferior, white or black.

"That's kind of you, sir, but it isn't the money. I just want to find a more settled life and I don't think I'll find it anywhere in Louisiana. I sort of dream of a small farm where I can settle down and raise some young 'uns. Somewhere away from all the killin' we seen these past years. Now that the war is over things are sure to change. I don't want to have to adapt to a new Louisiana. Maybe I'm just too old or settled in my ways. I'm sorry, truly. "

"Simon, you're leaving me in the lurch. The fucking niggers are becoming more and more arrogant. My wife is pregnant again and her parents are of absolutely no value. They eat, they drink and they shit. You're the only white man around here I can talk to."

"I'm sorry, Mister Rogers but I've made up my mind. You and your father were always kind to me. I wish you God's best." He turned and left.

Henry went to the window and gazed out at the manicured lawn at the rear of the house. It was still morning and he was already stressed and tired. What the hell am I going to do now, Henry wondered. I'm going to need help sharing these burdens.

His dreams of an easy life as a plantation owner and setting up a mistress for his occasional enjoyment had vanished as sure as his right arm. Life was not turning out as he had imagined. At least his cock still functioned. Losing that would have been worse than losing his arm. Elizabeth still hadn't learned how to please a man. She still made love lying there on her back as inert as unleavened bread. He had become quite creative, fantasizing unknown beauties who had bigger tits and great asses. It was only after he came and looked over at the sallow looking bitch his wife had become that the reality of his life returned. And the Williams! They had it so good here, why would they choose to leave?

Amy was maturing into a beauty. Too bad she continued to despise him. He'd like to suck those tits of hers. He'd watched them blossom this past year trying hard not gaze at them like an old lecher. Maybe if he screwed her she'd enjoy it and she wouldn't have so much animosity toward him.

Amy, on the other hand, was finding her life at Moss Grove increasingly meaningless. Thaddeus was gone. She wrote letters to him and he occasionally wrote to her although it seemed neither ever received the letters written by the other. Meanwhile, it was becoming increasingly difficult to avoid Henry and his ogling. He made her skin crawl. With Jedidiah gone, he and Elizabeth had moved into the master suite. It should have been appropriate but Henry would never be the man his father was. His arrogance and the demeanor she despised had returned.

She found if she spent time with Rose or Sarah she could learn something about cooking and herbs. It was something, at least.

Everything at Moss Grove seemed to wilt after Jedidiah died. There was a pall over the house and the fields. People moved slower and with a heavier step. Even the limbs of the trees seemed to hang a little lower as if, they, too, missed the presence of the man who had planted them.

Amy was careful to avoid Henry cornering her alone! She also began teaching some of the few children who remained at the plantation how to read. Josiah took to books easily. She would gather her nephew and the black children and together they would enjoy the spring weather reading the same books she knew that Thaddeus had enjoyed.

Elizabeth spent little time with her son. Her current pregnancy was progressing and, once again, she felt ugly. She'd spend hours preening herself in an endless battle to feel attractive to the husband who had become so remote. It was of no use.


"Congratulations, Henry, the war is over" Baxter Williams said, hoisting a glass of brandy. "Come, join me."

Henry stared at his father-in-law, disgusted with the man's almost constant alcoholic binge but happy to put it aside to toast the end of hostilities.

"Sure, Baxter, pour me one, too. All this damn war cost me was my arm, nearly my vision, the end of slavery and not enough cotton produced to end up with a profit this year."

"Well, maybe if they'd killed Lincoln sooner. But we'll never know. The paper says the war cost the nation millions of dollars and hundreds of thousands of fine young men, so now what happens?"

"Now the battle will shift to Washington," Henry said, sitting as Jesse came and helped him remove his boots.

"President Johnson understands the south. After all, he's a Tennessee boy. He's trying to get Congress to punish the Confederate leaders but give the rest of us amnesty."

"That sounds reasonable."

"Those fucking northerners will never agree to it. They want their pound of flesh and now that they are in a position to bleed us, they damn well will."

*President Johnson's continued attempts to help the southern states met formidable resistance from both houses of Congress. He allowed the southern states that had formed the Confederacy to hold Congressional elections in 1865 but neither the Senate nor the House would allow these Confederate representatives to be seated. Bitterness between Congress and the President reached a fever pitch. Johnson pushed for a speedy readmission to the Union for all the southern states but this, too, was blocked.*

*Meanwhile, southern states passed new racist laws, called 'Black codes,' including anti-miscegenation laws that prohibited black-white marriages. Indiana, Illinois, and other border states, passed laws that prohibited black immigration.*

*Freed slaves, now called 'Freedmen,' became a new southern class but leverage and power was still with the wealthy white establishment that needed a stable and submissive labor force.*

"Henry, we need to talk about Amy," Baxter Williams said, already on his second glass of port. Dinners had become less formal. Food was now limited to what the plantation could produce and trying to maintain the dress and decorum of the past seemed an anachronistic formality.

"She is growing up wild and spending far too much time with niggers here at the plantation. Sylvia and I hope that you will agree she needs to be sent to a finishing school."

Henry smiled. He and Elizabeth had already discussed it. It seems that his wife had noticed more than an occasional suggestive glance at her younger sister by her husband. It would serve everyone well if Amy were sent away. And the more ugly and fat Elizabeth felt, the less confident she felt having an attractive and virginal younger sister standing next to her for easy comparison. It was all too tempting for her husband's roving eye.

It was agreed that Amy would be enrolled in the same New Orleans school that Elizabeth had attended. It remained one of the few still open in this now northern controlled city. Amy wasn't thrilled. She would have preferred a school in Atlanta or even up north but those would only accept Yankee dollars and the limited northern money available to Henry was needed for the sustenance of Moss Grove. Amy would go where she was told.

Moss Grove needed workers, it was that simple. The plantation needed men willing to get their hands dirty in Louisiana's rich soil. Planting season was next month and if they didn't get seed into the ground promptly there would be no crop.

Slavery was over. A chance at freedom had decimated the traditional work force. Malaria and Yellow fever had never had such an impact. From a work cadre of more than a hundred field and house slaves, there were now less than ten who had stayed and continued to work. The biggest and strongest men had all left. Henry's eyesight had returned but he was otherwise limited in what he could do. With the harness Thaddeus had developed he could at least mount a horse and give orders. He was growing desperate for someone to give those orders to. The entire social structure with which he was familiar was in disarray. Confederate soldiers wandered the countryside, many with limbs missing, few able to return to their prewar lives. Men and some of their families that been slaves were even more disoriented. For the first time in their lives they were faced with making life altering decisions for which they'd had no experience.

Riding near the river Henry came upon four grown black men resting.

"You men are trespassing on Moss Grove property. Where do you belong?" Henry asked.

Nervously the men got to their feet. One man, less cowed than the others came forward. "We don't mean no harm, sir. We's tryin' to get back to our homes in Tennessee. We's jus tired and restin' but we'll move on if it troubles you."

"I need men to work the cotton fields. You boys interested?" Henry tried to smile amiably. It was clear these men had worked cotton fields somewhere at some time. "I'll pay you a wage."

"What kind of money we talkin'? Confederate paper's only good for wipin' yo' ass," one of the men laughed.

Henry really wanted to take out his side arm and shoot the brash nigger bastards lazing before him but it was a changed world. He needed Moss Grove to produce cotton and he needed damn niggers to do the work. If he couldn't buy slaves he'd have to hire them.

"I'll pay you solid Yankee dollars. I'll give you a place to live and we have a small store where you can buy food and supplies if you don't like what the kitchen cooks. You'll get one-half of what we get when we sell the cotton less rent and food. You can easily earn one hundred dollars for a year's work less the cost of your keep! We'll sign a legal contract. But if you don't work or finish the year you'll get a lot less."

"How we know you pay us?" The men were hungry and clearly needed a warm meal and place to live. They'd been on the road more than two weeks with less than one meal a day.

"Look, slavery's over. We all know that. Now you work, I pay. You don't want to work, get off my land. I need men to plant and then harvest the cotton. If you think I'm cheating you, you can take the contract to the sheriff. He'll make me pay you. But that isn't necessary. Moss Grove is a good plantation. Ask the folks who are still with us. They'll tell you we've always been fair to our people. We're adjusting, same as you. Follow me and I'll get you a good hot meal. We'll start work in the morning."

The men looked at one another and followed Henry back toward Moss Grove. Each was about to embark on a modified return of the lifestyle that had been theirs since birth. Henry had pulled the one hundred dollar figure out of the air. He had no idea whether these men would make anything but at this point he needed bodies and he'd work out the details later.

*Radical Republicans ranted at the spread of the Black Codes that were returning blacks to a new, modified form of economic slavery. They passed their own Civil Rights bill calling for 'perfect' equality between all black and white citizens and conferred full citizenship on all Freedmen.*

*President Andrew Johnson vetoed the bill. "This is a country for white men and a government for white men," he averred. For the first time in the country's history, a Presidential veto was overridden and became the law of the land. The elections of 1866 were a further repudiation of Johnson's philosophy. With many of the southern states still restricted from voting, militant Republicans were now in complete control of Reconstruction.*

Thaddeus and Matthew were released from their army service, paid in Union dollars and gathered their few belongings for a return to Louisiana. Captain Lindblade had already left without a goodbye. He would return to his life in Pittsburgh. He had done his duty for the Union and had little interest in what happened to the black people he'd fought with, or the slaves he'd freed. He had followed orders, nothing more.

Rufus Carmody decided to head west with his friends for awhile until he could decide what to do with his life. He had no intention of returning to New Orleans and the north held no interest for him.

The three took the best horses and loaded a mule with all the blacksmithing gear they'd been using. They tried to avoid the roads that had taken them through the midsection of the south where so much of the country had been reduced to ashes by Sherman's cut and burn campaign. They rode south toward Montgomery, Alabama. The city had been the home of the Confederate Congress but during fierce fighting most of those buildings had been razed.

Homeless Confederate veterans wandered the streets near the capitol building, hoping that some of the promises originally made to them might bring them some form of food or shelter. Nothing was forthcoming.

All three men had removed their Union blue uniforms. It would not have been safe to tarry in these surroundings without the protection of greater military support. Rumor had it that sizeable Union military units were on their way to supervise the south's reconstruction. Meanwhile blacks wandered throughout the city as well. They were unwilling to return to their slave jobs but they were growing hungry and winter would come soon enough.

The three ex-soldiers left their horses at a stable on the edge of town and walked back to have a meal at a café where blacks and coloreds could be served. For a change they wouldn't be subjected to Thaddeus' cooking. A large black woman, her apron heavily stained, a scarf covering her head and who obviously owned the café, eyed them suspiciously.

"Yo'all not from around here, are ya?" she asked, handing them each a hand scrawled menu.

"No, ma'am," Rufus said politely, "But we got money to pay for our vittles."

"Confederate money has no value anymore."

"We can pay with Yankee silver."

"Ah thought so. You boys are Yankees. Get out. We don't want no blue bastards in here," she stormed.

"Wait a minute," Thaddeus said. We're not in the Army anymore. Anyway, the war is over and we're jus' headin' back to our kinfolk in Louisiana."

"Your people burned our land and our homes. You and your kind probably did all of Sherman's burnin'. Black folk burnin' out homes of other black folks! It's a terrible sin. If the Rebs hangin' around figure you for Yankees they as soon lynch you as take a shit."

"We're tired. You gonna feed us or not?" Matthew chimed in. "I'm getting' so hungry even Thaddeus' cookin' sound good."

"No. No service. Jus' leave," The woman said as she picked up the menus and walked back to the kitchen.

Disgusted, the boys rose and left the café. Before they could decide whether to seek another place to eat or just get their horses, four white men approached them. One walked with a crutch, another had one arm, and the other two just looked plain mean.

"Jes' a minute, niggers," the one-armed man shouted. He wore a gray Johnny Reb cap and had a pistol strapped on his right hip, the hip that still had an arm hanging loose in an 'I know how to use this gun' swing.

"We're getting' our horses and leavin'," Rufus said, putting his hand up in a peaceful gesture.

"You're leavin' when we say you is leavin'," added the man on the crutch. "Yo'all fought with the blue-bellies, didn't yo? You nigger shitheads came down here and burned out our land and everything we loved."

"We fought for the Native Guards out of Louisiana. We fought for the south. We struggled through the same shit you did at Port Hudson and Vicksburg," Rufus shouted.

"You a lyin' nigger! If you fought with us where'd you get those Yankee dollars?"

"Stole'm off a dead Yankee," Thaddeus lied. "Matthew, go and get our horses saddled. We'll join you in a minute." If there was going to be shooting or violence, his younger brother had to be moved out of the way.

"Who'd you serve with if you was at Vicksburg?"

"I was up on Stockade Redan...General Pemberton ran the whole show...I was a sergeant, artillery, and we held off the Yankees for nearly two months. I lost more than half my men, some just to dysentery and shit rations. Now you believe us?" Sgt. Rufus Carmody shouted, reliving the horror of the battles he'd experienced and careful to avoid any mention of their switch to Union blue once Vicksburg had surrendered.

"I was up there, too," the one-legged white boy sobbed. "He's tellin' the truth. Let'm go," he said to his friends. "Sorry, fellas, we's jus angry and can't figure out what to do now there's no more Confederacy to feed us."

A small crowd of whites and blacks had gathered. Racial conflicts weren't unknown in Montgomery and the blacks, with fewer weapons, usually came out on the wrong end of the conflict. Emotions were even more raw now that the war had ended. Whites, rich and poor, had their traditional pedestal of authority shattered and they were now forced to coexist with blacks in an uncertain truce.

The three tired travelers arrived at Moss Grove on a Sunday. Everything seemed so different than when they left. It all had an eerie quality about it. Even the trees moved with less energy. Lethargy hung like a pall over the entire plantation.

They walked their horses into the stable, fed them, and set them in stalls. The forge looked as if it hadn't been used since Thaddeus and Matthew had left to join the army. Sarah was in the kitchen and turned as they entered. Her hands went to her mouth, tears filled her eyes, and she grabbed Thaddeus in a bear hug before they all began to laugh. Within minutes, Jesse and Amy joined them. Amy was home for a time from her school but she was due to return to New Orleans within the week. The celebration grew louder and happier but Thaddeus and Amy saw only one another. Tears were in her eyes as she looked at the boy who'd left, only to return a man.

It wasn't difficult for Thaddeus to notice the softness of Amy's bright red hair, tied back with a white bow. Her freckles filled in around smiling lips and green eyes that danced. She had developed curves that had been hidden in her coveralls but they were no longer possible to hide. Thaddeus had grown into a man, nearly six feet tall, handsome, with those steel blue eyes she adored in him and detested in Henry. As they stared at one another, the remainder of the family walked in on the reunion, Henry, a pregnant Elizabeth, and Sylvia Williams followed, holding a squirming Josiah. They had heard the loud noises coming from the kitchen and had come downstairs to find its cause.

"Well, well," Henry smirked. "The valorous knights of the Union army have returned. What makes you think you're welcome here?"

"Massa' Henry," Thaddeus said. "We never thought otherwise. Moss Grove has always been our home. Our kinfolk here. We be told that Massa' Jed died while we was gone and we want to offer you our condolences."

"My father would turn over in his grave if he knew that those he had provided for had sided with the enemies of Moss Grove and everything he represented. I'm master of this plantation now and I consider you both to be ungrateful niggers who are not welcome. Say your hellos and leave.

The plantation can manage quite well without you, both of you, and the colored Yankee friend you brought with you."

Henry turned and left. Elizabeth and Sylvia Baxter, wordless, trailed in his wake.

"Amy, please join us," Elizabeth said as she was leaving.

"No, I think I'd prefer to remain here," Amy said in a most firm voice, smiling at Thaddeus, as her sister and mother looked at her, aghast at the girl's rebellion.

"Matthew, Matthew, is that you?" Rose exclaimed rushing in from having collected the eggs from the hen house.

"Mother, I missed you so," Matthew said, once again becoming the young boy so lonely for the long months away from this woman who had protected him his entire life.

Amy pulled Thaddeus outside and away from the others. He went willingly and they held hands walking toward the river and their private place under the tree. The moon shed its light but the two knew the way by heart. They sat, their backs to the tree, and held one another. They watched the light play off the river and followed the course of an occasional steam boat plying its way north or south. Together they fantasized about its destination and where it might take them. They understood their absence would upset the others but this evening they didn't care. Thaddeus was back and he was with the woman he cared for more than he had ever cared for anyone in his entire life. It was the only love he had ever felt, white or black, allowed or forbidden.

"Is there a chance for us?" Amy asked, nestled in Thaddeus' arms as lights cascaded from the stern of an occasional boat.

"One day, perhaps. It is a new time, a fresh beginning. We'll just have to hope that someday soon, before we're too old, our stars will align," Thaddeus mused, thinking of all the white and colored folks he'd met marching across the country.

The men stayed until the moon descended, unwilling to separate themselves. They traded stories of the war and Moss Grove's transition from a home filled with happiness and a sense of stability while Massa' Jed was alive to an unhappy home laden with uncertainties under Massa' Henry.

No one wanted the reunion to end but as the early morning light arrived and a rooster began to crow it was clear the time to leave was approaching.

"We'll be fine," Thaddeus said, continuing to hold Amy's hand. "We been traveling on our own all the way from Atlanta. We'll find a place close by. We're back now and we intend to stay. The war is over and we aren't slaves no more. That's the important thing."

# Chapter Fourteen

"Massa' Henry, 'ah needs to talk to you."

Rose had mustered all her will to confront the man who had raped her when she was little more than a child. In all that time she had avoided him whenever possible. It wasn't always possible. She grew up in the cotton fields just as Henry had grown up riding through the fields with his father. Now that Massa' Jed was gone, this new blonde boss arrogantly rode alone through the same fields, inspecting the pace and quality of what the men in the field were doing. The Raffertys and Simon Hannify were gone and decent overseers were difficult to hire. Many had been killed in the war or had given up trying to boss blacks and headed west. Henry had to run things himself. It was just another way in which Moss Grove had changed, and not for the better.

The field hands dreaded seeing him up on a horse, a whip hanging loose over his neck, his only hand holding tight to the reins, his blonde hair protruding from below the gray felt hat he'd worn as a Confederate Captain. These days he always wore a new, modified harness that he'd had made out of leather. It was Thaddeus' design but stronger.

Henry had managed to avoid Rose as well. Their sexual encounter was an event of his youth, in the long ago past, and something with which he no longer wished to concern himself. He never thought of it as a rape. After all, she was just a nigger and the event would have been forgotten years ago had it not been for the birth of a colored child and his father's sentimentality that kept the boy, Thaddeus, around, serving as an ever present reminder. It's all bullshit. Moss Grove is mine and I'll run it as I please.

"Yes, Rose," he asked, his voice clear and sure. He probably shouldn't even have to converse with her.

"I wants you to let the boys come back here to Moss Grove," she said.

"You want? Who the fuck are you to want anything?" He said as his eyes opened in amazement at the sheer cheek of the black girl.

"Massa' Henry, you and me been avoidin' one another for a long time. You took a lot from me. I ain't never asked for nuthin'. Now, they is my boys and I want'em near me."

"Listen, bitch. You never asked for nuthin' cause you were the property of Moss Grove and property don't ask for nuthin'. You understand me."

Their voices rose as the self-enforced silence of more than a decade in both their lives burst forth. Elizabeth, Amy, and Sarah could hear them but none of them was unwilling to intervene. Sarah grasped her apron, froze over the linen she had been folding, and stared into the abyss of what her life was becoming since Massa' Jed and Miss Ruby died. Elizabeth had learned of Henry's child, Thaddeus, but knew better than to confront her husband about an incident that had happened so many years before Henry met her.

"I ain't a slave bitch anymore, Massa' Jed."

"You'll always be a slave bitch, Rose. No war or law is going to change that," he laughed. "You wouldn't even be working in the house if Sarah hadn't needed more help with Josiah and another baby on the way. You'd still be with the field hands spreading your legs for every nigger that wanted to get off."

She lunged at him but he caught her hand with his one arm and threw the smaller woman back.

"I should have put a knife in you years ago. You were no good then and you'll never be the man yo' daddy was," she snarled.

"Get out of my sight. You can leave Moss Grove and join your sons. You're all nigger trash. Get out! Get out!" he screamed.

"What we gonna do?" Rose moaned.

Rufus had built a campfire. He, Thaddeus, and Matthew sat rapt as Rose told them of her argument with Henry and his demand that she leave the plantation.

"I ain't never lived nowhere but Moss Grove. I's scared."

Matthew put his arm around her. "Don't worry, momma. We's got money. Yankee money! We be OK. He a bad man, that Henry Rogers! Always has been!" he said, looking at Thaddeus for confirmation.

"We could head west," Rufus said. "Lots of the men we fought with…

both sides, talked a lot of moving west, past Kansas and Missouri. There's the Oklahoma territory, lots of space there."

"Too many Indians! I like what little hair I have. Any other ideas?" Thaddeus asked.

"How about just finding a small farm here and working it? We do know cotton."

"I'd just as never see cotton again, if you please. I been pickin' that shit since I was old enough to stand up and pee," Matthew added to peals of laughter that even made Rose smile and relax.

They were sleeping soundly below a blanket of cold morning mist when they heard the rustling of leaves beneath the hooves of approaching horses. Rufus and Thaddeus grabbed their army pistols.

"Better stop, whoever you is. We got guns." Rufus shouted. All four rose and shook off the final dregs of the night's sleep.

"Don't shoot, for Lord's sake."

The voice was familiar and they could hear more than one horse but the figures still hadn't emerged from the woods. A few moments' later two horses appeared, the faces of the riders hidden by warm cloaks.

"Put those silly guns down," said Amy and she and Jesse drew close.

"What are you two doing out so early in the morning, wandering around. You lost?" Thaddeus asked, smiling at the two people in the world he was most fond of.

"Sarah thought you might be getting' low on food so we brung you some supplies," Jesse said.

"And Jesse felt it would be safer if we left while the rest of the household was still sleeping," Amy added.

"That's right kind of you, Miss Amy," Rose smiled. "Here let me help you. You all get down and rest and I'll cook up some coffee and grits for us."

"My mother's a good cook. Massa' Henry done us a good favor sending her here to us. We were getting' pretty sick of what Thaddeus called vittles. Even the horses turned up their noses to it."

Amy and Thaddeus strolled away together after sharing a hot meal midst caring friends. Morning light was beginning to peak through the overhead tree branches and they could hear small animals beginning to search out their own morning snack.

"I missed you something terrible," Thaddeus confessed with an unusual shyness. They hadn't spoken much when they'd seen one another at Moss Grove but that evening had brought forth the feelings they'd both sublimated for so long.

"At night when we'd marched all day and we camped under the stars I used to look up and imagine your face looking down at me."

"It was the same with me. Life at Moss Grove has become ugly and mean. I'd sit for hours under the magnolia tree near the river where we met. Usually I'd bring a book so everyone thought I was reading but really, that was our place. When it got dark I'd look up at the early evening stars and I'd know that somewhere you might be looking at those same stars. I felt you were with me. I was happy when they sent me off to school in New Orleans. Does that make any sense?"

"It makes sense to me. You were with me every step we marched toward that big endless ocean. I carried this image of the strangest girl I'd ever met, white or black. I'd never seen a tomboy, didn't know there was such a thing as a girl who liked to wear boy type clothes. I loved those silly overalls you liked to wear with your freckles and hair ribbons tying your red hair. Now you've become the prettiest woman I've ever seen. I worried that you'd only be a dream from my childhood. I look at you and nothing has changed. You still look and feel like the very young Amy that I met on the riverbank."

"I guess I'll always feel like that girl," she smiled. "You've matured as well. You're a grown man now. You've been a soldier and you're no longer the property of Moss Grove. That must be quite a change." She could feel the warmth of this man walking next to her as they moved effortlessly to hold one another's hands.

"Tell me what the war was like. I was so frightened the first time you ran off. Then you returned with Henry nearly dead in that wagon. He wouldn't even be alive today except for you and he certainly never showed any gratitude. He's a terrible person. And then you disappeared again. I kept writing you letters, never sure whether they ever got to you."

"I wrote you, also, but there was rarely anyway to send them."

"I guess our letters to one another are floating out there somewhere. Thaddeus, what's going to happen now? Is there any chance for us?"

"I'd like to think the answer is yes. Abe Lincoln may have ended slavery but this is still the south. We'll just have to keep that hope that somehow our stars will align."

The warmth of their bodies, so close to one another, blended with the heat of their emotions. They both understood that what they felt had always been forbidden and dangerous but at this moment it was all irrelevant. They were young, attracted to one another, and their hormones raged. They had imagined and yearned for this union for more than a year since that stolen kiss in the stable, never knowing whether they'd see one another again.

They embraced. There was no place to lie down. They found a log to sit on, never separating their bodies. He kissed her lips, her cheeks and her neck. She unbuttoned the top of her dress and he reached for her breasts, letting his hands roam as he embraced and kissed each one gently. She freed herself from her corset and he bent in front of her. His tongue moved slowly as their body heat grew and her nipples hardened. He knew he was fully erect and he struggled to control his urge to enter her. Their embraces lingered, and lingered, and lingered. Neither one of them wanted to break the magic of their coming together.

"Excuse us!" The voice seemed to come from a distant galaxy but it was repeated several times before Amy and Thaddeus realized that the rest of their group had come looking for them. The two stood and straightened out their clothes as their faces flushed. They were too stunned at what they'd shared to speak.

"You two must be crazy," Jesse spoke first. "You, boy, you gonna' get lynched. And you, Miss Amy, I don't know what they do to you, but it wouldn't be a good thing."

"Young love knows no color, Jesse," Rufus chimed in with a broad grin on his face. "I seen this lots of times when I was growin' up in New Orleans. White girls, colored boys and the other way, too! It ain't got no future though, kids, not in this country. Even the Yankees frown on it. Seems that only the Frenchies in Orleans don't care and neither of you is French."

"It was my fault," Thaddeus said. "Amy didn't do anything. My fault!"

"Don't be an ass, Thaddeus. We both felt something. I never felt this way toward anyone and I'm not ashamed of it," Amy said with a peck of uncertain confidence, as her fingers fumbled to re-button her blouse and she continued to straighten her clothes, more out of nervousness than necessity.

As they walked back toward the campfire Thaddeus and Amy continued to exchange glances at one another to the head shakes and frowns of their friends. As they sat together, drinking their hot coffee, no more was said of the couple's indiscretion. It was clear these two were in love, an illicit love that could doom them both.

"We need to decide whether we headin' west or buyin' a small farm," Matthew said.

"You boys are all good with horses. I seen you. Why not do somethin' with them?" Jesse asked.

"Baton Rouge is growing. I'm sure they could use another smithy," Amy added, eager to keep her friends close to Moss Grove.

"We got everything but the forge courtesy of the Union army," Rufus added. "I ain't too good with horses but we could sell feed and stuff. Union army might be here for awhile. We can tell the Yankees we fought with Sherman and we can tell the Rebs we fought at Vicksburg. If we do it right everyone'll want to buy from us." They all laughed at the paradoxical situation.

They talked awhile longer, Jesse and Rose making certain that Thaddeus and Amy were kept apart. They succeeded in separating them physically but it was impossible not to notice the continuing smiles and overt glances they exchanged. This dangerous liaison was going to require constant monitoring.


Less than three blocks from Baton Rouge's ornate Capitol, Rufus and Thaddeus found an ideal location to set up a business of blacksmithing and animal feed. They'd be close enough to stable the horses of all the government visitors but far enough away for any smells to be minimal. They'd also be able to catch wagons coming into town for supplies.

Matthew stayed at the site unloading and tending their goods while Rufus and Thaddeus went out to introduce themselves. Both men were light complexioned and they hoped that would make it a little more likely that white officials and business owners would accept them. Neither knew for sure what they might encounter.

"Better to be cautious at first," Rufus said. "If we're going to upset people, let's try and do it after our business is up and running. Just like we did before! We're Rebs to southerners and blue coats to our northern friends. Whatever you want...however you is...we're just the folks to do business with. Carmody & Williams Blacksmith & Animal Feed Store is open for business."

*Military occupation of the south by Union troops was established to ensure equality of opportunity during this post war period of reconstruction. To achieve this goal the Confederacy had been divided into five military districts. General Philip Sheridan commanded Texas and Louisiana. Sheridan had successfully led Union forces across the Shenandoah Valley at the same time Sherman was razing farms enroute to Atlanta.*

*Sheridan assumed his first problem was Texas and led his troops there to quell a small uprising. But he was wrong. While he was helping Benito Juarez rid Mexico of French troops, a race riot erupted in New Orleans. More than thirty blacks were massacred by rampaging whites. Sheridan returned quickly and took charge.*

*He interpreted the Military Reconstruction Acts sternly. He dismissed numerous officials and limited voter registration of former Confederate officials and only registered voters, including blacks, would be allowed to serve on juries. Union troops paraded daily in front of the Baton Rouge capitol building making certain their presence was felt within.*

Carmody & Williams thrived. Southerners would watch Thaddeus shoe cavalry horses and damn the Yankees. Union soldiers would relax around the stove in the feed store regaling Rufus and Matthew with war stories. The most serious problem was remembering whether they were 'gray' or 'blue' during each conversation.

Henry and Elizabeth's second child was almost due. Josiah had already learned to walk and he scampered everywhere. 'No' was not a word he chose to accept. He had inherited his father's aggressiveness and, unfortunately, his mother's looks. Sarah mused it would have been much better had the two traits be reversed but it was not to be. The little boy was a tyrant and Henry seemed to relish watching him. The old midwife wouldn't be around to help with the baby's birth this time. The woman had died the previous winter. It would be up to her and Sylvia Williams, if the elderly matron would stop drinking long enough. I suppose I could teach Amy so she could help, Sarah thought. If, and it was a big 'if', the girl would stay away from Thaddeus and Baton Rouge long enough to be of use and if she wasn't away at school.

"You want what?" Henry asked in amazement from astride his horse. It was his usual daily ride through the cotton fields. This time, however, he'd been accosted by several of his hired blacks. Only two of them had any history with Moss Grove. The others he'd found along the river or picked up wandering. When they'd been slaves they'd probably worked pretty diligently, he thought. Now you were lucky if you could get a decent half day's work from any of them. They seemed to believe that freedom from slavery also meant a freedom from having to work. Slavery or sharecroppers, they'll never be more than nigger trash, Henry fumed.

"We wants a share of the crops and better homes for our kin. These cabins always cold and damp. We ain't slaves. We is entitled to a bigger share of what the cotton crop brings," one spoke as the other eight hired blacks gathered around.

"You signed contracts. You agreed to work for a year at the wages we settled on," Henry's voice rose, his one hand tight on the reins. The horse began to rear with the subtle signal emanating from the increased tension, as the rider fought to control his temper.

"Yeah, but we learn a lot since then. And what we learned is that folks working other places got better places to live, better food, and a bigger share of the crop. We don't want any more than what we're entitled to," another ex-slave added.

"Listen, I had to borrow a lot of money from the banks to buy the seed for this planting. I had to pledge this entire plantation as collateral. What did you pledge? Not a god-damn thing. If this crop doesn't come in I lose everything…you niggers just move on."

"We don't know nuthin' bout that Massa'. We jus' knows what we is entitled to."

"I'll think on it and let you know," Henry insisted, the vein in his forehead beginning to throb with the fury boiling inside. "Now get back to work. This crop won't plant itself." He kicked his horse angrily in the flanks. The horse bolted and Henry rode off quickly.

Banks were nervous about lending in this post-Confederacy period. They had taken enormous losses when all that Reb currency had become worthless. Jefferson Davis had borrowed heavily to finance the war and his government demanded that the southern banks support the cause of Southern independence.

These same banks were now exacting difficult terms, demanding extensive collateral and charging high interest rates.

Henry would be facing that same obstacle. He needed to borrow additional money. He couldn't continue to use the depleting balances his father had wisely deposited into northern banks. He decided his best chance was in New Orleans where an old friend of his father, Abner Moresby, was President of the Louisiana Union Bank. It would be a break to leave the pressures of Moss Grove as well. With luck, Elizabeth might give birth while he was gone. She was becoming more and more irritating.

"Henry, come in. You must be tired after your long ride," Moresby said, an unlit cigar in his hand, forty extra pounds on his waist. "I'm so sorry I couldn't get to Moss Grove to attend your father's funeral. He and I went back a long way. Did you know I dated your mother, Ruby, before your father did? Once she met him, I had no chance," he laughed in a convivial way.

Henry sensed he was speaking to a man without a trace of sincerity in his being but the necessity of a good relationship made it essential he listen attentively to this familial bullshit.

"Mr. Moresby, thank you for seeing me. New Orleans certainly has changed, hasn't it? All these blue Yankee uniforms everywhere make me nervous. A lot more people milling about since I was here last," Henry said, trying to ease his nervousness with small talk.

"Can we speak frankly?" Henry finally asked when they were seated in Moresby's large and ornate walnut-paneled office. Pictures of Jefferson Davis had been set subtly aside, in a position second to that of Abraham Lincoln. The Confederate flag stood behind the American flag and both stood behind the Louisiana state flag, a blue and white banner of a sea gull feeding its young and bearing the motto, 'Union, Justice, and Confidence.' It was clear this shift from the Confederacy to the Union was complicated for the bank.

"Of course, Henry! Can I get you a brandy? Coffee? I must say I am impressed how well you are functioning with one arm. You're one of our authentic heroes, yes, you are.

"I understand you're married, nice family from Baton Rouge. Your father sent me an invitation but we were under siege by the damn Yankees. Anyway, I'm rambling. It's always so nice to see someone from the old times. Go on! I won't reminisce anymore. How can I help you?"

"Mr. Moresby, you've always been father's friend and I hope you will be my friend as well. Moss Grove is in my veins as it was in his. Times are very different these days. These past few years we've had problems planting, harvesting, and shipping our cotton. You know that. It's the same across the south," Henry explained as the banker nodded his head solemnly in agreement.

"I've had to hire niggers to work Moss Grove this past year. Without slavery and big black bucks to do our picking we've got costs we've never had before. We've lost one, nearly two, years of decent production. Our production has been smaller than it should have been and our capital has become really tight. I think I have the problem balanced now and cotton prices seem to be stabilizing. Everyone feels they are likely to stay that way the next few years while the back-up demand is met. Plain and simple, I need a loan…some additional capital to tide us over."

"Thought that might be why you came at this time. You aren't the first. I've had a constant string of long time friends here with the same problem. But let me share some other considerations," Moresby said, perspiring as he spoke.

The banker stood, took off his jacket and lit the cigar. What a contrast with his father, Henry realized. Jedidiah Rogers had taken care of his health all his life, working the plantation he loved. This man was obese, sweating profusely under each arm. But his nails were manicured, and he probably supported multiple mistresses living down in the French Quarter. To have such a man control his future made Henry angry. He would have preferred to run him through his fat gut with his Confederate saber.

"All the banks lost most of their capital investing in the Confederacy. We were obliged, not asked, mind you…obliged, to lend them money **AND** at minimal interest rates. Normally we share big loans with other banks, sort of share the risk, you know. Northern banks had no interest in participating. They could lend all the money they could lay their hands on at high interest rates. Northern factories everywhere were thriving and paid whatever the banks asked. Damn northern bankers made a fortune over this damn war. Now the only money we can find to lend comes from those same people and they're sticking it up our southern asses.

"The bottom line," he continued, as he pulled a linen handkerchief from his pocket to mop his brow, "I can get you money but it will cost you and cost you dearly. Figure out how little you can borrow, not how much I can lend you."

In the end, after much discussion, Henry borrowed fifty thousand American dollars at 11% interest, more than twice the rate his father ever had to pay. He was given two years to repay it provided all the interest was paid monthly. The bank's most difficult demand, however, was the obligation to secure the loan with the deed to Moss Grove. If he failed to repay the loan Henry could lose his home, his future, and everything it represented. He was certain that wouldn't happen but it was a gnawing feeling.

That night Henry entertained himself at a brothel in the French quarter. The dark red velvet drapes, the French provincial furniture, and a dapper young black piano player all set the tone. Eventually he found himself paying for the services of a young attractive high-cheeked mulatto girl, Melanie. They shared snifters of Napoleon Brandy before going upstairs for headier entertainment. It was the best sex he'd had in years and he realized how much he'd been missing, limiting his enjoyment to a very unimaginative wife and any fantasies he could conjure up. He climaxed three times before morning and woke, feeling starved, relaxed, and satisfied. Melanie joined him for a walk along the quay, stopping to enjoy a beignet and chicory-laced coffee. They could see the ships moving in and out of the harbour.

"I've always wanted to see the world," she said dreamily. "Henry, take me to Paris."

Henry laughed. "Not likely, my dear. You'll need to pluck a much richer and more available planter than me, at least for the next few years. But let us dream together. Perhaps we will have that opportunity in the future."

He paid her double her normal fee and climbed his horse, thoroughly satisfied with the results of his visit to the city, for the return to Moss Grove. He made it quite clear to himself, and to Melanie, that he'd return.

As he rode toward Baton Rouge, he had time to ponder the events and challenges he faced. Damn carpetbaggers…coming down from the north and fucking us over every chance they get. Tight money, high interest rates! I can run Moss Grove better than my father. I'll prove it. Maybe they think because I've got only one arm that I'm a cripple. Moss Grove is going to survive. Some of the money Jedidiah had deposited in northern banks still remained but it was his last cushion and no one, not Elizabeth and, certainly, not Abner Moresby, knew that it was there. It would remain his secret.

Floods had ruined most of the cotton and sugar cane crops south of Baton Rouge this past spring. The 'ol Miss had overflowed its banks and inundated the fields. Several of his father's friends that owned plantations in the area were wiped out. Fortunately Moss Grove was on higher ground and would be able to avoid their fate. These shortages did result in higher cotton prices and he might benefit from that. And the fuckin' darkeys. If their demands weren't enough, this troublesome weather made it seem that even God wasn't on their side. What was he going to do?

He had fewer and fewer people he could depend on. The few attempts he'd made to discuss his dilemma with Baxter Williams were met with blank stares. The man had become a doddering fool. Even the knowledge that he was about to become a father again didn't excite him. Elizabeth was a bore, content to eat chocolates and lie in bed. Amy was away in school. His only enjoyable moments came from spending time with Josiah. That boy will be a pistol when he gets older. He doesn't take crap from anyone…even me, Henry mused. As he approached Moss Grove his thoughts returned to Melanie and their evening together. He would definitely see her again. Meanwhile he'd have to get rid of his erection before he dismounted.

"Massa' Henry, Miss Elizabeth, Massa' Williams, come quick," Sarah shouted. "Mrs. Williams! She's not moving. I brung her tea this morning like always."

"She's dead," Henry declared, standing at her bedside, not feeling a pulse. Baxter Williams began to cry as he knelt beside his wife's bed. Elizabeth put her hand on her father's bent shoulders, realizing that her mother hadn't lived long enough to see her second grandchild born.

Baxter Williams continued to sob. Elizabeth knew that her parents hadn't slept together or even shared the same room in all these last two years at Moss Grove but she always felt her parents loved one another in that older generation way.

The funeral was a simple one but the trauma advanced Elizabeth's pregnancy. She was still early in her eighth month but her water broke two days after the funeral as she was putting fresh flowers at the graveside. She was rushed to the house while one of the servants hurried for the doctor, nearly a three hour ride away.

The contractions were coming more quickly now. Amy had returned to school after the funeral. Their mother was gone. Sarah continued to wipe the perspiration from Elizabeth's brow and call on the kitchen help for more hot water. The pregnant woman was becoming more and more agitated, demanding some relief from the pain.

The doctor arrived just as Elizabeth's screams grew louder and more agonized with each contraction. By the time he took off his frock coat and washed, the baby's head could be seen exiting the birth canal. Henry was in the library making liberal use of the brandy. He hated these 'women's times'. His silent companion, Baxter Williams, matched him drink for drink.

"It is eerie," the elder man opined, "We lose one generation and another arrives. God is truly mysterious."

"God is bullshit," Henry and the liquor responded. "Your wife, whom you ignored these past years of self-indulgence, died. Elizabeth and I have independently conceived a new child for ourselves who, God-willing, will share the bounty of Moss Grove. It may be a holy plan or a vast cosmic accident. Who the fuck knows? And, more concisely, who the fuck cares?"

The baby arrived and was cleaned of the placenta. Elizabeth had fallen asleep fitfully from her ordeal. Sarah and the doctor stood around the baby, staring at this new female Rogers, a gurgling baby girl. She seemed to smile as if she had arrived to deliver some ultimate joke. Words failed the three adults. It was clear they couldn't announce the arrival of the new child to the father until they had spoken to the mother.

Eventually Elizabeth began to stir.

"My baby, can I see my baby?" Is it a boy or a girl? I'm sure Henry will be fine either way this time now that we have Josiah? Will he have a sister or a brother?" she rambled, still in an exhausted haze.

"Here is your new baby girl, Elizabeth," the doctor said softly as he cradled the blanket-wrapped baby girl in her mother's arms.

Dreamily, Elizabeth smiled up at the doctor, holding her new gift lovingly. As she pulled the blanket back to see her new daughter, Elizabeth's eyes opened in disbelief. The baby was mixed, mocha-toned...not white like her mother and father, but unquestionably a colored infant.

"This can't be mine," she stuttered. "Where is my daughter? The one I just gave birth to."

"This is your baby, Mrs. Rogers. You will need a very good explanation before your husband sees this child," the doctor said sternly, obvious disdain in his voice.

"He can't think that I..." she stopped. That's exactly what he'd think... that she had been whoring around and that he still was unable to father another child.

"I never did. I wouldn't sleep with a nigga'. I can't imagine such a thing."

"Well, my dear. It was your body that carried this child," the doctor added with a sneer.

The men had heard the baby's cries and in a semi-alcoholic condition they had raced up the stairs and into the room, both men tilting drunkenly against one another precariously.

"I have a new child I understand. Elizabeth, my dear, is it a son or a daughter? Either shall suit me this time."

"It is a daughter, Henry, but there is a problem," she responded, as the tension in the room became palpable.

"Is the baby healthy...all her fingers and toes?"

"Yes, Henry but the child is...," she couldn't finish.

"Elizabeth, don't dawdle, what is the problem? Doctor, what is this problem that has my wife stumbling on her words?"

"Henry," he answered. "The baby is colored...got nigger blood. She is not a white child."

"Not a white child? Not white?"

The information seemed to overwhelm him before he turned to his wife, lying pasty-faced in the bed, now fully awake, her eyes red with terror.

"You whore," he screamed. "You fucking whore. You bore a bastard colored child into Moss Grove, our home." He turned to Baxter Williams. "And you, you fucking drunk. What kind of a daughter did you raise? I'll have both of you and that child out of here by morning."

"Henry, I swear I have never been with another man, not in my entire life. I can't explain this but I wouldn't do that to you...to us," she cried.

The room overflowed with conflicting emotion. Elizabeth continued to sob and profess her innocence. Henry continued to rant while Baxter Williams didn't know whether to support his daughter or condemn her.

Stepping from the tempest that engulfed the room, Sarah approached the side of the bed.

"Massa' Henry, I have been sworn to a secret my entire life but I believe keeping it is no longer possible. May Miss Ruby and God both forgive me."

"What are you talking about, Sarah? This can't possibly concern you. Pack my wife's things. She and the baby as well as her father and sister will be leaving in the morning." Henry, shoulders bent and drained of all emotion, turned to leave the room.

"Massa' Henry, that colored baby is your doin', sort of," she said as his hand grabbed the doorframe. He stopped and seconds passed before he turned to face her.

"You'd better explain, Sarah, and explain quickly," he spoke, his voice icy now, his hand shaking, his eyes glazed.

"It was your Mammy, Massa' Henry. It was Miss Ruby."

"You're crazy. My mother was French Creole."

"Creole, yes, but only half French. Her daddy was a French sea Captain, but her mother was already mixed. That make Miss Ruby a quadroon lady, one quarter black. But she so lovely and so light skin no one ever know, maybe not even Massa' Jedidiah."

"You're telling me that all the years my mother and father were married that he might have had no idea he was living with a colored woman. That can't be possible."

"I don't know whether your Daddy knew and never said anything. I does know that he and your Mommy loved each other from the day he brought her to Moss Grove to the day each of them died."

"But if my mother had colored blood in her, you're saying I do, too."

Sarah just nodded and the air went out of the room.

"And Josiah. What about my son? He has my blue eyes. He could be tainted as well," Henry protested weakly.

"Never know what come out," Sarah said. "God just sorta' plays roulette."

# Chapter Fifteen

Melanie enjoyed the warm afternoons. She didn't have to entertain gentlemen, some of whom could be quite demanding. She could breathe the clean New Orleans air, constantly washed by its magnificent river.

It was a time to dress and shop. The boutiques of New Orleans boasted the finest fashions. Some said they excelled those in New York. Melanie was tall, some said statuesque. She worked diligently to maintain her figure. She was always careful with her makeup, never too much. Her complexion, the color of the Mississippi's sand, was clear and silky. She abhorred the pasty look of too much powder or blush. She usually wore her soft brown hair up and pinned in a chignon. Unpinning it in front of her clients, allowing it to fall gently around her shoulders, was an eroticism her male guests never failed to appreciate. Her dark brown eyes seemed to glitter as she professed an undying interest in the dullest, most idiotic utterances of her evening's escort. It was important to her client's imagination that she looked natural, whatever that meant. The usual girls who walked the streets looked like trollops and their income reflected it.

Melanie thought of Henry Rogers, a one-armed bigot with a big dick and a bigger ego. At least he paid well. He'll definitely be back. She had made it a point to enter his interests into the notebook she kept. Most of the other girls were too ignorant to make notes but she was diligent and it rewarded her with well-paying repeat customers.

She was on time for her lunch date at Henri's, one of the finest restaurants in the Quarter. Her companion for the afternoon was already seated although he seemed more corpulent than the last time she'd seen him.

"Monsieur Moresby, it is so nice to see you," she smiled as the waiter took her boa.

"Miss Melanie," the banker stood, his napkin sliding off his lap before he could grab it. "You look ravishing, as usual."

Melanie waited for the Maitre'd to hold her chair as she sat and make his usual fuss over her. Without her needing to order, he brought her a Kir Royal.

"What's good today, Henri?"

They both settled on a turbot, lightly sautéed with chanterelles and a small endive salad. The wine was a French sauterne and the entire repast was far more pleasurable than the company, she realized as the two made small talk about the weather and the recent Mardi Gras.

Over sorbet and coffee she slipped an envelope to the banker.

"I believe you earned this, Monsieur."

"Not nearly as much as you did, Miss Melanie. Tell me! Was it difficult for him to have sex with only one arm?"

"Monsieur, you know I don't discuss the clients you send me. Discretion is part of the allure, don't you agree?" she smiled disingenuously.

"Don't play your coquettish games with me," he said snidely, leaning over the table. "I remember you growing up, doing the laundry, while your mother spread her legs in the upstairs rooms." She could see the evil leer in his eyes.

The girls had told her this overweight banker hadn't been able to get it up in years. His frustrations had turned to strange demands and sudden outbursts of anger. He had already been banned from a number of the better houses for hitting the girls and putting them out of commission, sometimes for weeks. The Madams made him pay for their losses but he was trouble they didn't need.

"Tell me," he continued salaciously, "Does he lick your brown twat?"

Melanie blanched before regaining her composure. She stood, her chair tipping back and crashing to the floor. They were an immediate center of attention.

"Henri, my wrap, please! Monsieur can enjoy both servings of sorbet. I must be somewhere else."

Her eyes never left the banker, still sitting, red-faced, facing the stares of the other diners, frozen over their meals.

While Melanie's outward demeanor remained icy calm and her face remained impassive, inside she was furious. She had worked hard to become a lady of means and respect but men like Moresby liked to drag her back to her origins and remind her of those early times when she was still someone else, someone she preferred to forget.

She found herself walking back along Bourbon Street. Many of the saloons weren't even open yet but their help was busy throwing buckets of water onto the walks in front of their premises and sweeping up from the urine and vomit that would create a terrible stench from the previous night's revelries, particularly on warm days.

Maybe she should just hire someone and have that Moresby asshole killed. Maybe not killed, maybe just shoot off his genitals! Yes, neutering him would certainly reverse their stations in life, and in an instant. She smiled as the thoughts eased some of her anger and tension. She could feel the muscles in her shoulder relax. She knew she'd do none of those things. Moresby was like too many men. Their brains were controlled by their erections. Anyway, why silence one of her most profitable sponsors.

Bankers seemed to know everyone. And men needed money even before they needed sex. She'd make that her best revenge. She'd already earned enough to buy a small farm for her brothers north about thirty miles. One of her clients, a notorious gambler, had needed quick cash. She had arranged for a third party to exchange the cash for the deed to the farm. The gambler would never have knowingly sold the property to a black or colored. Melanie didn't care. She'd succeed despite their arrogance.

She continued walking down toward the quay where the early afternoon breezes scented the air. She sat and stared out at the water. Music floated from nearby street musicians. She did this as often as possible, regaining her 'center' before returning to her evening's work. She didn't enjoy what she did but she was determined that it would never be who she was.

Amy had mixed feelings about the school she was attending in New Orleans. In addition to the snobbish southern girls from across Louisiana there were several northern girls enrolled. They were the daughters of Union officers stationed in the city. These girls didn't walk, they sauntered, their noses in the air, with the superiority of conquerors that professed to know everything and disdained everything they knew. They despised southern culture, fashions, and most of all, they hated New Orleans' humidity.

The privileged southern girls at the school made pointed efforts daily to insult or shun them completely. These girls had been reared to believe in the superiority of the Confederacy, just as their parents had. These invaders… this white trash, had come to New Orleans with the sole purpose of putting niggers ahead of white folk. Not where they were concerned. No, sirree!

Tension between the two groups might surface at any time. It was an unholy truce enforced by strict teachers whose own lives had been caught in the maelstrom of the Confederacy's rise and fall.

To Amy the shallowness of these southern girls was as unappealing as the snootiness of these temporary northern visitors. They all seemed to have the depth of a small puddle. In class they were more concerned with their hair and makeup or their monthly period than they were with their lessons. They each insisted on the rationality of their particular righteousness. They giggled a lot and spoke only of their beaus, real or pretended, and what sexual gymnastics the boys were trying at the moment. Amy sorely missed Thaddeus' maturity and presence but she understood the dangers of even mentioning her feelings for him to anyone.

One of the northern girls, however, seemed different. Brenda Summers was from Baltimore and didn't seem to connect with her snooty northern transplants any better than Amy connected with the southern belles. These feelings of being different from those they were assumed to be close with, drew them into an unlikely budding friendship.

Brenda had brown hair that curled at the slightest increase in the dampness of the day. The higher the humidity, the tighter the curl! She was quite short, barely reaching five feet. Her brown eyes had a constant searching in them, a 'wondering what comes next' sort of innocence.

It had begun quite by accident at lunch one day. Brenda had tired of the banality of the conversation within her group and moved to the shade of a large tree some distance away. Amy was already there, having become similarly frustrated earlier by the inane conversations of the southern debutante-wannabes, they perceived themselves to be.

"Mind if I join you?" Brenda asked.

"Free country, I'm told. Grab some lawn."

"You're Amy…Amy Williams. How come you aren't sitting with your friends?"

"Guess 'cause they aren't my friends. And you're Brenda Summers. How come you aren't with the rest of the pouty-faced northern girls?"

"Same reason as you…they aren't really my friends."

"I thought all you Yankees kind of stuck together, being in a foreign country and all that," Amy teased.

Brenda bristled. "Still one country, far as I know! Want an apple?" she said, offering the fruit, and eager to change the subject.

"Sure," Amy said, taking a bite of the proffered food. "Most of these girls are such ninnies. I'd almost forgotten how to hold a conversation with someone who might have a brain. I'll try to be friendlier."

"That's alright. Everyone I know is pretending to be someone other than themselves. Even my parents haven't figured out how they're supposed to act around people who really don't like them."

The two girls found they had a great deal in common. Amy found Brenda's quiet innocence amusing. Brenda was thrilled with her new friend's self-confidence and willingness to undertake anything new. Within a week they had erased that invisible barrier that so often separated teenage cliques.

"Tell me about Baltimore," Amy asked. "I've never been out of Louisiana."

"We only lived there two years. My father was stationed at Fort McHenry. He's in the Quartermaster Corps. They're responsible for all sorts of supplies from men's drawers to ammunition. My father likes to make jokes about being short of shorts. The jokes aren't really funny but we laugh anyway, my mother and two brothers. We did get to Washington D.C. once. We even saw President Johnson. He looked depressed and very lonely. My father was glad to see him go, called him a nigger-hatin' reb, whatever that is. We're all supposed to hope that U.S. Grant will be elected as our next President. My daddy says his initials say it all. He's a military man and will know how to run things."

Amy laughed. "You know, Brenda, in the few weeks we've come to know one another that's more words than I've ever heard you string together."

Brenda reddened. "Well, I guess, it's just been bottled up. What about you?"

"I don't know. I don't think I'm anything special. I like to fish and do the sorts of things boys get to do. I don't fancy putting on heavy petticoats and dresses but I don't mind the fact my breasts are getting bigger. That's kind of exciting."

"We're not to talk of such things, my mother says."

"Why not? We all seem to check out one another's boobs. Even the teachers stare, especially the men teachers. I do have one secret but you'll have to swear not to ever tell anyone, even your mother," Amy said nervously.

Her feelings about Thaddeus had been bottled up and she craved being able to share it with someone. She knew it was something that shouldn't be discussed, but writing his name in her notebook over and over again each day didn't assuage her urges. She knew she loved him and if she couldn't shout it from a rooftop, she'd share it with her new friend.

"I can keep a secret. Tell me...tell me," Brenda insisted.

"I have a boyfriend. He lives in Baton Rouge."

"Well, that's nice but hardly a reason to swear secrecy."

"This boyfriend is special. He's tender and he's bright and he has the most electric blue eyes," she paused. "He's mixed, but wonderfully handsome with his features and skin color and all."

"Wow! That would even have been a problem in Baltimore. Have you had sex?"

"Of course not," she said as if she'd been insulted. "We have hugged and kissed and once he fondled my breasts. I'd never been so aroused in my entire life."

"You're a lot more adventurous than I am. I've never gone that far with a boy. I'll certainly not tell a soul. But, what do you plan to do about it?" Brenda asked as they finished their lunches on the lawn under their usual shady magnolia tree that kept some of the heat and dampness at bay.

"I hope we can always be good friends. I'd like it to be more and I think about it far too much but I know the Almighty thinks that it's a sin, different races and all. I'm sure God is wrong but even thinking that is another sin. C'mon, we're late for afternoon class and I can hardly wait to see them dissect a frog."

*As Andrew Johnson's presidency ground to a complete standstill over issues of southern reconstruction and white superiority the country faced the off-year 1866 elections. A coalition of whites and southern Democrats campaigned vigorously on their platform that the United States should forever remain a nation of white men. They were soundly defeated by equally adamant Republicans.*

*Within a year Congress launched impeachment hearings against this President who had separated himself so completely from those who had successfully prosecuted the war. For the first time in the country's brief history an energized effort to eject a sitting president moved through the Senate and the House. The vote was close. A two-thirds majority was required to convict a President of the 'high crimes & misdemeanors' of which he was accused. In the final tally seven republican Senators broke with their party and a junior Senator from Kansas, Edmund Roth, cast the deciding vote against impeachment. The effort left Johnson isolated and humiliated for the remainder of his term.*

*Ulysses S. Grant easily won the election of 1868. He had carried the Union's military banner triumphantly to victory. His Democratic opponent, Horatio Seymour, campaigned on a platform of 'This is a White Man's Country, Let White Men Rule.' The war had been over for nearly four years but the wounds were still raw. The streets of both New England and the Carolinas were still pock-marked with men standing idly with amputated limbs and blank stares wondering where their next meal would come from. Resentment and racial divisiveness deepened.*

Elizabeth named their new daughter, Clara. Henry wanted nothing to do with the child and wouldn't countenance naming the child after a family member. Clara seemed to be the least offensive name she could come up with.

The baby girl remained in her room. No Baptism was performed as it had been for her brother, Josiah. Except for Sarah and Amy there was no one to hold the infant. The servants discussed it amongst themselves and then turned silent if either of Clara's parents approached.

Elizabeth was uncomfortable holding her daughter and refused to even consider breast feeding. Instead, a slave woman was found to nourish the newborn. Henry spent less and less time at home. He worked the fields or got drunk. He ignored his daughter entirely and his wife predominantly. If he exhibited any positive feeling of affection it was reserved for his son, and even those occurrences became more and more rare.

"Henry, Clara is still our daughter," Elizabeth insisted. "What are we to do?"

"She is not my daughter. I do not have a daughter. I want her out of this house by the end of the week. I don't care what you do with her. Drown her in the Mississippi. That would be the best solution."

"I didn't create this situation. If there is shame it is with the Rogers, not the Williams," she persisted, in a rare state of temper. "I don't want to raise a nigger either, but I will not see her killed."

"Sarah, come in here," Henry shouted from the doorway. "Now!"

Sarah rushed up the stairs and nervously entered the room. She had heard the shouting but that had become rather commonplace between these two hotheads who now ruled over Moss Grove.

"We want you to take this baby and find a new home for her....away from Moss Grove. You are to tell no one who her parents are. Just say she was abandoned. Do you understand?"

"Yes,suh, Massa' Henry. I'll do it today," she said meekly, knowing that any suggestions from her would be ignored.

"And when you go downstairs, have Celeste cook up some of that jambalaya I love for dinner."

"But Massa' Henry. Celeste gave her notice two weeks ago. She be leavin' Moss Grove."

"Why wasn't I told? For Christ's sake, Celeste's cooking is the only thing that made eating meals here palatable. Elizabeth," he said, turning his attention back to his wife. "Did you know about this?"

Elizabeth looked at Sarah and then at Henry. She was chagrined at his anger.

"Yes, Henry. But I didn't want to bother you with a household matter. You'd always said you had no interest in such matters."

"Elizabeth, sometimes your stupidity amazes even me. Do you plan on doing the cooking yourself?"

"No, of course not, but I've been told Celeste has been training one of the kitchen women. Since your mother died, Celeste hasn't been happy here."

"Now I understand....one fat Creole and one nigger mixed Creole... they probably shared their secrets. Fuck them! Let her leave! Good riddance!" he said as he stormed out of the room and closeted himself with a bottle of brandy for the evening.

Celeste Montaigne turned and gazed at the plantation that had been her home for more than a decade. Tears fell on her cheek as she thought of all the happier times. Mister Rogers had always treated her with respect and often complimented her on both her cooking skills and the attractiveness of the food she served. And Mrs. Rogers...Ruby! They had more than a working relation. They had a friendship.

The wagon in which she rode contained more than her clothes and personal cooking utensils. It also carried a tiny baby, carefully blanketed, lying hidden among boxes and crates. Moss Grove's departing chef was carrying Clara somewhere, to a new life. This was an innocent child who was also Ruby and Jedidiah's granddaughter. Clara would continue to connect her to those happier days.

Once Sarah had explained Henry Roger's decision to get rid of this embarrassment, the heavyset Creole cook offered to care for the baby until she could find an appropriate home and parents who would love her. The child deserved to be away from the rancor that pervaded this once peaceful plantation.

"Amy, I need to buy a new frock for a party this Saturday," Brenda said. "I hate to shop alone and my mother is busy. Will you come with me? These southern shop owners treat us northerners as if the war is still going on. They can be so rude. I think some of them even raise their prices. Maybe, if you're with me, I won't feel so cowed."

"Sure, c'mon. We'll take 'em on together," Amy smiled. Usually she hated shopping but helping Brenda might prove to be a fun outing.

After unsuccessful efforts at several stores they opened the door to Maison Frere. From the moment they entered the boutique they knew the clothes were going to be a lot more expensive than Brenda's budget. Amy pushed her timid friend ahead anyway.

"Be confident," Amy said, sensing her friend's nervousness.

"We need a dress for an important party," Amy declared to the sales woman. "Something not too expensive! For my friend, not for me."

Amy sat on the heavily padded settee as Brenda went to the dressing room. A few minutes later she returned wearing a ball gown even her mother would have rejected. She stood in front of Amy and a full-length Louis XIV mirror as they stifled their laughter. Back again to the dressing room, repeating the process several times with diminishing enthusiasm on each occasion.

"These are all dowdy. Don't you have anything with more style?" Amy demanded. Brenda nodded in dejected agreement but seemed to have lost her voice.

"Perhaps I can help." The two girls and the sales woman all turned.

"Mademoiselle Melanie! How nice to have you in our shop again," the store's owner rushed up, pushing his sales girl aside.

"Bernard, I believe these young ladies need some help. Your woman has been showing these young ladies dresses that are more appropriate for their mothers. Perhaps one of those Gautiers that recently arrived! One of those should fit her beautifully," she said softly, turning toward the wide-eyed teens. "Pardon my intrusion; I do hope you won't think me rude."

"No, we're grateful," they both said, words tumbling over one another, their eyes not leaving this exquisitely attired mulatto woman standing before them who appeared to have come to their rescue.

They introduced themselves and all sat, awaiting the flustered store manager's return from the back. The two young girls stared at the dress he brought out. It was a sleeveless lilac satin, trimmed in white lace.

"Please, please. Try it on. It was made for you, I'm certain," the manager gushed, holding it carefully in front of Brenda but never taking his eyes off Melanie.

Melanie's eyes beckoned Brenda to try it on as Amy still gaped at the change in the attitude of the store's personnel. Tea and small cakes emerged from the back and were set before them on a filigreed silver tray.

When Brenda returned from the dressing room her eyes were moist.

"I've never seen myself look like this. I feel so pretty," she cooed.

"You are pretty," Melanie offered. "Here," she said, now standing, "If you pin your hair like this it will make you look taller and a little older. I have no doubt that you'll achieve the sophistication you deserve."

"My gosh, Brenda, you are a knockout. Those young soldiers will drool over you. Your dance card will be filled in the first five minutes," Amy laughed. Her friend looked amazing.

"But the price," Brenda said, hesitatingly. "I'm sure it is way too expensive."

Bernard began to mention the price when he looked askance at Melanie, one of his best customers. She simply smiled at him innocently. It was a look he understood. He'd have to take a loss on this dress to protect his relationship. Oh, well! It was a cost of doing business. They settled on a price less than half its retail value and the girls couldn't stop bubbling as they mingled outside the store, Brenda's package gripped tightly under her arm.

"Would you ladies care to join me for a latte?" Melanie said. "If you have the time, of course."

Brenda might have hesitated. She had never actually spent much time with a person of color who didn't clean her home or do menial tasks for her father. Those people were nice but usually not very well spoken and certainly none ever had the lovely persona of this woman. Was it acceptable to be seen in public with a colored person? She was always very worried about embarrassing her family but Amy seemed to have no such hesitation. Her friend was smiling from ear to ear at being able to converse with a colored person other than Thaddeus. Maybe this was the new South.

"We'd love to," Amy gushed. "Wouldn't we, Brenda?"

Brenda smiled and nodded with uncertain confidence.

Not wanting to end this fortuitous encounter the three new friends walked across the narrow street to a small café.

"Melanie, you were so wonderful in there. We could both tell poor Monsieur Bernard was about to have apoplexy. His reddened face was beginning to clash with the lilac dress. How much would this dress normally sell for?" Amy asked.

"A little more, perhaps. But I'm a good customer. He will make up for it on another sale. I wouldn't worry about Maison Frere's profit. Bernard earns enough to have several mistresses and young children spread around the city."

This brought gales of laughter from both girls.

"What will you be doing this weekend, Amy, while your friend is breathing fire into the hearts of young men?" Melanie asked conversationally.

"I may hire a carriage to take me to visit my sister or friends in Baton Rouge."

"Perhaps we can travel together. I have family just south of the capital. We have a farm there and I have been most delinquent in visiting."

"That would be wonderful."

# Chapter Sixteen

The entire Fineman household fitted easily into the single wagon that carried them into Baton Rouge. Captain Eli Fineman and his wife, Ruth, sat in the front while their two young children sat in the back, cushioned by furniture on all sides. Rachel, their nine year old daughter, had had her mother's dark eyes. Her hair was neatly plaited into two braids, each adorned with a perfectly tied yellow satin ribbon. She wore a blue gingham dress that, too easily, gathered the dust kicked up by the horses. Next to her a toddler squiggled from the shaky ride, an unruly five year old boy, Stewart, who looked too ready to find mischief doing something he was told not to. Fineman had been assigned by the Union Army to be the Central Louisiana's first Manager of the Freedman's Bureau.

The Finemans were Jews by faith. Eli had been born and raised in Vermont. The Jewish community there was quite small but they practiced their faith as their parents and grandparents had done in the small shetls of Europe. Fineman decided to remain in the Union army after the war ended rather than return to his family's small tailor shop where he had learned the needle trade from his immigrant father.

Most of the men he served with had never seen a Jew. Some wanted to make certain he didn't have horns under his military cap. Their Christian religion had often taught them Jews were horned devils who had killed their Savior. Others had been taught that they were God's chosen people. To most they were just a curiosity. They weren't niggers but they weren't good Christians either. This would be the family's first time in the south and stories they'd heard about the zealousness of Southern Baptists made them concerned for their children's safety.

Ruth Fineman's parents were old-country devout as well. Her stern father was especially confused when he learned that his very Jewish son-in-law wanted to remain in the Army. Where his family had lived, the army meant Cossacks who burned and pillaged, bringing terror on horseback. How would their daughter be able to maintain a Jewish home or celebrate Shabbat? But Ruth had followed Eli as an obedient Jewish wife. He was a good man, a decent provider, and a loving father. Now they had traveled to a land and a culture as foreign as if it had been across the ocean.

They drew their wagon up to Carmody & Williams.

"You board horses?" Eli asked the young black man that approached them.

"Yes,suh. We the best place to do that in all of Baton Rouge," Matthew answered. "Looks like you folks come a long ways and is plannin' to stay."

"Yes. Good day to you. My name is Fineman. Captain Eli Fineman, U.S. Army! This is my wife, Ruth, my daughter, Rachel, and my son, Stewart. The Army sent me here to oversee the Freedman's Bureau and since we will be here for awhile we've brought all our belongings."

"Well, don't worry none about your horses or things. We'll cool' em down and feed 'em good."

"Your little ones look as if they might enjoy a cool drink, if you'd care to sit a spell," Rose offered, standing in the doorway of the adjoining house. Without hesitation Stewart and Rachel jumped from the wagon, happy to be anywhere else after a day sitting in the cramped wagon.

Eli Fineman shrugged, climbed down and stretched from his long ride, happy to have arrived at their destination. Rose soon returned with a pitcher of lemonade.

After the horses were released from the wagon and given water, Matthew and Thaddeus joined Rose and the Finemans. They shared the shade under a nearby copse of Spanish moss. Rachel kept chasing her younger brother, who much preferred to run under the horses without fear, emitting a loud, contagious laughter that kept the adults smiling but made the horses skittish.

"We've been seeing more and more Union soldiers around here. Seems a little odd now that the war is over," Thaddeus said.

"The government is going to be sending nearly two hundred thousand soldiers spread across every state that was part of the Confederacy."

"Why?" Matthew asked. "We's free now. Slavery is over."

"President Grant and the Congress are apparently afraid that unless there are plenty of Union troops around, the old Confederate mindset won't give this new racial equality idea a chance to succeed. And, we lost too many good men to let it fail. Anyway, one of the groups they established to oversee this reconstruction was the Freedman's Bureau to help blacks move into the mainstream. I'm in charge of Baton Rouge and the northern Louisiana parishes."

"That's a lot of land to protect," Thaddeus said.

"How do you think the whites and blacks will react?" Eli asked

"Simple. Most of the whites will hate what you're doing and the blacks and coloreds will welcome it."

"Massa' Henry will definitely hate it," Rose said, gritting her teeth as she named her nemesis.

Thaddeus and Matthew laughed in agreement.

"He ran the plantation where we were slaves," Thaddeus explained.

"Well, my orders come directly from General Sheridan to report to Baton Rouge. That massacre last month in New Orleans unsettled both blacks and whites. I'll have two companies of Union troops to keep the peace and a lot of discretion in how to do it. My task is to maintain the peace and promote equality both here and north to the Mississippi border."

"Well, we sure hope for your success," Thaddeus said as Rose and Matthew nodded in agreement.

An hour later, well-rested, the Finemans said their goodbyes and climbed back onto their wagon, now with well-rested horses, for the short rideto his new headquarters that consisted of nothing more than several large tents adjoining the state capitol.

Melanie and Amy laughed as their small buggy moved along the road from New Orleans toward Baton Rouge. As the sun moved overhead and the heat of the day became more oppressive, Melanie pulled out an umbrella to keep the hot rays off of them.

"Land sake," Amy said. "I seen women in New Orleans with these here parasols but I always thought they was just for show."

Melanie smiled. "At your age you don't think anything about your skin, but you should. Those strong summer rays and all that dampness bring wrinkles. You stay out in it too long and you'll look like your pappy's shoes, all dark and crinkly."

"Your skin is beautiful. Actually all of you is beautiful. Me, I'm the ugly duckling in the family, freckles and all."

"Actually you have no idea how beautiful you can be. Your hair is striking, and if you let me fix you up, you'll look even lovelier."

"Maybe, sometime! Maybe when I care more! Right now all the girls who spend so much time on themselves seem to be brainless and I wouldn't want to be lumped in with them."

"I understand. When you're ready! Meanwhile, let's stop for lunch. I had this lovely picnic basket prepared for our trip."

They stopped along the north side of Lake Pontchartrain and spread a cloth on the riverbank as a light breeze lapped the water nearby. Amy described her growing up in Baton Rouge as a tomboy and their family's move to Moss Grove as Union troops were approaching the city.

As Amy proceeded to describe her sister's wedding to the scion of Moss Grove and his return from being wounded in Confederate battles, Melanie realized there could only be one tall , blonde, and blue-eyed man with one-arm, named Henry in all of Louisiana. Amy described her intense dislike for her brother-in-law. Melanie smiled to herself, pleased that her new friend's judgment paralleled her own. Melanie remained silent about her own interaction with Henry. She had never actually explained to Amy how she earned her living.

Melanie didn't recall her client ever mentioning Moss Grove in their long evening together and Melanie's lunch with Abner Moresby had been cut short by his rudeness. Had he not been such a boor she might have learned her new client's last name and more about Moss Grove.

The two women decided they would stop at the Carmody & Williams Feed Store and Stable first before Melanie continued on to her family's farm. Amy could either stay or continue on to visit her sister. They reached Baton Rouge in the late afternoon just as summer clouds darkened the day and flashes of orange lightening lit up the sky.

The rain and their buggy arrived at the stable at the same time. Thaddeus rushed out first, helping Amy down, and giving her an embarrassing hug before she pulled back to introduce him to her new friend.

"Miss Melanie," Thaddeus said, "You are the loveliest thing to ever visit and if it weren't for my feelings for Miss Amy, I would immediately throw myself at your feet."

The ladies smiled.

"Thaddeus, you keep growing taller and I can certainly see what working on that forge has done for your muscles. You are definitely a good looking young man **but**, and I do mean **but**... you have definitely spent too much time with horses. That is the smoothest manure I have ever heard you spread," Amy chided as Rose, Rufus, and Matthew joined them.

"Come in from the rain," Rose said. "You all jus' standin' there like dumb mules. Miss Melanie, you ain't goin' nowhere tonight. This rain is fixin' to stay around for awhile. We'll make you comfortable here and you be fine in the mornin'."

"Let me escort you in where it's warm, Miss Melanie," Rufus Carmody said, pushing Matthew aside and escorting this beauty toward a comfortable chair. She blushed, took his hand, and looked into a strong, smiling face. She was used to men staring at her but this wasn't the same. None of the lasciviousness was there. This look was more an appreciation of soul mates. They knew within minutes that this would be more than a chance encounter. They both shared a mixed race experience in a white dominated world and there would never be a reason to verbalize what that meant.

They remained, hands held, through most of the evening. Rose and Matthew could only smile at one another, surrounded on one side by Amy and Thaddeus, and on the other by Rufus and Melanie.

Outwardly Rose smiled, happy at sharing the warmth of her sons and their friends but on the inside she hid nervous fears of where all this might be heading. She was going to make certain that she determined the sleeping arrangements. There were just too many raging hormones floating through the room for it to be left to the young ones.

The next morning the damp grass and the dripping of leftover rain from the trees was all that remained from the surprise downpour. Rufus had decided to take the day off and drive Melanie to her family's farm. Pleased by the attention of this attractive and well-traveled colored man, she didn't object and her driver got an extra day to relax. They left early before anyone got around to teasing them. Meanwhile, Thaddeus insisted on taking Amy to Moss Grove. He hadn't seen Jesse and Sarah for nearly two months and, while they had exchanged brief letters, he missed seeing them in person.

Rose took him aside before they left, "You listen, and you listen good. You have Ms. Amy sit in the back of the buggy...not up front with you. Maybe you ain't no slave no more but that don't mean white folks attitudes changed none. I lost my Faris to angry white folks and I don't want to lose you, too."

"Don't you worry, Momma Rose. I'll be a right proper darkey, yes I will."

He turned to Amy and extended his hand.

"This way young Missy. Ah' is your courteous driver today. Now, you just climb in the back there, tuck this blanket over your legs and let this here nigger take you to your plantation."

"Don't get silly, Thaddeus," Rose said. "Just be careful."

"What's going on here?" Amy asked. "What's all this silly chatter?"

"Miss Amy, you be careful, too," Rose added. "Roads are full of angry folk and they don't like what they think of as 'uppity' niggers. You stay in back and let Thaddeus drive. That way I know you'll get to Moss Grove safely."

The two young lovers nodded their heads in reluctant agreement and set off. If the roads weren't too muddy they'd be at Moss Grove in four hours and leaving this early might enable them to avoid meeting anyone on the road in search of trouble.

Two hours north of Baton Rouge they got down from their buggy to stretch and share a small snack Rose had packed. Before they got settled three scruffy looking white men on horses rode up.

"Nigger, what you doin' sittin' next to that white girl?" a large pock-marked man said from astride a pinto that looked as if it had served in the same Confederate cavalry as its rider. The other two men, silent, just sat their horses with grim dirty faces.

Thaddeus started to stand, fury rising in his throat, but Amy acted more quickly.

"This is my darkey, gentlemen. He's here to protect me from any danger we might meet on the road. I thank you for caring. We're heading to Moss Grove to visit my sister and brother-in-law, Captain Henry Rogers. Perhaps you know him?" she cooed in her best Southern manner.

Their scowls softened. "Henry Rogers? Yeah, we know him. But Missy, don't you let this nigger boy get too friendly, you hear. You make him keep his place. And you hear me, boy, you take care. I don't care much for that look on your face. I've killed niggers who've looked at me like that, and I don't care much if you think you free now. You a nigger and that says it all."

Before Thaddeus could respond the three men turned and rode off.

Rufus took his time driving to Melanie's family's farm. He was just enjoying himself too much. In all his travels he had never met anyone like the woman sitting next to him. She was just plain warm and beautiful and he felt like a schoolboy.

"How long have you known Amy?" she asked, wanting to keep the conversation harmless.

"Since Thaddeus, Matthew and I returned from the war. I'd seen her at Moss Grove the first time I passed through but she was just a scrawny tomboy then. Not much more than a year later she'd blossomed and I watched her and Thaddeus struggle to control how they felt."

"You like Thaddeus, don't you?"

"He's my closest friend and we've become closer than brothers," Rufus admitted. "But tell me about you. You know you're special, don't you?"

Melanie just smiled. She wasn't about to confess her profession to this man she just met.

They reached the farm before lunch. It was well off the regularly traveled roads surrounded on two sides by a grove of magnolia trees. You would have to know the farm was there or you'd miss it completely.

"My goodness," Rufus smiled. "How'd you ever find this place?"

"It isn't too complicated," Melanie said sweetly. "A gentlemen friend had a long, very bad turn at the tables and needed to clear his debts quickly. A mutual friend arranged to act on my behalf by providing the money he needed in exchange for a deed. There wasn't much here at the time but the land looked rich and there was plenty of water close by."

Rufus put his back and chuckled. "Does he know he sold his property to a 'colored'? That you are his new neighbor?"

The glint in Melanie's eyes made it clear no one knew. "I'm sure he just believes the Chartier family is an absentee owner. He had never asked me my last name. I guess he assumes the people living here are share croppers."

"I love it. I knew you were beautiful but you're clever as well."

Marie Chartier, Melanie's mother, came out to meet them. She was an older version of her daughter. Shorter by four inches, she possessed the same sculpted high cheek bones. Her dark deepset eyes and wide brows couldn't mask her delight at seeing her daughter. They hugged effusively.

"Mother, this is my new friend and Galahad, Mr. Rufus Carmody. He wouldn't allow me to drive here without his personal protection."

"Well, what do I call you, Galahad or Mr. Carmody?" Marie Chartier smiled as she separated from Melanie and looked at her daughter's friend with a practiced eye. She knew what her daughter did to earn the money that allowed them to live safely and comfortably on this farm. They had never discussed it. Marie had never wanted to embarrass her daughter. She knew instinctively that it wasn't who her child really was and as the three of them stood there she continued to clasp her daughter's hand tightly.

"Let's just make it Rufus, Mrs. Chartier, just plain, old Rufus."

"Only if you'll call me Marie, she said, taking their arms and leading them inside."

As evening and dinnertime arrived, Melanie's three brothers came in from the field. They each shook Rufus' hand with an excessive firmness. They were wary of strangers and protective of their sister. Able was the eldest. He was as tall as Rufus but much darker. He was a serious man who relished his role as man of the family and his look said it all…don't trifle with my sister.

Benny was the middle boy. He exuded a happy, carefree air but it was clear he was the brains of the family. He knew the cost of cotton seed and anything else they needed to buy. Charlie was the youngest. He deferred to his two older brothers. They were his heroes. Melanie was the only girl in the family and had been born two years after Benny. She had grown up under the protection of these brothers.

Their father had been killed during New Orleans racial riots ten years earlier. A friend of his had been accused of insulting a young white girl. It had never happened, but thirty whites had gotten drunk and dragged six blacks from their homes and began beating them with clubs. Melanie's father was one of the six. All of them ended up being savagely killed. Melanie had promised herself then that she'd get the family as far away from angry ignorant white folks as she could.

The next day Rufus joined the brothers as they plowed and planted. There was always more work than hours on a small farm. But in the middle of the morning there was a scream that brought everyone running. Birds fluttered from the trees and horses began kicking in their stalls. When they got to the scene Charlie was writhing on the ground, blood gushing from his leg.

"What happened, Charlie?" Able said as he and Benny slowly lifted him.

"Jes clearin' da ground like you tol' me to. Musta' stepped into a hole cuz' nex' thing I know I'm goin' one way and my leg's goin' another."

"The bone is protruding. He's got a bad fracture. Any doctor around to set it?" Rufus asked.

"None closer than Baton Rouge and he don't like to tend black folks anyway," Melanie said.

"I saw a lot of bad stuff like this in the Army. Let's get him back to the house. Carry him carefully. Don't move that bone," Rufus ordered. "Melanie, can we send someone to get Mama Rose? She knows a lot about medicines and herbs that we're going to need before a fever sets in."

Benny headed off on his horse to get Mama Rose while Able and Rufus carried Charlie back as carefully as possible. Getting him settled in the house, they cleaned the break and put the bone back into its place, using clean clothes and rigid boards to keep the leg from moving. Charlie had fallen asleep, sweat continuing to drip from his forehead. Marie Chartier kept up a steady change of cold damp cloths.

Rose arrived later in the afternoon and after the briefest of introductions examined Charlie's splint and temperature.

"He's got a fever," she said, feeling his forehead.

As Rose examined Charlie's bandages one more time, Rufus took Melanie aside.

"I need to return to Baton Rouge but I hate to leave you."

"I understand. Send my driver for me. I'll need to get back to New Orleans as well."

"Charlie's going to have a rough night. We should get some potions into him. It'll help him sleep more calmly and fight any infection. Rufus, you did a good job resetting the bone."

"Will he be OK?" Able asked.

"He's strong and with some strong prayers and a little luck, I think so."

They passed the night together, awake mostly, drifting in and out of sleep. By morning Charlie was beginning to stir.

"Fevers down," Rose said.

"Thank the Lord," Marie murmured. Her son would make it.

"Will I see you again?" Melanie asked.

"You'll get tired of seeing me," Rufus smiled, looking into her eyes. "Now that I've found you, I have no intention of losing you."

Her eyes met his and without words he knew that she shared his feelings.

Rose and Rufus returned to their home in Baton Rouge. Melanie waited for her carriage and returned to New Orleans. It was never a good idea to leave her clientele unserviced too long. They might begin to look around for someone newer or younger. Charlie healed slowly with a limp that he'd have the rest of his life.

# Chapter Seventeen

"Ready to go riding this morning, Josiah?" Henry asked, as one of the new house servants helped him put on his boots. Henry stood, set down his coffee, and grabbed his riding crop. Elizabeth sat quietly nearby, never sure what sarcasm her husband would direct her way. But Josiah jumped up, thrilled to be able join his father for an outing.

"Yes, father. I'll put on my boots." The boy leapt up the stairs noisily.

"I will be back this afternoon," Henry said brusquely, not caring whether his wife even bothered to reply. She didn't.

Josiah sat cramped between his father and the pommel of the saddle. He no longer wet his pants like he did the first few times he was hoisted up, frightened by being up so high on a live, breathing, moving animal that liked to snort and shake its head energetically. He was still nervous and bit his lip to keep from crying. He didn't want to act like a baby in front of his father and ruin the morning.

"Will I be able to get my own horse soon, father?" Josiah asked.

"Perhaps in another year! You need to be a little bigger. I like that you are no longer afraid. Rogers men have always been good horsemen."

"I was a baby then, but I'm big now."

When these father-son mornings first began nearly a year ago, his father's infrequent gentleness quickly gave way to immediate disgust as his son's fear suddenly became pee drifting down the horse's neck. But Josiah was a little older now and once he was able to control his fear and embarrassment, he began to enjoy the outings, particularly the smells. The odors of damp earth blended with the cooking smells from the black kitchens. They tickled his nose. At first he'd kept sneezing but now he found the odors pleasant. His yellow hair was a mass of curls long down his neck. Henry wouldn't let Elizabeth cut it. He found it reminded him of his own hair at that age and it felt good to relive those happy years through his son. His missing arm was still an inconvenience but it was no longer an impediment. When he lifted his son up to the saddle he loosened the shoulder strap enough to embrace his son as well.

Crows flew overhead, picking seeds wherever they could find them, usually hidden between the flowering cotton plants. This was the time Henry loved best, when the hibiscus-like buds of embryonic cotton turned from white to pink to brown in the weeks before bursting open to reveal their fluffy treasure. Sometimes, for no discernible reason, the birds would suddenly take flight and make Henry's horse skittish. Only his tight hand on the rein would keep the animal in check.

"Josiah," Henry admonished. I told you not to wave or acknowledge the niggers that are in the field. These men are there to work, not wave."

Josiah watched the glistening black field hands sweating as they bent over, planting seeds in the spring or pulling the white puffs off in the fall. Sometimes the men would stop, stand, drop their sack, and wipe their foreheads. They rarely smiled.

The penetrating heat and summer's uncomfortable humidity were still weeks off. Today they could enjoy a cool spring morning, the kind of day where thoughts of anger and worry were locked away, where deep lung-filling breaths of fresh air and the rays of the sun against a clear blue sky coalesced to raise endorphin levels and make smiles flow so easily. But these were white smiles…privileged smiles, and those without property, black and white, were forced to toil long hours, with no time to enjoy God's bounty of a beautiful day.

Whisper ran beside them. Henry had bought his son the brown female hound dog as a puppy and the two had bonded instantly. As an unintended bonus to Henry, the dog barked or snarled from the get-go at blacks working in the field. Its ears would flare in a fearsome way. No one was sure why the animal acted this way but Henry found it most entertaining while it made each field hand stop and get ready to flee each time this white boss and his young 'un rode by with their damned dog constantly yipping.

"Good morning, Thatcher," Henry hailed to his new overseer.

"Mr. Rogers," Thatcher acknowledged. He knew this white boss expected him to say 'sir' but slavery was over and he'd be damned if he'd give the man the satisfaction.

Thatcher was medium height but stocky. He rarely smiled and he didn't like these Henry Rogers or any other interruption that might delay the day's work. He did happily acknowledge that if the cotton came in at today's prices he'd make a sight more than runnin' his own small spread. He was the first black overseer ever employed at Moss Grove. It was something that Jedidiah had always been able to avoid and Henry resisted. But there weren't any white overseers to be employed. Henry doubted there was any left anywhere in Louisiana. At least Thatcher had once owned a few slaves himself and understood growing cotton.

"Planting going well?"

"Yes. We even got another ten acres along the back in greens. It was too late to plant cotton."

"Good…good!" Henry acknowledged, continuing on.

Thatcher was glad to see him leave. He was still upset about the steady stream of complaints he had to deal with from the sharecroppers. They're always get'n riled over somethin'. If it wasn't the damn dog that upset them, it'd be the vittles or the housin' or what got took out of their pay. We was all better off when blacks was slaves, he mused…even the niggers were better off. Everything was much simpler.

Riding with his son was one of Henry's few pleasures as the pressures of running Moss Grove continued to mount. He smiled as he envisioned the boy growing up as a younger version of how he had looked before he lost his arm. Their morning ride over, he sent his son to be bathed and begin his daily lessons. Henry hoped that Josiah would take to books and be a better student than he had been. He knew that his father had always been disappointed Henry hadn't applied himself more diligently.

He closed himself in his study and lit himself a rare cigar. This certainly wasn't the life he had imagined for himself. He wanted to shout at someone and scream out his frustration, but all he could do was grit his teeth and pour another drink.

The economics of Moss Grove was one of increasingly treacherous clouds. If it wasn't figuring out how to pay and feed his sharecroppers, it was worrying about the weather or the price of cotton. First, there was not enough rain, then there was too much. Cotton futures went to new highs, then into the crapper. He could only hope that in another three months when this crop was ready to harvest, conditions would be more stable. If not, he'd have to either get another bank loan or withdraw more from his dwindling hidden bank accounts. That was his only nest egg and he was reluctant to keep tapping it. Meanwhile most of the value of Moss Grove was already pledged to Moresby.

He was planting less acreage than he would have liked but the damn nigger workers just up and left, sometime in the middle of the night. Hiring Thatcher had helped some. The man had a small spread of his own, barely enough to feed himself, his wife and their four children. It wasn't difficult to convince him that he could do a lot better at Moss Grove if he could keep the sharecroppers working and not running away. The previous overseer, Spencer Hannify, couldn't make the adjustment from bossing slaves to dealing with blacks who were liable to walk at any time. The man just came in one day and said he was moving out west. He wanted nothing more to do with cotton. Henry was hopeful that Thatcher would be able to keep things under better control.

Elizabeth was no help. She was baffled by the problems of running a plantation home. To her, all darkeys were plain lazy and more than once this past year her scolding resulted in some of the staff up and leaving. She'd never seen so many uppity niggers in her life and that seemed to include every one of the house staff.

She still fretted about her lost daughter, Clara. She knew she would have never been able to raise the baby girl but knowing the child was still out there somewhere, made her perpetually anxious as to where the infant was and how she was faring.

She and Henry hadn't shared a bed since the eruption over their daughter's birth a few months ago. They were driving one another crazy and rarely even took their meals together. He had taken over the rearing of Josiah, the one bright light in both of their lives. Elizabeth tried to inject herself into her son's life but she never seemed strong enough to confront the domineering husband she'd wanted so badly and who she now feared. She had seen the anger and violence to which he was capable.

Henry poured himself another brandy and began to rub his stiff penis as he recalled his last visit to that brothel and Melanie...that was her name. He definitely needed to see that nigger beauty, and soon. He certainly needed to fuck someone other than his bitchy wife. It wouldn't hurt to see Moresby again either! He'd definitely enjoy blowing off steam in New Orleans.

"Henry, we need more money for provisions," Elizabeth said, entering his private sanctuary and shaking her husband from his fantasy.

Fortunately he'd finished and rearranged his pants before she'd entered unannounced.

"We have no money. I've told you that," he shouted. "Our god-damn confederate money is worthless. Might as well wipe our asses with it! You'll have to make do."

"How do I do that?" she asked tearfully.

"We've got pigs we can slaughter, maybe even trade some. We've got potatoes. It might not be what you're used to but we won't starve."

"Henry, how long will this all last?" she moaned.

"I wish I knew. Taxes are sky high. Plantations are being taken over by the banks. Niggers are wandering all over the land. It's damnable anarchy."

Eli Fineman sat across the desk from Major John Shipley, his commanding officer, and Commandant of the Southern District military command. Shipley was the immediate report of General Philip Sheridan.

> *Congress was determined to invalidate the Black codes that many of the Confederate legislatures had passed. These laws had the same effect as returning blacks to slavery. Maybe they were no longer property but economically they would continue to be treated as indentured servants.*
>
> *To ensure some measure of opportunity for the freed black slaves, President Grant and the Republican Congress backed their determination by dispatching large military forces across the South. But changing the white Confederate mindset that had evolved over more than a hundred years would not be an easy task.*

Shipley had ridden up from New Orleans to meet this Jewish officer who was assigned to head The Freedman's Bureau in the upper part of Louisiana. He'd never met a Jew before. Imagine, a Jew, in the Union Army. He couldn't understand why the military brass would countenance such a thing. They must have been really hard up for recruits. And an officer! This guy had better be really special or I'll court-martial his ass, Shipley thought, determined to show his subordinate how a Christian officer handles responsibility.

"You'll be fine, Captain. You've got money, authority, and troops to support your programs," Shipley said, sizing up his new subordinate. "Just remember, these assholes lost the war and cost our country far too many young lives. So while we are not authorized to punish them, I, personally, don't feel the least bit sorry for them, particularly the wealthy plantation owners who made all their money off the backs and the sweat of slaves for generations.

"Now that their plantations are falling apart from high taxes and bank loans, your job is to get some of this wealth into the hands of the ex-slaves. Forty acres, a little seed, a couple of chickens and maybe a mule and they'll make out just fine.

"You'll need to set up schools, hospitals…even banks. We're remaking the culture, from the bottom up and it won't be easy. Are you up to the task?"

"Yes sir, I am," Eli answered, with all the conviction he could muster, although within him he had no idea how to proceed.

"It's a blank slate, Captain, and you get to be Michelangelo."

"I may need some help," Eli confessed.

"What kind of help?"

"Teachers, doctors, or even nurses! Baton Rouge is a small town and the area is even more rural as you head north. Many of the blacks, whites, and the few colored I've met are mostly illiterate. The ex-slaves are almost all uneducated. Remember, they had laws that made it a crime to teach slaves to read or do numbers. What I need is a little yeast to help leaven this raw dough you've assigned me to work with."

"You're a Jew, Fineman. I don't pretend to know much about you and your kind but I'm told your people walked across a desert without yeast or time for leavening. Think of this as another Sinai."

"Touché, Major! Too bad I don't have forty years."

"No, you don't. I want to see definite results and I want to see them quickly. Meanwhile I will see if I can coerce some of what you need from people in New Orleans."


"Mr. Carmody! My name is Dr. Louis Roundanez. I'm the publisher of the New Orleans Tribune. It's the first newspaper in Louisiana that focuses on us blacks and coloreds. It has been a long time coming and we are very proud of it. This gentleman with me is Mr. P.B. Pinchback. He is running for Lt. Governor at the next election and we've come here to solicit your help. We have been led to believe that you and your partner know a lot of the new voters in this area."

"Whoa, gentlemen! How did you even get my name?" Rufus asked, coming out from behind the counter where he'd been busy restocking shelves.

"Well," Roundanez smiled. "I believe we may have mutual friends. Your name, as well as that of Mr. Thaddeus Williams, was mentioned to us. We met Major Shipley and Captain Fineman of the Freedman's Bureau in New Orleans recently. They suggested we come and talk to you. Captain Fineman was impressed with what you and your partner have accomplished."

"We run a simple stable and feed store," Rufus replied. "Rose," he said, smiling and turning aside, "You'd better get Thaddeus in here before these slick folks steal our goods with their sweet talk."

He gathered his guests around the stove. Sitting, drinking hot coffee, allowed them all to relax and chat informally.

"I don't need to tell you that our nation has been permanently altered," Roundanez continued. "Louisiana has been changed and none of our lives will remain 'simple' any longer. The black man is free. He is free from hundreds of years of slavery. Thank the Lord the Union Army has come to our state to help us implement the necessary changes. A few concerned white men and a few educated coloreds are all we have to lead this revolution. You and your partner know how to read, do numbers and run a business. There are not enough of us with those skills and it is the obligation of us few to spread that knowledge and lift up those less fortunate."

Thaddeus walked in, wiping his hands. His heavy apron was still blackened from the ashes off the forge.

"Gentlemen, this is my partner and friend, Thaddeus Williams," Rufus said proudly. His affection for his younger friend was evident. He had watched Thaddeus grow from that first night at Port Hudson into a fine self-confident man. Their soldiering together had strengthened their bond. They were brothers in the strongest sense of the word.

"Mr. Williams," Pinchback asked as he stood to greet this light complexioned man who stood several inches above him, "One of the properties that have become available in Baton Rouge is a home that was owned by someone with the same surname as yours. Is there a connection?"

"Please, call me Thaddeus. The connection is rather loose. I was a slave, the property of the Rogers family who owned Moss Grove. When I ran away to fight in the war someone asked me my last name. Actually, I think it was you, Rufus," he smiled. "The only name that came to mind that wasn't connected to the plantation was 'Williams' as one of their family had become an acquaintance of mine. When Union troops approached Baton Rouge, that family moved in with their cousins at Moss Grove and the families intermarried. I became friends with one of the younger girls, Miss Amy Williams."

"We were thinking that since it was available for just the unpaid taxes, we could acquire it and use it as both a school and medical clinic. What do you think of that possibility?" Roundanez asked.

"I only know the home from Amy's description but I know of no reason why it couldn't be adapted," Thaddeus responded.

As they talked both Thaddeus and Rufus became imbued with their visitor's enthusiasm for the opportunities that lay ahead. These were important men of color who truly believed that black equality was achievable.

"What do you think, Thaddeus?" Rufus asked after the two men left to return to New Orleans.

"Hard to know! They could have just been smoking something stronger than a cigar," Thaddeus laughed. "I was a slave just a few years ago. The blacks I knew were mostly picking cotton. The whites in this state aren't going to take this without fighting, I don't care how many troops they station here."

The Williams house was acquired. Thaddeus agreed to train a replacement for himself as blacksmith and take charge of the embryonic school. The limited education Jedidiah and Ruby had provided him would now be able to benefit others. He wished that he was more learned but he would make it a point meanwhile to study as much as possible.

Rose would come with him and use her knowledge of herbs to provide a little medical solace to the community by a small clinic they would establish at the same site. Pinchback would search out a trained doctor to come to the area a few days each per month for more serious ailments. They would each receive a small stipend from the Freedman's Bureau which would also send them as much schooling materials and medical goods as could be gathered. Fineman would also get trained army medics from nearby Army units to help. The entire effort might take months but their first small step had been taken.

# Chapter Eighteen

C eleste Montaigne continued on to New Orleans and stayed the first few nights with friends. It had been easy to become emotionally attached to Clara. The older woman enjoyed the smell and gurgles that only emanate from a well-fed, well-hugged baby. Celeste's heart cried out when she looked at this sand colored little girl that had arrived with a complete innocence, only to be greeted by total hostility and complete rejection from the two people that were supposed to love and care for her. It was unnatural. It did convince her, however, that getting away from Moss Grove was the right decision. Without Ruby and Jedidiah to spread their warmth, there was no longer any pleasure in preparing her sauces and special dishes and overseeing the plantation's kitchen.

Her first task now was to get Clara settled. Then she would worry about finding herself a position befitting her culinary skills. One of Celeste's closest friends from her earlier life in New Orleans had gone from training as a sous-chef to becoming a nun. The girl was now a novitiate at the Catholic School for Indigent Children.

The end of the war had created serious problems for the small school. It was severely overcrowded and, at the same time, it was terribly underfunded. There were just too many people across the state without homes and too many women and children without men to support them. Children suffered the most, and more than once, the morning arrived with another basket at the front door of this sanctuary, a brief note of despair pinned to a tattered blanket, and a small baby within.

Celeste offered to cook at the home until she found a proper placement for herself but a day became a week and a week became several months. They needed her and the job brought her both satisfaction and a chance to stay close to Clara. The child was thriving. There was always someone eager to hold her. Perhaps things would turn out well.

The days were long. There was rarely enough food to prepare anything but bare sustenance and Celeste had no qualified staff to help her. Most of the girls were ex-slaves and illiterate, never having been allowed to learn how to read or do numbers. If they had any experience at all it was in slave kitchens with simple fare. But the girls were eager to learn, sometimes too eager.

One evening, quite late, one of the new girls was experimenting with a sauté pan and a little cooking grease. A small fire erupted, spreading quickly onto the floor. The dry wooden walls lapped the flames like a starving man. The kitchen was situated in the back of the buildings but breezes off the Mississippi blew embers back into the building. The upper floors of the school didn't have a chance.

Celeste and Clara were asleep in their second floor room and were quickly overcome by smoke and flames. Their only exit would have been the single staircase already collapsing. The entire building was consumed in less than thirty minutes.

A small crowd gathered in front of the school to watch the flames and keep them from spreading to neighboring structures. Not everyone cared about the destruction they were witnessing.

"Good riddance," a short white man, wearing coveralls that had been worn without washing for way too long, spat out.

"Yeah! God knew what to do. Most of them kids was niggers or coloreds. We don't need 'em to grow up. We got enough of 'em already. "Maybe we should throw more timbers on the fire, just to make sure."


"They're dead…both of them, along with forty other children and twelve nuns," Melanie said to Amy, getting her excused from her classes.

Amy sobbed, tears pouring down her cheeks, trying to understand what she was being told.

"There was a fire at the Catholic School for Indigent Orphans near the Quarter. It was the middle of the night and nearly everyone was asleep. They think it started in the kitchen but no one is really sure," Melanie said. She had driven to Amy's school to share a casual afternoon together.

"I didn't even know they'd settled there. I'd known that Celeste hadn't wanted to continue at Moss Grove after Miss Ruby died and that she'd left. She'd never gotten along with Henry but that was no big surprise. My sister had no experience running a plantation and even less understanding on what it took to run a kitchen staff. I'm sure that Celeste got frustrated. And Clara, my baby niece, oh my God," Amy said, explaining her sister's shock at having given birth to a mixed child.

My God, Melanie thought to herself. Bigoted Henry…colored blood. How deliciously ironic.

"How did Celeste and the baby connect?" Melanie asked.

"If I had to guess, I'd assume Sarah asked Celeste to find a home for the baby when Henry demanded she be taken out of the house and drowned or given over to some similar fate. It all happened about the same time but I don't really know for sure," Amy posited.

"Looks like your wonderful brother-in-law got his wish after all."

"I've got to get to Moss Grove and tell my sister. She was still Clara's mother. She may not even care but she does deserve to know. Oh, this is terrible."

Once again they hired a wagon and driver to take her to Baton Rouge. She hoped that Thaddeus, or someone else she could rely on, would take her the rest of the way to the plantation.

Thaddeus wasn't at the stable when she arrived but Matthew offered and the two headed off with a fresh horse after Amy filled them in with news of the tragedy that had occurred. Meanwhile Matthews' return visit to Moss Grove would produce a lot less anger than a visit by Thaddeus' in the event Henry was around.

Amy found Elizabeth napping in her day room. It was clear that her older sister had become a frequent user of laudanum to dull the frustrations and pain in her life. It took a few minutes for her to waken to Amy's shaking. Sarah, meanwhile, knowing what was to come, had brought in some tea.

"Lizzy, I have terrible news," Amy began.

"I don't want any bad news, Amy. That's all I hear these days. I want things to be like they were when we lived with mommy and daddy in Baton Rouge. I didn't think I'd ever miss those days but I surely do," she moaned as she tried to sit up.

"Would you like some fresh tea, Miss Elizabeth?" Sarah asked. "It'll get your insides up and moving."

"I'd prefer some brandy. Bring me some brandy, Sarah."

Sarah looked at Amy and then moved across the room where a ready carafe of brandy rested, half empty.

Elizabeth sipped the brandy as Amy moved next to her on the settee, holding her hand.

"Clara is dead," Amy said. "She died in a fire where she'd been placed!"

The brandy glass dropped and rolled onto the carpet as Elizabeth seemed to go rigid, breathless at the news. The entire room became a frieze, the three women, motionless, waiting for further reaction.

Elizabeth slid to the floor and began wailing. "My baby...my baby girl. I let Henry send her away and now she's dead. I'm to blame." She began sobbing, tearing at her clothes, inconsolable.

When Henry returned several hours later he found the house in a state of mourning. All mirrors had been covered with black cloth.

"What's going on here?" he asked.

Amy met him near the entrance. Josiah was beside her carrying blocks they'd been playing with.

"You need to go upstairs and comfort your wife."

His forehead furrowed and a scowl came over his brow. He wanted to ask more questions but the dislike between he and Amy precluded it. Instead he turned and went upstairs.

Elizabeth was well into a hazy emotional 'nether land' produced by the combination of drugs and alcohol. Tiny droplets of perspiration balanced precariously on her forehead and cheeks. Henry's rising voice and stronger shaking finally brought her back to consciousness. Her eyes opened to see Henry standing over her.

"We killed our daughter, Henry. We killed her. As sure as if we'd done it ourselves! She's dead, damn you. You made me give her away," she screamed.

Sarah, still in the room, quietly explained to Henry the tragedy of the fire. It took a moment for him to absorb what they were telling him but his reaction was unexpected. He began laughing, first quietly, and then louder and louder, throwing his head back in utter glee.

"You were right, Sarah. You were so right. God does play roulette with us. This isn't a fucking tragedy. That baby shouldn't have been born and now God, or fate, or whoever you want to blame, has corrected the mistake."

He turned to his stunned wife. "We should be celebrating, you stupid cow. Get up, let's dance. Sarah, get rid of those black shrouds over the mirrors. Get some of the good wine from the cellar."

"You are truly an evil man, Henry," Elizabeth seethed. "You are a bastard!"

Henry needed to adapt to new challenges and new rules. He would do so. He would not let Moss Grove go the way of his neighbors. He would weather this storm until life returned to some degree of normalcy. His wife would probably remain a drugged out cow who he could no longer count on. So be it! He appointed another house servant to oversee the kitchen. Sarah could train her since it was a much smaller staff these days. With Thatcher acting as overseer, he would manage. By now he had twenty families share-cropping. He'd get his rent, ten percent of their gross income, and still charge them for whatever food and supplies they needed to buy from the plantation commissary Thatcher had wisely enlarged.

He closed off some of the back acreage. It was less fertile soil and until he could set up more share cropping arrangements there was no one to plow and tend that land. If he could find a buyer, he'd even sell it, but there weren't many buyers around these days for anything other than property that had been foreclosed. Like the rest of the growers he'd been paid in Confederate currency for his crops during the war years and now all that money was worthless. If cotton prices stabilized, he'd survive. He would need some help from the weather but God couldn't be against the white man and the south forever.

His only respite was time with his son. Josiah had become a mature toddler, on his way to becoming a fine little man. A tutor came three times a week to give Josiah his lessons and the boy's face lit up each time. It did look as if his son would be a better student than Henry had been.

Jesse died quietly in his sleep. He was nearly sixty years old. No one knew his exact age, not even Jesse. He had been captured by slave traders as the son of an important tribal shaman in Angola and carried with hundreds of others across the land to waiting ships. There, along with two brothers, a sister, and a cousin, they were crammed into the bowels of a ship that reeked from the human stench of previous voyages. He was deposited on the beach of an island he would learn was called 'Jamaica.' His sister and a brother died on the boat and were simply thrown over the side into the endless rolling ocean. The respect of a tribal burial for his siblings would have to be left to Jesse's memories recalled from his boyhood training.

The young Jesse was sent to the cane fields to work. He grew, learned some Spanish and French, and he waited. One morning, working near the edge of the island, he, his remaining brother, and cousin, ran…and ran…and ran. For months they hid from the dogs and the teams sent out to track runaways. His cousin was caught, having hidden in a tree he had climbed to reach some bananas that would supplement the meager food they'd been able to forage. They never saw him again.

Jesse and his brother stole a boat and headed away from the island. They didn't care where they'd end up at, as long as it wasn't that bedeviled Jamaica. A week later, dehydrated, they were picked up by a French naval ship. They were still slaves but now in French, rather than Spanish, hands.

They were deposited at the slave market in New Orleans, tall, strong bi-lingual. He and his brother were separated and never saw one another again. Jesse found himself the property of Massa' Samuel. This new white master was taciturn. He'd bought some land with a small house on it north of Baton Rouge and he set to work to develop it. Jesse became his right-hand and a quiet respect evolved between them. The years passed. The plantation grew and acquired a name, Moss Grove. Additional slaves were acquired. Massa' Samuel bought Sarah and Jesse was told that he would marry her. The two grew to love one another but no children survived and eventually it became too dangerous for Sarah to conceive.

Samuel died and his son, Jedidiah, became the master of Moss Grove. He and Sarah took over the running of a home that could now rightfully be called a plantation. Massa' Jed found himself a new beautiful young wife, Miss Ruby, and life was good. There was no violence, no whippings. There was plenty to eat. Their livin' was cool in the summer and warm in the winter. The last ten years he and Sarah had the extra joy of raising Thaddeus. It fulfilled them in pleasures they'd long assumed they would never share. Perhaps in death Jesse would finally be reunited with his brothers and sister. At minimum he would no longer be a slave.

Sarah took Jesse's death in silence. He had shared her bed for more than thirty years and she had loved him mightily. Now that her husband was gone, now that Miss Ruby and Thaddeus were gone, Moss Grove remained a house of ghosts and she could no longer stay. She never said goodbye to Henry or Elizabeth. Slavery was over and she was no longer their property. She owed them nothing, and in whatever months or years that God allowed her she wanted to be close to Thaddeus. Early one morning she wrapped her few belongings in a shawl, climbed into a wagon going into town for provisions and rode away from the only home she'd known all her adult life.

# Chapter Nineteen

The Baton Rouge home that the William's family had vacated as the Union army approached the city was now the Freedman's School and Clinic. As soon as her school year was over Amy began working there. She had no desire to return to Moss Grove. Sarah, now free of the ghosts of the past, joined her, wanting to remain active enough to control the sadness that overwhelmed her if she relaxed. Jesse had been her life and that hole was going to remain. She needed to move forward by doing good.

Rose was treating patients with ailments that ranged from childbirth to malaria to tick bites and she was pleased to have Sarah and Amy to help her. Thaddeus was busy getting his school underway. And one of his first students was Melanie's brother, Charlie. The Chartiers had decided that if the boy couldn't carry a full load in the field, because of the injury to his leg, he should be the first one educated so that he would be able to oversee the farm's finances.

The Army had lived up to its commitments. Doctors assigned to Captain Fineman stopped by weekly and could be summoned in an emergency. Major Shipley had sent both medical and school supplies, much of the latter donated by free coloreds and scalawags from New Orleans. Scalawags was the denigrating name applied to those white southerners who had opposed the war and championed the Republican party's efforts to promote equality and opportunity in the south. They were in a distinct minority detested by the more traditional white southerners.

Melanie sent word that she had accumulated furniture and supplies for the school. Rufus wasted no time in hitching the horse to the wagon for the trip. Miss a chance to see Melanie…not likely! Charlie, Melanie's brother, and Matthew decided to join him, and, after considerable prodding, they convinced Thaddeus to join them. Matthew had never been to New Orleans and was as eager as a prancing pony to see the city.

The four of them laughed as they traveled the road along the river in just a few hours. Traffic on the road had become much lighter since the war. People sat along its banks the entire distance. Some of them were ex-Confederate soldiers that stared angrily at four dark hued people riding and laughing, without a care in the world. If it had not been for the frequent presence of Union soldiers the trip could likely have had ugly consequences.

"Leave the wagon," Melanie told them after warm embraces all around. The one with Rufus was particularly warm, and particularly emotional, a situation that gave rise to raucous comments from the others.

"There is a meeting at the Mechanic's Hall. It's just a few blocks from here. They're going to discuss the details of how black and colored men can now vote. I'll just stand in back but this could be really important. Imagine finally being able to elect officials that look or think like us."

"Melanie, trust me," Rufus laughed. "None of those politicians will look like you."

The four of them walked the short blocks to the hall. There were a few hundred black and colored men milling around. Scattered here and there were a couple dozen scalawags. The speaker was Captain James Ingraham, the colored President of the Louisiana National Equal Rights League. During the war he had served with distinction in the Confederate Native Guards.

As he began to speak, a group of whites entered through a side door brandishing clubs and sticks. Their shouting drowned out any attempt to keep order and within minutes a melee ensued. Punching, kicking and screaming rocked the hall as people tried to flee.

"Charlie, get Melanie out of here," Rufus shouted, taking command once again as he had in the Army.

Once he was certain that she'd be out of harm's way he turned his attention to the fighting. He, Thaddeus, and Matthew stood back to back moving forward and giving two for every blow headed in their direction. Thaddeus had a moment to look at Rufus and grin. As before, they fought well standing together. Matthew took a hard stick to his shoulder and dropped to one knee. The blow had glanced off the side of his head and blood was beginning to trickle down. Thaddeus was there before the white thug could throw another blow. Matthew brushed him aside and threw his right fist. He connected with the man's chin. The blow had been struck with all of Matthew's weight behind it and the man dropped like a sack.

The riot lasted twenty minutes before Union troops and local police arrived to separate the combatants and disburse the crowd. Hundreds were jailed as police stormed the building and the surrounding areas. Thirty-four blacks and three whites were killed, hundreds were injured.

"These white southerners are not going to move toward equality peacefully," Ingraham shouted as the Police pushed him into a van filled with smiling black-skinned rioters.

The three of them had managed to avoid arrest as they hobbled back to Melanie's place grinning through black eyes and cut cheeks.

"Never hit a white man before," Matthew said. "I thought it would feel different but it don't. Guess that makes it a little disappointin'."

Thaddeus laughed and then stopped. "Hurts when I laugh. Don't make me laugh, little brother."

"Your little brother isn't so little anymore," Rufus added.

"I'm so glad you're all back safely," Melanie said. "I really worried about all of you."

"Well, thank you, Melanie. I'll take that as meaning that you care for me," Rufus grinned, and then winced, as she applied extra astringent to clean a gash in his arm.

"I care for all of you, you big oaf," she said.

"Yes, but you care for me most, don't you?" he persisted.

Their eyes connected and they both knew it was true. So did the others in the room.

"I'm going to stay in New Orleans," Matthew declared, as they all began to relax from the busy evening. The smell of antiseptic hung in the air and mixed uneasily with the scent of sweet ginger tea. His brow was furrowed as he spoke.

"I know this seems to come as a surprise but I've given it a great deal of thought. As we were coming into the city I knew I belonged here. There is an energy and a power all around that excites me."

"But we need you with us," Thaddeus objected. "Although I must say that watching you hit that white guy made me a lot more respectful of messing with you."

"I'm not sure if I was seeing red...or maybe it was white, but that man definitely needed some racial sensitivity. I'll miss you all, and I won't be far away, but I want to learn more and accomplish something. I'm too learned for a beginning school and too dumb to teach. I don't want to spend my life at a forge or in a store."

"What do you want?" Rufus asked.

"I'm not sure. Remember, of the three of us I was the only one who was truly a field slave. My daddy was burned to death for trying to find a better life. I want to make him proud and I need you all to support me on this journey."

"Matthew, we're brothers. We share the same mother. I'm happy to support whatever you do," Thaddeus said.

"We all will," Rufus added, as they all clasped hands together.

Over the next few days they loaded the wagon with all the supplies Melanie had coerced from her clients and friends. She had even reestablished her tenuous relationship with Abner Moresby, the banker, and convinced him a make a $500 donation toward medical supplies. She knew it was his way of apologizing but 'whatever it took' seemed to express the motto of the day. She and Matthew waved until Thaddeus, Rufus and the loaded wagon disappeared north.

"We will not allow these niggers to think they are our equals!" The deep resonant voice addressed less than three dozen intense white men sitting before him.

"My name is Alcibiades DeBlanc...Colonel Alcibiades DeBlanc," he emphasized, his dark eyes blazing with the fire of a zealot. "I fought in Virginia and I was wounded in the battle of Gettysburg defending this white man's country against these inferior blacks and carpetbaggers that have come into our midst telling us that they are equal to us. They are not!

"We may have lost the military battle with the Yankees but as long as there is blood coursing through our veins we will continue the battle to retain our rightful place in our society."

"How you proposin' to do that?" a well-dressed man asked, moving a thin cigar from one side of his month to the other and back again nervously.

"Every one of you here fought in the war, same as I did. Many of you come from good, solid, white families. We are part of the elite that was the old south and I ask you today to pledge your lives and well-being in a new, different war. This war will be fought to return our land to the white control we earned by the sweat of our brow and the efforts of our ancestors.

Are you with me?" he said in raised voice, blood vessels protruding across his cheeks as he became more animated.

The roar of support was unanimous. These men had lost their homes, their wealth and their standing in society. They were not used to defeat. The Knights of the White Camellia was formed, officers were appointed, and codes to communicate with one another were established. They understood that they would be working outside the law. They understood that the Union Army, the Blacks, the Coloreds, the Carpetbaggers, and the Scalawags were all their sworn enemies. The Knights were prepared to wage an ongoing guerilla war. They would neither be defeated nor dissuaded.

Rufus, Thaddeus, Rose, Matthew, Amy and Melanie stood on the front porch of the frame home adjacent to the Carmody & Williams Feed Store and Stable and watched the sky light up. There was shouting and cheering. People were laughing and patting one another on the back. Ulysses S. Grant, 'US' Grant, the man who had carried out Ol' Abe's plan and won the war, was goin' to be their new President.

> *The Republicans had won again. The decision was made easier by the fact that Texas, Mississippi and Virginia had not yet been readmitted to the Union and were not permitted to vote, but who cared. Bottom line was, the war was over, the government was still committed to enforcing equality in the south despite the hatred of the vast majority of the southern whites, and the country had now elected a leader to implement these convictions.*

"A lot of people are wandering around this town not cheering," Thaddeus noted.

"Louisiana didn't go for Grant," Rufus said. "A lot of the Rebs either didn't vote or didn't sign the Union allegiance card they needed to so they could vote. New Orleans paper say that some fellow from New York named Seymour, a Democrat, got nearly 48% of the vote. He say 'This is a White Man's Country, Let White Men Rule.' I guess that played pretty well in this state."

"Even got lots of white votes up north," Matthew noted. "We won and the law say we equal but I don't think white folks are necessarily gonna be good with that here in Louisiana. Now that the election is over a lot of whites that had been on the sidelines are going to be joining the Klan, the White Camellias or those other hate groups. People I know are worried what might happen."

Carmody & Williams was doing well. The horses they boarded were walked, rubbed down, and fed. The stables were mucked and kept clean. Their prices were fair and until recently they had done business with both whites and blacks. Now, except for some occasional business from the military, their business was becoming more and more focused on the blacks and coloreds around Baton Rouge. It was a good thing several black businesses had opened or their business would be very slow. On the other side of town a new stable and blacksmith had opened, Diedenbach's, with a sign, "Whites Only", prominently displayed.

Sven Diedenbach was a huge Swede with arms the size of anvils. He was blond, towering well over six feet. His wife, Hilda, was a tiny German woman, and jokes about what gymnastics they might share, caused snickers among the men. Sven didn't mind. His five children, all under eight years old, gave testimony to the success of their gymnastic fertility. He was an unlikely candidate to participate in the brewing racial battles but he had fought for the Confederacy.

The white plantation owners that had joined the Knights of the White Camellia provided the capital. They befriended Sven. One of the group's early operating principals was to avoid black businesses wherever possible… even drive them out. There just wasn't enough business for two stables so close to one another.

And both businesses had to operate by extending large amounts of credit to their customers. There was little actual money around and everyone ended up stretching their debts like a tight rubber band. Every business waited for the cotton crop to be harvested and sold. That's when debts would be settled, not before. The only customers with money were either the soldiers or those who worked for the government.

Sven had a large family to feed and finding food and shelter for them was as tenuous for him as it was for most of the other hundreds of thousands of ex-Confederate soldiers. He was willing to accept any offer that wouldn't be a sin in God's eyes. If he had to trumpet white superiority, it was a small thing. Blacks were certainly lazier and dumber than whites anyway. He'd seen that during the war. He knew the coloreds across town ran a nice business and he didn't wish them bad, at least as long as he could keep his family warm and well-fed.

# Chapter Twenty

New Orleans had, indeed, changed. There were blue uniforms everywhere. Blacks and coloreds walked with a new, more confident gait. Many even dressed like white folks. They didn't avert their eyes, or drop their heads when they passed a white. They didn't cross to the other side of the street. And some of them, grown men, could gaze at a white woman with a look that would have brought instant lynching just a few years earlier.

Henry noticed these changes as he rode into the city. This new insolence riled him and brought back memories of the arm that no longer hung from his shoulder. He would have liked nothing better than to dismount and horsewhip one or two of this new colored trash. He knew he couldn't but it didn't stop the seething he felt. He had come to the city to get away from Elizabeth and he needed to see Moresby, the banker. He knew it was important to keep that relationship cordial even though he detested the slovenly, obese man who continued to profess so much friendship for Henry's father. The insincerity just dripped.

Abner Moresby greeted him with the same 'bon ami' as the last occasion and they shared coffee together in an obsequious, but leisurely, manner. Moresby had a habit of speaking in a didactic way, as if teaching basic business principles to an inferior. Henry just gritted his teeth and smiled.

"Cotton prices had dipped a little on the world market. But production was beginning to increase after the disastrous final years of the war. The large plantations were producing more cotton per acre using new double row planters that had come on the market and larger, more efficient cotton gins were yielding a cleaner product. Share-cropping was forging new relationships between plantation owners and field hands and despite frequent, and violent differences, it was being made to work. The south would survive." He seemed to speak without taking a single breath.

The banker explained to Henry that as long as the interest on the loan was kept current, the bank would be patient and wait until the crop was harvested and sold. Henry assured him that Moss Grove was functioning in this new economy. He had signed share cropping agreements with more than twenty families. It was different than the way he'd been raised…a lot more complicated. He detested the righteous attitude of most of these niggers but Moss Grove, too, would survive.

"You're one of the lucky ones, Henry. Foreclosures everywhere! And instead of us getting the property, the Union military takes it, breaks it into smaller parcels and doles it out to the blacks. How many black families you have as new neighbors, Henry?" Moresby asked.

"More than I like. We keep our distance from one another. I heard about the riot at the Mechanic's Hall. Quite a ruckus!"

"It won't be the last! Angry ex-Rebs joining groups! Blacks joining groups! Union Army already has its groups. It seems like everyone is picking sides and tempers are boiling over. Too many folks still fighting the war! They don't like the way Louisiana is heading. Blacks voting! Some even got elected and are up in Baton Rouge running the state government," his voice rising in righteous indignation.

"It's hard to blame the whites whose families built this state. They didn't come to Louisiana for this sort of thing. Louisiana voted overwhelmingly for Seymour no matter how many blacks the Republicans managed to register and vote. The intelligent white males came out to vote. Yes, they did. Seymour's call for this to stay a white man's country resonated. But I'm not optimistic, no I'm not. This racial divisiveness will not be resolved easily."

"Well, Miss Melanie, it is indeed lovely to see you again. It has been way too long," Henry cooed with an obvious sexual connotation.

Now that he was finished with Moresby, it was time to enjoy a few days relaxation from business. He was eager to visit old friends like Philip Lunstrum and others from Knoxville. Several of these men had died in the war but Philip had returned unscathed.

"I heard what happened, Henry", Philip said over lunch. "Actually, you were pretty lucky. A lot of the men we knew never made it back at all.

Fitz and Kennedy both fought against Sherman all the way to Atlanta but they finally each took a bullet.

"And remember that pimpled kid, Malcolm? You cracked his nose over that card game."

"Sure! Got his horse after he accused me of cheating."

"You were cheating," Lunstrum laughed.

Henry just smiled.

"Anyway, he must have gotten another horse…rode with Jeb Stuart all the way to Gettysburg."

"But you survived."

"Lucky! Personal aide to Jefferson Davis! Good man, I guess, but surrounded by a lot of assholes."

"And now?"

"I'm part of the new South. Aren't we all welcoming our black brothers?" Philip said in a caustic, icy tone.

"Not in my lifetime," Henry sneered as he waved to the waiter for another drink.

"Nor me."

After they said their goodbyes he walked over to the same Gentlemen's Club he'd met Melanie at on his last visit. Melanie wasn't at the Club when he'd arrived and he waited, getting impatient and now on his third brandy. He saw her as she entered, greeting the staff with laughter and a smile. He knew a similar smile would be his when she realized he was waiting for her and he felt himself get an immediate erection. Physical needs that had been unsatisfied for so many months, surfaced.

"Henry," she gasped. Seeing him after so many months and knowing so much of what had transpired in his life, made her stammer uncharacteristically. She had developed such a keen sense of how to control her demeanor. She never lost it in front of her clients. At least not until now!

"Henry," she repeated. "You look well. It's been quite a long time since you visited."

"Life has been challenging," he said, unwilling to spoil the moment with details. "Will you join me for a drink…and the evening?" he added.

The idea was revolting. Her friendship with Amy, Thaddeus, and the rest made any thought of spending time with this man abhorrent to her but he could never know that. She had her image and status to maintain.

"I'd love to, Henry. I really would but I have an appointment elsewhere this evening. I'm sure I can find someone perfect for you. A number of our girls would be thrilled to be with you."

"I'd prefer that you change your plans, Melanie. I recall that you and I shared something special."

"Yes, and I'd like that too, but it just isn't possible with such short notice. Perhaps another time when I know you're going to be in town," she scrambled to make her lies seem credible.

"Melanie, I'm not used to be rejected. It just isn't in my nature," he said as his voice acquired a more strident tone and his eyes tore into her.

"I am not rejecting you. You are a gentleman. I know that. A gentleman occasionally has to acquiesce to a lady's request. I'm asking you to understand that I'm just not available for your warm and gallant company this evening," she continued to smile but a nervous tremor that couldn't be hidden, brought her voice up a pitch.

"If you won't drink with me or entertain me, I will take that as a rejection and since this is a business arrangement, as well as a pleasurable pastime, I am doubly upset. And I assure you, upsetting me is definitely not a good thing to do. I will pay you twice your normal fee for the evening. That should persuade you. Now sit down, have a brandy, and talk to me," he demanded as he sat and slapped the pillow next to him as an encouragement for her to join him.

She stared down at him. He had obviously had too much to drink and was becoming quite testy. Leaving or staying wasn't an easy decision. Staying and earning money was what she did. Some of the men she had to spend time with were terrible people. Some were evil! Some smelled bad! Some played rough! Henry wasn't the worst but she detested him for everything she'd learned about him. She wouldn't be able to face her new friends if they learned what she'd done.

"Goodbye, Henry," she said, pushing her shoulders back as she continued to meet his gaze. "I will ask them to find you someone particularly amiable for you this evening." She turned and hurried off. She knew his eyes watched her exit.

"Melanie," he said to himself. "You cunt", he seethed. "You colored bitch! You will regret tonight's decision."

A few weeks after Henry returned to Moss Grove he had a visitor. Colonel Alcibiades DeBlanc stepped off his buggy as Henry stood at the front entrance, Whisper stood at his side, emitting low guttural sounds that made the approaching stranger reluctant to move forward. DeBlanc no longer wore his gray uniform adorned with gold braid stretched through the epaulets. Now he was attired in a fashionable gray suit and a wide brimmed felt hat.

"Explain to your dog that I come as a friend. My name is DeBlanc. I've ridden up here to meet with you, Mister Rogers, as well as some of the other large plantation owners. I believe I've come on a mission of supreme importance to us all."

"Come in, Mr. DeBlanc. Whisper, down! The parlor is cool this time of the day," Henry said. He had heard about DeBlanc from Abner Moresby. They had discussed the emergence of these 'white only' groups and whether they were worth the trouble they were causing.

After they were brought drinks, Henry closed the doors to the parlor to ensure their privacy.

"I represent the Knights of the White Camellia," DeBlanc began.

"I know who you are. A friend explained your organization and its goals. I'm in sympathy with you and your people but your fight is in New Orleans and Baton Rouge. I and the other plantation owners that didn't lose our land are busy just surviving. It hasn't been easy."

"I should say. Niggers don't want to work and everything the white man did to develop this land from swamps has been trivialized. We brought industry and God. Without our ancestors there'd be nothing here but swamps and 'gators."

He spoke with the eloquence of a man of the cloth. His words and tone had a reverence to them. Henry began to understand why lesser men would be willing to commit violence in support of what the man was preaching.

"My grandfather," Henry nodded in agreement, "Samuel Rogers carried the Cyprus timbers from the swamps to use for the foundation to Moss Grove. He plowed the first furrows. By the time he, and then my father, died, we were employing nearly four hundred people. Now if there are one hundred fifty working the land and tending the house, we're lucky. At least we're still here. My cotton production is down by more than half."

"Then join us. Make our struggle your struggle. All we want is to return our great state of Louisiana to the white man."

"And how would you propose I do that?"

"You have influence. Invite your neighbors here. We have power in numbers. We can bring these niggers down. We're doing it elsewhere.

"I'm not sure I want violence in this parish. I could lose the sharecroppers I worked so hard to find. They aren't the best workers but they are a sight better than having my fields lie fallow. I will, however, agree to host a meeting for you to talk to the other plantation owners. If you can convince them, I'll consider joining your crusade."

One month later DeBlanc returned with five serious looking strangers and a sixth man, Philip Lunstrum. The old college roommates smiled broadly as they shook hands and laughed. Nearly two dozen men from nearby plantations joined them. Henry tried to get Elizabeth cleaned up so he could introduce her. He would have liked to be able to present a proper wife but it was no use. She staggered around the house; her eyes glazed over, and remained in her upstairs sitting room.

Josiah played in the corner while the men gathered. He shouldn't have been there but Henry wanted to show off some member of his family. A wife would have been better. A son would have to do. Once again the doors were closed and the house servants were sent to work in the far corners of the house.

"Gentlemen, let us begin," Colonel DeBlanc began. "Thank you for coming and my special gratitude to Henry Rogers for hosting this meeting. It is a pleasure to be in a room with the type of men who built this country and who, so recently, fought to defend its ideals.

"It is better that we not know one another's names so I won't ask you yours nor will I introduce the men who have joined me. If you have any questions to ask or information to impart, please contact Henry Rogers and he will contact me. What we are proposing to do is outside the law but these are not laws that we white men enacted and we will not abide by them. Suffice to say I believe you all share my concerns about Louisiana and the white man's place in it.

"We are not the only white group being formed in the south but we are different from the Klan. They just want to kill and destroy. Most of the men putting those white sheets on are poor ignorant whites not wanting to compete with blacks. We support them but they are men who would have worked for us performing menial tasks."

The men raised their glasses in support. There was no disagreement here. Henry was swayed by the unanimity of purpose among these men who felt a strong need to remedy the privileged life they'd lost.

"We prefer to harass and torment, get the blacks back fearing their white masters and understanding their proper place in a white society. In other words, the way it was before the war. Once they give up some of these new dangerous ideas the carpetbaggers are selling them, we can make them good workers again.

"Our goals are to disrupt and destroy black businesses and those who frequent them. Fire, lynching and general mayhem are all acceptable tactics. White Camellia groups elsewhere in Louisiana and other states will be undertaking similar tasks.

"We will encourage them," he declared, "For they do our work, the Lord's work. Let us pray for divine support before we return to our homes."

"Melanie and I are getting married," Rufus said, as Rose, Sarah, and Thaddeus sat around the table. There was complete silence that seemed to last forever but it was only a few seconds before they each understood what they'd been told.

"Aren't you happy for me?" he asked, just as everybody burst into joy and laughter and hugs.

"Of course we're happy for you," Rose said.

"We're not sure we're too happy for Melanie though," Thaddeus laughed. "Obviously I need to explain some of your less known traits to her."

"You leave it be, boy," Rufus smiled, knowing that Thaddeus, especially, would be happy for him. "My charm swayed her and when I sways someone, they stayed swayed."

"Well, we think it's just grand," Sarah added. "We need to plan a nice wedding. Have you and Melanie given any thought to how soon you want to have the wedding?"

"Now that's a small problem," Rufus confessed. "I haven't actually asked her yet."

"And you're telling us, why?" Thaddeus asked.

"To get your help! I do love that lady and I think she's fond of me. But she is so classy and I'm just your marginally educated but terribly good lookin' colored fellow."

"And modest," Matthew added. "Let's not forget modest."

They had welded into a family. Events at Moss Grove had given them a shared experience. The war and the peace had linked them together. The business kept them connected but it was mutual affection that sealed their friendships.

They all assured Rufus that if Melanie had the good sense they were sure she had, she would accept his proposal enthusiastically.

Charlie drove his wagon filled with supplies back toward their farm. He had taken a break from his classes at the Freedman's school but the two books he would need to study sat on the seat next to him. He promised to practice his reading and numbers every evening. He was getting pretty good at it.

He'd relaxed at Carmody & Williams while his order was filled. He enjoyed spending time there. Rufus had confided to him his feelings for Melanie. All the Chartiers agreed the man would be a wonderful husband for Melanie. It was good to be able to buy the things you needed from people you liked without wondering whether they'd given you fair measure.

He should have gotten started earlier so he could arrive at the farm before dark but he and Rufus had started arm wrestling. Charlie won one of the matches. He might limp a little but he wouldn't concede arm strength to anyone.

About two miles from the farm as the last light of the day failed and the early evening stars appeared, Charlie found himself confronted by five white riders. They blocked his path. He could feel their hostility, even in the dim light. Two of the men wore remnants of old gray uniforms. A third man wore a wool Reb cap. They weren't very old but he knew instinctively they were set on violence.

"What you doin' on this road at night, nigger?" one asked.

"Jes goin home."

"You got a home near here?" another asked.

Charlie grew afraid to answer. He knew that their farm was off the beaten path and whatever was going to happen he didn't want it carried to his brothers. He sat silently.

"Nigger lost his tongue."

"Bet if I looked I could find it, maybe even cut it out for a souvenir."

"Look, I ain't hurtin' anyone. Jus' let me pass," he said, unmistakable nervousness in his voice.

"Get down. Get down quick. Let's see what you got in that wagon," one man ordered as he drew his horse closer. Now Charlie could see parts of three stripes on one part of the uniform that hadn't been torn. If these men had anyone in charge, it was probably this man.

He had to make a quick decision. If he got down he was sure they'd not only steal his wagon but kill him. If he ran, they might catch him. If he could surprise them and get closer to the farm, his brothers might be able to help without revealing where their farm was situated.

He pretended to get down and suddenly yanked on the reins and gave a scream. The horses leapt forward. The men scattered, one thrown from his horse, his leg caught in the stirrup and dragged off. One of the men went to help him while the other three gathered themselves and headed off to chase the wagon.

Charlie could feel the men close behind. He wasn't sure how well the men knew these back roads, definitely not as well as he did. There was a stream off to the left. He began shouting; even screaming, hoping his brothers would hear him although he knew he was still pretty far off.

The chase only lasted a few minutes when one, then a second pistol blast went off. It missed him but the bullet continued into the back haunch of his horse. The animal's rear legs collapsed and the wagon careened to a stop. Charlie just sat there as the three remaining riders rode up brandishing their guns. One of the men dismounted and pulled Charlie from the wagon, cuffing him with a blow that sent him to the ground. As Charlie writhed on the ground the others dismounted as well.

"Dumb fuckin' nigger. We mighta' let you live if you'd been respectful. Now you're just gonna be hog-feed."

They tied him facing a tree and ripped his shirt. Charlie recognized the whip they pulled out. He'd had to watch runaways being whipped. He wouldn't scream. They could kill him but he wouldn't scream.

The pain seared across his back as each stroke tattooed criss-cross lines across his back. He bit his lips to enforce his self-imposed oath of silence. Two of the men soon lost interest in the whipping and moved to the wagon.

"Let 'em go," one man offered. "Good lesson for other niggers."

"Dead'll give them a better message," the man holding the whip insisted and swung the leather strap again at the now comatose form.

A gunshot wrung out and the whip flew out of his hand as the man grabbed his shoulder. "I'm hit," he screamed.

Without another word, the men raced off taking the wagon with them. Able and Benny came through the thicket. Benny tried to reload to get off another shot while Able dropped his gun and raced to the tree.

Charlie was unconscious, his breathing shallow. As gently as possible they carried him to their small cottage. Marie screamed as she saw the blood covering her youngest son.

They laid him on the bed, cleaned the blood from his back and applied salve with as light a touch as they could. His back was shredded. The leather weapon with the tiny knotted ends had found their mark. In the earliest morning light they'd send Benny to get Mama Rose. She might have herbs that would speed the healing but by morning it was no longer necessary. Just before dawn Charlie stopped breathing. He'd awakened for a moment to see his brothers and mother.

"I never screamed." They were his last words.

# Chapter Twenty-One

"I love you, Rufus, but I can't marry you. Not now," Melanie said softly as she and Rufus held one another's hand. He nodded. The timing couldn't have been more wrong. He knew they'd wed eventually and that would have to satisfy him.

They were at the farm. Charlie had been buried that afternoon. Anger and sorrow hung heavily over the small family and few friends that huddled around the grave. The minister's words rang hollow. He hadn't known Charlie. He never knew the teenage boy's good nature and his easy laughter. A remote and uncaring God had taken gentle Charlie from them. Without cause, without sense, he had been whipped worse than an animal. Even as free men they were being treated as slaves.

"We cannot change yesterday, we can only hope for a better tomorrow," the minister said. "The war has changed 'yesterday' and given us hope. The better 'tomorrow' we hope is ours may be an unlikely dream that will take longer to achieve. We will not allow them to snatch it away so easily."

"I'm so sorry for your loss, Mrs. Chartier," Captain Fineman said. He and his adjutant had come to pay their respects. "I have a squad of men searching the surrounding area. I'm sure the men that did this come from around here."

"It's gracious of you and your men to come, Captain," Marie responded. She was dressed in black. The Chartier family didn't have a great deal, but Charlie would be sent to the hereafter with respect. Mirrors were covered and food was laid out for the guests.

"Captain Fineman," Thaddeus asked, "How worried do our friends living here have to be? What should they be doing?"

"There are hundreds of unemployed ex-Confederate soldiers wandering the countryside. Many of them are ex-slave owners. They might have owned one or two on a small spread before the war. For them, that's all gone. In some places they've formed groups, raiding countrysides, burning farms, raising hell. But, we're also catching them. My men are good. Sometimes finding them is just luck but most of the time we can track them. These dirt roads leave hoof marks that can be followed."

Less than a week later the five men involved in Charlie's death were ridden into Baton Rouge surrounded by two squads of Union soldiers. It was a cool fall day. The town was crowded, some with government business, some hoping to find work, others just watching their children play in a nearby park. As they rode slowly toward the military arsenal and jail crowds began to gather and follow them. At first there was silence. Then there were murmurs.

"It was a good killin'", someone shouted.

"It was murder. String these killers up!" came another.

A rock was thrown at the troops but two blacks standing nearby saw who threw it and wrestled him into the ground. More troops arrived and broke up the scuffle. The prisoners were quickly herded into the jail, but the crowd, larger, but now more orderly, just waited.

An officer exited the jail and faced the crowd.

"The men who have been jailed are being accused of the murder of Charles Chartier, a Negro citizen of the State of Louisiana. They will be put on trial and they will have an opportunity to defend themselves. Until that happens and the law has taken its course, I suggest you all return to your homes or get on with your business."

With that brief statement he turned and reentered the building.

"They ain't gonna' get a fair trial if there's blacks on that jury," one man shouted.

"And they'll go free and get a parade if there aren't any blacks on the jury," a black on the other side of the crowd hollered.

Amy divided her time between teaching at the Freedman's school and helping Rose and Sarah in the Clinic. Even Ruth Fineman, Captain Fineman's wife, worked and spent time there. Her children, Rachel and Stuart, were each a year older than when they'd arrived in Baton Rouge and they felt quite at home among the mostly black and colored children who came and went. It made sense since it was their school as well. It was certainly a better school than what the military could provide. There just weren't enough military wives and families in Baton Rouge to justify them having their own schoolhouse.

As more and more black legislators were elected to state-wide office, a small, professional, black society began to evolve. These parents wanted their children educated and they wanted their family's health watched over. The city's humidity made the possibility of yellow fever, tuberculosis and other serious diseases an ever-present hazard and the children were easily susceptible.

Black, colored, and white members attending the White & Tan Convention descended on the Baton Rouge capitol building to write a new Constitution. Blue-coated Union soldiers could be seen everywhere and the Carmody & Williams stables were filled. Rufus recommended to some of the recent arrivals that they stable their horses with Sven Diedenbach. He even offered to walk the horses there himself. The huge Swede was tentative at first but he was grateful for the business. They shook hands as Rufus left and looked one another in the eye. What Sven saw was not the type of colored man he was supposed to hate.

Matthew had traveled from New Orleans for the upcoming convention but since it wasn't scheduled to begin for another day he visited Thaddeus at the Freedman's school.

A few months earlier Matthew had gotten a job as an assistant to Oscar Dunn, a New Orleans attorney and one of the state's leading colored delegates.

"Imagine," Matthew said, sharing a late afternoon drink with Thaddeus, sitting in his classroom, "Integrated schools…blacks holding political office, and civil rights for everyone. Mr. Dunn says we are clearly in the eye of the tornado with opportunities unimagined just a decade ago."

"It sounds as if you admire this Mr. Dunn," Thaddeus noted. He was cleaning off the chalkboard as Amy entered.

"Nice reunion," she smiled, gave Thaddeus a light kiss on the lips and turned to give Matthew a hug. "You are looking mighty fine…what do I call you now?"

"I am now officially Matthew Carmody. I needed a last name. I knew I didn't want to be a 'Rogers' so I asked Rufus if I could use his name and he loved the idea. So let me introduce myself to you both.…Matthew Carmody, at your pleasure. Mr. Dunn helped me change it legally." He gave a small bow as Thaddeus and Amy punctuated his courteous movement with laughter and applause.

"Matthew was telling us about Oscar Dunn, his employer AND politically important delegate. Our boy seems to be much taken with him," Thaddeus teased with a broad smile.

"He started life as a slave, just like me," Matthew continued, ignoring his brother's obvious sarcasm. "Ran away one time when he was sold and joined the Union Army. He became a Captain really quick! He told me that right after the war when they promoted an incompetent white man to be major over him; he resigned from the Army and set about making some money. Seems he was good at that also. Now he's here at the Convention to make sure all this equality is legal and written into the Constitution. Yes, he's quite a man!" Matthew avowed. "But enough of this! Let's have dinner. I want to hear about your school and your clinic. I hear good things about it all the way down in New Orleans."

Several very pleasant restaurants had opened on the side streets near the capitol. They were certainly not the caliber of New Orleans but for people who grew up on the slop from slave kitchens, it was a gastronomic odyssey. And what could be better than enjoying an evening dining with friends. Most of these restaurants made no distinction as to color, although some diners were very uncomfortable seeing an attractive young white girl with lustrous red hair dining with two equally young and handsome men, one colored and one black. Bile could well rise in the throats of those whites who cringed at the mental image of white women being debauched by dark skinned men. The entire city was a rainbow of humanity. Since blacks and coloreds were able to hold elective office, trying to operate a 'white only' establishment would have been financial folly.

The three friends were clearly enjoying themselves. Thaddeus understood, better than his companions, that their presence was making some of the other patrons uncomfortable but he kept this to himself, not wanting to dampen Amy or Matthew's evening.

The tables surrounding them were filled with notable scalawags, Union officers, and an array of government officials. At a table adjacent to theirs sat Monroe Baker, just elected Mayor of St. Martin, a parish just south of Baton Rouge. This middle age businessman was the first black ever elected to run an American city. But with all that, Thaddeus and Matthew were focused on Amy and what a beauty she'd become.

Diners two tables away included Alcibiades DeBlanc and some of his friends. Every delay in serving them, every dish not to their satisfaction, and every waiter smiling at Amy or her escorts infuriated them. Finally, they could bear it no further. They stood as one, their chairs tumbling backwards as they threw down their napkins in obvious disgust.

DeBlanc loudly announced to the entire restaurant, "We will not frequent any restaurant that allows whites and blacks to dine at the same table. It is an affront to God. I urge all of you who think of themselves as good Christians to join us in leaving this heathen establishment."

Patrons at two other tables stood and exited as well. The rest, both white and black, shouted, "Good riddance," and continued their meal.

Matthew left his brother and Amy as they approached the school after walking the short distance from the restaurant.

"I'm off to my hotel room. I love it when the three of us are together. You two stay out of trouble," he said, looking at them with knowing eyes.

Amy and Thaddeus watched him leave and grabbed one another's hands in the dark.

"Let's not go up yet," Thaddeus said. Amy nodded as the two walked toward the children's play area. Swings stood quiet as they found a bench and sat.

Neither of them moved for two eternities. The moon hung in the sky, the planet Venus obediently close by.

They turned toward one another and kissed. The kiss lingered until a noise in the distance broke them apart. Amy's eyes glistened with the dampness of tears as Thaddeus brushed a red hair back from her face.

"I love you, you know," he said.

"I know," she said in a voice so soft that only the quiet air stirred with emotion.

They moved to a dark area of the playground. Thaddeus took off his jacket and spread it on the dirt. Together they lay down and embraced.

"This is so dangerous," he warned. "But you are the woman I have always loved and I need us to be as one."

"If I were to die tomorrow, my life would have been a waste unless we can connect our love. I am willing to live with the risk of what could follow."

As quietly as they could, the stars overhead their only witness, they expressed their love and murmured… 'one day, some day.'

*That year more cotton was produced and harvested than in any year since the war ended. To the great relief of plantation owners, share croppers, bankers and the rest of the small stores that had extended credit, a financial catastrophe had been averted. The price had stabilized.*

*This conversion of cotton to currency didn't bring parades and celebrations so much as it brought an easing of the financial tension that had pervaded the temperament of whites and blacks alike.*

*Share croppers received their shares as well but after paying ten percent to the land owner for the land and paying the commissary for the extra food and necessities they'd consumed they had considerably less than they'd planned for. Still, they had survived another year, and it was better than slavery.*

Some of the sharecroppers pooled their small stake and took advantage of the eighty acre grants of Federal land that were being offered. If share cropping was better than slavery, owning one's own small plot was better still.

Henry looked around Moss Grove. He'd paid off Abner Moresby, sent some money to replenish his secret northern bank accounts and hired a full-time tutor for Josiah. But he'd also lost three share cropper families who had just disappeared one day after his overseer had settled with them. This same 'vanishing act' occurred on several nearby plantations. His closest neighbor also found several important pieces of planting tools missing with them.

Elizabeth had slowly shaken her drug induced lethargy. She had lost weight and began to look more matronly. She familiarized herself with the kitchen and her obligations. She was even able to develop a small social life with the women from the other plantations, and most important, she and Josiah had developed a closer emotional bond.

They had a few months before next year's planting would take place but there was a lot to do before then and too few workers to do them. Cabins needed to be repaired, fall vegetables needed to be harvested and stored, pigs needed to be slaughtered and the land needed to be cleared from corn and sugar debris before any winter frost set in.

Thatcher, 'Big George', as everyone called him, had done a good job as overseer. Even Henry respected the job this strong, stocky black man had accomplished. He had arms with the girth of a small oak tree and in strength he reminded Henry of Faris. Some of these blacks, Henry thought, had to have sprung from a race unlike any he'd ever seen.

'Big George' was planning to leave. He had taken one of the field girls as a wife and their baby would be born in a few months. He thought they'd head toward Oklahoma and get himself some of the free land they were offering.

"Stay another year, George," Henry asked. "You did well, real well. Now you've got a child coming. You and your young wife don't want a newborn in a wagon during the winter, traveling to unfamiliar places and trying to find a place to settle. Another year, you'll have more money saved, the baby will be healthier. What do you say?"

"Massa' Henry, I'm jus' not sure. Let me talk to my woman, Bessie. She was kinda' set on goin'."

"Big George, don't forget, you're the man and you've got to make the decisions for your family. Women are too soft, too emotional, to make these important choices. You stay; I'll throw in an extra one percent bonus. That'll certainly increase your nest egg."

"That's kind of you, Massa' Henry," George sighed, scratched his head, and smiled. He didn't like the man but he did respect the fact that this boss functioned with one arm as well as most men with two and he did get a smile out of seeing he and his son together.

"I'll do it then. I'll stay one more year. I'll tell Bessie. It'll be better for the baby."

That decided, the next thing Big George had to do was replace the lost share croppers. He climbed on his horse, a sizeable mare, but dwarfed by George's size, and headed north. He and Henry had figured there might be more unsettled workers closer to Natchez where a lot of the river boats unloaded their sugar and cotton for the trains heading into the north. Now that the cotton crop was harvested the bales were on the move both toward Natchez and south to New Orleans. The world was waiting.

The Louisiana state constitutional convention did its work efficiently, albeit without the support of a large portion of Louisiana's white population. The new white governor was a young man who had arrived in New Orleans several years earlier as a Civil war veteran and organized the state's Grand Army of the Republic as a wing of the Republican Party. He recruited nearly five thousand whites and freed blacks. Henry Clay Warmoth's politically astute efforts had now earned him the state's highest office.

Matthew's mentor, Oscar J. Dunn, was elected Lt. Governor, and became the highest elected black official in the country. Dunn had a talent for elaborate oration, hewn listening to actors reciting their lines in his mother's boarding house. To a booming voice he'd added an elaborate mustache and put on the weight that marked successful men of the day.

"I've come to meet with the Governor for a few days and if you have a clean stall, I'd like to board my horse with you." Rufus stood there, his mouth agape. There was no mistaking the speaker. It was General James Longstreet, long beard and receding hair line. This was Robert E. Lee's "War Horse" and military right-arm. From Bull Run to Antietam to Gettysburg his military prowess was a thing of legend.

Longstreet had been personally pardoned by President Grant, his old adversary. With no more battles to fight or troops to lead, he had retired to run a successful cotton brokerage business in New Orleans. His conversion from rebellious military leader to temperate speaking Republican was clouded in controversy. The Picayune paper had published a portion of one of Longstreet's speeches urging those who remembered him to 'save what little is left of the south.' Since Blacks now had the vote, he had urged, southerners 'should exercise such influence over that vote, as to prevent its being injurious.'

"Yes, General! Yes sir!" Rufus said firmly, bringing himself to an erect military posture.

"At ease, mister..." Longstreet paused, inwardly pleased at the recognition.

"Carmody, sir. Formerly Sgt. Carmody, first of the Native Guards and after Vicksburg, attached to General Sheridan."

"It's all in the past, <u>Mister</u> Carmody," he said, emphasizing the title. "All our military exploits are in the past, thank heaven. I'm sure you tired, as I did, of seeing so many of our fellows dead or broken. I'm in Baton Rouge as a private citizen trying to add a small voice of reason that might allow us to move forward without violence."

"Well, leave your horse in confidence, General, eh, Mister Longstreet. He'll be well cared for and rested when you are finished with your business," Rufus said with a smile, taking the reins from his customer. Rufus watched as the general walked off, a small bag in his hand, his shoulders a little bent from age and weariness.

# Chapter Twenty-Two

Thaddeus found himself adrift from his friends and family. Matthew was working with Oscar Dunn preparing for the upcoming Convention. Rufus was running the feed business and waiting impatiently for Melanie to get over the melancholy of her brother's violent death. The Freedman's school and the adjoining medical clinic were both functioning well. But he was finding it more and more difficult to see Amy every day and not be able to act on his feelings.

He'd look for excuses to visit the clinic. He wanted to see Sarah or Mama Rose. He needed to reorder supplies. Amy looked for the same pretenses to seek out Thaddeus. Each time she arrived she'd get to her task by whatever hallway took her past her friend. It was impossible for either of them to think of the other as just a friend any longer when their entire being ached. They both struggled. They conveyed their love in touches and in their eyes but each of them knew what danger they would bring to the other if they continued to act on these feelings.

"One day," he'd mouth silently to her.

"Someday," she'd respond.

The quality of Thaddeus' teaching began to suffer and, while he struggled to maintain his enthusiasm, he became curt and testy. Ruth Fineman was one of the first to notice and discussed it with her husband.

"Thaddeus, let's get out of here for a few hours," Captain Fineman suggested. The local Union officer had found an excuse to visit the school at his wife's request as he brought a wagon filled with used desks. He and Ruth had grown fond of Thaddeus and his extended family. It was a pleasant fall morning and he had found Thaddeus in his tiny work area shuffling papers in an absent-minded way.

"Any reason?" Thaddeus asked, curious at the sudden offer. "I don't have any classes but I do have work to do."

"No reason! I want to check up on some farms to the west and I'm tired of military guards. They can stay and unload the furniture we've brought. I thought you might enjoy getting away for a few hours as well."

"Sure," he answered, standing and setting his papers aside. "I can use the diversion."

The two men rode side by side, speaking very little, until they stopped and dismounted. They stretched their legs and walked slowly over the carpet of leaves beneath their feet as their horses drank from a small nearby stream.

"Ruth tells me you seem upset lately," the Union officer finally confessed.

"Is that what this is all about?" Thaddeus laughed. "My seeming to be upset?"

"Kind of! You know women. They sense when something or someone seems off kilter."

"Off-kilter," he smiled. "I imagine that's as good a way to phrase it as anything. Well, she's right. I've tried to keep my feelings to myself but it isn't working too well. I may have to leave the school for awhile."

Thaddeus described his feelings for Amy and how many years he'd been in love with her, from that first episode on the bank of the river. Eli just listened. Eventually they both sat. Eli lit up a small cheroot, a habit he'd acquired since coming to Louisiana. The smoke drifted through the air.

"Funny, isn't it?" Thaddeus finally asked. "We coloreds may now be equal but we are still different."

"That's our society, I'm afraid," Eli Fineman admitted.

"It isn't very different being Jewish in a world of mostly Christians. Your skin color separates you, our culture separates us. Most people don't like 'different', either way."

"That's right! You're a Jew. I never met a Jew until you. At Moss Grove we heard all sort of stories, you're God's chosen people, you won't eat certain foods and, strangest of all, you cut off the tip of a baby boy's penis. Weird things!"

"The little caps we wear are called 'yarmulkes'. We wear them as a token of respect to our God. We do have dietary laws and we do remove the foreskin of the penis when the baby is born. It's called circumcision and it's done for sanitary reasons. Sorry to disappoint you. I could tell you a few more stories that aren't true either. People tell such falsehoods about

Jews, Blacks, Italians…makes no difference. They just don't know, so they make things up."

"So, what do I do about me and Amy?" Thaddeus asked sadly, already knowing there was no magic answer.

"I'd like to tell you I have some special insight. True love will triumph and all that but I don't think it's true, at least not in Louisiana, at least not in this century. At best you would both be ostracized, at worst you would both be killed. Either way you can never be together safely. I'm sorry."

"I know," Thaddeus acknowledged. "But it isn't easy to deny something that has always felt so right."

"No, it isn't," Eli said sadly. They sat there silently, each in their own thoughts, the only sound, the lapping of the water from the breeze and the rustling of the tree branches overhead.

"Why not put some distance between yourselves for awhile and see if it makes matters a little less complicated?" Fineman suggested.

"I'm sure Major Shipley can take advantage of your skills. He's my superior officer down in New Orleans. You're bright. Those energies and talents are in short supply and we need to find more black people to educate and equip them to be able to function for themselves and prepare the next generation. You and I both fought a war for that cause and a lot of men died. Even Ol' Abe lost his life to stop men from owning other men."

Thaddeus' goodbyes were as brief as he could make them. He wouldn't be gone long, he explained to Rose, Amy, and Rufus. No one believed the reasons, especially Rose, who instinctively understood his son's love for this smiling red haired white girl. But she understood it was the best thing, the only reasonable decision, for them both.

Amy followed him out toward the main road, unwilling to just say a simple goodbye.

"It's because of us," she asked, "Isn't it?"

"It's for the best. We're both happy being close to one another and terribly miserable not being able to be closer and share the pleasures that most couples do. That night we had was so wonderful but it made things even more complicated. I want to be with you like that forever and knowing I can't, makes my life a complete hell."

"Your leaving won't make me love you less," she said, tears cascading down her cheeks.

"I know, but for now we both need to try," he said sadly as a single tear lodged in the corner of his eye.

"I see you next to me every night as I climb into bed," she said, barely above a whisper.

"Amy, I've loved you since that first morning. You and your freckles! Who can't love those freckles?" he teased.

"I expect you to remember them while you're gone."

"Amy," he said, as he stopped walking. He dropped the reins and grabbed her hands.

"We both need to move on. You need to find some handsome successful young white guy who can love you without risk. It can't be me."

"It has to be you," she sobbed openly. "It has to be you. I don't want anyone else. Remember our pledge... 'some day'!"

"'One day'," he acknowledged without conviction this time, a hollowness in the pit of his stomach.

"Amy, please. This is so hard. In our hearts we'll always have one another."

"Thaddeus," she pleaded. "We could go to California, or Mexico, or even Europe."

"We can't. Don't think I haven't dreamt of the same thing. I'm going to New Orleans and I'm going to try and forge a new life with people my own color. It will never change how I feel."

Thaddeus kissed her, freezing on the face he never wanted to forget. He mounted his horse, kicked its flanks, and didn't turn back.


"I want you to take me to New Orleans," Elizabeth said firmly. "I am sick and tired of this plantation. I want to dine at a fine restaurant and shop and listen to good music. Please, Henry. I need it, you need it, and we definitely need it."

Their relationship had matured. It hadn't aged like a good wine but it had avoided becoming vinegar. They shared Josiah and the responsibilities of Moss Grove. Neither spoke again of the birth and loss of their daughter, Clara, nor did Elizabeth ever dare to raise the issue of what had caused it. The cotton harvest had allowed them to avoid financial ruin.

Perhaps it would be pleasant, he thought. His mind turned to Melanie. At one time those thoughts of a trip to New Orleans might engender an immediate erection but no more. He would never forgive her rejection.

A week later they set out in the large carriage with a driver. Elizabeth had spent most of that time selecting what to take with her. She hadn't shopped in so long; she knew that even her best frocks were out of style. She didn't want to embarrass Henry by looking dowdy and open the wounds between them that had already taken so long to heal.

They waved goodbye to Josiah standing in the portico next to his tutor, their house nanny, and Whisper, tail wagging furiously. It was the first time they'd left him. They saw the tutor, Julian Rabot, whisper in his ear. Josiah smiled and immediately began an energetic wave.

It had been years since Elizabeth had been to New Orleans. She'd been a young schoolgirl then, and the city was gay and robust. Now, nearly seven years later, nothing looked the same. The city had survived the ravages of the war and become the biggest and busiest metropolis in the south. It teemed with whites, blacks, coloreds and blue uniformed soldiers moving hurriedly in every direction. Crews of workers scurried along carrying lumber, nailing boards, laying bricks. New buildings would be erected in days. The school she had attended wasn't even a school any longer. It was part of a new hospital.

They had dinner that evening with Abner Moresby. He was pleasant and attentive to Elizabeth. She'd been able to find an appropriate dress for the evening, a lavender off-the-shoulder chiffon with a very low cut bodice. Henry noticed the banker ogling his wife's breasts more than once. He found it more amusing than offensive. Let the fat man drool, Henry thought. As long as the bank is there with money when Henry needed it, which fortunately wasn't at the moment, he'd put up with the obnoxious man's bad manners.

As they began to exit the restaurant Moresby stopped to acknowledge another client, a famous one.

"James, good evening," he gushed. "How nice to see you. I'd like to introduce long-time friends. This is Henry Rogers and his lovely wife, Elizabeth. They own Moss Grove, a large plantation north of Baton Rouge.

"Henry, this is James Longstreet, formerly General Longstreet of Confederate Army fame. Now he's a successful cotton broker."

As Henry stepped around the table to shake the General's hand, it froze in mid-air, the blood drained from his face. The General's dinner companion was Thaddeus.

"Don't bother to introduce me, Mr. Longstreet," Thaddeus said as he remained seated. "This man and I have a rather long and tumultuous history together."

"You're still a nigger brat. But I understand you've been making improper advances to Amy and that gives me enough reason to kill you."

Thaddeus stood and faced his tormentor, their identical blue steel eyes only inches apart.

"Henry Rogers, I am no longer your slave nor am I the property of Moss Grove. Those days are gone and good riddance. I believe you and Mrs. Rogers were on your way out. Please don't let us delay you."

Henry's temper snapped and he backhanded Thaddeus across his face.

"If you were a gentleman, I'd challenge you to a duel but since you're a nigger I think I'll just arrange to have you strung up."

As Longstreet rose in anger, Moresby spoke first.

"Henry, let's just leave," he pleaded. "Your lovely wife doesn't need to share all this."

"Mr. Moresby, if this nigger is dallyin' with my sister, he deserves to be horse whipped or more."

"No one is dallying and no one is going to be horse whipped. Abner, take these people away, our dinner is getting cold," the General ordered.

"We aren't done with this," Henry said as Moresby grabbed both his guest's arms forcefully and let them toward the door.

Longstreet and Thaddeus sat quietly for several minutes, their food untouched as the younger colored man slowly regained his composure.

"I don't think that man likes you," Longstreet smiled, trying to lighten the mood.

"He's my birth father. He raped my mother, a young Moss Grove field hand, when he was in his teens."

"Ah! That helps explain the blue eyes...and the hatred. And who is Amy?"

"The woman I love. We've known one another since the early days of the war. She is also Elizabeth Rogers' younger sister."

"You certainly challenge the traditional southern morality. I raise my glass to you, young sir."

"Henry, my apologies," Moresby said as he helped Elizabeth into a carriage. "General Longstreet is a scalawag to be sure, but a gentleman. Who is the colored boy?"

"Too long a story, Abner. Suffice to say he is a canker that has festered under my skin for far too long."

They spent five more uneventful days in the city. Their rooms were at the posh Royal Orleans Hotel in the French Quarter with its wrought iron filigreed balcony overlooking Bourbon Street. They had a formal picture taken by Jules Lyon, the city's most prominent photographer. Lyon, a life-long free- colored, had introduced the daguerreotype process invented in Paris. The picture would be a wonderful keepsake to pass on to Josiah and his children.

Elizabeth was more than successful in replenishing her wardrobe. She walked the aisles of the D.H. Holmes store and the smaller shops along Canal Street. She even purchased bright new fabrics to replace worn drapes in several rooms.

Her only disappointment was her inability to locate her sister. She wanted to talk to Amy about her relationship with Thaddeus and how it was ruining her reputation. It seemed that Amy was no longer at her school and no one was sure where she'd gone. In frustration Elizabeth began questioning some of the girls that might have been in Amy's classes. Eventually she connected with Brenda. Brenda explained how Amy had gotten involved with a new school and medical clinic in Baton Rouge.

It wasn't too hard to figure out that this Freedman's Clinic was their former home. Elizabeth tried to discuss it with Henry but he made it clear he had no interest in anything to do with Amy. She wanted to press him into having them stop by the school on their way through Baton Rouge but their visit to New Orleans had gone so well she didn't want to risk his anger.

She and Henry had made love twice in the plush bed of the hotel's lavish suite. That was more than they had in the previous two years. It was nice to have an intimate relationship with her husband again. Henry had been solicitous and sober and mildly grateful that his wife's daily use of laudanum had lessened. It wasn't hot passionate sex but it seemed to signal a truce. At least they no longer openly detested one another.

They drove through Baton Rouge without stopping. Elizabeth knew that they were passing only a few blocks from their old home and that Amy would likely be there.

As they approached Moss Grove they could see smoke. Henry told the driver to hurry. The black liveried servant cracked the whip and raced the horses past the turnaround toward the stables. Henry jumped from the carriage and ran. He could see that flames were engulfing several of the shacks. Thank goodness the fire was well away from the main house.

Thatcher was ordering men everywhere. People were scurrying at a frenzied pace. More water…over there…keep the flames away from the chicken coop. He saw Henry approach out of the corner of his eye but he didn't stop. Finally, what was going to burn, did. The kitchen, the smoking shack, and two slave cabins were gone. Smoke-filled eyes of those who had fought the flames surveyed the scene as light breezes lifted flickering red embers into wafting elliptical circles before giving up and falling again.

"What happened, Thatcher? What damn fool let this happen?" Henry demanded. "I leave this place for less than a week and your ignorant no-account blacks' burn part of the place."

George Thatcher slowly removed the neckerchief he always wore around his neck and wiped his face. The cloth immediately turned black with soot as the overseer gathered his thoughts.

"Mr. Rogers, you is my boss, sure 'enuf, but you ain't my master. You got no right to shout at me that way."

Big George gathered up his frame and just stared at this white man with the head full of long flowing blonde hair and a manly physique, only slightly diminished by the absence of one arm. Henry stared back, taking the measure of this immense man before him, and suddenly realizing there was no longer any fear in the eyes of a righteous black man.

"You're right, Big George. I shall choose my words more carefully in the future," he said contritely, sublimating the anger seething in his intestines. "What happened?"

"Apparently it was your son, Josiah. Mr. Rabot said the boy had finished his lessons and could get himself a treat. The boy ran outside to the kitchen where the women were working. He had to get up on a chair to reach whatever it was he wanted. No one saw him fall off the chair and turn over a pot that was rendering hog fat until it was too late. The flames spread quickly. We was lucky to keep it to just a few buildings close by. Could have been much worse. You saw the results. One of the women isn't doing too well, though. She's got burns over a lot of her body where the liquid fat splashed up when the pot fell to the floor."

"Josiah? Oh, my god. Where is he? How is he?" Henry ranted, no longer caring about Thatcher, the woman who had been burned, or the loss of a few buildings.

"He's with Mr. Rabot and the house staff. He got frightened when the pot fell and some of the fat kicked up and got on his arm. He might have some scarring but he'll be alright."

Henry rushed off, pulling Elizabeth with him as she, too, had run toward the fire and smoke.

"Josiah's been injured," Henry blurted out as they skirted back toward the house. "He's safe but they say he started all of this by accident."

Josiah was sitting at a small table near the pantry eating a piece of cake and drinking a glass of milk. His arm was bandaged but he seemed in good spirits.

"Josiah," Elizabeth said, grabbing her son and turning over the glass. "Are you OK? What happened?"

"Mommy, you spilled my milk," the boy said, oblivious to the concerned adults all around him.

"I'm so sorry this happened," Rabot said contritely. "He almost always gets himself a treat after his morning lessons. I will stay with him from now on."

"Yes, that would be best," Henry said, clearly wanting to blame someone, anyone other than his son.

Fires weren't uncommon at plantations. It was the primary reason kitchens were not connected to the main house but rather fifty to one hundred feet away, preferably on the side where prevailing winds blew smells and smoke away.

Within days the kitchen had been rebuilt. None of the cast iron pots had been damaged but they did need heavy scouring. All other work at the plantation was put aside while new structures were built. The girl, who had been scalded by the boiling hog fat, died. She was buried quietly in a small ceremony. Neither Henry nor Elizabeth attended her funeral and their absence was clear proof that these were terrible white folks. Those who had been at Moss Grove for a long time knew that neither Massa' Jed or Miss Ruby would have been so uncaring.

Because the fire had been started by Josiah, however, and not one of the servants, Henry and Elizabeth tried to be extra considerate as a way of apology. Their efforts were so obvious after their failure to attend the funeral that, rather than engender feelings of gratitude, the dislike for this couple who financed their everyday lives, was reaffirmed.

Big George had returned from his short trip months earlier with three new share cropper families trailing behind him with their meager goods. It wasn't the ten families he wanted to bring. That would have brought him a much bigger bonus. But it was a start and would enable them to plant more acreage. The workers in this caravan had little farming experience, and none growing cotton. One family had just arrived from the Dominican Republic. The other two families were related. They were cousins and were slowly making their way west from Alabama. All in all there were three grown men, four workable sons, wives and daughters and four more screaming young 'uns.

George had taken his stand with Henry Rogers at the fire and there would be no stepping back from their new relationship. George Thatcher was illiterate but he wasn't stupid. He knew he had been sweet-talked into staying another year but he did get the commitment of an additional bonus and he and his young bride really weren't sure they should be traveling with a new baby, so all in all it worked out. He'd just have to watch this oily white boss.

# Chapter Twenty-Three

Amy cried herself to sleep the night that Thaddeus left. The man she loved was gone. She felt more alone than she ever had. When she lost her parents she was filled with a sense of sadness but they were getting older and one always assumed you'd eventually lose your parents. This was different. It felt as if a piece of her very soul had been torn from her body.

She never expected to lose her connection with her always self-absorbed sister either. Elizabeth was never bright, but she had always been so full of life. Now Amy felt as if she'd lost her sister to the husband from Hell. It was impossible to visit Moss Grove and have any type of sane connection with either of them. Amy got chills whenever she felt Henry looking at her. It was always such a visceral stare. Then she even lost a niece, Clara, who she would never be able to cuddle or spoil because of reasons that had never made sense to her. Josiah was cute but his resemblance to his father sometimes made it uncomfortable to warm to the child.

Thaddeus had been her anchor. She felt safe with him. They could talk about anything and they'd both smile. They could sit and share nothing but silence and that felt right, too. There was nothing in her life that seemed to matter anymore, certainly nothing worthwhile. She drifted off, her head lying on a pillow made wet by her tears.

When she awoke the sun was drifting through the glass window. Her body ached. Dried tears matted her cheek. She had no desire to get up and face the day. Tired of remaining in her bed she moved to a chair by the window, continuing to be distressed over the turns her life had taken.

She thought of going to New Orleans and seeing Melanie and Brenda but it would almost be as if she were following Thaddeus. She finally needed to rise, do her morning ablutions, and gather herself. She rinsed her body in cold water, tied her hair back with a ribbon, and pulled on her favorite overalls and gingham shirt. She walked down to the river where she and Thaddeus would spend hours lounging. This wasn't underneath their personal magnolia tree but at least it was the same river flowing by. She breathed the heavy damp air as small flies flitted about. From time to time bubbles would emerge from the quiet water. It was likely a catfish stirring up the waters in search of a little snack. She knew she should be back inside working at the Medical Clinic. They were always shorthanded. She wiped her eyes with her sleeve and stood, straightening her clothes and fluffing her hair. She walked slowly back to the house and the tasks that awaited her. She smiled as she remembered what Thaddeus had told her. He said that Daddy Jesse had said when things were bad you could take fifteen minutes to fuss and complain. If something really terrible happened you could have one hour. After that you had to get up and get on with your life.

Thaddeus stood before Major John Shipley as the Union officer read the letter of recommendation written by Captain Fineman. This tall, handsome, latte complexioned man seemed to have led a most unusual life.

"I find some of what Captain Fineman has written to be a little difficult to believe, especially since he wasn't there when these events occurred. Perhaps you can clarify some of these things for me. You were a slave and you ran away. You fought for the Confederacy and brought your Master's son, who had been badly wounded in the battle at Port Hudson, back through Union lines, nearly sixty miles. Weren't you afraid of being hung as a runaway?"

"I didn't really have a choice, Major," Thaddeus replied, uneasy at having to discuss his past.

"You could have let him die. You could have stayed and continued to fight with your unit. You had choices," Shipley insisted.

"The battle had been lost when we left. My sergeant, now my friend and partner, Rufus Carmody, helped me. And," he hesitated, finding it difficult to voice the words, "I knew that Henry Rogers and I were connected in some way. I learned later that he was my father."

"Oh," Shipley said, finding himself embarrassed at pushing this most personal revelation. Seconds elapsed before he could continue. He cleared his voice.

"Then you became a Union soldier, fought with Sheridan's unit and distinguished yourself. When the war ended you established a successful business and now you have been teaching and organizing the school set up by the Freedman's Bureau. I was right. You've led an amazing life for one so young!"

"Slavery and war mature a person quickly," Thaddeus noted. "Would you feel the same way if these things had been done by a white person?"

Major Shipley stared into the steel blue eyes glistening before him. It was a stare of self-confidence. "If you are implying that I am more impressed because you're colored, the answer is yes. I don't think that makes me insensitive. It would have been difficult for any young man to have all the adventures you've had. For a man of color to have done so much strikes me as being even more unusual. I suggest you take it as a compliment and not read anything else into it."

"Then, all I can say is 'thank you,'"Thaddeus replied.

Shipley's Jewish Baton Rouge officer had done him a fine turn by sending his young man to help him. There weren't enough educated blacks or coloreds to teach a population starving to learn how to read and do numbers and earn their own keep.

The two men spoke for another two hours. Shipley wanted to know more about the school and medical clinic they were operating. He was impressed and vowed to see it for himself soon.

"Do you think you can accomplish similar results setting up or expanding the schools here in New Orleans?"

"I don't know but I'm willing to try."

Five men rode through the quiet, deserted streets on the outskirts of Baton Rouge. They rode slowly without talking. They had put out their cigarettes to avoid any small light flickering from them. Their only illumination came from the sliver of a moon. They had carefully chosen this night. A full moon might shed enough light to make their detection too easy and no moon might make it difficult for them to do their work.

Four men got off their horses while the fifth held the reins. All five donned white hoods with slits cut unevenly for eyes, nose and mouth. The hood came to a point at the top, not unlike a dunce cap children might be forced to wear for unruliness in class. But these men weren't unruly. These men had a mission…a mission God had given them. It was a mission to re-assert the superiority of white Christians.

Using a small flint they generated a spark and lit a packed pile of dry twigs. The buildings of Carmody and Williams stood before them. This nigger business would be their most aggressive attack in the area. Their like-minded kin in Alabama and Mississippi had been doing this sort of thing for months and it didn't pay to make them 'crackers' feel they were better Christians than us here in Louisiana, no sir.

As the first flames lit up the walls of the stable, the horses inside began to neigh and kick noisily, panicked by the smell of smoke filling their sensitive nostrils. Rufus Carmody emerged from the house with his rifle and side arm and began firing. Two of the hooded men continued to spread the flames while the others grabbed their guns and fired back. Rufus had the advantage. These bastards had the light from the burning fire framing them and making them perfect targets. The two Klansmen who were firing, fell, hit by Rufus' shooting. It was a skill he had honed by years in the Army. The other three men dropped their torches and fled on their horses.

Sarah, Rose, and two workers who had been asleep in the barn had already begun pulling the horses to safety and drawing water from the well to douse the flames. There was no wind that evening and they were able to save the store and the house. The stables were lost. The straw had burned quickly and taken the building with it. When they were finally able to stop and catch their breaths they realized that Sarah wasn't standing there with them. They set off in separate directions trying to find her.

"Sarah! Sarah! Where are you?" Rose shouted.

They found her lying unmoving on the far side of what remained of the barn. The wet timbers still smoked. Sarah had apparently tripped on a fallen timber and suffocated from the heavy smoke.

Rufus carried her into the house and set on her bed. He closed her eyes and cleaned the soot from her face. He sent a worker to find Thaddeus and Matthew. He sent another worker to find Captain Fineman, or any Union troops that might be in the area, and advise them of what had happened. He had no intention of touching the two dead white marauders. He'd let the army deal with them.

Sarah's funeral was held a few days later. She was dressed in her best going-to-church dress. She looked serene and ready to join her husband, Jesse. Captain Fineman and his wife, Ruth, were present. Fineman had sent a telegraph through military channels to New Orleans relating the events at Carmody & Williams and Sarah's death. Without hesitation,

Thaddeus, Matthew and Melanie had already dropped everything to be there. Amy had arrived the morning after the fire and had stayed to help. Mrs. Chartier, Melanie's mother, and two brothers had ridden over. Everyone pitched in rebuilding burned out buildings or assisting with the funeral arrangements.

Thaddeus was distraught. Mama Sarah had raised him. She was the only mother he had known growing up. Now unnecessary stupid violence had brought about her death, years too soon.

Everyone stood silently at the graveside and said their good-byes. They wept as the casket was lowered into the brown earth. All that remained to mark her life was a simple headstone:

> ### *Sarah, nee Rogers*
> ### *Beloved by Jesse and Thaddeus*
> ### *Born a slave, died free*
> ### *1821 – 1870*

Those assembled walked back to the house, their heads bowed, holding one another's hands as they struggled to comfort one another. Melanie and Amy helped Rose set out food at the back of the house. The army had removed the bodies of the two dead clansmen but dried blood still pooled where they had fallen.

"They were members of the Klan, the KKK, Ku Klux Klan, whatever name they go by," Captain Fineman explained. "They're angry violent white men, usually ex-Reb soldiers. They're stirring up trouble all across the south. They aren't averse to killing and we have lots of run-ins with them. We caught the three you didn't kill and they'll be put on trial. Until then, we've got them in jail. They'll have lots of company in there to share hate stories. You're lucky, Rufus. They might have killed all of you."

"I began sleeping with loaded guns nearby right after they caught up with Charlie and killed him."

"This might not be their last attempt," Eli warned.

"We'll be better prepared if they show up again," Rufus promised.

It had been nearly four months since Thaddeus had left the Freedman's school and Baton Rouge. Now he and Amy found themselves sitting side by side trying hard to bridge the chasm of time that had strained them both so emotionally.

"Are you enjoying New Orleans?" she asked, softly.

"There certainly is plenty of work to keep me busy. They have access to a lot more resources than we have in Baton Rouge. Ships come and go continuously, unloading and loading people, sugar, cotton, pianos, and all manner of things.

"I never realized how many people there are living in the city who have my coloring. Sex was obviously a popular pastime in what some folks call the Crescent City. I'm not really sure why they call it that."

"Thaddeus, you're beginning to ramble," Amy said, smiling now at her friend's obvious discomfort.

"If you want to know whether I've stopped missing you, the answer is, no, I haven't," he confessed.

"The same with me," she admitted as they instinctively reached for one another's hand, grasping tightly, knowing that this brief interlude really didn't change anything. Eventually, maybe in hours, maybe in a day or two, they would, once again, have to say their goodbyes and face their separate worlds.

"Rufus," Melanie said, "If you still want to marry me, I'm ready."

"Ready," he grinned, dropping the glass he was holding and embracing her tightly in his arms. "I've been ready since the day I laid eyes on you," he whispered in her ear, letting his lips brush the side of her face."

She blushed and it startled her. With all the men she'd known in her life, she'd never blushed. The realization of how much she loved this truly wonderful man spread through her body and she returned his embrace with emotions she had consciously buried throughout her life.

"My life," she said nervously. "There are things I need to tell you… things I need to explain."

He embraced her. He could feel her tears on his cheek and her body shake. She felt so young and frightened.

"Melanie, I love you. I love who you are, not what you needed to do. Just love me a little of how much I love you and I'll be happy."

He lifted her chin and wiped away a tear. She tried to stifle a sniffle and they both smiled.

She knew everything would be alright and she clung tightly to this man she loved with every pore in her body.

Rufus turned to the others. "Hey, everyone, I know this is a time to mourn but it will also be a time of gladness. Melanie and I are going to be married."

Their friends gathered around them, ecstatic in this day of sadness.

"When's the wedding?" Matthew asked.

"The sooner the better so she doesn't change her mind," Rufus answered to the nods and laughter of his friends.

Two months later the Reverend Walter Dinsmore climbed into his buggy and drove up from New Orleans to perform the wedding ceremony at the Baton Rouge's small Methodist Church now renovated from the war damage it had suffered. The Confederates had used it as a Quartermaster Supply depot. Later the Union Army did the same. Only the color of the uniforms that rested on the shelves changed. Now peace had returned the building to a house of worship.

Dinsmore was a founder of the Union Normal School, Louisiana's first black college. Melanie was one of his frequent parishioners. But she was special, often doing extra work with his elderly black congregants, making them a little more comfortable, paying for things they might need from her own purse. He knew how she made her living but he never judged her and they never discussed it. With God's grace she'd finally be able to leave that sinful life and have a family of her own to love.

Matthew was escorting two young ladies to the ceremony. One was Amy's friend, Brenda, who remained in awe of Melanie from that day they'd helped at Maison Frere. The other girl was Sheila Stokes, who Matthew rarely let out of his sight these days. They made a handsome couple. Sheila was attending Straight University, studying nursing. Straight was the only other black college in Louisiana. It was smaller than Union Normal, orienting itself more toward nursing and medicine.

The two had met when Matthew accompanied Oscar Dunn on a tour of the school. At the same time he noticed her taking a patient's pulse, he found his own pulse quickening.

Sheila and her family had come to New Orleans from Mobile, Alabama. They were free blacks in a state that didn't much tolerate 'uppity niggers'. A spate of KKK bombings and fires encouraged them to leave their business and friends for someplace they hoped would be safer.

Sheila, like Matthew, was as dark as night. She was quite short, less than five foot tall, and when she stood next to her much taller beau, the difference was striking. Sheila didn't mind. She would gaze up at Matthew with a mixture of affection and the sharing of a secret between them that no one else understood.

Amy and Brenda each let out a squeal as they saw one another. They hugged and laughed. Amy had been so busy at the Freedman's school that she had been unable to return to New Orleans and it had been months since they'd seen one another.

"Brenda, you look stunning. You have to be overwhelmed with men chasing after you," Amy said.

"I confess there have been a few, but most are Southerners that my father rejects. It is a little flattering, however, having some options. I'm having a wonderful time being courted. And you?" she asked. "Where is Thaddeus? I saw him once in New Orleans but I didn't get a chance to say 'hi'. Are you two still together?"

"It's a long story, not for today. Come, let's find Melanie," she said, happy to change the subject.

The Chartier family smiled, hugged, and clasped the hands of each guest, some more than once. Able and Bennie were nattily attired with suits their sister had insisted on providing. Marie Chartier looked as stunning as any fine lady who strolled the quay at the French Quarter. She was thrilled to play the role of the bride's mother.

Before the wedding Melanie had taken Rufus aside.

"I love you and I will live anywhere you choose," she said tenderly. "But if you want to give me the wedding gift I would desire most, it would be to remain with you here and be close to my mother and brothers."

"And I would follow you to the ends of the earth, my dearest," he responded tenderly. "Staying here is what I'd prefer in any event."

Delicately he didn't mention that he preferred to be as far away from his wife's prior life as possible. They had never discussed her work in New Orleans Gentlemen Clubs but he knew what her life had been, and she knew that he knew. It remained unspoken between them and she loved him even more for never bringing it up. Now that they were marrying, Rufus had no desire to accidentally encounter any of Melanie's former clientele. He'd probably have to kill them.

"Another thing," she smiled. "There is a parcel of land available that adjoins the farm and I'd like us to buy it. Eventually we might decide to raise a family there and until then Able and Benny can farm it."

"Looks as if you've got our life all planned. I'm glad I was in your plans," he laughed.

"There was no plan without you" she said, kissing him. "Now, shall we entertain the guests with our wedding vows?"

Matthew, Sheila and Brenda returned to New Orleans a few days later but Thaddeus and Amy both decided to remain through the end of the week. It wasn't just that he wanted to be close to her…he did, but Sarah's death, the loss of that wonderful woman and surrogate mother who raised him, brought him considerable grief. He just wasn't ready to return to his responsibilities.

He also wanted to help Rufus rebuild the barn. He was still a better smithy than anyone Carmody & Williams had been able to train, and with so many of the horses spooked by the fire, the hired help needed to devote a lot more time walking and calming them down.

While Thaddeus walked outside with Rufus to assess the damage, Amy helped Melanie clean up once the guests left.

"You miss him, don't you?" Melanie asked, folding the beautiful bed linen they'd been given as a wedding gift by the Finemans.

Amy nodded and turned away. Any discussion of her feelings for Thaddeus inevitably brought tears. Melanie stopped what she was doing and took her friend into her arms.

"You are both such special people," Melanie said. "It is so clear that you're meant for one another and it's so sad that you are both feeling such pain. It isn't fair." Together they sat on the bed and cried.

The newlyweds and their guests ate their meals together during the next few days but both Rufus and Melanie were careful to keep the conversation light and their friends occupied with tasks as far apart as possible. When the eyes of the two young lovers connected, both their love and their pain was palpable.

Each night Thaddeus and Amy went to their separate rooms after saying goodnight to Rufus and Melanie, still glowing from their wedding. Thaddeus waited a discreet amount of time and then walked quietly to a waiting Amy.

This was their time. They wouldn't fall asleep until the early morning hours. They savored one another, touching, kissing, exploring with their fingers, their lips, and their tongues, each discovering new feelings that aroused them both and took them smiling to new erotic highs.

Then they would lie there in one another's arms, satiated by the other's love.

'One day...some day, when our stars are aligned' were living, viable words for the first time. They also understood that this was a magic moment and not an ultimate answer.

When Amy missed her period she wasn't too worried. She was often a few days late. But a week passed, and then another and she could no longer ignore the possibility that she was pregnant.

"Ruth, I need to speak with you in confidence," Amy said, as she took Ruth Fineman aside.

"Of course!"

"I may be pregnant!"

Ruth nodded sympathetically. There was no need to ask who the father was.

Within days, with the help of a compassionate Army doctor, Amy's pregnancy was confirmed. She decided to visit Melanie. That evening the two sat alone on the small porch.

"I'm pregnant, Melanie. With Thaddeus' child! I'm ecstatic but I don't know how he'll react."

"I'm sure he'll want the two of you to marry but you both know what kind of a life you'd have. I do have my own news, although I haven't told Rufus."

"You, too?" Amy smiled.

Melanie nodded, an enormous grin spreading sparks of joy.

"Oh, my gosh. That's so wonderful. I wish the four of us could share these next months together."

Amy agreed to remain with her friends for a few days hoping against hope that solution would present itself.

"You'll have to give up the baby," Melanie concluded a few days later.

"I can't! I just can't walk away. This child was conceived out of love."

"Think of Thaddeus. You love him. White men wouldn't hesitate to lynch him. He can't know. And, unless you give up the baby, he'll know immediately."

Amy sobbed. She was torn between her love for Thaddeus and her love for their unborn child.

Melanie tried to console her friend.

"I have a crazy thought, Amy. Rufus and I could raise the child as ours. Our due dates are close enough. We'd just say I had twins. Of course, Rufus would have to agree, which I know he would. You and I would just have to stay out of sight until both babies were born."

Amy sat silently, sifting through her limited options as she dried her damp cheeks.

"At least I'd still be close enough to see the baby often. Are you certain this is something you'd be willing to do? It's obviously a really long term commitment."

"Without question!"

Amy packed a few things with little explanation at the school, settled in with Melanie and Rufus.

Rufus' emotions had roller coasted from a high upon learning he'd soon be a father to the realization he was being forced to withhold the truth of Amy's pregnancy from Thaddeus. He didn't disagree with the reasoning. It was just a tragic shame.

Both pregnancies went smoothly.

Michelle Carmody came into the world with the arrival of spring, the first child born at Carmody House. The baby girl came out smiling, confident it was her world to conquer. Marie Chartier and Amy took turns taking care of the six pound, four ounce gurgling baby girl, who announced her arrival with gusto.

Baby Stephen Williams joined Michelle five days later, making it quite clear that it was the first and only time he'd come in second.

Stephen was a funny looking infant. He had Amy's lips and smile. He also had his father's blue-green eyes, a comfortable blend from his parents. But it was his skin color that enchanted his birth mother and adoptive parents…lighter than colored, but less than Southern pasty white. He was the color Jedidiah might have been after a summer riding in the fields. If the baby's coloring remained, he'd be able to live in either culture.

Two weeks later Amy said a teary goodbye and returned to the Freedman's Clinic.

# Chapter Twenty-Four

Matthew watched as Nurse Sheila Stokes played in the children's ward. The children loved her. She was able to put them at ease even while they were sick, often from terrible afflictions. She had a small pile of raggedy dolls that she would distribute but first she'd hug each doll and pass it to the child with instructions that they were to hug it each time they felt a pain.

"Sheila," he asked as she exited from the room. "Where do you get all those dolls?"

"From my daddy! He sells them in his store. They make them in Mobile where we lived. The children adore them. Why are you so interested in dolls? I can get you one if it's important but I thought you wanted something a little older," she said flirtatiously.

"Why are all the dolls white children?" he asked.

"What do you mean?"

"Why aren't there any black children rag dolls?"

"I don't know? I guess 'cause nobody makes them," she responded.

"That's what I mean. Whoever is making them has probably been making them that way forever but now there are more black folks who are educating their children. Wouldn't you want a black doll for your black child?"

"You're funny. You're always looking for something different," she smiled.

"Well, I found you, didn't I?" he laughed. "Give me one of those dolls. I have an idea."

Three weeks later a small package arrived. He handed it to her with a smile on his face, confusion on hers.

"Black raggedy dolls! Aren't you something! These are wonderful. How did you make this happen?" she laughed, grabbing an armful of the dolls and dancing around the room.

"I sent your doll off to my mother with a note explaining what I wanted. She's terrific at making things, and guess what?"

"What?" she said as she stopped dancing.

"We're going to make some to give to the children and enough more to sell them. Give a few of these to your father and see what he thinks. Tell him I'd like our first order to be from him."

"Mr. Stokes, so nice to see you again," Matthew said as he and Sheila walked into the parlor.

"And you, too, Matthew. You've made quite a stir with those dolls."

"A good stir, I hope."

"They're wonderful, Matthew," Penelope Stokes, Sheila's mother, remarked as she entered the room holding one of the rag dolls. "Everyone I've showed them to wonders why no one thought of it sooner."

"Matthew thinks about things differently than most people," Sheila added proudly, as Matthew smiled back at her.

That exchange brought a knowing glance from Sheila's parents but they were not at all displeased. Matthew looked to be a fine choice to join the Stokes family.

"I'm going to go out on a limb and order five hundred," John Stokes said. "Can you produce that many in a reasonable time?"

"I'm sure we can."

"Ship them to me as soon as they are ready. I'm going to send them to stores across the south. You don't mind that, do you?"

"No…my mother and her friends are enjoying making them. You can take care of the selling. I do want the right, however, to give some of them away to the children in the hospitals and schools."

"That sounds not only fair…it seems quite noble."

The men shook hands as their women looked on proudly.

That evening, on his way home, Matthew stopped by the telegraph office to send a wire.

*To: Rufus Carmody, Carmody & Williams, stop. You are now in the rag doll business, stop. Initial order for 500, stop. Begin production and don't stop.*

Major John Shipley rode into Baton Rouge to make his monthly inspection. He never told his subordinates when he might show up. He wanted no special preparations. Better to find things the way they are, without pretense, he thought.

What he found was that Captain Fineman was doing the same, touring his area of responsibility as far north as Natchez. He'd be gone at least one more week.

One of Fineman's sergeants recognized the Major and offered to assist in whatever the senior officer might require. Shipley sat at the Captain's desk, fingered a few files and decided to wander around on his own.

"Can I help you?" Amy asked the unfamiliar Union officer peaking in drawers and opening doors.

Shipley stood and stared at the girl with the bright red hair and green eyes resting atop freckled cheeks. He disliked freckles on women but not on this girl. Here they just seemed to sparkle.

"My name is Jipley," he stammered, "Shipley, I mean. Captain John Shipley."

"Do you always stumble on your own name," she laughed.

"Only when I am rendered speechless by someone so fair."

She laughed more loudly and curtsied. It was the first time since leaving her baby with Melanie and Rufus that she had reason to laugh.

"I am not used to such compliments, Major, particularly when I'm working. Let me introduce myself. I'm Amy Williams and I work here. Now I realize who you are. I've heard your name mentioned. You work with my friend, Thaddeus Williams. He's spoken of you."

"Actually, since no one has ever accused me of being modest, Thaddeus works for me."

"I stand corrected," she said. "But you and Captain Fineman work together. His wife, Ruth, often works here as well."

"You won't appreciate me saying so, but Captain Fineman works for me as well. He's my subordinate officer in charge of this area and I'm up here making an inspection."

"My goodness then Major," she smiled sarcastically. "You must be quite important with so many people working for you."

"I like to think of myself as having a wide swath of responsibility. But your point is well taken, Miss Williams. I shall endeavor to present a more humble countenance."

"A difficult task I would imagine, Major Shipley. However, on second thought, you do look formidable enough to meet the challenge."

The Major bowed and laughed. He hadn't met a girl with this much sauciness during his entire posting in Louisiana.

"If you will dine with me this evening, Miss Williams, I will begin my military campaign of conquering my lack of humility. Perhaps you can assist me in planning my strategy."

"Another time, Major. I am not in the habit of having dinner alone with strange men."

"I promise I will be a perfect gentleman and I'm sure both Captain Fineman and Mr. Williams would vouch for me. I promise to have you safely tucked in by nine, if that suits you."

"That would be nice...but I think I'd prefer to tuck myself in," she smiled again.

John Shipley smiled, kissed Amy's hand and left. Over the next several months he continued to return to the Freedman's school on the excuse of seeing Captain Fineman. The reasons were becoming more and more farcical.

Amy was forced to accept her situation and John Shipley was proving to be a pleasant diversion. They began having dinners together but the conversation was always light and it allowed Amy to feel no conflict regarding her love for Thaddeus.

In New Orleans Thaddeus' efforts to establish more school in and around the city were meeting with success thanks to the protection of Union troops. On a few occasions, however, the staff arrived in the morning to find the school burned to the ground.

Julian Rabot was able to restart Josiah's lessons now that the boy's arm was healed. Elizabeth had raged at him in a senseless tirade. She wanted him fired for allowing her son to get burned so carelessly. If the man had watched the boy more closely, none of this would have happened, she railed. She might have succeeded except that Josiah had developed a close attachment to his teacher and argued on his behalf.

What a bitch she is, Rabot thought, relieved for the moment. Josiah's parents are both miserable people. I do need to find another posting but unless I can get a letter of recommendation from one of them, no decent position will ever be forthcoming, not with my troubled history.

Tutor and student sat together reading a book on the Greek wars when Henry entered. The father stood quietly at the door, admiring his son's reading. Rabot and Josiah would read a page or two, often stopping to clarify difficult words or passages. Then they would put the book down and discuss what they had read. Henry's eyes lit up at his son's quick mind. The best thing in my life, he thought.

Josiah sensed his father standing there, threw down his book, and ran to him.

"I don't want to interrupt you. Josiah, you seem to be doing quite well."

"I'm learning all about Homer and Jason and everything, father. Did you know that they traveled the seas for years and years," the boy gushed.

"No, Josiah, I did not know that," Henry laughed.

"He is a good student, Mr. Rogers. And he is a fine young man," Julian beamed. Perhaps the father might be more willing to write a letter for him when the burn incident is not so fresh in everyone's minds.

"To your credit, Mister Rabot! I was a terrible student. I always hoped Josiah would not inherit the same tendency."

"He has not. You need not worry on that score. Josiah is rather like a sponge and absorbs knowledge easily."

"Well, I will let you men return to your tasks. Josiah, keep up the good work and learn what Mr. Rabot teaches you," Henry said in his best paternal voice as he turned to leave.

"Mr. Rogers, a moment please. I have a small matter I'd like to discuss with you."

The two men walked together to the door. Rabot wore the dark frock coat that he always wore. It seemed to be his only outfit. Standing next to Henry, the teacher seemed to shrink in stature. It wasn't just his height and slight build. Julian was shorter by several inches. And whenever he stood next to someone with a dominant personality he seemed to retreat.

Julian Rabot loved standing next to Henry Rogers. He loved being close enough to smell the man's essence. He knew he was physically attracted to the man and could never do anything about it. These sorts of feelings had cost him his tutoring job in Richmond as well as two jobs in Ohio. He continued to move west, always just ahead of the stories that plagued him. He never acted on his feelings, he would never do that, but the tension his feelings engendered always ended up making his patrons uncomfortable, and that incident in the cold cellar with the teenage son never should have happened.

"Mr. Rogers, Mr. Thatcher has asked me to teach some of the black children when I'm not busy with Josiah."

"He did what," Henry stormed. Henry's blue eyes turned icy, the furrows on his forehead deepened. "The effrontery of that man! How dare he?"

"I'm sure he meant no disrespect. It would be in the evening, on my own time," Julian said in a cowering voice.

"I don't give a shit what time of the day it is. We don't teach niggers to read. Not at Moss Grove, we don't," he said, storming out of the room and slamming the door behind him.

That went well, Rabot said to himself, shrugging, and returning to the small boy standing across the room, shaking slightly at his father's sudden outburst.

"Mr. Thatcher, a moment please," Henry said. It was early in the morning although the sun was already giving evidence of its intention to exude a full measure of heat that day. The Moss Grove master alit from his horse, put the leather harness over the saddle and walked the two rows over to where the overseer was trying to fix a part on a broken plow. Big George stood, wiped his hands, and faced the obviously upset white boss.

"Somethin' wrong, Mister Rogers?" he asked, his voice, as always, soft and controlled.

"I understand you have asked Mr. Rabot to teach some of the nigger children to read."

"Yes, I did. When he wasn't teaching your son and only when the children's chores were done. He seemed to think it was a fine idea."

"I don't give a fuck what he thinks. I pay him to live here and teach Josiah, nothing more."

"Mr. Rogers, I don't want to have upset 'tween you and me. It ain't a good thing for either one of us but teachin' black chilun' to read ain't 'gainst the law no more and these new sharecroppers I brung you got young 'uns they want educated. You say no, they gonna' leave. Your choice!"

"Let 'em go. They can go to hell for all I care," Henry fumed.

"You ain't thinkin' this through, Mister Henry. The acres they tendin' means lots of extra cotton. They go, the cotton go. You sure you want to do that?" George said, smiling to himself. He knew this white bastard liked money more than his old slave-owning principles.

Henry was too agitated to say another word. His stomach was knotted. "Make sure he only works with them when they're through with their chores." It was all the rebellion he could muster.

He needed to return to his refuge in Moss Grove but he had difficulty mounting his horse. In his anger he had twisted his shoulder harness. It took him three strained attempts to climb up. George Thatcher stood quietly, neither saying nor doing anything. He simply watched this man who was his employer but who would never be his boss.

Henry knew he had no choice. He'd be giving up thousands of dollars for his principles. Fuckin' blacks think they hold the cards now, do they? We'll see. I'll give them the use of that faggot, Rabot. They deserve one another.

The owner of Moss Grove sat in his palatial dining room overlooking the front portico. He recalled vividly the ritual of arm wrestling with his father. It had always brought a smile to his father's face and frustration to the growing boy. He'd bested the old man just before he went off to war and he remembered that rather than be disappointed, his father had smiled. Henry never understood the reaction until he watched Josiah read. It was paternal pride. His father possessed it and now he did as well. He had so few fond memories of his relationship with Jedidiah Rogers. Everything he recalled reinforced his conviction that the old man was a cold taskmaster.

The war had taken his father and his good right arm. There was little left in his life that brought him warm memories. His mother had deceived him his entire life by hiding a background so onerous that if it ever became public knowledge, his life would be ruined.

Henry knew he could sit in this room and parade most of the significant events of his life but he was Henry Rogers, owner of one of the largest plantations in the parish, and it didn't behoove him to act mawkishly. There were important things to do.

He turned to the small stack of mail that had arrived and leafed through it casually. One letter caught his attention. He rose and walked to the sideboard to get himself another cup of dark black coffee ground especially for him on those occasions when he was near the French Quarter. It had a hint of chicory that never failed to awaken his palette.

The letter was from Alcibiades DeBlanc, posted from New Orleans. It reviewed the progress that the White Camellia Society was making in soliciting new members and organizing new chapters. It also discussed the actions of the KKK along with its successes and failures. The letter ended with a plea for more energy and action from Henry and his friends. DeBlanc was disappointed that nothing seemed to be taking place in their parish and that such inactivity was unacceptable if their goals were to be accomplished. Henry knew he was being rebuked and yet, DeBlanc was right. Like his neighbors, he had cotton to grow and sell, and that was the priority for them all. But they were going to need to act. It was their duty if the old social order was to be reestablished.

Henry greeted the men that arrived with silence and an acknowledging nod of his head. There would be six of them meeting. The five men who arrived dismounted and handed the reins to the waiting stable boy. Henry led them into his private study where drinks awaited them. He closed the door and sat at his desk facing them.

"We are being embarrassed by our lack of action. I received this letter from DeBlanc, criticizing us, and urging us to do more," Henry declared.

"Easy for him to say! He's in New Orleans where he can lose himself among a hundred thousand people. Up here whatever we do, they'll know it was us and I don't need any of my sharecroppers scurrying off because they're afraid. I need those black backs bent and working the fields."

The man who spoke, Alfred DePue, owned Fraser House, a small plantation up the river about five miles. Henry didn't know him very well but what he said resonated with the others as each man voiced the same opinion.

"Alright, Mr. DePue, what do you suggest we do?"

"I don't know. I don't need my niggers killed. I don't mind seeing other of the monkeys killed or tar and feathered but not mine. Mine need to work."

"I'm sure we all feel the same way," Henry said, wanting to regain control of the meeting and needing to reexert his leadership.

"I have given this matter considerable thought since receiving Alcibiades' letter. I suggest we each donate money, perhaps $300, to a work fund, and hire some of the poorer white farmers to harass the black farmers, the ones the Freedman's bureau gave land to. Maybe not kill them, just burn them out. They aren't working our lands. Who the hell needs them here to infect our sharecroppers? We'd be doing ourselves a doubly good turn."

Their unanimous agreement came easily. They could be seen to be doing something and not get their hands dirty. Alfred DePue knew some roughnecks across the river in Natchez who would be perfect. He would take responsibility for getting it started.

A month later Henry was happy to send the leader of the White Camellias a letter recounting the incidents of harassment and burning that had taken place in three northern parishes. Five separate homes were burned and their families routed. It was unfortunate that one nigga' had brandished a rifle and had to be tarred and feathered. Another uppity black teenager had to be whipped. One pretty young colored girl had been raped. The man who had done it had been drunk and sent back to Natchez without pay. The Union Army had chased the men but lost them at a river crossing. Henry was satisfied that DePue had used the money wisely.

# Chapter Twenty-Five

*The election of 1872 was not a difficult one to predict. The wounds of war were healing. Slaves had been freed. Equality had been proclaimed. Why change? Ulysses S. Grant was reelected easily. The Democratic and Liberal Republican candidate, Horace Greeley, died shortly before the election but the outcome had never been in doubt. The country was continuing to regale in a peace dividend. Cotton prices were stabilizing in the south. A railroad spanning the country from New York to California was completed and the nation was beginning to truly believe in the inevitability of 'manifest destiny'. The nation would continue on its course of reintegrating the south and raising the status of its black citizens.*

In addition to being a successful stable and feed store, Carmody & Williams had become successful manufacturer of dolls. Rose was employing from twelve to twenty women sewing boy and girl Negro cotton rag dolls. Their popularity was a surprise to them all, at least to everyone except Matthew.

"Matthew, these dolls are continuing to sell," John Stokes suggested as the two men balanced their accounts at month's end. "Perhaps we can expand the line, add some new items."

"I expect so. This whole doll thing is already a lot bigger than I ever expected it to be."

"Well, now that Oscar Dunn died, you are out of a job. You could run this doll business full-time."

"I don't think I'm cut out for business," Matthew said.

"How did your friend Oscar die? There are lots of rumors flying."

"Some said he was poisoned but no one knows for sure. Pinchbeck is governor now and all I've learned is that black politicians possess neither more, nor less, integrity than their white counterparts.

"I don't know what to do. I don't want to be in business and I'm burned out on politics," Matthew said.

"We're even beginning to receive orders from Europe but I'm nervous about sending merchandise across the Atlantic before I get paid and the white bankers aren't interested in helping a black business grow. I'm sure they believe it will anger their white customers."

"We need a black bank. That's what we need!" Matthew averred. "Maybe Major Shipley can help us."

"I met a friend of yours, Miss Williams, on my recent trip to Baton Rouge," John Shipley said to Matthew, as he unbuckled his military belt and unbuttoned his jacket.

"I just realized she and Thaddeus both have the same last name. Is that a coincidence?"

"No," he said, uncomfortable having to explain his brother's history. "I assume it happened accidentally when Thaddeus needed to adopt a last name. That's how I became Carmody. As you know none of us slaves had surnames."

"Tell me about Miss Williams. She's very attractive. Does she have a beau? What about her family?" he asked in an unleashed torrent of questions.

"Major, I've come to ask your help in setting up a black owned bank. Please do not ask me to assuage your personal curiosity," Matthew insisted.

"You are right, Mr. Carmody. It was unprofessional of me and I apologize, although I confess it has become rather difficult to get her out of my mind. As regards your bank, I have little experience, but I do know who can help us, General James Longstreet. He knows a great deal about both banks and bankers. I'm sure he'll be pleased to meet with us."

"I would like Thaddeus to join us. He has already met the General and he has a good understanding of what we might need."

Gaston's was a small French eatery located just off Bourbon Street near to the quay. Early each morning Rene' Gaston, the owner and chef, walked the short distance to where the fishing boats unloaded their catch. Pelicans hovered noisily overhead while he carefully selected the best of the seafood that had been caught that day. The restaurant only had fifteen tables but they were filled every night with those who favored an unusual dining experience. His specialty was a 'black paella' that rested languidly on the taste buds. His wine cellar featured only the best French Bordeaux.

James Longstreet was a frequent customer and a close friend of Rene'. Monique, Rene's wife chatted with the diners and ran the business. The two had migrated from Marseilles when Napoleon commandeered him to be his personal chef enroute to his invasion of Russia. Instead they caught the first ship out of the harbor and found themselves in New Orleans.

Longstreet never ordered. Menus didn't even exist. Rene' knew the preferences of each of his guests and even took the liberty of selecting the appropriate wine. This night the General was accompanied by Major John Shipley and two handsome young men, one colored, one black and a fifth man, older, and unfamiliar to everyone but Longstreet. Only in France, or in New Orleans, might he have the opportunity to entertain such an eclectic ensemble, the Frenchman mused.

"Gentlemen, let me introduce Mr. Julius Freyhan, one of our city's most successful merchants. When I heard you wanted to discuss banking I asked my friend to join us. However, I refuse to discuss anything until I've had my sherry and my dinner. If you will all indulge me, you will be amply rewarded," Longstreet insisted.

They dined without discussing business. Gaston would have been terribly upset if all of his gastronomic efforts were forced to compete with talk of money, cotton or shipping. Discussions of commerce would have to wait for coffee and cigars. When the dinner was complete, nearly three hours later, Gaston pulled across a heavy drape that would ensure his guest's complete privacy.

"A bank," Longstreet said, "A black run bank, what do you think, Julius?

"Why not?" Julius laughed. "Us Jews have been lending money for centuries. Who do you think financed the English victory over Napoleon? I'll tell you. It was the Jews. It'll certainly twist the tale of the white Goyisha bankers, and don't they deserve it.

"You're Jewish?" Major Shipley asked.

"Is that a problem, Major?" the middle aged business man asked back.

"No, I rather find it humorous. I had never met a Jewish person in my entire life and now I find myself connected to two within a few months.

You see, Mr. Freyhan, my immediate subordinate is Jewish and very proficient. Captain Fineman runs the Freedman's Bureau in Baton Rouge and the northern parishes."

"And it surprises you that someone could be a Jew and also be proficient in their job?"

"No, of course not! I meant it as a compliment. I am not a worldly man. I had never left Michigan until the war came along and I was able to buy myself a commission. Since then I've had the pleasure of meeting all manner of people, good and bad in every persuasion. It just so happens that my limited experience with Jews leaves me with quite a good impression."

"Then on behalf of all the Jews you may meet in the future, let me thank you," Julius Freyhan said, smiling. "We will need a bank that will work with all the people but especially the black and colored folks who have few places to go. It will be a lot of work. Many of them don't understand banking and don't trust it. Will you be running the bank, Mr. Carmody?" he asked.

"Me?" Matthew asked, stunned from his reverie. Brandy snifters and cigars were something new to him. A few years ago he would have been happy with collard greens and a small piece of pork. "I don't think so. But perhaps Thaddeus would consider taking it on."

"Why not you, Matthew?" Thaddeus asked. "I never thought of it but you'd be terrific. You've acquired a decent financial head on your shoulders and you know people. Look how successful your doll business has become."

"That's you? I am impressed," Freyhan said.

"We can hire some people to assist you, Matthew, people familiar with banking procedures," Longstreet added. "And if you allow ex-Confederate officers and Jews to do business with you, both Julius and I will be happy to be your first depositors."

"A toast, then, to the state's first black bank," Thaddeus said, hoisting his glass.

"I hope it will be as easy to run as you imply" Matthew said, unsure how he'd been conscripted into this new position.

"A few years ago I couldn't spell 'banker', now it seems I am one."

"Amy, we just received a very disturbing report that the Mississippi Ku Klux Klan forced a white teacher out of the school where she was teaching blacks and beat her," John Shipley said on another visit to review Captain Fineman's efforts and see Amy.

"The Army is afraid the Klan will try the same thing in other places. They've gotten very good at getting publicity about their adventures. We think some of the groups are even competing with one another. I worry for your safety."

"That's very considerate of you, John, but I'm not spending much time teaching and this is not Mississippi. Most of my time is spent in the medical clinic."

"Amy, I have other news, and it isn't good. The government is closing the Freedman's Bureaus, all of them, and before the end of the year."

"That's terrible. These clinics are vital. Some of the people have nowhere else to go for basic medical services. We've been able to accomplish so much and help so many people."

"It doesn't make much sense to me but they only give me orders, not explanations. The reason might be money or the Federal Government deciding that it's time for the south to move forward on its own. Regular army troops will still be stationed throughout the south but I'm going to be reassigned."

"Now you've made a bad day even worse," she sighed.

"Amy, I know we haven't known one another as long as we'd like and under normal situations I'd ask your parents if I could be permitted to court you, but these aren't normal times," Shipley's nervousness grew and his palms became damp.

"Will you marry me? I will work all my life to make you happy," he pleaded.

Amy fell into the closest chair and stared into the face of this very pleasant man. She'd enjoyed his company these past few months but she didn't love him. She thought about Thaddeus and about their infant son and tears filled her eyes. Her love for them both hadn't diminished and she clung to a faint ray of hope that some way might be found for them to be together.

John Shipley was taken aback. He'd always assumed that proposals of marriage were accompanied with joy and mutual expressions of love. Then he realized how ignorant he'd been. He just didn't have any experience with courtship. Give him a knotty military problem to solve and he could determine the best strategy quickly. But women? They were all so alien.

He'd never told Amy how much he'd loved her. They'd only kissed a few times.

He knelt beside her and took her hands.

"I've been a fool, Amy. Please forgive me. But I love you so much and I'm not sure I'd ever told you."

"Oh, John, it isn't that. You are so sweet and funny and I know you love me and I wish things in life could be that simple."

"But it is that simple. I love you, you love me. We get married, raise a family, and live in blissful harmony."

"John, I adore you. I feel good when I'm with you," she paused. "But I don't love you. I've always been in love with someone else."

John fell back in surprise and sprawled on the floor. Their immediate shock at John's reaction, now sitting nonplussed on his rump, changed to open laughter.

"Get up, John! You'll get your uniform dirty…and you look so silly."

They moved to chairs and sat as Amy held John's hands and gazed into his eyes.

"I've been in love with someone I met when I was very young but we can never marry."

"Why not? Is he a priest? Is he married?" John asked before getting a troubled look in his eyes. "He isn't one of those men that likes other men, is he? We had a few of them in my unit at Antietam and some of my men used them as cannon fodder. They didn't last five minutes standing directly in front of Confederate artillery."

"John, that's terrible. But the answer is no, none of those."

"Then why?"

"John, it's someone you know. It's Thaddeus."

"Thaddeus?" he said, his voice rose in eerie disbelief. "But Thaddeus is colored. You're in love with a nigger?"

"John, you know Thaddeus. You admire him. You've told me that. Can you really think of him as a 'nigger'?" She said, hurt and sad.

"No, you're right," he said contritely. "But thinking of you and someone of color making love distresses me."

"It shouldn't, and I'm terribly hurt by your reaction. I thought you would have reacted better. You know Thaddeus. You know what a remarkable man he is and what he's accomplished. Why is the color of his skin even an issue?

"Because it is! Just because I fought in a war to end slavery doesn't mean that I think the races should mix."

"John, it's a skin color. It isn't who the person is inside," Amy insisted.

"Maybe you're right but being thrown into this new cauldron that treats Jews, Blacks and Coloreds the same as whites isn't how I was raised and I'm having a lot of trouble getting used to it."

"Thaddeus is far more concerned about this than I've been. We both realize it is something that can never come about."

"Young love! Shakespeare! Romeo and Juliet! A tragic tale," he responded with a sarcastic bite she hadn't heard before.

"They killed themselves. I hope you aren't planning anything so drastic."

"No, John. Don't be an ass. This isn't old England. This is Louisiana. I didn't think I was going to receive a wedding invitation this morning and I was ill-prepared to handle it."

They sat silently for several minutes. John would begin to say something, and then stop. He'd stand, pace the room, look at Amy, and sit down again.

"John," Amy said softly. "I do thank you for your proposal of marriage. I am very flattered. You will make a fine husband for some very lucky girl."

"Amy, I'm not a very complicated man. If the war hadn't come along I'd probably have been a farmer or worked in a store. All I know for sure is that I still love you and I would still like you to marry me."

"Even knowing that I don't love you?" she asked querulously.

"Yes, even knowing that you don't love me. I am convinced you will come to love me. Perhaps not as you love your Romeo but I can't imagine sharing my life with anyone else," he said, holding her hands and looking at the freckled face he adored.

"John, you are so sweet," she cried and he embraced her, afraid to let go, afraid to let the world intrude. "I need some time to decide. I will need to talk to Thaddeus."

John smiled, looked lovingly into her green eyes and kissed her with a surprising tenderness.

"Melanie, John Shipley has asked me to marry him." Amy had decided to visit her son and talk over this strange turn of events before discussing things with Thaddeus.

"John Shipley? That Union Major? How did that happen? When did that happen?" Melanie rifled off, stunned by the news as she sat, breast-feeding Michelle while Amy jiggled Stephen on her lap.

"I'm not sure. He'd come up often to see how Eli Fineman was doing and stop by to see me. We had dinner a few times and then, zoom, he proposes."

"And you told him...?"

"Well, I didn't tell him about Stephen, of course but I did tell him I'd always loved Thaddeus."

"What did he say?"

"He fell off his chair onto the floor in surprise."

By the time Amy left a day later she was still confused.

"Amy," Thaddeus asked. "What are you doing in New Orleans? Is everything OK?" She was sitting in John Shipley's office. John had discreetly absented himself.

"Thaddeus, John Shipley has asked me to marry him," she said.

Amy could see her lover's blue eyes glaze as he attempted to control the emotions coursing through his body. She could sense him waver and then strain to take control.

"John is a fine man, Amy. I'm really happy for you."

"I've told him about us. I've told him I've always loved you."

"Why? Why would you do that? What we have is personal to you and me."

"Knowing how I feel and how much we love one another, he still wants to marry me. I don't quite understand why, but unless you have found some magic way for us to be together I need to consider his proposal."

"I wish that I had. I keep hoping our stars will align. I wish for it more than anything but I have found no way for us to be invisible to the rest of the world. I hope you don't mind if I sit and try to absorb this, do you? If I had sea legs, I'd have lost them by now," he jibed, wiping his eyes and trying to regain his composure.

"Thaddeus, what should I do?" she asked.

"I think you should marry him," he said, the words sticking uncomfortably in his throat.

"Will you be OK with this? I couldn't go through with it if you didn't support me. I want to have a family. I would prefer that the family be our family, but absent that, John seems to be a decent man."

"You'll be the most beautiful bride in the parish and it'll be a spectacular wedding," he said, standing and holding her now in a more chaste embrace.

"Congratulations, Major. I wish you and Amy nothing but happiness. Truly, I do," Thaddeus said, extending his hands to John Shipley.

The three of them were in Shipley's office at the Freedman's Bureau. Amy sat, as demurely as possible, hiding her nervousness. It was the first time the three of them had been in the same room together. Each of them were having difficulty making eye contact, their palms perspired.

Amy's love for Thaddeus nearly burst across the room. She knew the pain she was feeling, agreeing to this compromise. He was having the same sense of loss, she was sure of it. She bit hard down on her lip.

"Thank you, Thaddeus. I promise you I will do everything in my power to care for her and make her happy."

"I know you will. I know you are a good man and I hope you will always count me as a close friend."

They agreed to hold the ceremony at the chapel near Carmody & Williams in two months. There would be a great deal of planning to do.

"John, have you told Thaddeus that the Freedman Bureaus will be closing before year's end?" Amy asked.

"Thaddeus, the Freedman Bureaus will be closing before year's end," John said with a silly grin on his face.

"Thank you, Amy. I'd nearly forgotten," he teased, still euphoric that this beautiful freckle-faced girl with the green eyes had agreed to marry him.

"I can tell I'm not wanted. I am going to find Melanie and my friend, Brenda. You'll find me at my hotel later."

"This has been the best assignment I've had since joining the Army. Now, just as I am planning to wed, that task will end," Shipley said as he and Thaddeus sat alone, across from one another.

John Shipley, Michigan farmer, was forced to reassess so many things he'd been taught and believed. Amy loved this man sitting across from him and there was no question he was an unusual person. So why does skin color make a difference, he pondered. If Amy was ever to grow to love him it was an attitude he would need to understand and change.

"You've done a good job, Major."

"You must call me, John. This has been such a whirlwind of events;

I prefer to think of you as a friend and not a subordinate. We only have a few months to figure out how your programs can move ahead with the Bureau behind you."

"Where will you be assigned next," Thaddeus asked, fearing that it could be so far away he'd never see Amy again.

"I have no idea. The Army likes to keep us in the dark until the last minute. Some General in Washington will eventually let me know."

"Do you think that's entirely fair to Amy," he asked, knowing he was treading on dangerous ground.

John looked across the desk at the man Amy loved, less friendly than moments earlier. He was angry that someone was already injecting themselves into his life and distraught that, in truth, he, now, did need to consider whether his posting was appropriate for a married man.

Eventually his only response was, "I don't know."

"Does Captain Fineman know?" Thaddeus asked, eager to move the subject away from thoughts of John and Amy moving to some remote Army post.

"Yes! Captain Fineman has chosen to resign his commission. He's decided to remain in Louisiana. I'm not sure what he'll do but he's bright and resourceful so I'm sure he'll be just fine. Yes," he smiled, "Fineman will be fine."

"You know you can lose your commission for making bad puns," Thaddeus smiled, eager to ease any tension between them.

Three musicians strummed their instruments and sung songs that blended French and slave rhythms while the Mississippi River moved to the beat rhythmically in the background, and the sun flickered with the wake of paddle wheelers passing by. A hat lay on the ground in front of the men, already laced with coins from smiling passersbys. Nearby, waiters ran back and forth carrying lattes and strong New Orleans coffees, small beignets, and glasses of wine. It was midday in the Quarter.

"How are the children?" Brenda asked. "Imagine having twins. Do twins run in your family? I understand it's more common then."

"They're fine. They even play together although they always seem to want the same toy," Melanie answered but holding tight to Amy's hand as she spoke.

"Stephen and Michelle, isn't it?"

"Yes. Michelle is five days older. They've made Rufus and I very happy."

"Your wedding was beautiful, Melanie. I just hope mine can be almost as nice," Amy said, eager to change the subject, as she, Melanie, and Brenda lunched.

"I'm sure we can make it even lovelier since we can have it in our new home. Rufus did such a wonderful job building it and I've had such fun decorating each room. Hosting your wedding will make us both so happy. Now, let's talk about the wedding. We need to begin with a color," Melanie said.

The three were thrilled with the news after a doleful beginning to their meeting. They'd all shed tears as Amy described John Shipley's proposal and the complete and conflicting love she felt for Thaddeus. If anyone could help her see happiness in her current situation it was Melanie and Brenda.

"Isn't white appropriate?" Brenda asked. She had lost weight, gained confidence, and shed all her concerns regarding snobbishness. School was behind her and she was working for a large cotton broker. She would have liked to work at Matthew's First African-American Bank. They had launched it with a great flair, champagne and all, but Matthew explained that they needed to give preference to the hiring of blacks or coloreds who had so few opportunities other than farming.

"I don't think I want white," Amy said sheepishly, thinking of the son she wasn't able to rear.

"Why not?" Brenda asked.

"Perhaps an ivory or egg-shell color would work as well," Melanie interjected, understanding her friend's concern.

"With Amy's bright red hair we also need an accent color, something that will pull it all together."

"How about blue, a soft powder blue?" Brenda agreed with a nod from Amy.

"Wonderful," Melanie said enthusiastically, "Powder blue it will be. Do you think Bernard at Maison Frere' would be happy to help us select an appropriate wedding dress?" she laughed.

"We're such good customers, I'm sure he'd be delighted," Amy agreed.

Although Melanie didn't shop quite as often these days, the three women trekked into Bernard's store arm-in-arm with smiles on their faces. By the time they left, nearly two hours later, Amy had tried on nearly every appropriate dress in the store before settling on a traditional ivory lace floor length dress adorned with thousands of baby pearls individually sewn across the bodice. Bernard's girls would make the small size adjustments to have it fit perfectly.

They returned to Amy's hotel, shared a casual dinner, and continued discussing every aspect of the ceremony and the party to follow. They also learned that Brenda was seeing a nice young man who worked at the same company and their relationship was beginning to get serious. They all looked forward to planning her wedding the following year.

Melanie was winding up her business in the city and would leave permanently for Baton Rouge in the next few weeks. Rufus was completing the construction of a new home for them and had ordered her not to return until it was finished. Meanwhile she was busy buying drapes and furniture. The extra days would also give her some time to spend with her mother and brothers. They complained they didn't see her often enough.

"Amy, the more we talk, the more excited I become. It will be such a blessing, both for you and for us. I know Rufus will agree. I can't guarantee that everything will be completed but this will certainly give him an extra incentive."

"That will be marvelous. I don't think a marriage is a marriage unless you're surrounded by family and friends. Oh, my gosh," she gasped. "What about Elizabeth and Henry? Do you suppose they would accept an invitation to come?"

"I don't know. Wouldn't they want you to be married at Moss Grove?" Brenda asked.

"Elizabeth would, but lecherous Henry is another question."

"A wedding? A fucking wedding? With all the people I dislike? Are you crazy?" Henry ranted. "Why would I go to such a wedding?"

"Because it's my sister! My only sister," Elizabeth screamed back. "She and I are all that's left."

"Your sister hates me, Rose hates me, and then there is Thaddeus and Rose's nigger kid. They hate me and everything I represent. But frankly, I detest them as well. They are destroying everything our life has always stood for, everything my grandfather, my father, and I have built."

"You aren't too different from them, remember," she said softly, knowing she was treading on never-to-be-mentioned ground.

Henry's blue eyes flashed white as his arm pulled back and he struck his wife across the face. She fell to the ground, stunned. She reached for her cheek and felt rivulets of blood trickling down toward her chin and falling onto her dressing gown.

"If you mention that again, I'll kill you," he seethed and stormed from the room.

Captain Eli Fineman would soon be Mr. Eli Fineman, ex-Union Army officer, unemployed, with a family to support. Fortunately he had a few months before this chasm would be reached and he had come to know quite a few people. He and Ruth had talked long into the night on several occasions, discussing a myriad of options. They lit the Friday night candles and prayed over the bread at Shabbats. There were three other Jewish families that had settled in Baton Rouge and opened various stores. All three urged the Finemans to stay. Each wanted desperately to enlarge their small Jewish community.

Thaddeus had returned from New Orleans and was helping Rufus build his new home. He'd lost much of his motivation since Amy and John had announced their nuptials. He ceased being able to organize and motivate and he moved with a lethargic gait that made people avoid him rather than flock to him as they always had.

Construction of the house was proceeding. Large numbers of Cyprus logs lay on the ground waiting for their use as beams. A short distance away other men were busy planting oak and magnolia trees. A large carved plaque lay on the ground. It would grace the entrance with the proud name, 'Carmody House'.

"I think your new wife is going to be thrilled with her new home. Can you use another hand?" Eli Fineman asked as he climbed down from his horse.

"Sure can," Rufus shouted. "Nice horse. Think the Army will let you keep it when you leave?"

"I'll be lucky if they let me keep my drawers," he laughed. "Hey, Thaddeus, you men are making major progress. Almost looks as if the first floor is entirely done."

"Except for the windows! They'll be coming up from New Orleans next week after the ship docks," Rufus said proudly. "I ordered them specially made all the way from London."

Thaddeus climbed down from the ladder and wiped his brow as he studied the Army horse.

"Horse needs shoe'n," he said. "Want me to do it?"

"No, I'll let the Army use their energy."

"How're the children?" Eli asked.

"They're wonderful. Marie's taking care of them while Melanie and Amy are busy buying out the shops in New Orleans."

"Let's ride over and have dinner with them after work. What do you say?" Thaddeus asked. "I haven't seen them since they were new borns."

"I have too much work to do," Rufus objected. Having Thaddeus spend time around the son he didn't know was his, made him really uncomfortable.

"We'll help you with the work," Eli added. His wife had explained the conundrum and his curiosity on how the children were faring energized him.

Rufus was outvoted.


"How're you handling all this? Are you alright?" Eli asked, as the three rode to Melanie and Rufus' home after a long day's work. The sun was just fading from the sky and the first stars were beginning to appear faintly in the southern sky.

"It's better than slavery, even on a good day, but aside from that, it's pretty miserable. And it isn't just the wedding. That would be bad enough. It's the fact that Shipley's going to be reassigned and the Army could take them anywhere. I'm eager to see Amy happily married and John Shipley is as good as any white man she could find. But that doesn't mean I want her to disappear from my life."

"Let's hope he isn't assigned too far away. He knows this part of the state and there will be Union troops that remain. Meanwhile what can I do?" he asked.

"Rufus can always use help laying brick. What do you and Ruth intend to do once you leave the Army?"

"We're not sure. We just decided we needed to settle down, find some place nice to raise the children. Rachel is a young lady already and Stuart just grows into being a bigger handful every day. Ruth needs me around more. We like it here. I'll try and find a business. There must be something in my military career that qualifies me to be a civilian."


Marie smiled as her son-in-law, the Jewish Captain, and Thaddeus got off their horses. The two children were playing on a rug in the living room and both looked up when the men entered.

"Dada," Michelle called and began a speedy crawl toward her father. He swooped her up and kissed her. One second behind her Stephen followed. He gurgled more than spoke but it was clear that if Michelle was going to be picked up, he wanted to be held as well.

Thaddeus got to him as he was pulling himself up on Rufus' leg. Stephen struggled for a minute and then stopped, looking directly into Thaddeus' eyes. The baby sounds stopped.

"Dada," Stephen said. It was the first clear words he'd ever spoken. Rufus stared, his jaw agape.

For a long moment Thaddeus and Stephen stared into one another's eyes. Thaddeus felt a sensation he didn't understand...an emotional tugging.

"No, that's your Daddy," Thaddeus he laughed, breaking the moment and pointing to Rufus. "And that's your sister, Michelle."

"Dada," Stephen repeated.

"Here, you take Michelle and let me hold him," Rufus said, hoping to lighten the situation.

Eli Fineman watched the exchange silently. It was a scene he would long remember.

# Chapter Twenty-Six

*It arrived like a sirocco blowing across the desert destroying everything in its path. It began with the collapse of the Vienna stock exchange. It was followed by the collapse of Jay Cooke's banking empire in Philadelphia when they could no longer sell bonds to expand the Northern Pacific railroad.*

*It was aggravated by an unprecedented outbreak of equine influenza that crippled every city's transportation system; Union cavalry in the west was forced to fight Indians on foot. Men pulled wagons because their horses were too sick. The post-Civil war expansion and economic boom had run its course. Neither goods nor people were moving. The Panic of 1873 had arrived.*

By the time the financial crisis reached Louisiana prices for every product had declined and violence was erupting. Cotton prices dropped nearly thirty percent. Businesses were being shuttered and the once busy harbor of New Orleans was strangely quiet. Paddle wheelers up and down the Mississippi stood idle.

Sixty miles due west of Natchez and eighty miles north of Baton Rouge was the embryonic town of Colfax, named after Abraham Lincoln's first term Vice-President. It was a rural and bucolic town that had rarely had anything eventful occur. But a contested election between a black and a white candidate for a local office simmered without resolution before erupting without warning. The violence dwarfed anything the nation had seen since the Civil War ended nine years earlier.

Armed Black freedmen and state militia were overrun by organized brigades of whites armed with small cannon. It became a siege that lasted nearly two weeks. The blacks, led by a former slave and Union army veteran, William Ward, organized into squads, dug entrenchments, stored ammunition and supplies, and readied themselves for a pitched battle. The whites were led by C.C. Nash, an ex-Captain in the Confederacy. He drew every KKK member and white supremacist in the northern part of the state into the fray.

Henry Rogers and his associates rode hard to reach Colfax. They arrived there on the fifth day of the siege. Given his experience supervising artillery, he was immediately assigned to direct four small Napoleons, cannons that were now no more than Confederate war relics. They shelled the black positions repeatedly. C.C. Nash and other white leaders insisted on the surrender of the blacks and all the positions they were fortifying.

Before order was restored one hundred fifty blacks had been killed. More than fifty of those were massacred after they had been taken prisoner. Only three whites lost their lives. It took the arrival of two companies of Union troops to quell the riot and restore peace to the town. The guns no longer shelled one another but racial hatred froze in the souls of both races.

The wedding of Major John Shipley and Miss Amy Williams at Carmody House, the newly built home of Mr. and Mrs. Rufus Carmody, was a personal and social success. Everyone they loved was in attendance. Melanie was Amy's Maid of Honor. The bride would have preferred it to be her sister, Elizabeth, but there had never been any response to the invitation Amy had sent. She doubted anyone from Moss Grove would attend. She was unaware that, after weeks of having to listen to his wife's unabated sobbing, Henry relented enough to let Elizabeth go and take Josiah.

Allowing his wife to take their son was almost as big a battle as the first but the rapid decline in cotton prices was making him nervous and being alone for a few days to better focus on Moss Grove's survival might allow him to better concentrate on the wide array of problems facing his large plantation. He had just returned from the siege at Colfax and the debacle that followed. Fortunately he'd left a scant two hours before the Union troops arrived. One of the slower moving plantation owners had been captured and was now facing criminal charges.

Matthew and Sheila Stokes watched the ceremony hand in hand. Rose looked at him and smiled. Whenever she looked at her grown son she saw Faris. She was so proud of what he'd become and she knew Faris was sharing that pride looking down from above. All traces of the sickly boy she had raised had vanished. Matthew was a man, not as big or as tall as his father but bright and accomplished. Imagine! A banker! And handsome, Rose thought. He was a fine looking man and with Sheila on his arm, they were a visual delight.

Brenda and her beau were there. He had never been at such a multi-racial, multi-cultural wedding and his eyes struggled to take it all in. He found new affection for this beautiful girl on his arm that was clearly more cosmopolitan and self-confident than he'd thought.

The entire Fineman family was there along with James Longstreet and Julius Freyhan, who had ridden up together. Louis Roundanez from the New Orleans Picayune was there, and even the controversial governor, P.B. Pinchback, made a brief appearance. Melanie's mother and brothers were there and it was impossible for it to be anything but a festive occasion.

But outside of the marrying couple, the day belonged to an unexpected late arriving guest, Josiah. He was a handsome boy and every adult made a fuss over him to Elizabeth's delight. The boy still had a mass of curly blonde hair, rarely cut, and his father's blue eyes. He had a self-assurance and swagger that both amused and unnerved those who knew his father.

"Are you feeling alright, Elizabeth?" Amy asked, still grasping her new husband's hand.

"I'm fine, and I'm so happy for you both," she replied.

"We're glad you're here," John added. "I'm sorry your husband couldn't be with you but you have brought a most charming escort," he added, admiring the young boy standing protectively next to his mother.

Amy and Elizabeth stole glances at one another. Amy had never told John anything about Henry. She worried that if she told him everything he might change his mind about getting into such an unbalanced family.

"There is so much to do running a large plantation, he sends his regrets," Elizabeth added delicately.

Carmody House was beautiful. The furniture had arrived unmarred from France and England. All the mirrors and windows had been hung and set in place. The foliage, still in its infancy, gave evidence of its eventual splendor. Rooms with rugs adorned each bedroom and guest area. Each bedroom had a flush commode. Rufus' room also had a new-fangled gadget for washing called a shower. He'd seen a picture of one in a magazine and it had been a surprise gift from Melanie that only Thaddeus was aware of.

Thaddeus wandered through the throng, nodding to everyone but avoiding conversations that might provoke an embarrassing question. He noticed Josiah standing with Stuart Fineman at the dessert table. The two youngest guests had formed a quick friendship. In their wake, following them everywhere, were Michelle and Stephen.

"Can I help you children select something for your sweet tooth?" he asked casually.

The older boys nodded and pointed while the younger two stretched to see what delicacies were just out of their reach.

"I agree," Thaddeus said. "Those small berry pies are especially tasty. How about I grab one for each of us and we enjoy them under that tree?"

The boy's faces lit up while Michelle and Stephen shouted their approval. Stuart and Josiah ran to find a comfortable place nearby where they could all enjoy their treat.

Together they lounged and 'oooh'd' as they enjoyed the pies, leaving a ring of purple around their lips.

Thaddeus stared at the blonde tossle-haired toddler and noticed his blue eyes for the first time. The realization startled him and a cold chill drifted through his body. This was another half-brother he was looking at. It was an unworldly feeling that had never even occurred to him. He wanted to tell the boy that they were related but at this age it wouldn't mean anything. Imagine, he thought, sharing the same father with this cute little white blonde boy.

Seeing Thaddeus sitting with the children and their son drew Amy away from John. She hadn't had a chance to talk to him yet.

"Sneaking pies, I see," she laughed as she dropped on the ground next to them.

"You'll get your beautiful dress dirty," Thaddeus said as he helped her straighten her elaborately beaded skirt.

"It's the tomboy in me," she said, instinctively grabbing Stephen and setting him in her lap. "I guess I'll never grow out of it. I know Stuart and Michelle, and Stephen here, but who is this other young man?"

"We already met, Aunt Amy," Josiah said, wiping the berry stains with his sleeve.

"Oh, it's you Josiah. I didn't recognize you with all that pie on your face. Didn't your mother teach you to put the pie in your mouth and not on your face?"

"You're silly," he said.

"She's always been a little silly," Thaddeus added.

Amy stopped suddenly and looked at Josiah. Then she stared at Thaddeus and shared the same realization that had captured him a few minutes earlier.

"Thaddeus," she whispered. "This is your half-brother."

"I know. I just realized the same thing. Do you think your sister has realized it?"

"I don't think she or Henry thought of it or they definitely wouldn't have exposed you to the boy or the boy to you."

"You look good holding a young child although I think you're definitely going to find berry stains on that dress."

"Stephen is a handsome young man, don't you think?" She was unable to hold him without tears welling up inside. And this was the first time she, Thaddeus and Stephen had been together. How strange that it took her wedding to John to make it occur.

Thaddeus took Michelle on his lap and wiped the berry stains from her mouth.

"Imagine Rufus and Melanie having twins and the two children don't look anything alike. Even their skin colors are quite different." As Thaddeus talked he began looking at the two children with a more critical eye. Amy knew if he continued he would, at some point, guess the truth and the thought frightened her.

"Thaddeus, help me up please. I should get back to John. Josiah, should we spend some time with your mother? Come, we'll bring Stephen back to his mother."

But Stephen had other ideas. As Thaddeus helped Amy to her feet, Stephen decided he wanted to join Michelle and stay with the remaining pie eaters.

Thaddeus picked him up and as Amy turned to leave she could see the father in the young son and it was no longer possible to keep from crying.

"Mr. Rogers, thank you for seeing me," Eli Fineman said as he was shown past the front entry hall into Henry's office.

"Southern courtesy, nothing more," Henry said, motioning his guest to sit. "I'm sure it's no secret that I wasn't particularly supportive of your efforts at the Freedmen's Bureau and I am most pleased that the Congress has now seen the error of its ways and has begun closing them down."

"Yes, I understand your feelings but the Bureau's efforts were quite productive in assisting ex-slaves to adjust to their new status."

"It certainly succeeded in driving the entire black labor pool from the land and nearly ruining our cotton based economy."

"Actually, it's about that economy that brings me here today. General Longstreet has long thought that an energetic cotton broker could thrive here in the midst of so many successful plantations north of Baton Rouge. He and I felt that we could make it easier for you growers to dispose of your cotton without having to deal with people in New Orleans. Now that I am no longer associated with the Union Army I have agreed to open such a business. We can offer you the same price you'd pay in New Orleans without the bother or shipping costs to get your bales transported there. And with the drastic decline in cotton prices I'm sure every dollar per bale that you can save is critical."

"A Jew and a scalawag in business together, how appropriate. Mr. Fineman, Captain Fineman, whatever you call yourself now. I don't like niggers, I don't like Union soldiers, and I don't like Jews. Please show yourself out. I don't believe either I or my friends will be interested in your business offer, even if your services were to be offered free of charge."

"My best to your wife," Eli said as he rose to leave, refusing to acknowledge the taunts of his host.

"How do you know my wife?" Henry said turning back to the man he'd dismissed with insulting pleasure.

"I met her at the recent wedding of Major John Shipley and Miss Amy Williams. I believe they are sisters. I'm sure your wife described to you what a lovely affair it was. Everyone was also most taken with your son, Josiah. Good day." Eli turned and opened the door, not wanting Henry to see the smile on his face. Good riddance you bastard, he said to himself.

Despite Henry's assurances that no one would do business with him, Eli Fineman succeeded. The depressed cotton prices made it all the more imperative to save the time and cost of moving the goods to the mouth of the Mississippi. By the time the bales arrived there, the planters worried, the price could have dropped further.

To protect himself against the vagaries of brokering, Eli also set up a clothing store in Baton Rouge that specialized in practical everyday clothing, such as overalls, work shoes, and the like. Ruth ran it and did the buying. It wasn't for the fashion-minded. Those customers preferred to shop in New Orleans, anyway. They also carried clothing that was appropriate for the government employees who made up an increasing percentage of the city's population. Ruth Fineman made no distinction as to how colored, black or white customers were treated and this was their greatest asset, a willingness to treat everyone equally. Fineman's Clothing Store would succeed and be a legacy to Rachel and Stuart when they grew up if they desired to follow in their parent's footsteps.

The First African-American Bank had done well at the onset making loans to blacks and coloreds wanting to buy land or open small businesses. The financial underpinnings of its business were the cotton contracts of an increasing number of cotton brokers. Matthew worked hard to learn the banking business but concepts of collateral and security were foreign to him.

Furthermore, at least once a week he'd arrive at work in the morning to find all the front windows shattered by bricks. The bank was turning out to be a perfect target of the KKK hoodlums. And by the time the Union soldiers arrived, the miscreants were long gone. Now with financial panic seemingly everywhere the bank was under new pressures. Cotton prices were at their lowest in nearly twenty years and the bank was forced to call loans and put pressure on the very people they had set out to help.

Thaddeus returned to New Orleans determined to forget Amy and move on with his life. The first problem he encountered was the refusal of the parents of the Creole children to attend schools that had integrated blacks and coloreds from its inception.

"We are white, monsieur," Juliet Pouton said, dragging her nine year old daughter behind her. "We no longer want our daughter thought to be anything else."

"Madam Pouton, I don't understand," Thaddeus asked, standing next to the class's teacher. "Your daughter does wonderfully in school. Why would you take her away?"

"It is you who does not understand. When the war ended we all stood together with thoughts of equality and fraternity. We would be more like France. But it is not turning out to be that way. White children tease colored children. Colored children tease black children and black children get angry at them both. We Creoles have our own culture and I do not want my daughter in the middle. I thank you, but I am going to enroll her in a school where she will be safer and among her own kind."

Within days Thaddeus learned that much of the same thing was happening all over Southern Louisiana. It wasn't just the Creole children. Wherever they could find an alternative, parents sought out schools where their ethnicity dominated. Everything he built was splintering, and with the government's funding for all the Freedman schools ending within months, the outlook was bleak. They would definitely need more financial help from the state and city if they were to continue to function.

Thaddeus sat in the middle of the church agonizing over his job and his life. He had had so much optimism just a few years ago when he and Rufus launched Carmody & Williams. He never doubted that Amy would always be an integral part of his life and the sea of white, colored and black faces coming to their school would be endless.

He was lost in his thoughts when a man who looked slightly familiar, dressed in black and wearing the white collar of a man of God entered through a side door.

"I hope I'm not disturbing you. I'm Reverend Dinsmore. I believe we met at the Carmody wedding. You were an usher or best man, if my aging memory serves me."

"Best man, and you have a fine memory," Thaddeus replied. "Thaddeus Williams! I hope you don't mind my sitting here. I'm trying to work through some insolvable problems I seem to be facing all at once."

"That's what the church is for. Somehow I think God can hear you a little better when you talk to him from a house of worship. Is there anything I might be able to help with? I'm told I'm a very good listener."

"I'm not sure. May I just sit here awhile longer?" he asked, looking up at the man on the cross to whom he had rarely confided.

"Certainly! I'll be in my office if you change your mind."

Thaddeus continued to sit without resolution. His conundrum just seemed to whirl through his mind in an endless loop. The light from behind the only two stained glass windows the church had ever been able to afford began to fade as evening approached.

"I'm going to go home for my dinner," Walter Dinsmore offered as he exited his office. "Would you care to join me? It would give me great pleasure."

"Are you certain your wife won't mind?" Thaddeus asked. The alternative of returning to his own room for a solitary evening gave him no pleasure.

"I'm sure neither my wife nor my children will mind. They relish guests and they are quite used to me bringing them home unexpectedly."

The two men walked around the corner to a small house attached to the church and entered a small, clean, but neatly furnished, alcove.

"Hester, I've brought a guest, Mr. Thaddeus Williams. Mr. Williams, this is my wife Hester, my daughter, Sarah, and my young son, Jesse. I met Mr. Williams at a recent wedding over which I presided."

"Welcome to our home," the matronly Hester Dinsmore said in a warm greeting. But Thaddeus was only half-listening. How strange that these two young people bore the exact names of the parents that raised him.

As they sat for dinner, daughter Sarah gave a short prayer of thanks.

"Thaddeus, are you alright? A very strange look came over you a few moments ago," the preacher asked.

"It's just such an unusual coincidence. I was raised as a house servant at a plantation north of Baton Rouge called Moss Grove by two wonderful parents whose names were also Sarah and Jesse.

"They're Biblical names, loving reminders," Hester noted, smiling at her children.

He and young Sarah changed smiles throughout the dinner and for the first time he wondered if he might be able to put Amy in a separate corner of his heart and move forward.

Sarah was dark-skinned with the loveliest high cheek bones he'd ever noticed, each one with a deep dimple. She smiled with both her lips and her eyes in a way that lit up the room. Her voice was soft, but resonant, and the prayer she had spoken at the beginning of the meal had an almost lyric quality. She had her father's height and her mother's warmth.

"Thaddeus," Jesse asked, "How come you so much lighter than us?" It was a question only a twelve year old boy would have had the nerve to ask. Jesse had the same lanky quality and tight natty hair as his father.

"Jesse, that's a rude question to ask our guest," his father interjected.

"No, that's alright. Jesse, I had a white father. Most of the people of color you meet will have some white blood in them from somewhere back."

"OK! Mom, can I have more potatoes?" As quickly as he had asked the question, he changed the subject with the normal span of attention of someone not yet in their teens.

# Chapter Twenty-Seven

"It's colder than a witch's tit this morning. I worry that some of our vegetable plants might freeze," Henry said.

"Come back to bed," Elizabeth pleaded. "It's cold and it's New Year's Day. Happy 1874 to you!"

Loud noises outside made it impossible to return to the warm bed. Henry donned a robe and descended the circular staircase.

"What's all this noise," he asked. "Don't you think it's the wrong hour to be celebrating," he asked as he headed toward the noises in the pantry. Thatcher and several others were standing there.

"What's this all about? Why are you all here?"

"Boss," Thatcher said. "You better come to the stable with me. Your dog, Whisper, woke us all up with barking and running around. He found something terrible. Trust me, this is somethin' you're gonna' wanna' see."

"Let me put some clothes on. Wait here."

Within minutes Henry had put on his boots and jacket and followed his black overseer toward the stable. Others followed at a respectful distance but the murmur of their voices gave the cold air an eerie pitch.

There, near the entrance, was Josiah's tutor, Julian Rabot, naked, dead with his genitals removed and lying next to him. On the other side was the prostate body of the black teenage son of one of the shareholder families, also naked.

"Jesus Christ, almighty," Henry blanched. He started to retch but then caught himself, leaning against a beam. "What the hell is this all about? Who did this?"

"I 'spect we ain't never gonna' find out, but I hear before that this is punishment for breakin' God's commandments in a terribly sinful way," Big George proclaimed.

"Did you do this?" Henry asked.

"No, sir. I don't take another man's life 'cept in self-defense. But," he added, "I ain't condemning it either."

"Somebody put a blanket on these two and get them buried. No ceremony, just get them buried before news of this incident spreads," he said as he turned and moved slowly back toward the house, his breath leaving trails of steam in the air as Whisper heeled next to his master, satisfied with his morning's work.

"Not a particularly happy note on which to launch the New Year, is it Elizabeth?" he asked rhetorically as he and his wife shared a rare breakfast. "Do you suppose Rabot ever touched Josiah?"

"I don't think so, but we can never know for certain without questioning him and I'm not comfortable doing that. We certainly must be more careful finding a replacement to teach him."

"He's almost old enough to send away to a school. Not as far as New Orleans, perhaps, but there may be something appropriate in Baton Rouge. The city certainly has grown and there are enough government parasites with children that also need schooling. I shall try and find out what might be available that would be suitable for our son."

The frost continued another few days. The day it broke, Big George Thatcher arrived at the rear entrance of the main house and asked to speak to Henry.

"How did the corn survive the frost?" Henry asked.

"Lost some, but most'll make it through. We should have the soil ready for planting by the time spring arrives."

"Good! Is that what you came to tell me?"

"No! I've come for my year-end bonus we talked over and to let you know that me, my missus, and my young 'un will be leavin' so as you can get a proper replacement. I can recommend one or two men if you like."

"George, there's no bonus. I went over the books as soon as the year ended. Cotton prices fell into the crapper, you know that. And all the extra supplies and things you and your wife took from the commissary when the baby was born. You owe me money. So do most of the sharecroppin' families. I've had to borrow from the banks again to keep from goin' under. Now I can't keep you from leaving but if you do, it's without any bonus money."

"Mr. Rogers, that's not the agreement we had. You owe me my bonus like we agreed. What about the sharecroppin' families and the money you owes them?" he said as the muscles in his neck began to tighten and he clenched and unclenched his fists.

"Those tenants are entitled to most of the money from the sale of the cotton but the cotton didn't bring much this year. Here, look yourself," Henry he said, thrusting papers toward his angry overseer.

"You knows I don't do numbers very well."

"Then after the cotton is sold, I deduct for the rent that we all agreed to and the things each family used from the commissary. If we'd sold the cotton for what it brought last year everyone, including me, would have made a profit. But it didn't, so there is no money. You need to understand and explain it to them."

"I'll talk to them but they ain't gonna be any happier than I am," he said, turning and walking out in a gesture that said clearly this matter hadn't been resolved.


A few days later Big George once again approached Henry Rogers. This time it was at the smoke house, where the slaughtered pigs were still hanging. The slow burning fire emitted a strong pleasant odor, tinged with the smell of the maple wood burning beneath it ever so slowly. Occasionally cedar, or sometimes oak, chips were added to give extra flavor, but Moss Grove had always favored using maple.

"Mister Henry, we all talked it over and if you ain't gonna' pay us fair wages, we all gonna' leave. We decided we'd give you a week to give us an answer. If you still not goin' to pay us, we'll find work somewhere else. We ain't gonna' be cheated."

"You and your families won't find work anywhere," he said, unsuccessfully keeping his voice from revealing his anger.

"The damn state is nearly bankrupt. No one wants cotton. Maybe things will be better next year. You want to leave now, go ahead." He turned and walked back toward the house.

"One week, Mister Henry," Thatcher said to the back of this white owner who, he was convinced, was trying to cheat them again.

"We'll wait one week," he repeated to himself silently.


Henry grabbed the brandy and a glass and poured a heavy drink as Josiah entered.

"I miss Mr. Rabot," the boy said.

The drastic change of subject spun him around. He looked at his son, not knowing whether to dismiss him or question him. The silence hung heavy as the boy waited for some response.

"Mr. Rabot is gone. He had to leave suddenly," Henry sighed, unwilling to raise the delicate issue.

"But he didn't say goodbye. He was my best friend. Now I'm lonely again. You don't want me to play with the nigger kids. I sometimes see them from my bedroom window down by the river playing and I wished that I could play with them."

"You aren't a nigger. Remember that! No matter what people ever say to you in life. You are not a nigger," he said, raising his voice and realizing his son wouldn't understand a word he was saying.

"Go take Whisper for a walk. Go ahead. Daddy has a headache."

By Friday the tension at Moss Grove had risen precipitously. The house slaves moved with extra quiet, not wanting to set off an unprovoked tirade from either Massa' Henry or Miss Elizabeth. The two owners had barely spoken to one another since the gauntlet with the field slaves had been thrown.

This time it was Henry who walked over to the overseer's house. It was the first time he had been there since George's baby was born, almost six months earlier. He nodded at George's wife, smiled at the baby, and made eye contact with its father. They stepped out to the porch together.

"When it's this cold in January it usually bodes well for a rainy spring and a warm summer. The kind of weather cotton likes," Henry said, trying to make small talk. Big George just stood silently, letting the man talk. He'll get around to it eventually, George thought.

"I can't pay your bonus, George. I just don't have the money and the bank isn't in a lending mood. I can't pay your sharecroppers either but I do have an offer and it's as good as you'll find in these parts. I'm sure you know that Moss Grove isn't the only plantation having troubles."

George did know. They'd sent men to plantations as far as thirty miles in each direction. It was the same everywhere. He also chose to not acknowledge his awareness of the situation with this bigoted white man who stood in front of him and who had broken his word.

"The only thing I'm able to do is forgive everyone's debts at the Commissary. I don't have any money; you and your workers don't have any money, so we all take a loss. What do you say? Everyone I talk to says this problem should be over by summer and with a decent crop we'll all be a lot better off by fall."

George listened and said nothing. He knew he was trapped again and would have to stay another year. He hated Henry Rogers for that.

"I'll stay, Mister Henry. You ain't left me no choices but I'm not happy about this and if I discover that what you're tellin' me ain't true, we will leave with or without my money."

"Thank you, George. What about the sharecropper families?"

"I don't know. I'll tell 'em what you said. They's each gotta' make their own decision."

In the end all but one family agreed to stay. That family was the parents of the boy who had been found in the barn with Julian Rabot. They still had three other children and, even without money, they weren't equipped to be reminded every day of their son's awful ending. They knew that no one would look very hard for the men who did the killing.

It was still winter and not yet time for planting but land had to be cleared, pigs slaughtered, food canned, and buildings repaired. Everyone had work to do and the anger at feeling cheated was stored in the 'bad' memory bank of each of them. It wasn't until nearly a week later that the story of the beating of the family that had left Moss Grove reached them. The family had decided to follow the river and look north for work. The third night out, some forty miles from where they'd begun, they were confronted with six men wearing white hoods and brandishing a burning cross.

The family tried to run from their attackers. They even tried to hide in the thickets but with the river at their backs there was no place to go. Five hours later the women had been raped and the men beaten. They were still alive but it would take them a long while to recover. For now they were being cared for by Union Army medics.

Big George knew that in some way the evil hand of Henry Rogers had instigated this terror and he now assumed personal responsibility for seeing that man rot in hell.

Thaddeus needed to clear his head. It was a good reason to visit Rufus, Melanie and their family. His career was in turmoil; his emotions were in turmoil and his friend represented one of the few points of stability he could connect with.

"I'm thinking we should open another feed store up north, maybe Alexandria or St. Francisville," Rufus said as they walked the grounds of Carmody House, reviewing each new embellishment.

"We've trained some pretty good folks and with us guiding them I think they could make a decent living out of it.

"Sounds fine with me, Rufus, although I'm here so little these days we should think about removing the Williams name and just calling it Carmody."

"I'd never do that, my friend. We started this business together and we won't change it."

"Well, let's do this then. I'll continue to be part of what we built here but whatever new locations you open will be entirely yours."

"That's typical of you. You're always looking to stretch what's fair to favor the other person. Now, aside from business, how're you feeling … emotionally, I mean? Amy-wise, I mean?" he said, clasping his younger friend around the shoulders.

Rufus' hair was beginning to turn grey at the temples and his body had a few more aches in the morning than he'd remembered. Now with a daughter and a son to care for, he was feeling older and more paternal. Those feelings easily included his affection for the man standing beside him who he'd first met at Port Hudson more than a decade earlier. So much had happened in the years since then but his feelings for Thaddeus had only grown. He hated that his friend hadn't been able to marry the woman he'd always loved. He rarely thought of Stephen as anything but his own son except in times like this when he felt his friend's pain.

"I've met a girl, the daughter of the Preacher who married you, Reverend Dinsmore. She's nearly as black as an ace of spades but with a smile and a voice that are special."

"So you've already gotten past Amy and moved on?"

"I'll never get past Amy. She'll always be there with a special place in my heart. Right next to you, you big oaf who's now a daddy! But I do smile a little now, when I think of Sarah and I think she likes me a little, too. It isn't the same intensity but there is an easy comfort I haven't ever experienced."

"Do you care that's she's really dark-skinned?" he asked a little hesitantly. "I mean, you did mention it."

"I know we all want to be a little whiter in our family tree but that's not important to me. I didn't love Amy because she was white. I loved her, and still do, because she's Amy. I think I'm beginning to feel the same way about Sarah."

"Does Amy know?"

"There isn't anything to know yet. If and when there is, I'll tell her."

Thaddeus stayed for dinner that night and watched Melanie with Michelle and Stephen. Both children had become toddler chatterboxes and loved their Uncle Thaddeus.

At bedtime he read to them as they both snuggled under their covers. His eyes twinkled. He loved them both but he continued to have a special feeling for Stephen. Maybe because he's a boy, Thaddeus thought, knowing it was something more.

"Mr. Henry, come quick. Something's wrong with Miss Elizabeth," Chloe called as she ran to find the master of Moss Grove in the field overseeing the spring planting. Chloe had been managing the house since Sarah left, but as hard as she tried she'd never been able to develop any rapport between herself and the plantation's white owners. She had even prayed over it, but to no avail.

"What's the matter, Chloe? Can't you see I'm busy?" he said as he tried to pull a large root that had clogged his new prized seed planter. Having only one arm made it especially difficult. One side of the rope was tied to the root and the other to the pommel on his horse's saddle. It wasn't giving in easily.

"Miss Elizabeth is real ill. She's throwing up and her skin is cold as ice."

"I'll be right there. You'd better send someone for the doctor."

Elizabeth's skin was clammy and her eyes were glassy when Henry finally arrived nearly an hour later.

"Do any of you know how treat her?" he asked Chloe and two of the other house servants standing nearby.

"We can give her some tea and some laudanum but we don't know herbs the way Rose did."

"Never mind Rose! We'll wait for the doctor. Keep her clean and comfortable in the meantime."

With no one else easily available to go for the doctor, George Thatcher decided he could do it as quickly as anyone. In just over two hours, he left his horse to get watered and fed at the Carmody & Williams stable and ran the few blocks to the Freedman Clinic.

As he was explaining the problem to the woman in charge, he was overheard by Amy. She had stayed in Baton Rouge to be close to Melanie since John had to report back to his Army post.

"Excuse me, did I hear you're from Moss Grove?" she asked.

"Yes, ma'am. Ah's the overseer! Miss Elizabeth is real sick and I need a doctor to come right away."

"I'll get the doctor. You go to the feed store and ask for Rose. Explain what you know about Miss Elizabeth's condition and tell her to give you some medicines. I'll get the doctor and we'll go there separately. Now hurry!"

Amy and the doctor were on their way as soon as a horse was hitched to the wagon. Thatcher returned to the feed store and stables where his horse was being cooled down from the harsh ride. He introduced himself to Rufus and Rose.

"I've always wanted to meet you Miss Rose. A lot of the folks talk mighty kindly about you back at Moss Grove."

"I'm sure that doesn't apply to Massa' Henry, does it?"

"No," he laughed. "It surely does not."

"How is everyone there?" she asked as she handed the big man a steaming cup of coffee and a roll.

"Not real good, now you ask. Cotton prices way down and that white man sure is ornery."

"Always was, always will be. I know it ain't godly but I do hope he end up in the fires of hell."

"Ah shares that particular point of view," Big George said, his head nodding in complete agreement.

Elizabeth was tossing and turning when they all arrived at the plantation. Josiah had tried to get into the room to see his mother and he wasn't at all happy that no one would let him. He struggled to hold back his tears. He just knew something was terribly wrong and there was no one to reassure him. He ran to find his father who had gone back to the fields. Chloe was the only one in the room with the ashen woman lying on the bed. She smiled with relief when Amy entered with the doctor.

"Lizzy, it's Amy. I'm here. I've brought the doctor. Can you tell him what's wrong?"

"I feel hot and cold at the same time and I can't hold anything down. Please do something. I'm frightened. I feel as if I'm going to die."

"I'm sure you aren't going to die. Please let the doctor examine you."

Amy left while the doctor made his examination. She told Chloe to let Henry know that she'd arrived and she watched as another girl followed the instructions Rose had sent on how to prepare the herbs George Thatcher had brought.

The doctor came out of the room as Henry returned.

"Hello, Amy," he said icily.

"Henry," she nodded.

"Your wife has a very high temperature and is badly dehydrated from diarrhea. It looks to be a case of Yellow Fever. I've already seen a few at the clinic," the Doctor said seriously.

"Daddy, will mommy be OK?" Josiah asked, clinging to his father's pants leg.

"She'll be fine. Go take Whisper for a run. And don't cry, for God's sake," he said impatiently.

"If you wait outside, Josiah," Amy intervened, "I'll come with you. Just give us a few minutes."

Henry stared at his arrogant sister-in-law. How dare she intervene with his son? He uncharacteristically held his tongue and turned his attention back to the doctor.

"What should we do?" he asked.

"Keep her as cool and comfortable as possible. Give her the laudanum if she's in pain, otherwise liquids. And I have no objection to giving her some of the herbs Rose prescribed. We doctors don't understand how they work but they sometimes have an unusually beneficial effect. Send a rider if you need me to come back, otherwise only the will of God and some luck will prevail. Amy, will you be returning with me?"

"No, I'm going to stay and try to help. Assuming that is acceptable to you, Henry?" she asked with a tone that clearly said that she was staying and he'd better not oppose her.

Henry just nodded and walked the doctor to his wagon.

For an hour Amy and Josiah walked through the trees bordering the planted fields while Chloe remained with Elizabeth. Whisper scampered ahead of them easily covering twice their distance. The boy's nervousness was gone. He had a friend. He and Amy had not seen one another since John and Amy's wedding. Amy was sure he'd grown inches in those few months and she delighted in getting to know the boy. Here was another mixed child that reminded her of her Stephen.

For the first time Josiah no longer reminded her of Henry. He was becoming his own person. By the time they returned it was time for Josiah's bath and dinner. Amy returned to her sister's bedside. The bed was soaking wet and no one was around.

"Chloe! Chloe! Where is everyone? Why is no one here with Miss Lizzie?" Amy shouted.

"Massa' Henry said you going to take care of her so we could go do our other chores," the house maid said as she dashed up the stairs.

"I need help. The bed is soaking. Go get clean bed linens and help me cool off my sister."

"But Massa' Henry say…"

"I don't care what Massa' Henry say. I'm here now and I'm telling you to help me," Amy said angrily.

Chloe ran to get clean sheets and fresh cool water. It took more than an hour for things to get settled down.

"Thank you, Chloe. I appreciate your help. I'll explain things to Mr. Rogers."

"Thank you, Miss Amy. I just don't want to get into trouble with Massa' Henry."

Amy sat in the chair opposite the bed, too tired to even light the candles in the room as the evening approached. Within minutes she had dozed off.

"How is she?" Henry asked. Elizabeth was still sleeping. Amy had no idea how long her brother-in-law had been standing there. Finally, he began lighting candles.

"Clean and resting, no thanks to you," Amy said.

"Don't get snippy with me. You come into my home and begin giving orders. So," he paused and smiled, "If you want to care for her, she's all yours."

"This is your wife, Henry, and Josiah's mother. Don't you want her to get well?"

"I'm sure you'll do everything you can to care for her. Certainly better than the house niggers that sometimes work here. Ask the girls to prepare some food for you if you're hungry. I'm going to my room." He left haughtily without another look at Amy or his bedridden wife.

Elizabeth lingered for nearly a week with a fever that hovered between

102 and 105. Chloe assigned one of the other maids to be available to Amy if she was needed and the younger sister rarely left the room.

"Amy, is that you?" Elizabeth called weakly from the bed in the middle of the night.

"Yes, Lizzie, it's me. Can I get you anything?"

"Did you know my baby girl is dead and I killed her?" she sobbed.

"Clara died in a fire, Lizzie. You didn't kill her," Amy said softly, caressing her sister's arm.

"Henry sent her away and I didn't stop him. He sent her away 'cause she had nigger blood. I should have stopped him, Amy. I should have stopped him."

"Lizzie, you're distraught and not thinking clearly. I knew you sent the baby away and that she had died in an accidental fire. It wasn't your fault. But Clara wasn't colored. How could she be? She was your and Henry's daughter," Amy stopped.

"Liz, you never….."

"Of course not! That's what Henry thought until Sarah told him that his mother, Ruby, had mixed Creole and black blood in her. I think it was Henry's mother and Henry's father may or may not have known. I'm not sure; I get confused easily these days."

"Henry has black blood? Bigoted Henry? Who else knows?"

"No one. Henry swore he'd kill anyone who told his secret. I assumed Sarah told you after she left here."

"She never told any of us. Oh, my god Elizabeth, how terrible for you to have lost your daughter for such a stupid reason."

But there was no reply. Elizabeth had drifted off to sleep while Amy sat, trying to absorb the startling revelation she'd just been told. When the first morning light peeked into the room, Elizabeth was breathing more easily and Amy was sleeping, dreaming terrible images of having had to give her Stephen away because he was mixed, just like Josiah and her Thaddeus. By the time Amy awoke it was morning and she was still tired from the emotional kaleidoscope of mixed races that paraded through her mind.

Elizabeth's fever came down and seemed to improve but as it did she began to demand more and more laudanum. It made her thoughts and speech foggy and her eating erratic. Henry stopped by only once, looked in the door, and left again. Josiah was permitted to visit for short periods and as long as he and Amy read a book together he was entertained.

A week later, believing her sister was resting quietly, Amy stretched and went down to have the first real meal she'd had in several days. Josiah was there, dropping food to Whisper, who waited anxiously under the table, his tail wagging furiously.

A sound startled them. Amy's and Chloe's eyes made contact and they both raced up the stairs.

Elizabeth was lying on the floor, a table turned over, and blood on her forehead. Carefully they picked her up and set her back onto the bed.

Only half-conscious she mumbled something that sounded like 'Clara' but Amy couldn't be sure and Elizabeth fell into a deep stupor. The women tried everything they could think of, cold cloths, medicines and massages. They took turns trying to waken her but nothing worked and by morning, drained of every bit of energy in their being, they stopped.

"She's gone," Amy sobbed. "My sister is dead, my only sister." She knelt by the bedside and wept openly. Chloe pulled a sheet over Liz's face and left to tell Massa' Henry.

The funeral was held a day later and Elizabeth was buried in the small cemetery reserved for members of the Rogers family. Henry barely spoke to anyone. He didn't cry, he didn't eat, but neither did he raise his voice. It was impossible to discern what he was feeling, if he was feeling anything. He moved in a dream-like state and it frightened the staff. This was not the loud bigoted man who was universally disliked. This was a man who had just lost his wife and deserved sympathy.

Amy spent most of those next days comforting Josiah, who knew something important had happened, but all he understood was that his mother had gone on a trip and would not be returning for a long while. With his father acting so strangely, the small boy found solace in his aunt and his dog.

"Henry, John and I are prepared to raise Josiah if you will allow it. Without a mother to care for him, he will not fare well," she said the day after Elizabeth had been buried.

"Josiah and I will be fine. Goodbye. I prefer you not come back to Moss Grove. Your presence is not wanted." He stared at her icily before even she wilted under his angry gaze. She said her goodbye to Josiah, hugging him and wiping away his tears.

"I'll miss you, Aunt Amy. Will you come and visit me?" he sobbed.

"I'll try, Josiah. I really will. I love you."

She left Moss Grove knowing Josiah was watching the buggy until it disappeared from view.

# Chapter Twenty-Eight

Spring burst forth from a rainy March and the puffy scented flower of the hibiscus cotton plants burst optimistically across the state. With luck, it would move smoothly through its maturing process before opening to reveal the soft fluff of its cotton boll.

Henry had to use most of his secreted northern bank reserves to avoid a third loan from Abner Moresby and his New Orleans banker friends. Moss Grove had grown increasingly lonely since his wife had died. He now chose to remember his relationship with Elizabeth as a loving one. The house staff moved in silence through the empty rooms and he had little to say to them. He invited Lunstrom to visit with him for a few days but their lives had taken separate directions. There really was no one with whom he could have a conversation. Moss Grove simultaneously felt too big and too lonely and, at the same time, too small to embrace his frustrations.

The expectation that he and Josiah might grow closer hadn't materialized, rather the opposite. The boy seemed to grow more afraid of his father and more reticent to laze around the kitchen and servant's quarters. Mostly he remained in his room, his dog, Whisper, his only companion.

Henry had no concept of how to raise a son by himself on the few occasions it even crossed his mind. Chloe tried to make him aware that there was a problem brewing but the father's concern was fleeting. Thatcher noticed it, but, he, too, chose to remain silent. This was not a white man who took suggestions from a black man, no sir.

Henry badly missed female companionship, and he missed sex, the type of hot, sweating from every pore, sort of sex. He remembered his first times with Melanie. That type of intense fucking…that's what I miss, he thought.

He made a sudden decision. It was time for a visit to New Orleans. He'd take Josiah, leave him with a nanny, or even Amy, and go enjoy himself.

Amy kept her pregnancy a secret as long as she could. She hadn't even told her husband, John, that she had already missed two periods. He was busy with his military duties and often away for days at a time. If he knew, he'd worry and couldn't do his job, she thought. This was her second pregnancy; she knew what to expect and this time she wouldn't have to hide.

She also held the belief that the shorter the time people realized she was expecting, the more rapidly the nine months would pass. She hated being pregnant. Everything in her tomboy nature reasserted itself, although she was thrilled with the thought of her and John having a baby. Maybe they'd be able to spend more time with Stephen at Melanie's home. The Shipley's had settled on the north side of New Orleans in a small house. There would be a sunny small room for their new addition.

Major John Shipley was still under orders that all the Freedman's Bureaus across Louisiana would be closed by year's end. He had no orders beyond that. He knew Amy had a strong desire to remain in the area where she'd grown up and always lived. He knew if he had to take her up north, or even worse, out west, that she'd be miserable.

This past week he and a company of his men had chased nearly two dozen men they believed to be Klan members through the Bayous southwest of New Orleans. They captured two and the rest either escaped or became a meal for the 'gators. Troops were already being withdrawn in some of the other states, but in places like Louisiana, Mississippi and Texas, they were still authorized the same number of troops as when they arrived.

The problem was that a lot of men were resigning every week and not being replaced, reducing their actual numbers. These men, like Eli Fineman, realized their military responsibilities were coming to an end and they were forced to make other plans with their lives.

Amy disliked being alone so she would often take the buggy north to Baton Rouge where she could visit her friends at the School and Clinic. This week, however, she planned to do some secret shopping for the baby and dine with her friends.

Amy hadn't seen Thaddeus for awhile and she was taken aback when he came to dinner escorting an attractive dark black girl she'd never met. It was equally awkward for her long-time friend as he made the introductions.

"Amy, this is Sarah Dinsmore. Her father is Reverend Dinsmore who presided at Rufus and Melanie's wedding. Sarah, this is Amy Shipley now. She used to be an ugly freckle-faced tomboy named Amy Williams," he smiled.

"Hello Sarah. I'm sorry John can't be here with us but he's off somewhere chasing white hooded hoodlums," she said as they made themselves comfortable around the table. She tried to keep her voice calm. Her old feelings stirred within her and she wasn't sure what they were. It seemed to be a pinch of jealousy meshing with happiness for her lover. It was clear that Thaddeus had never explained their relationship to this sweet girl he was escorting.

Matthew and Sheila Stokes arrived quite late, out of breath and noticeably unnerved. They apologized for their tardiness, made their greetings and sat, obviously still rattled.

"They tried to burn Sheila's father's warehouse last night", Matthew said with an unfamiliar anger in his voice.

"The bastards got away but we had enough warning to stop them just as they were getting started. Maybe a few broken heads will convince them there's no way we're going back to being slaves." He spoke with a new maturity. He had become the ultimate banker, suitably attired, replete with swinging gold key chain, but through the façade, it was still Matthew.

He and Sheila had become engaged. The bank was struggling and Matthew felt he needed to get it on an even keel before getting married. Sheila wanted to have the wedding in June, just two months away. She wasn't thrilled with this uncertain postponement but her love for Matthew was so apparent, it was clear she would be as patient as circumstances demanded.

"The people in my father's church are getting angrier and angrier," Sarah said. "All this violence is forcing peaceful people to organize and fight back. It's not a good thing."

"Let's not allow all this distressing news to spoil our being together," Thaddeus said.

"We have so little opportunity to enjoy one another's company and get caught up. I propose that we are only allowed to discuss good things during dinner. We can always wait for dessert to chat about distressing subjects when a good soufflé may overcome the news. All agreed?"

The mood brightened and everyone began chattering at once. Amy had originally planned to tell Thaddeus of her pregnancy when they were alone but his obvious comfort with Sarah made her change her mind. Maybe Thaddeus didn't even love her anymore. He certainly seems to have moved on. Truly she didn't know what to believe and it bothered her. All she knew was that she had to tell this group of friends that she was expecting.

"I have several things I want to share with you," Amy began, "But under instructions from our friend, Mr. Williams, I shall only disclose the good news at this time. I'm expecting. John and I will have our first child in the late fall."

Immediately Thaddeus' deep blue eyes connected with hers and they were alone. The happy din of the others was there but neither of the two locked lovers saw nor heard them. She searched for his acknowledgment that it would be alright. She needed him to know that it didn't change, would never change, her feelings. Finally, his eyes lit up and she knew they could both move forward. And most important, she knew that he still loved her. She thanked him in silence. They both understood that they would continue to love one another. He might have Sarah just as she had John but their connection, their love, was forged forever.

No, they hadn't yet picked out a name. No, she hadn't told John yet. She hadn't wanted to worry him when he was so preoccupied with his Army duties. No, they still had no idea to where they might be reassigned.

Matthew and Sheila told their friends of their engagement and Matthew's desire to postpone their marriage at this time because of his business uncertainties.

"I know I'm new to this group," Sarah said, "but if you love one another those sorts of troubles are to be shared whether you're single or married." Amy nodded her head in agreement while Thaddeus joined in supporting his brother.

"You don't take on the commitment of a wife and family until you're sure you can support and care for them," he said.

Ultimately they realized it was a difference in how men and women felt about such things, always had been, always will be.

By the time the soufflés arrived they were sated with Amy's news and a good meal.

"OK," Thaddeus directed. "You may now share your negative stories.

But do try and lace them with some degree of hope. I would hate to have our stomachs lose that wonderful meal to a cold floor."

"That's actually pretty disgusting," Matthew smiled.

"I know you've all heard that my sister, Elizabeth, died last month."

"I'm so sorry," Thaddeus said. "I wish I could have been there with you."

"It was all so strange. She was getting better from the yellow fever but she'd been taking so much laudanum that she was perpetually woozy. I was downstairs when she got out of her bed and fell. She hit her head on a table near the bed," Amy sobbed softly, reliving the still-raw memory.

"Shortly after we put her into the ground Henry told me to leave Moss Grove and never come back."

"I'm glad to see he's still the bastard he always was," Matthew said, while Thaddeus sat in stony silence. "What about their cute little son, Josiah?"

"He says that Josiah will remain there, without a mother. I offered to take him but you know Henry. There is something else that I was told, something I found very difficult to believe.

"In one of my sister's few moments of clarity we talked about Clara, the daughter she and Henry had. The baby was immediately given away," she paused, trying to verbalize the unlikeliness of what she'd been told.

"Clara was colored. Henry and Elizabeth had given birth to a racially mixed child. Elizabeth said that Henry accused her of being a whore. He was ready to throw her out of the house for having had an affair with one of their slaves when Sarah stepped in and told him that it happened because of his mother, Ruby, and her Creole parents. One of them had been black. She didn't think Jedidiah ever knew but she wasn't sure. He might have known and not cared but either way Henry never knew. Late in life Ruby confided the truth to Sarah but even Sarah's husband, Jesse, had never been told."

"My god," Thaddeus said, momentarily stunned by the news, before putting his head back in an enormous gale of laughter.

"That bigoted son of a bitch! My white father…colored. I have to tell Mama Rose. This is so ironic. It should give him more than ample reason to kill himself. And what about Josiah?"

"Him, too!"

"Lordy, oh my," Matthew smiled. "What a little drop of blood does to one's family tree."

The horse pulled up to what had been the William's family home in the more peaceful pre-war days. It continued to house the Freedman's School and Medical Clinic. It had been an uncomfortable ride from Moss Grove. Josiah was too big to ride between he and the pommel and the boy was too fidgety to ride behind him. He really does need his own small horse, Henry realized.

Henry hadn't been to the William's house or this part of Baton Rouge since he had cavalierly whisked Elizabeth and her family away from approaching Union troops and brought them to Moss Grove. It seemed like several lifetimes ago, he reminisced, recalling how dashing he looked in his uniform and the hungry puppy eyes that Elizabeth had cast at him. It should have all turned out so differently.

"I'm going to leave you here for a few days, Josiah. I have business in New Orleans. Your Aunt Amy will take care of you," Henry said as he and his son climbed down carefully. Two on a horse was uncomfortable for such a long distance. His arm and both legs ached. When the adult rider had a single arm it was doubly difficult even though Henry's single arm had become quite strong through the years, often having to do the work of a man with two arms.

Amy came down the stairs when she was told she had a visitor. Seeing Henry and Josiah was the last thing she expected.

She could no longer hide her pregnancy. Her husband finally realized his wife's condition. John had been ecstatic about becoming a father but he was apoplectic about what he was supposed to do or how he was supposed to act. Now the Army had sent him off again on another assignment.

"Hello Henry! Hello Josiah! My, how you've grown. You must be a full foot taller than when we last saw one another," she said, earning a broad grin that revealed a gap where two of his baby teeth were missing.

"My dear sister-in-law. I see you've replaced your boyish coveralls. I imagine congratulations are in order. I will be an uncle. How quaint!" he smiled.

"I would take it as a kindness if you would care for Josiah for several days while I conduct business in New Orleans."

"Of course! Josiah and I will do quite well together."

Henry kissed the boy and the two shook hands in a schooled formality. Without another word, Henry hoisted himself onto his horse, gave it a hearty kick in its flanks, and galloped off.

Henry arrived in a once again bustling New Orleans and took a large, comfortable suite at the Royal Orleans. The recent resurgence in cotton prices had put smiles on faces that had been downcast only a few months earlier. He had already arranged to meet Alcibiades DeBlanc for dinner but he hadn't expected three other serious looking bearded men to be with him. Even before they were introduced Henry knew these were ex-Confederate officers. They carried that haughty bearing that he, too, had manifested early in the war.

"Gentlemen, this is Henry Rogers. Captain Henry Rogers lost his arm in the battle at Port Hudson, where he served with distinction," De Blanc said.

"Henry, this is Major Arthur Pemberton, Lieutenant Charlie Philipson, and Lieutenant Casper McKenzie. They were also Confederate officers who served in numerous battles against our blue coated brethren. They are influential members of the White League here in Louisiana."

"I've read a few things about your group in the Picayune. One article even made the front page," Henry said as they all shook hands, carefully taking one another's measure.

"Yes," Pemberton said. He wanted to make it clear he was in charge.

"We're not as bashful as you Knights of the White Camellia. We don't hide behind masks like those Klan fellows either. We're going to return this state back to the whites, the way God intended. We have no intention of allowing these black monkeys to run the government. We've already organized active chapters in Alabama and Mississippi and we have men ready to go in Tennessee and South Carolina."

The Major's diatribe brought back Henry's memories of the young cocky officers he served with who preened rather than train their men. Those arrogant men were now dead.

"Major Pemberton, with all due respect," he said. "I'm sure you fellows can cause considerable havoc but as long as federal troops and state militias are around, there is going to be a lot of bloodshed and some of it will be your people."

Henry sat back and eyed the men around the table. He took a moment to sip his brandy. When he set it down he picked up the lit cigar in the ashtray in front of him and blew lightly on the end. As he puffed he allowed the smoke to drift while he gathered his thoughts.

"Look," he continued. "The Klansmen are burning homes, beating niggers and driving small farmers off the land. I don't have any problem with all that. Our group prefers bigger fish. We go after large businesses and all of us joined the fracas at Colfax. We're doing our share."

"Perhaps you misunderstand the purpose of this meeting, Henry," DeBlanc interrupted. "No one is criticizing what the Camellias are doing. We all need to do more. We also want to see if there is any way we can coordinate some of the more aggressive actions we are planning."

"We have something significant in mind," Pemberton said in a conspiratorial tone. Neither of his subordinate lieutenants had said a word but their expressions said they were not pleased with the tone of this one-armed blonde ex-Confederate officer. They had seen too many of these pretty officers at Vicksburg, Gettysburg, and Bull Run. War was a game to these rich, pampered men, not a cause. Most had purchased their commissions, not earned them through success in battle.

"We intend to take over a parish in the northern part of the state, up near Coushatta. Our men are all trained soldiers who still believe in what the Confederacy stands for. Since we'll be riding through your area, we would like your support for our men, for our horses, and for whatever supplies we might require."

"I am quite willing to commit for all the White Camellias in our parish. Let us know when you intend to arrive and we will put everything we have at your disposal. We try to avoid direct involvment in our area, however, as we are too recognizable. If we were caught, the Union troops could seize our plantations and everything we possess."

"Our men are risking their lives, Captain," Lieutenant Charlie Philipson interrupted, in an insulting tone. "Surely that matters more than your property."

"You're out of order, Lieutenant. Perhaps you and Lieutenant McKenzie had best wait outside. We shall not be long," Pemberton said sternly before Henry would voice a retort. Henry's steely blue eyes had flashed at the obvious insult. DeBlanc knew Henry had a quick temper. He was also an excellent marksman and a duel between like-thinking men was the last thing they needed at this point.

"I'm sorry, Captain Rogers," Pemberton said, hoping that a reference to his rank might make Henry remember he was still a subordinate officer. "The lieutenant was out of order. Our group will appreciate whatever support you can provide."

Angry, but mollified, Henry allowed the tension at the table to ease and a few moments later they parted company.

It wasn't difficult to find a woman strolling seductively along the quay in the evening. There were dozens of every hue. Offers came from the dark in French, Spanish, Creole, and English. Voices might ring out with a southern twang or a Jamaican lilt. None of these were the type of woman Henry was seeking. He always preferred a woman who looked good on his arm and was creative in bed.

For these talents the hotel was most accommodating in describing several options. He settled on Les Femmes, a Gentlemen's club he had frequented occasionally in his school days. It had been refurbished after the war but it still retained its old worldly charm sensualness. Soft, dark red velvet chairs, Louis XIV tables, gold inlaid mirrors and well-placed candles enhanced its charm. Somewhere, unseen, a piano played Debussy and Mozart. Henry was introduced to Suzanne, tall, with dark eyes the color of coal. She was a French Creole with skin the color of the cotton boll just before it blossomed.

They enjoyed three drinks sharing the type of small talk that presaged an evening's love making. Eventually, and unevenly, he rose to follow Suzanne up the circular staircase. He knew there were other couples enjoying comparable activities but each room was arranged for maximum privacy and the only blacks he saw were there to cook and change the linens.

Suzanne helped Henry remove his clothes and admiringly complimented him on the size of his member, no longer flaccid. She excused herself behind a dressing screen, removing all but the minimal lingerie. Her rich, dark brown hair, which had been pinned into a chignon, now hung to her shoulders. As she approached the bed she put out several of the candles that lit the room and joined Henry.

He was hard now, fully erect and, as she massaged and cooed to him. He realized how long it had been and how badly he'd needed this evening. By the time he entered her, his entire being was screaming. He didn't want to climax so quickly but he couldn't control himself.

"I am sorry, my dear," he wheezed in an exhausted voice. "You deserve a more patient lover."

"Do not worry yourself, Monsieur Henry. We have all evening. You will have plenty of opportunity to redeem yourself," she laughed.

Suzanne had been well-trained. Most of the better quality courtesans knew one another. She had heard about this one-armed blonde man from Melanie. Several of the women had thrown a small party for their long-time friend before she left, beaming jealously over her pregnancy and new life. She hadn't spoken well of this 'Henry,' but business is business and he would pay well for this one night.

# Chapter Twenty-Nine

Coushatta was located in the northeast corner of Louisiana, just south of Shreveport. It was a small, quiet, rural village and bore few scars from the war when a Mr. Marshall Twitchell arrived to serve as head the Red River parish Freedman's bureau. Twitchell was a Union army veteran from Vermont. He had never lived in the south but he had his orders and he would follow him. Major John Shipley, his immediate commander, was nearly three hundred miles away and seemed to have little interest in this part of the state. Captain Eli Fineman was closer but he'd already resigned his commission and hadn't been replaced.

Twitchell loved what he'd found in Louisiana. He would no longer have to face Vermont's long cold winters. He settled in and began to think of Coushatta as a place where he could marry, settle down, and raise a family. He learned how to farm cotton and got himself elected to state office. Everything seemed peaceful.

But while he was away at a Republican convention, several dozen armed White League members had ridden into town. They shouted, brandished sabers, carried Confederate flags, and stormed Coushatta's government offices. They were looking for uppity blacks, scalawags and carpetbaggers. They were there on God's mission of reasserting the superiority of the white race.

Six whites and twenty freedmen were held at gun point and taken outside. There, Major Pemberton forced each of them to sign statements that they would leave the state. Then, while they sat on the ground, arms tied behind them, they were all murdered…shot in the back of the head at close range. It was a massacre. Pleased with what they'd accomplished, Pemberton and his men departed Coushatta. Four days after having stopped at Moss Grove to rest before heading north, they returned, their boots barely scuffed. Pemberton and his officers shared drinks on the veranda, continuing to chat amiably about their recent success.

"You should be pleased, Major. The telegraphs are already buzzing," Henry said, more casual and self-confident after his respite in New Orleans.

"We accomplished our goal. Damn niggers will be nervously looking behind them for a long time to come. But the battle will continue. We're going to get rid of that damned Republican governor, Kellogg. Every group of decent white men is joining us. I hope that you and your friends in the White Camellia will consider participating."

"Normally I would be delighted but I have just returned from New Orleans and I have plantation business to attend to."

"Apparently you do not like to fight any more, Captain," Lieutenant Philipson said snidely. "Perhaps in losing one arm you have lost your courage as well."

"This is the second time you have made scurrilous accusations. At the restaurant I was dissuaded from action, but this time you go too far," he said as he walked up to the man and slapped him.

"I demand satisfaction," he said, his eyes in a frozen glare.

"Gentlemen, please," Pemberton said, trying only mildly to stop this nonsense. Inwardly his military experience was curious how this would all turn out

"I will have neither my honor nor my courage questioned by this oaf. Major Pemberton, I ask you to organize the field and provide the necessary pistols. We will settle this matter in one hour," Henry said as he walked away.

Lieutenant McKenzie was selected as Philipson's second and another officer was chosen to second Henry. At the appointed time all the parties assembled near the back veranda.

Every task on the plantation had come to a stop. Thatcher tried to insist that the field hands continue to work. Chloe had tried to get the house staff to ignore what was going on. Both found their orders falling on deaf ears. The workers gathered behind bushes, on the balcony, and wherever they could, to follow the proceedings. The outcome could well affect their futures.

"Gentlemen," Pemberton began, wearing his full military regalia, caught up in the formality of the proceedings, no less than the two duelists. This was the south at its best, he thought. Proud! Unyielding!

"I must ask you to abort what you are about to undertake. I do not wish to have either of you harmed."

"I am ready to proceed," Henry insisted, never taking his eyes off his enemy.

"I, too, am ready," Philipson said confidently. "I have a girl in New Orleans waiting for me."

"She will wait a very long time, Lieutenant, a very long time," Henry seethed.

"Ten paces each of you. If either of you turns or tries to shoot before then I am prepared to kill that man. Is that understood?"

Heads nodded and the two men stood back to back. Except for the sounds of the men breathing, all sound in the universe stopped. Even the birds were quiet, as if, they too, were curious about the event ready to transpire.

"One, two, three, four, five," Pemberton called in a cadenced tone as the men separated themselves a few feet at a time. "Six, seven, eight, nine!" The tension was palpable as everyone watching was mesmerized at what was to come.

"Ten!"

The two men turned. The smile never left Henry's face. He could see the tiny beads of perspiration on Philipson's forehead. The lieutenant fired first and the bullet passed where Henry's missing arm would have been. Without hesitation, less than a second later, Henry fired. Time stopped as the bullet traveled the twenty paces between them. The single shot entered Philipson's throat just above his military collar. Then it was over. Philipson lay dead on the ground; his eyes still open in surprise. Henry handed his pistol back to Major Pemberton and walked toward the house.

General Longstreet and Julius Freyhan met with several influential leaders that included the Editor of the New Orleans Picayune, three prominent bankers, and a variety of businessmen. Major John Shipley had already indicated his support. Now the only problem was the candidate.

They had asked Thaddeus to join them at a small café on the pier that served shrimp, shrimp, and shrimp. It also sold wonderful beer, icy cold from ice that had been brought all the way from Minnesota. It was the antithesis of the lavish restaurants in the French quarter. The three could talk without being overheard or recognized.

"The best shrimp on the Gulf," Longstreet chimed, cleaning sauce from his elaborate grey beard. "You people aren't supposed to eat these things, are you Julius?"

"I eat. I just don't tell my wife or the Rabbi. I'm sure with all the craziness going on that God doesn't have time to fret if some Jew eats 'traif'."

Thaddeus smiled. He had never met two white men whose company he enjoyed more.

"What is 'traif' Mr. Freyhan?"

"'Traif' is any food that has been forbidden by Jewish law. Shrimp that crawl along the bottom of the sea are scavengers and considered unclean. But they are tasty, aren't they?" he grinned like a little boy caught doing something wrong, but enjoying it.

"Thaddeus, Julius and I and several others want you to run for public office in the upcoming elections. You're well-known. You're young and good looking."

"And I assume I'm the proper 'shade'?"

"Yes, that doesn't hurt either," Freyhan admitted.

"That's the world we're living in," he continued. "Dark blacks make whites nervous and whites make new black voters nervous, in the middle, color-wise, is the best thing to be these days for public office."

"But I have work to do with Major Shipley before they close the Freedman's Bureau."

"We spoke with the Major and he thinks that you would be a strong positive voice in our state. He has a great deal of admiration for you."

The picture of John Shipley and Amy at home snuggling together flooded into his thoughts and it took him a long moment to reconnect. He thought about Sarah and what she would think. He knew she would support whatever he did; she was that kind of a woman.

He thanked them and asked if they would allow him a few days to consider their proposal. As they started to order one final beer, all hell broke loose.

The city erupted in violence. The New Orleans Metropolitan police had learned that a delivery of arms to the White League was about to take place and, as they tried to stop it, the first shots were fired. League members had been gathering in the city in an effort to rout its scalawag governor and replace him with their Democrat, McEnery.

Five thousand White Leaguers faced more than three thousand police and state militia. The latter was no match against the seasoned ex-Confederate soldiers. The Governor was ousted and the League took control of the government offices. President Grant ordered Federal forces in the area to restore order and, as various Union military units approached, the League discreetly left. It had made its point and it wasn't interested in a pitched battle with seasoned and well-armed troops.

Rose had a lot of time to think about the twists and turns her life had taken. From such an ugly childhood, God had blessed her with memories of a wonderful husband and pride in her two amazing sons. She felt truly blessed. She had to laugh as she sat cross-legged on a pillow fixing one of the black raggedy cotton dolls. Now that there were so many women sewing them with all types of faces and poses, she decided that she would inspect them before they were packed into boxes. This particular doll had a loose button that would certainly come off the moment a child began playing with it. Who would have thought she would have progressed from bending over picking cotton to inspecting dolls.

She hadn't been feeling well lately and she'd brewed some of her own herbs. They'd always had a calming effect on her but they didn't seem to be working this time. If she didn't feel better in the next few days she'd stop over at the Freedman's clinic next week. Maybe their doctor could recommend something stronger. They were always discovering new fangled things.

She got very tired, set down the needle and the doll and put her head on a nearby pile of dolls awaiting her keen eye. In a moment her eyes closed and her breathing eased. She seemed to be asleep. A few of the women saw her but didn't think it was anything unusual. Perhaps Rose was just tired. When they realized it might be something more serious and they couldn't awaken her, they ran to the feed store and screamed for Rufus.

Rose was unconscious, not dead, but barely breathing. Rufus picked up her frail body and carried her to her room in the house. He sent someone to get Melanie and another to ride as fast as they could to New Orleans to fetch Thaddeus and Matthew.

They determined that she had had a stroke. Rose lingered between life and death for a day and a night. By the time her two sons arrived it was near midday the second day after her collapse.

"Momma," Matthew cried. "Don't leave us. We need you. Please!"

"My boys! You're both here. I was afraid I wouldn't see you before I join Faris," she said weakly.

"Mama Rose, you can't go yet. I have something very special to tell you. It should bring a big smile to your face," Thaddeus said.

Rose tried to sit up and take some nourishment but she lacked the strength.

"We all know how you were treated by Henry Rogers when you were just a young girl and what an evil man he is. We know how much hatred you've carried with you all these years. You can let go of that hatred now.

"Henry Rogers isn't the white man we all thought he was or that he thought he was. Mama, he's part colored. Seems he didn't even know it until he and Elizabeth had a dark child. One of Miss Ruby's parents was black. Can you imagine? All of his sense of white superiority now destroyed. He has finally gotten worse than he gave."

Rose smiled and looked into the eyes of her two very different, very similar sons. Henry Rogers was no longer important. Her life had turned out well and she felt a fulfillment she had never felt before. She grabbed the hands of her two sons, closed her eyes and drifted off to a happier world.

The funeral was a simple affair. A few of the people Rose had worked with at the clinic, Thatcher and two others rode over from Moss Grove and stood amidst Rufus, Melanie and the children. Thaddeus and Matthew stood in front of the simple cross that had been erected.

Reverend Dinsmore had arrived with his family to conduct the service. Amy was too far along in her pregnancy to attend but had sent a loving note to both Thaddeus and Matthew.

As Rose's sons stood at the graveside of this woman who had given them life and would soon be lowered into the ground, young Stephen left Melanie's side and moved between the two brothers. He took both their hands and the three of them stood together. No words were said. None were needed.

*The debate was fierce, not only in Louisiana, but across the entire country. Each of the rebellious Confederate states had been readmitted into the Union and the dominance of the Republican Party that had spanned two decades had waned. Numerous corruption scandals within Grant's administration were a national embarrassment. The Democrats gained control of the House of Representatives in an overwhelming landslide.*

Thaddeus campaigned vigorously for his own election. If he won, he'd be one of several colored Representatives serving in the Louisiana State Assembly. The newspapers were reporting repeated incidents of racial harassment across the state. More than a dozen Blacks had been killed with the typical explanation that they'd been stealing cotton seeds. Thaddeus knew that each of the men who had been killed was a Republican. He had met two of them at a campaign meeting in East Feliciana. He was convinced that their deaths were no coincidence. White militants, all Southern Democrats, were not going to lose gracefully.

Thaddeus got what help Longstreet and his associates could provide, but his greatest support came from Matthew and Rufus. They were everywhere, encouraging people to vote, and to cast that vote for Thaddeus Williams.

As they headed home late one evening after a particularly boisterous meeting, they found themselves facing a half-dozen whites, clustered in front of them, brandishing clubs.

"This nigger ain't goin' to get elected and go to Baton Rouge. He goin' to Hell," one man shouted.

"Let us pass. We have no argument with any of you," Matthew said as calmly as he could.

"Listen, boy. It's the tall one we want so why don't you other two monkeys go shimmy up a tree and leave him to us," another extolled, to the snide laughter of his friends.

Rufus pulled out a pistol he began carrying two years ago when Charlie had been attacked and killed.

"Don't make any rash moves." he ordered. "Like my friend said, we don't want any trouble."

"Niggers are cowards, proved that in the war. I'm going to wrap that barrel around your head," the first man said, trying to regain the upper hand and moving forward without fear.

The bullet found him high on his right shoulder and he dropped, screaming and holding it with his left hand to halt the bleeding.

"The bastard shot me. He shot me. Kill 'em but save the one with the gun for me to finish. I'm gonna' make it slow and painful."

Four of the men rushed forward, their clubs poised overhead but Thaddeus, Matthew and Rufus were ready. Everything they had learned in the Army flooded back. They side-stepped the first onslaught and knocked the clubs away. They exchanged blows. One man struck Thaddeus with a fist clenched around a piece of pipe. It put a gash in his cheek and dropped him to his knee before he could gather himself and return the favor with a leg kick to the man's knees, knocking him to the dirt.

Matthew kicked his opponent squarely in the groin as the man rushed him. As that man fell, Matthew put all his weight into a right fist across the man's face. He thought he heard a crack as the man fell unconscious. The other two men were trying to subdue Rufus as Matthew rushed to his side and pulled one man away.

Within ten minutes the scuffle was over and the three friends hurried away from the scene. In this uncertain time they didn't want to be accused of creating the assault, a white jury would never believe anything they'd say.

"They take their politics seriously around here, don't they," Rufus jested as they sat in the Dinsmore's kitchen. Hestor Dinsmore was busy cleaning the cuts and liberally applying bandages where necessary.

"You got quite a gash there, big brother," Matthew said, one eye black and turning color from a blow he'd taken.

"Sort of makes you look rakish. Maybe it'll appeal to the voters that aren't too scared to vote."

Walter Dinsmore walked in, looking tired and depressed as he listened quietly to what had transpired. "What you men confronted is going on everywhere. Listen to this letter three hundred Blacks in Vicksburg wrote and sent to President Grant:

> *We are intimidated by the whites. We want to hold meetings, but it is impossible to do so, if we does, they will say we are making an invasion on the city and come out to kill us. When we hold church meetings, they breaks it up, our lives are not safe in our houses. Now we ask you who shall we look to for protection…We are in the hands of murderers. There will not be peace here until troops come to unarm them.*

"The letter was released and reprinted in the Picayune. General Sheridan is on his way to take over the entire city of New Orleans and all of Southern Louisiana, if necessary."

"Philip Sheridan is a good man. Both Thaddeus and I served with him. If anyone can fix things, he will," Rufus declared.

Thaddeus won the election by a small margin over three other candidates, including two whites. Amy, Sarah, Sheila, and Melanie had joined the men in canvassing the entire district, urging people, black and white, to vote. Amy even convinced some hard core whites to give it a chance by electing the best person. There had been one additional man running for state office, a black man named Big John Cutler. They found Cutler hanging from a tree on the outskirts of the city. No one was ever able to determine who had done it.

Once the vote count had been ratified, Thaddeus traveled to Baton Rouge and took over his old room in the home adjoining Carmody & Williams that Rose, with the help of Sarah, had kept for him and Rufus. It felt strange to walk the rooms and expect to hear their voices, cheery, going about their daily chores. Rufus no longer lived there. He and Melanie were now comfortably ensconced at Carmody House along with their beautiful daughter, Michelle, and their son, Stephen. He planned on visiting there tomorrow but he needed an evening of solitude to think about where he was and what he was supposed to be accomplishing.

In the morning he dressed and walked the few blocks to the Capitol. People were running in all directions but all were hoping to put as much distance as possible between them and violence. There were gun shots and screaming. He quickened his pace.

"What's happening?" he asked a man running in the opposite direction.

"Whites with guns have taken over the building and the government. Black militias are rushing to get their guns to take them on. Everyone was taken by surprise." The man pulled his arm from Thaddeus' grip and continued his hasty departure.

A group of Blacks, now armed, had set up a barricade and were using it to shoot from while the Whites were using the windows of the building to fire down into the crowd.

Thaddeus grabbed a gun from a man who had fallen, made sure that it was loaded and sought out his target. There, on the second floor, laughing, a bearded white man, wearing a frayed gray felt cap, looked for another victim. The man's eyes connected with the well-dressed colored man below just as a bullet rose and caught him in the forehead. He pivoted for an eternity before falling through the window and onto the ground in front of both battling groups.

The rebellion continued for two days. The Black Militias tried to rush the building and were met by ex-Rebs with guns and sabers. This battle was very personal.

In the end the whites vacated the Capitol, convinced they'd made their point. Sheridan's troops were on their way from Vicksburg and those who had who had taken over, once again, preferred to avoid any direct confrontation. By the time the battle had ended and order was restored, twenty-seven people had been killed, many in close combat. Thaddeus had been there the entire time, catching a few moments sleep only in the hours after midnight when there was no light to guide their aim. It was Port Hudson all over again.

Thaddeus didn't get to Carmody House until nearly a week later. It had taken that long for things to settle down among the elected officials. Most kept looking over their shoulders expecting armed white militants to reappear.

Michelle Carmody was the image of her mother, Melanie. Stephen didn't look like either of his parents, or, perhaps an unrecognizable blend of them both, Thaddeus thought.

"And thank the lord my daughter looks like her mother," Rufus laughed. "She could have looked like me. That would have probably guaranteed her spinsterhood."

He cradled both his children with loving pride while Melanie stood next to him, clearly adoring her family. That night Matthew joined them. Melanie felt the kinship among these three men and sat quietly in the corner of the room as they traded reminisces of war stories and adventures they had shared together.

"Rufus, you've been busy, I see. You've opened another Carmody & Williams and you've kept the doll production going even though Mama Rose is gone," Thaddeus said as he stood to stretch his legs and pour himself another cup of coffee.

"I have a lot of good people to do the work. Mama Rose was always good at training people. Look how many women she trained on how best to minister with her herbs. She did the same thing with the dolls. There were other girls ready to step in. As for the feed and stable business, you did a terrible job of training a replacement blacksmith so you need to come back," he laughed.

"At the moment that job offer is sounding pretty good. Certainly better than engaging in warfare at the Capitol," Thaddeus smiled.

"How're you and Sarah doing?" Matthew asked.

"She's wonderful and we could probably build a life together but there is one big problem."

"Her skin color?" Rufus asked.

"No, I'm embarrassed I even ever mentioned it when she and I had first met. I'm way past that," he admitted.

"No, the problem is that I've never told her about Amy and me."

"Oh! That is a problem, big brother. Did you ever tell Amy about Sarah?" Matthew asked.

"I haven't done either. I'm really nervous about telling either of these women I love about my feeling for the other one. Before Amy agreed to marry John, she came to me and wanted my approval. She had already told John about us. It unsettled him but he decided he loved her so much that he wanted to marry Amy anyway, hoping their love would grow. She and I agreed it wouldn't affect the special love that she and I have and we both felt John would give her a good life. I'm afraid if I try and have a similar conversation with Sarah, she'll go away and I don't want her to do that. I love her but it's a different love than I feel for Amy."

"Melanie, you've been sitting there, quiet as a church mouse. Do you have any thoughts or insights on Thaddeus' dilemma?" Rufus asked.

"I do have one. It's not complicated, Thaddeus. You need to talk to Amy, and then you'll likely have to explain everything to Sarah."

Thaddeus smiled and nodded. If he couldn't talk to the women he loved, he'd never be able to move forward.

The week that Amy had spent with Josiah had been wonderful. She imagined what Henry might have been like as a young boy before his arrogance overshadowed more pleasant traits that could have developed. She saw traits of Elizabeth in him during those special quiet moments when she and her blonde-haired nephew would read together. She imagined being able to sit quietly and read to Stephen. Melanie had told her how her son had gravitated to Thaddeus and Matthew at Rose's funeral. He had to have acted instinctively. None of them knows the truth.

And, she felt the life continuing to grow within her. The events made her better understand the importance of motherhood and the knowledge and morals she would need to teach. It helped that John Shipley was a good and moral man. She wouldn't need to do it all by herself.

Henry picked up his son and returned to Moss Grove. He never said 'thanks.' He greeted Josiah, pulled him up onto his horse, nodded at Amy and rode off. Josiah, first happy at seeing his father, had given his aunt a tight loving hug before he was whisked away.

Thaddeus found Amy at the school, reading to the young children. She was sitting in a rocker holding eight children entranced as they sat in a circle at her feet. Given the advance state of her pregnancy, sitting was so much less exhausting than moving around.

She spotted him standing at the door smiling.

"How long have you been standing there?" she asked.

"Let's see. I think I arrived on Tuesday and today is Thursday. That sounds about right," he laughed. "You do tend to concentrate pretty intently when you're reading. Will you have some time for me soon?"

Amy left the children with another teacher and joined Thaddeus in a shaded picnic area that was deserted in this late afternoon hour.

"You're looking radiant, Amy. Pregnancy looks good on you. How much longer?"

"Another eight weeks, unless the baby decides to pop out earlier. John is trying to arrange his schedule to be close by. Are you alright? You have a grey pall that you always get when something is bothering you."

"I'm thinking about asking Sarah Dinsmore to marry me," he blurted out.

Amy looked at the man she loved and thoughts for and against cascaded in her mind. He's mine, he loves me, and I love him. I have John and a new baby coming. Thaddeus needs someone to love. He has so much to offer a woman.

"Sarah is lovely, Thaddeus. You couldn't have picked anyone better," she said, barely above a whisper after a long moment of silence.

"Amy, we both agreed that your marrying John didn't change how we felt about one another, remember?"

"Of course, I do."

"And you were surprised that John wanted to marry you anyway."

"Yes, I was…very surprised."

"Marrying Sarah won't change my love for you but I doubt that Sarah will be as understanding as John. I can't imagine her wanting to marry a man she knows continues to love another woman."

"You've never told her anything about us, have you?"

"Nothing! Amy, what should I do?"

"I'd like to suggest that you not tell her but going into a marriage with a lie likely won't bode well for its success. You have to tell her, and hope that she understands."


Sarah Dinsmore and Sheila Stokes had become friends. With Matthew and Thaddeus gone so often, it was natural for the women to seek out one another. They would often alternate whose home they would favor with dinner. Their mothers enjoyed the girls and the happiness they brought into one another's home. It wasn't surprising then that the girl's conversations would eventually lead them to discussions of marriage. Sheila and Matthew were still engaged but Matthew was unwilling to set a wedding date as long as the situation at the bank was so volatile. Sheila, pressured by her parents and her own desires, continued to urge Matthew to have the marriage sooner rather than later.

"Has Thaddeus discussed marriage, Sarah?" Sheila asked one evening as the two girls washed the dishes after dinner at Sarah's house.

"No, he hasn't. I know he loves me and I'm sure he knows I love him but he seems wary at the idea of having to make a commitment."

"If you could move him along, we could have a double wedding. After all, we would be marrying brothers. Would you mind if I got Matthew to bring it up with him?"


A week later the two couples were able to schedule an infrequent dinner for the four of them. Matthew was still having problems keeping the bank afloat and had only half-listened when Sheila tried to solicit his support in talking to his brother. Meanwhile Thaddeus was busy traveling between New Orleans and the Capitol in Baton Rouge and was rarely settled at one place long enough to have such a personal conversation.

They'd settled on a newly opened Italian restaurant, La Fontina. It offered its diners an understated intimacy and reasonable prices. The décor was accented with murals from Italy and the faux lattice work on the ceiling was made to look as if guests were dining in a Tuscan grape arbor. The only wines offered were Italian.

"We have something important to discuss with you both," Sheila began. She was slightly older and a little worldlier than her new friend.

"We think the four of us should be married at the same time in a double wedding. There, I've said it." She stopped, out of breath. Matthew blanched and a look of stunned awe was evident on Thaddeus' face.

"But Sarah and I aren't even engaged. Matthew, did you know about this?" Thaddeus asked.

"Not exactly! Certainly nothing about a rush to be married soon! Look, Sheila, you know the problems at the bank; we've discussed them. Blacks borrowed and can't repay the loans. A lot of them just gave up from all the harassment and have become share croppers. Some have left the state. We've done better with the people that opened small businesses but there are fewer of them. I just think we need to wait until this financial mess stabilizes."

"And Sarah, we haven't discussed marriage. You and I need to have a conversation," Thaddeus said.

Nothing more was said and by the time the dessert was served, each one, for his or her own reasons, was eager to end the evening.


"Sheila, I love you. But I can't marry you until we talk about some things we've never discussed." They were sitting in her parlor. It was late and her parents and brother were already in bed.

"Thaddeus, if you're concerned about events that went on before we met, those aren't important. I love you. I'm sorry Sheila pushed the subject this evening. It was partially my fault. She and I got into discussing her and Matthew's wedding. We got rather carried away with the idea of a double wedding."

"I'm not blaming anyone. This is all my fault for not discussing things with you sooner. Please sit down. This is going to take awhile."

Sarah sat, a worried look on her face, her hands clasped.

"Since I was a young boy at Moss Grove, Amy and I have been in love but because she's white and I'm colored we both knew it was something that could never be."

Sarah sat silently, trying to absorb what she'd just been told.

"Sarah, please, say something. Tell me you still love me and that we can plan a life together," he pleaded.

"Amy? You've been in love with Amy all this time and you never told me?" Sarah said as she began to cry.

"Does John Shipley know? And if he does, why hasn't he had you shot? And if he doesn't, then Amy is despicable."

"John knows. Amy told him when he first proposed. He loved her enough to still want to marry her, even understanding that she and I had a separate kind of love for one another. And, apparently he loves her enough to not have me shot." Thaddeus tried to say the last thought with a lightness in his voice but Sarah was oblivious to his tone. She was busy trying to absorb the full impact of Thaddeus' deception.

"Well, I am not quite as understanding. You are telling me you love me but you also love this white girl, this pregnant white girl. Is it also your child she's carrying?" Her voice quivered with terrible hurt.

"Of course not. Please Sarah; what Amy and I have is different. It's you I want to marry and have a family with."

"I love you, Thaddeus. You are one of the finest men I've ever met and I was thrilled that you loved me. But this! This is wrong. It is so wrong and what you have done is hurtful. Please don't call on me again," she cried and ran from the room.

He had lost Amy and now he had lost Sarah.

# Chapter Thirty

"Matthew, I'd like to introduce Mr. Charles Nash. Mr. Nash is the first man of color elected to the United States Congress from our great state," James Longstreet said proudly. "Charlie, this is the young man I've been telling you about, Mr. Matthew Carmody."

The three men seated themselves in Longstreet's business office as Matthew studied the man he'd heard about but never met. Nash's dark nappy hair was all combed to one side in an attempt to cover some bald spots. He had a heavy mustache and was a full figured man, definitely overweight and made more pronounced by the fact he was nearly six inches shorter than Matthew. But it was his eyes and his almost cherubic smile that drew you to him. He was a man you liked the first time you met him.

Nash had been a bricklayer in his earlier life and the strength of his hands was still evident in his handshake. He had ended his service with the Union Army as a Sergeant Major. Now he had risen to be unique among every man of color in the state and less than a dozen in the nation.

"We didn't want to meet at the bank, Matthew, given all the difficulties you're having," Longstreet opined.

"You aren't the only banker, or the only bank, facing these same problems," Nash added. "Banks that were set up with the help of the Freedman's Bureau are closing in many communities. Some are the victims of bad loans but many might have survived except for the financial panic that spread across the country last year. Businesses everywhere suffered and we're now just beginning to dig our way out. This is a very resilient country."

"I thank you, but I don't find that very consoling. I was given responsibility for the bank's success," Matthew said ruefully. "I'd hoped I could save it but now I am doubtful, and the white bankers will be happy to say 'I told you so'."

"We need to move forward. We have far more serious problems. The recent election gave the Democrats overwhelming power in Washington. And that means that Southern Democrats will be more than ready to return us to economic slavery. Good Republicans stayed home and didn't vote. They were obviously angry at the financial debacle and by the corruption that's been uncovered involving so many of President Grant's cronies.

"If we don't do something to energize our party before the next election, we could end up with a Democrat in the White House. We'd have a President AND a Congress who would not be very friendly to our people. We could lose the gains we've made and we'd face increased violence across the south defending what we've already achieved."

"And you've invited me here, why?" Matthew asked.

"I want you to come to Washington with me as my aide. I want you to work with me to do whatever we can to convince our good friends in the northern wing of our party that we are important allies in this battle."

"I appreciate the offer, Mr. Nash, and the confidence of both you gentlemen but, frankly, I'm a little taken aback. I had hoped this meeting was going to provide a magic amulet on how to save my bank. I'm also getting married later this year and I'm not sure my new bride is ready to pick up and leave her family."

"Congratulations on your upcoming marriage. It is Sheila, I assume. You two will be a lovely couple," James Longstreet offered, having been silent during the exchange of these two men he admired.

"But let me say something, Matthew. As someone older who has seen enormous social shifts during my lifetime. You have no option. Given everything you've accomplished since being born a slave, you are obligated to do what you can to further similar progress for your people. Without individuals like you, it can all be lost. Please think hard on this."

The decision was not an easy one. He had been correct in his assumption that Sheila was less than thrilled with the idea of moving a thousand miles to the east. She would be far away from her parents for the first time. It was her father, John Stokes, who helped convince her. As a business man who had already moved his family because of white prejudice he understood the importance of what Matthew was being asked to do.

"We will visit you and you will visit us. Matthew has been asked to assist in a most important undertaking and you should be pleased that others have such confidence in the man you are about to marry."

Amy and John had a hefty baby girl with the same red hair as her mother. John managed to be present at the birth. He seemed to be traveling more and more as the realization that the closing of the Freedman Bureaus was about to effect people across the state. So many had come to depend on the support and largesse the Federal Government had provided.

The Army doctor who happened to be available was one of the few who had experience with pregnancies. The baby weighed in just over six lbs and nearly seventeen inches long. She was as pink as a carnation. She had her father's brown eyes but in every other way, she was a tiny version of her mother. They named her Bess, after John's mother, who he hadn't seen since he left Michigan to join the Army. Amy had thought briefly of naming her after her mother, but given her ongoing guilt about her child with Thaddeus, she willingly deferred. John walked around in a state of euphoria. It hadn't been a difficult birth and within days Amy was up and around.

John had been ordered back on patrol but now he wore a perpetual smile on his face. Amy, much stronger and enjoying her new maternal responsibilities, decided to introduce Bess to her friends. Melanie brought Stephen and Michelle. Brenda had joined them and with the baby wrapped comfortably in her basket, the three women friends, their tiny children in tow, headed north along the lake.

Between running the store, the toy business, and the small acreage they'd planted in corn and cotton, Rufus was busy from dawn to dusk. He enjoyed seeing all the women he adored, so happy together. He stayed for a few moments, and then retired to work at his desk.

The stuffed doll business had slowed with the general turndown in the economy and he was thinking of turning it over to John Stokes. Meanwhile, however, it was here, and with Rose gone, it was another responsibility. Most of the construction effort on Carmody House was finished. He was pleased with how it turned out but now he felt the urge to enlarge it. They wanted another child, hopefully a brother for his little girl, Michelle. He loved his daughter as he loved her mother. It was like watching a miniature as she copied her mother's walk and her expressions. But she was definitely her daddy's girl and she would be a handful when she discovered boys, he mused. And Stephen, he couldn't love him more if he were his natural father. Each day he saw more of Thaddeus and Amy in the child. Would he ever be told who his real parents were? How complicated we've all had to make our lives.

Invitations, floral arrangements, music, menus, and an infinite number of small details occupied the women for weeks. Seamstresses were brought up from the city to help with the bride's dress. The Stokes seemed to invite every customer, vendor, and competitor from Mobile to Shreveport. Second and third cousins no one had seen in a generation were invited. Tents and privies were set up all over the area. More than two hundred guests were expected to attend.

"So this is Washington, our nation's capitol," Matthew said as he got off the final leg of the very long train ride. He was happy to be away from the minutia associated with planning a large wedding. He'd return to Baton Rouge in four weeks, just in time to learn his vows and smile appropriately during the ceremony.

The train ride had taken nearly a week. The last time Matthew had left Louisiana it was as a kid, a runaway. He was a foot soldier in the Union Army and he got to walk across the country. That was more than ten years ago. Everything seemed so different. He knew part of it was the fact that he was looking at it with older eyes. But it was a lot more than that. The entire landscape of the country had changed. There were fewer men wearing uniforms. Blacks walked more erect, and once they left the south there didn't seem to be as much fear and nervousness in their persona.

He followed Representative Nash into the building that housed all of the Congressional representatives and their staffs. He was introduced to the people he'd be working most closely with, including his secretary, Linda, and two assistants. Linda was a matronly woman from Maryland. Two generations earlier her mother had been a slave.

"I am so happy to meet you, Mr. Carmody. Congressman Nash has told us so much about you. But you're so young," she smiled.

"I'm told I'll age rapidly here in Washington," Matthew responded.

"We now have thirty-eight states in the Union and 293 Congressmen, actually 292 plus me. We have two Senators from Louisiana, one Republican and one Democrat. We'll meet them soon. We will begin our meetings and our work next Monday. Linda will see to your needs. Take the next few days to get familiar with the city," Nash said and walked into his private office.

Rooms had been arranged for him in Georgetown, a primarily black neighborhood. Matthew unpacked a few things and got restless. He wanted to see the city. Horse-drawn streetcars would take you anywhere in the city for two cents. He walked Pennsylvania Avenue and poked through the corridors of the Smithsonian Institute. But he was most in awe of Howard University. The school was less than a decade old and already had a prestigious reputation. Its goals were to educate blacks to compete with whites in all the advanced fields of science, economics and medicine. He wandered the corridors seeing young men and women. The snippets of conversation he heard made it clear they were drawing people from across the country. He laughed when he heard one boy speak with a definite Irish accent.

"Matthew, I'd like you to meet Senator Blanche Bruce of Mississippi. Senator, this is my new aide, Matthew Carmody," Nash said, as they toured the Senate offices, larger and more ornate than those of Congressmen.

"Senator Bruce is the first man of color elected to the United States Senate and so he will forever hold a position of distinction."

"Good morning, Senator," Matthew said. "I've heard your name often. You are a beacon to many of us."

"A beacon?" Bruce laughed. "You may be right, Charlie. The young man knows how to turn a phrase. He may be a natural politician himself."

"We've come on serious matter, Blanche. If we don't reenergize the party in the next two years we will lose the White House **AND** Congress. With the Southern Democrats back in control there is no telling what will happen. I hear your state has already passed a law separating blacks from whites in schools. They've even enacted laws separating the races on streetcars and trains. They mean to put us back in shackles if they can. This could mushroom and all the Union troops in the world parading down southern streets won't be able to help us."

"You've stated the problem, Charlie. Now tell me the solution."

They chatted for nearly an hour before Matthew volunteered a suggestion.

"Having been in the banking business this past year I know that a great deal of frustration around the country has been in the decline of the economy. If we can improve people's sense of financial well-being and have

Congress and the Republicans take credit for it, we can regain a lot of the voter's confidence our party lost in the last election."

"Keep talking, son," Bruce smiled. "You picked a good one here, Charlie."

In the next two hours they laid out a plan to meet with every banker throughout the northern and western states that had supported a Republican candidate and get their suggestions as to what the government could do. They would also meet with President Grant to garner his support. When the meeting ended, it was with smiles and an enthusiastically supported plan. This effort might take them the next two years but they were determined that their efforts would not fail from a lack of energy.

Alfred DePue had traveled down from Fraser House to visit his friend, Henry Rogers. Of all the neighboring plantation owners DePue came closest to understanding the frustrations of growing cotton under these share cropping labor conditions. Workers might just up and leave in the middle of the night, sometimes with tools or a mule or a bag of seed that didn't belong to them. You never knew what was going on until it was too late to rectify it.

He admired Henry. Why not? Henry had a bigger plantation. He was a handsome man's man and he came from the kind of 'stock' that defined the Southern patriarchy.

"Your duel with that Confederate Lieutenant from the White League has tongues buzzing from here to Natchez," he said. "Remind me not to upset you."

"I killed more than enough men in the war but this was very different. I won't be insulted, particularly in my own home. My son, Josiah, was in the room and I will not have him think his father a coward.

"It's always nice to see you Alfred. If you can stay a few days we might go shooting and see if we can bag some birds as they head back north this time of year."

"I'd like that. And, with cotton prices up this year I feel a little more relaxed about leaving Fraser House in the hands of my overseer."

"Speaking of which, my overseer, Big George, needs to see me. Come, we can walk over together."

George Thatcher was talking to three field hands when Henry and Alfred approached. Josiah had joined them, quiet, several paces behind.

"Mornin' Boss," he said as he also nodded his head to the man with

Henry. "Sirs, this is Lionel, Little Pete, and John. They is good sharecroppers that been workin' here goin' on two years."

"Hello boys. Good crop this year. God brought us the right amount of sun and rain. I guess all our praying worked," Henry smiled as he assumed the tone of someone talking to those he deemed inferior.

"Sure did. Now my missus and I's finally gots to go. She's already got kin in Texas and they wants us to join them. I been explainin' to the boys here what to do if I'm gone before you hires another overseer."

"That's responsible of you, George. I've been happy to have you here and I wish you and your family good luck."

"Wait, Boss," he said as Henry turned to leave. "We need to settle my bonus. Cotton prices up so I figure my settlement should be enough to get us where we's goin'."

Henry turned, his jaw set, his steel eyes icy blue. It was a look Josiah had seen too often, a look that always frightened him. He retreated behind the wall of the overseer's house.

"I did the books George," Henry spoke softly, each syllable carefully chosen, as he faced the bigger man.

"I added in every percent and bonus we agreed to. Then I subtracted the rent for this here house. I subtracted for the doctor we had to bring when your wife gave birth to your second child. I subtracted the cost of everything you and yours used from the commissary. I took off the cost of the wood and labor you had to use to rebuild the kitchen and smoke house after the fire."

"The fire was your son's fault. T'aint fair to charge me," Thatcher said angrily.

"You were in charge. Your kitchen staff should have been more careful. The bottom line is you can leave as soon as you pay me what you owe. It comes to $257. Until then, you stay and you work, or I'll have the Sheriff and his men put you in jail. Is that understood?"

In that moment George Thatcher snapped. This white man had no intention of ever letting him leave. He'd find a way to twist every commitment he'd ever make. He screamed and rushed Henry Rogers, grabbing him by the throat.

"You is a hateful man and you deserve to die," he said in angry, guttural tones as his hands spanned Henry's neck. Henry could feel the pressure on his windpipe and his eyes begin to bulge as he struggled to breathe.

For a moment everyone stood, frozen, not knowing what to do. The three blacks moved forward, hoping to pull their friend off the struggling, gasping plantation owner. But an instant later, without hesitation, DePue grabbed the pistol he always carried and shot one of them, believing they, too, would attack his friend. The one called Little Pete fell, the bullet tearing into his chest from a shot at such a close range. The other two men, Lionel and John, turned and ran.

George Thatcher's huge legs spread across Henry's body, not willing to lessen his grip. Henry kicked and tried to free to push this crazy nigger off him. He'd be dead soon if he didn't act immediately. He gave up trying to get George's hands off his throat with his single left arm. Instead he reached down into his boot, pulled his Remington derringer and fired a single shot into the side of the man's head. Instantly the pressure on his throat eased as the huge black body collapsed on top of him.

"Alfred, get this nigger off me. I'm damn near suffocated," Henry gasped.

As he stood and rubbed his neck the color began to return to his cheeks. "That son of a bitch almost killed me. Thanks for covering me," he said hoarsely, as he eyed the other field hand lying in a pool of blood.

House and field workers had begun to gather at the sound of the struggle. Now they hid in the background, frightened at the scene they had witnessed.

"Chloe, gather the entire staff and have them assemble in the back of the house. And, I mean everyone. I want the wives and children. Have them here in one hour and please get some of the men to get those two bodies ready for burial. One hour!" Henry commanded.

He suddenly remembered that Josiah had likely watched the entire episode as it unfolded.

"Josiah," he shouted. "Josiah, come here!" There was no answer. He went to the boy's room but it was empty.

"The boy's gone. I'm sure he'll be back. Noises must have frightened him. Sometimes I worry he has his mother's temperament, way too gentle. Meanwhile I need a drink. Pour one for me, will you please, Alfred? And one for yourself, if you want."

"I'll have a double," DePue answered, walking to the sideboard where the carafes rested. "That was all pretty unnerving. Good thing you carried that pistol."

"Always carried one. You never know when you might need an extra measure of safety."

They sat together, resettling their nerves, as every field and house servant at Moss Grove began to gather just outside the house.

"Are you sure your son will be OK?" Alfred asked.

"I imagine so. I gave him his own horse a few months ago and he's got his dog with him. The boy is a real loner. He and I have had more and more difficulty connecting since his mother's death," Henry admitted in a moment of reverie.

"Everyone's in the back, Massa' Henry," Chloe announced nervously.

Henry stood, gathered himself, and walked purposefully to the rear of the house. He put down a small box and stood on it.

"George Thatcher just tried to kill me and I shot him. There were witnesses, both black and white. I want you all to know that. When another man tried to help him, he was shot as well. We'll bring in another overseer but in the meantime you each know what your jobs are so I expect you to do them. Are there any questions?" he asked, fully in control as the lord of Moss Grove.

"Sir, what goin' to happen to Big George's missus and chillum?" a girl he recognized from working in the kitchen, asked.

"We'll send them on their way unless one of the single men wants an immediate family. Her man tried to kill me. I don't owe her or her children a thing."

Silence and muttering sent waves of discomfort into the air.

"We had a good season. Most of you covered what you owed for rent and commissary and such. Some of you families even have a little money due to you or you can take it as a credit on what you might need this next year. We want you to stay and we want you to tell your friends we're looking for more croppers," Henry knew he'd have to pay out a little of what he owed, to keep peace. He couldn't kill them all.

"But if any others of you intend to leave, I want to know now or the contracts you signed to work a year automatically extend for another year. That's the law. Now go back to work." He remained where he was, staring out at the dark faces of these people he detested but needed.

Josiah kept riding long after he left the confines of Moss Grove. He stayed along the river and headed south. He'd never traveled this far from home alone and he had to keep wiping his eyes with his sleeve from the tears that had been falling steadily since all the shooting had frightened him.

His father had almost been killed by George Thatcher. George had always been so gentle with him, so patient. I wonder why he got so angry with my father, Josiah wondered. And then George was dead. I didn't know people could die so suddenly, he thought. My mother lingered for weeks when she was sick.

The young boy had no idea where he was going. Whisper darted in and out of the trees chasing squirrels or birds or possums or whatever might be in the underbrush.

He was getting very tired. He knew he'd been riding a long time and it would be dark soon. He didn't want to return to Moss Grove. He thought he was near the road he and his father had taken a few months ago when he got to spend time with Aunt Amy. If he was right, he knew where he wanted to be and who he needed to be with.

Amy wasn't at the clinic when a tired young blonde boy arrived but it wasn't difficult to recognize him. Several of the staff had seen him before. They took him in, cleaned his tears, fed him, and put him to bed. They even set out a dish for the dog who would growl menacingly if anyone approached his master. The next day, Josiah's horse was tied to the back of a wagon and boy, dog, and horse were brought to the Carmody house where the wedding plans were underway.

"Josiah," Amy said in total surprise, looking up. She and Stephen had been tying ribbons, while little Bess napped close by. Stephen's bows were a little lopsided and for everyone Amy tied, he would untie two of them. It had become a silly game that made them both laugh.

"What are you doing here? Does your father know where you are? Is everything OK?" she peppered him with questions before he could answer.

"I'm sorry, Josiah. You gave me a shock. I am so glad to see you. Take a minute and then tell me what brought you here."

Josiah hugged his aunt and didn't want to let her go. She felt his entire body quiver as his crying flooded back. She held him as he emptied the tension he had held in the past two days. Even Whisper whimpered, not knowing how to react. When the boy's crying eased, Amy wiped his eyes and runny nose. She continued to hold him as he told her the story of what happened. Once started, Josiah gushed out the loneliness he felt with his mother gone and the fear he had of his father. When he was finished, he was empty. He laid his head on Amy's lap and cried himself to sleep.

Amy sent a rider to Moss Grove to explain to Henry that Josiah was safe and that she'd appreciate being able to keep him with her for a short time. She wanted the boy to enjoy the festivities of the wedding but she thought it better to not mention those details.

Henry, worn out from his near-death experience, sent a return message that Josiah could stay and that Henry intended to find an appropriate school for him as soon as practical.

Thaddeus enjoyed his work as a State Assemblyman now that the Capitol grounds in Baton Rouge were secured by Union soldiers and he could focus on learning his way around. He was hopeful he could make a difference. In all the states surrounding Louisiana, laws were being passed that favored blacks or whites. Not a single southern or border state seemed willing to have a civil dialogue between the two races.

As more and more disputes were settled by the courts, their decisions were isolating the races more and more. The Federal courts were making an overwhelming number of their decisions in favor of the white majority. The new Constitutional Amendments that were passed to guarantee equality were interpreted as applying only to Federal, not state, situations. The southern states, it seems, would be free to pass whatever laws they wished regarding race relations.

Thaddeus was distressed when the Supreme Court decided that whites who had broken up a black political meeting couldn't be tried because the meeting related to a state election. He hurried to propose a state law that would correct such injustices but the white Democratic bloc was strong enough to defeat it. Similarly the black bloc was strong enough to block the passage of the extreme discriminatory laws being enacted in Tennessee and Mississippi. Few men and fewer legislators were willing to cross the color barrier with either their actions or their votes.

Thaddeus' personal life was not going much better. He'd lost Sarah. She hadn't forgiven him for the revelation of his past love for Amy. And Amy was at Carmody House. Just as well, he thought. He'd occasionally visit with Rufus but his friend was also busy running the business. Those times when they'd worked together had certainly been happier times.

Plans for Matthew and Sheila's wedding were proceeding with happy anticipation. Because of the need to travel, many of the guests arrived a day or two before the ceremony, some coming hundreds of miles. Extra gardens of spring flowers had been planted or brought in and the colorful scented blossoms adorned and cheered every room in the house. Platters of food and drinks were arrayed on tables both in the house and near the kitchens where teams of cooks prepared large quantities of food.

Rufus' chest burst with pride. His wife was still gorgeous and a marvelous hostess. Michelle was the little lady, already dazzling admirers. Carmody House never looked more exquisite and here he was, hosting a wedding for his closest friends. And that wasn't all. Stephen was an amazing handful. He had already learned to ride a horse but worse, he had become most proficient at manipulating him, Melanie and Michelle. And, always with a smile. This son of his was anxiously awaiting the birth of his new sibling, demanding that it be a brother. Yes, his life was overflowing.

"How do you like Washington?" Thaddeus asked his brother, as they tried to stay out of the way of the frenzy of all the preparations.

Both brothers had made their way to Carmody House just days before the ceremony. It was a time to reconnect.

"It's like nothing I've ever experienced. To actually be at the very soul of what makes our country function. It's a little humbling."

"Well, if you feel humble, that must be a first," the older brother laughed.

"I'm so sorry about you and Sarah. Sheila had always hoped that tomorrow might have been a double wedding ceremony."

"I don't blame her but I certainly still love her. I had to tell her about Amy and me and our feelings. Once I did that, she was crushed."

"Would you mind if I spoke with her? I'm not sure it would help but at this point there's nothing to lose either," Matthew said, putting his arm around his older brother.

"Hi Sarah," Matthew said as he caught her arranging fresh flowers that she had just been brought in from the garden.

"Matthew, how nice to see you. Are you getting excited? I mean, Sheila said she can hardly keep food down."

"They won't let us see one another. Some foolish rule that someone thought of a long time ago and now no one can remember why. The house looks beautiful. And so many people!"

"How is Washington? Sheila is a little nervous about living in a strange city."

"It's a beautiful place and there are a number of hospitals that would be thrilled to have a nurse with her experience. Sarah," he said, adroitly trying to shift the subject. "Can we talk about you and Thaddeus? He loves you and he is so unhappy. The thought of losing you is tearing him up. Is there any possible way you two can make this thing work between you?"

"Oh, Matthew, I just don't know. I do love him so. But you tell me, how do I give myself completely to a man who openly tells me he also loves another woman?"

"I guess you believe him when he says it is a different kind of love that doesn't diminish what he feels for you. You know Amy. She moved on with her life because she had to. There would never have been a life for the two of them…not here in Louisiana or anywhere else. She is the one that convinced him to move on with his life. It wasn't easy until he met you. Will you talk to him?"

Slowly, trying to hold her emotions in check, she nodded. Matthew put down the flowers she had been holding, took her hand and walked her across the yard to where Thaddeus was sitting.

He stood as they came closer. Matthew passed Sarah's hand into Thaddeus waiting palm, smiled at them both, and walked away. Neither said a word. Their eyes connected and they embraced.

"I promise we'll make it work," he said confidently.

"I can't tell you I know how to deal with all this. What do I say to Amy? What do I say to her husband? Do I tell my parents? Being a child in my parent's home was easy. This is hard."

"We can only trust what we feel for one another. I love you and I'll work hard to make you happy."

"If you shout Amy's name while we're making love, you're a dead man," she smiled.

"I love you," Thaddeus laughed.

"Dearly beloved," Reverend Walter Dinsmore began, in a commanding voice, hoping to get everyone's silence and attention. This ceremony was special, he knew. He was performing at the wedding of his daughter. How many men are blessed to be able to do such a wondrous thing?

Before him stood four beautifully attired, accomplished, young people. Thaddeus Williams and his own daughter, Sarah, looking every bit as beautiful as his wife, Hester, looked when they'd married more than twenty-five years earlier. They'd both been so young and uncertain as to what the future might bring. And Matthew and Sheila, another accomplished young black couple, looking at one another, truly in love. They are all so self-assured, so filled with the hopes of tomorrow. How far we've come in such a short span of years. It gave hope for the future.

Walter Dinsmore was touched by the decision to make this day a double ceremony. When he looked past the couples to his wife, he saw that she, too, was touched by what she was witnessing.

He finished the ceremony, not even aware that he had gone through the entire text without being conscious of the words until each 'I do' was said and everyone shouted and threw flower petals at the married couples.

Amy handed Bess to husband John. She wanted to talk to Thaddeus and it took some doing to extricate him from his new bride and all the well-wishers. They walked through the garden but it was hard for him to ignore the handshakes and pats on the back from guests wandering the grounds. They finally found themselves alone well away from the house. They could still hear the music and the partying but for a brief moment they were in their own world.

"Congratulations, Thaddeus. Sarah is a lovely woman. You couldn't have found someone better," she said, and then realized that, although unspoken, they both knew the two of them would have been 'better.'

"She obviously loves you enough to overcome what you and I feel for one another. You and I have been blessed to be loved by two such amazing and giving people.

"But I needed to see you. We've received some distressing news and it is terribly unsettling. John and I will be leaving Louisiana sooner than we thought. His orders finally came through and he is being reassigned to a Cavalry unit under General Crook at Fort Leavenworth, Kansas. He is being promoted to Colonel and that entitles him to bring his family. I guess the Army thinks as highly of him as I do. He will be leaving the end of the week. I'll follow as soon thereafter as Bess and I can tie up all the loose ends of our lives that we'll be leaving behind. I may not get another chance to see you."

"I can't imagine not being able to reach out to you. Even from New Orleans to Baton Rouge we could connect. You've never been out of my mind, you know that. Now all we'll have is our memories. We needed the stars to align but they never did." he said, unable to contain the heavy loss he was facing, despite his conflicted love for his new bride.

"No, they never did. And no matter how I try to put you into a special vault in my heart, you keep peeking out. I imagine you always will. Be as happy as you can, you know I will always love you. And when I look up at the sky at night, know that we are sharing the same stars."

They grabbed one another's hand and held tight. Both knew that an embrace at this point might last forever and weaken an already shaky resolve. Amy finally brushed his cheek with her hand and walked back to the wedding party.

# Chapter Thirty-One

As both political parties energized their supporters for the upcoming presidential election, Thaddeus and Matthew campaigned to become Republican delegates from the State of Louisiana. Much of the work on their behalf was done by supporters.

In addition to his ongoing work for Congressman Nash and Senator Bruce, Matthew enrolled in classes at Howard University, taking classes in Law and Economics. He worried that his educational background was too spotty for him to keep up with his lessons but the professors displayed an amazing empathy for their southern students that had always been deprived of the same educational opportunities as their northern brethren. Meanwhile both Blanche Bruce and Charles Nash were more than happy to act as mentors. They were able to add a real life interpretation to academic theory.

He and Sheila rented a larger flat in Georgetown. She had begun working at the local hospital. Both their schedules filled days and evenings but they always found time on Sunday to enjoy walks along the Potomac or visit the ever changing sights of the city. It was the happiest Matthew had ever been.

They took an over-filled train in May to attend a boisterous flag-waving celebration of the nation's centennial. Imagine, he thought, our country is one hundred years old. No expense had been spent on the Philadelphia exhibition. The President of the United States and the Emperor of Brazil would officially open the gates to more than one hundred thousand visitors the first day. In total the Centennial would host more than eight million people, and the country, now recovered from the wounds of war, honored the city that had united the original thirteen colonies.

The Republican convention was held in Cincinnati in the midst of a hot, muggy June. It rained constantly and in those rare moments when the sun appeared, the humidity made the delegates hope that the rain would return.

Thaddeus and Matthew, having won their race to become delegates, shared a room and met with delegates from the other states. The Republican favorite for President was James Blaine from Maine. The man had enjoyed a long and stellar career in Congress. He led a moderate group of supporters called the Stalwarts, who were in favor of eliminating patronage and replacing it with a merit system. But questions of his health, and his ties to a bankrupt railroad investment, left him twenty-eight votes short of winning the nomination. Instead, a dark horse candidate, Rutherford B. Hayes, a reform Governor from Ohio, edged him out to secure the nomination.

Neither Thaddeus nor Matthew had ever met either candidate. They were quite willing to support whoever Senator Bruce favored. They shifted their efforts when he did. On the seventh ballot, Hayes was approved by acclimation.

The Democratic Party convened in St. Louis one week after the Republican meeting ended. The leading candidate was Samuel Tilden, a well-known New York Governor whose stature had risen as a result of his success in dealing with the corruption of Tammany Hall and the conviction of its leader, Boss Tweed. He was chosen on the second ballot and the battle was joined.

The campaign was heated, particularly in the south. Illiterate voters cast their votes with symbols on the ballot instead of names, but Republican and Democratic symbols were often intentionally switched. Voter fraud were widespread.

Blacks were being threatened and coerced throughout the south. Thaddeus had returned to Louisiana charged with the responsibility of giving blacks in the northern part of the state the confidence to cast their vote. When several blacks were maimed and three were killed, his job became both more difficult and more dangerous. He crisscrossed from Baton Rouge to Tennessee, both east and west, usually accompanied by Sarah, who would sit with the women while Thaddeus would speak solemnly to the men about the dangers they would all face if Tilden and the Democrats were elected.

*When the electoral votes were tallied, Rutherford B. Hayes had won, but only by a single vote. Cries of fraud and ballot errors were raised by the Democrats and the nation held its collective breath. The ballots of more than a dozen states were disputed. Under the Constitution the task of resolving this issue was delegated to the Congress but the issue had never before arisen in the country's hundred year history.*

*Another dispute arose as to whether the Senate or the House retained final authority to determine which questionable votes were to be allowed. That decision was crucial as the Senate was controlled by the Republicans while the House of Representatives was controlled by the Democrats.*

*After furious debate it was agreed that a fifteen member Electoral Commission would be impaneled to resolve the problem. There would be five members from each house of Congress joined by five members of the Supreme Court. Each chamber would choose three majority members and two minority members, making five Democrats and five Republicans chosen by Congress.*

*The Supreme Court selected two Republicans and two Democrats. These four would decide on the fifth, and deciding, member. The man chosen to be the pivotal fifteenth, and deciding vote, was Justice Joseph Bradley, thought to be the most impartial member of the court. Bradley had voted consistently with that court's Republican majority most of the time. Thaddeus and other black activists began to feel cautiously optimistic.*

*Bradley had begun his professional life as an educator but soon switched to law. He became quite wealthy, specializing in patent and railroad law. President Grant appointed him as an Associate Justice of the Supreme Court in 1870. As he'd aged, he acquired the air of a distinguished grey-haired patrician and a reputation for possessing a keen legal mind.*

*As the date for inauguration neared, everyone awaited the resolution of this **'Compromise of 1877'**. The members of the commission reviewed the duplicate sets of ballots submitted by Louisiana and three other states. Thaddeus was chosen to assist in preparing the argument for the state's Republican slate. In the end the Commission gave South Carolina to Hayes by 887 votes and Florida to Hayes by 537 votes. Fourteen members of the commission had split* *evenly along party lines. As predicted, the final and deciding vote, cast by Judge Bradley was for Rutherford B. Hayes. Hayes would be the next President of the United States and Samuel Tilden would become a footnote in history. The Republicans would retain the presidency.*

*The decision, however, would always be tinged with the stench of a smoke-filled backroom compromise. Implied in the settlement was a tacit agreement to remove all Union troops stationed in the south whose sole purpose was to enforce equality and opportunities for Negros. The 'compromise' further ensured that legislation would be enacted that would accelerate the industrialization of the more rural southern states.*

*President Grant began the process of withdrawing Union forces stationed in what had been Confederate states before Hayes took office. A month later, the new President Hayes ordered the final troop removals from South Carolina, Florida and Louisiana.*

*The Civil War was over. Slavery had ended Reconstruction had ended. It was a pyrrhic victory. The hearts of men had been hardened and fused into a renewed conviction that race mattered.*

# Chapter Thirty-Two

Thaddeus joined Matthew and Sheila in celebrating the inauguration of another Republican President. They dined as guests of Senator Blanche Bruce and Representative Charles Nash in the lavish surroundings of the National Hotel. This was where President Lincoln had enjoyed his last dinner before continuing on to Ford's Theater on that eventful night. Mementos of that fateful night decorated one corner of the room. Tonight all those attending should have been euphoric; their candidate had won.

"Something isn't right," Senator Bruce warned. "I'm smellin' a polecat. I don't have any facts but this should just have been a clear and simple election victory, not some political compromise."

"I hear Grant is preparing an order to begin removing Union troops from all Confederate states. I hope I'm hearing wrong," Charles Nash said with a tinge of sadness in his voice.

"I don't know about the other states, but if they pull the Union troops from Louisiana we'll have a blood bath," Thaddeus averred.

"It would be the same all over," Bruce warned.

"Can we stop it, or even slow it down?" Matthew asked.

"Unlikely. But I fear our joy over electing a Republican President may not shower us with the benefits we all worked so hard to protect. The signs are quite ominous."

Thaddeus decided to stay in Washington another week before returning to Sarah and Baton Rouge. Sheila and Matthew proudly announced that Sheila was pregnant. Thaddeus would be an uncle right after the New Year. The news sent them all into a screaming frenzy as onlookers thought the three young people had lost their senses.

The three transplants from Louisiana toured the city, enjoying Thaddeus' obvious awe at seeing everything the nation's capitol had to offer.

A few days later Matthew returned to his work at the school. Thaddeus went with him and was introduced to Edward Smith, the President of Howard University. Smith was a tall man, towering over six feet. He wore heavy rimmed glasses that framed a light complexion and a full head of grey hair. His goatee was neatly trimmed with the black and white peppering that gave him the presence of a mature and serious man. His dress was appropriately conservative. He carried himself with a permanent cloak of academia but he had a reputation in Washington for being an aggressive solicitor of funding for the school.

Matthew had to leave them to attend his classes. Smith seemed fascinated by his mocha-colored guest. Most visitors to Howard University and Washington D.C., in general were from nearby states. And, except for Matthew and a few others, visitors from Louisiana were a rare occasion. He invited Thaddeus to join him for dinner so they might continue their conversation. They talked late into the night. Smith explained his goals, beginning with the addition of new colleges in both the sciences and the arts. Thaddeus described how he and Matthew had begun their lives and the paths they'd taken. As the evening wore on, the conversation became more personal. It was late in the evening before they stood to say their goodbyes.

"Thaddeus, I would like you to consider joining the staff of the University. I'm sure we can find a program that would permit you to pursue classes at the same time."

"President Smith, you hardly know me. I'm not sure I'm University material."

"This dinner was no accident. Matthew had solicited several letters of recommendation on your behalf including a Senator, a Governor, and several Louisiana business associates. They all say the same thing. You can do any job set before you in an exemplary fashion. I knew within a short time of our meeting that you could assist me in encouraging Congress to accelerate funding for the school. You and your brother are exactly the type of persons we are here to develop."

It was an offer that would be difficult to reject but it would depend on Sarah. She had been hesitant about leaving her family in New Orleans for a move to nearby Baton Rouge. Asking her to move another thousand miles further wouldn't be easy. And Amy, already packing for her move to Kansas. Would he ever see her again? Would their stars ever align?

"Matthew, please come in and sit down," Charles Nash said from behind his desk. "We need to talk."

"Yes sir, how can I help you?" Matthew asked. His mentor had lost a close election and their interconnected jobs would soon end. He took a seat opposite the man who had mentored him so much.

"I've decided to leave Washington. The pace has become too much for my family. My wife and I have decided we want a quieter life with people who are friendlier and not always looking for a way to line their pockets.

"At first I was personally disappointed I'd lost the election. We'd all worked so hard and we were so committed to the work we still had to do. With a Republican President we might have been able to put more empathetic people on our courts. But not Rutherford Hayes! We might as well have a Democrat for all the good he's doing us. Now our future is back in God's hands. You and I are only too aware how many Republican black officials were defeated by white Democrats in this recent election, despite the aggressive campaigning we did."

"The people of Louisiana and the Congress will be the worse for your loss," Matthew said.

"I guess I feel a sense of dread almost as much as you do," the younger man continued. "Sheila and I are also beginning to make plans to return to Louisiana. We'll probably wait until the baby is born and strong enough to travel. I would have preferred to stay in Washington and keep fighting. I also hoped to continue my part-time schooling at Howard. I had hoped to get my Law degree."

"That's why I wanted to speak to you. I'm going to accept a position as Postmaster of St. Landry Parish, near where I grew up, but you don't have to leave if you don't want to," Nash said with a wry smile.

"Senator Bruce would be delighted if you would agree to join his staff. He admires you and the work you've done. I'd consider it a personal favor if you'd agree and accept his offer. He has indicated he will give you time to continue your schooling and earn your degree."

Matthew was startled by the offer. It was a chance to work with a Senator whom he admired and a chance to continue his education. He felt as if a huge burden had been lifted from him for the first time since the election. He could almost feel himself tearing. He hurried to wipe his eye before he was embarrassed. He and Sheila both wanted to remain in Washington. The baby was almost due, his final exams were next month, and now he could stay and do the type of work that thrilled him, trying to make a difference.

Amy looked around her house as she packed her things. She'd grown up around Baton Rouge. She'd met Thaddeus at Moss Grove and they'd conceived a child together at Carmody House. Now she and John would travel hundreds of miles to a different, more raw, part of the country, out west. She stopped, grabbed her bonnet, picked up Bess, and left the house. She needed to see Stephen one more time.

Rufus wasn't home. He always spent long days overseeing the multiple feed stores and the toy business. Melanie and Michelle shrieked when they saw Amy's wagon pull up.

"Oh my gosh, what a delightful surprise. I thought you might leave without saying goodbye."

"I couldn't do that."

"Can I watch Bess for awhile?" Michelle asked. "I'm big enough now."

"You certainly are. But be careful! She's starting to crawl everywhere."

"Aunt Amy...Aunt Amy," Stephen cried running helter-skelter, hands covered in mud.

"Stephen, you'll get your Aunt all dirty. Go wash up first," Melanie cautioned.

"C'mon Stephen, we'll wash up together," Amy laughed.

"Did you bring me anything? Did you?" he said, wriggling from the soap and water splashed across his face."

"Aren't I enough? Bess and I came to say goodbye for awhile." The words caught in her throat. Goodbye! What a terrible thing to say to your child.

They stayed the night. Amy clung tight to both her children, willingly them to know one another and desperately wanting Stephen to not forget her.

Rufus had come back late and stayed to share the difficult goodbyes, not knowing if they would ever see one another again.

Josiah was back at Moss Grove. He had been happy being with Aunt Amy and Uncle John but they were leaving for Kansas and he had nowhere else to go. Henry knew he had to get Josiah enrolled in a school. If the boy ran away once, he'd run away again. The boy needed a mother but there was no one Henry felt like marrying. On occasion he'd visited other plantations or found himself in the company of an eligible young miss but they were either too willing or too timid and his patience for games of seduction had waned. He'd prefer to pay for his sexual pleasures and not have to deal with the whims of unstable women. As far as he knew, they were all damned unstable.

He finally selected a school for his son. The West Baton Rouge English & French Academy was a preparatory school where Josiah would have the company of boys his age from the proper sort of families. He had, with considerable reluctance, thought of seeking help from Amy in finding an appropriate Boarding School, but their history with one another made it too difficult.

Fortunately, others at the Freedman's School remembered Josiah and offered to help. Amy had brought him to the school often while she worked in the clinic and the blonde boy had made friends with both teachers and young students.

"Josiah, I shall visit you often. I will expect you to do well in school," Henry said in his sternest voice as their wagon approached the school. "I will have no slacker for a son. You are a Rogers, be proud and do well."

"Father, I really don't want to be here. I'd much rather be back at Moss Grove," the boy said in a quaking voice. "I won't run away again. I'm sorry I did that, but I was frightened."

"There was no reason to be afraid for me," his father said confidently. "I was never in any danger."

Josiah listened and said nothing. It wasn't a fear of his father being killed that had sent him running. It was the simple brutality of two men attacking one another. He'd once seen two dogs attack one another in that same way and he had watched, transfixed, as one dog's throat was wrenched open, blood on the maw of the surviving dog, fangs bared, guttural sounds filling the air, as it stood over its victim. The violent scene had stayed with him. The struggle between George Thatcher and his father brought all that horror flooding back.

His father didn't understand and Josiah knew in his boyish way that he and his father would never really understand one another.

"I'm glad you were alright. I'll miss you. They said I could keep Whisper if I took care of him. May I? Please," he begged.

"If you do well in your classes, I will have your dog sent to you."

They parted, not as the father and son type of farewell the

boarding school matron normally watched, but respectful and remote. Mrs. Sylvia Noresby watched, a tear forming in her eye as a cold chill passed through her body. She wasn't sure why either reaction had occurred but she was a superstitious woman and she sensed it didn't bode well.

Thaddeus was glad to be home. He and Sarah embraced, promising one another that neither wanted to face such a long separation again.

Whites, Blacks and Coloreds in Louisiana and the surrounding states were permanently nervous and frightened from a spate of recent violent attacks that might spring up anywhere. Even bystanders were getting killed.

The Ku Klux Klan had burned a business not far from her father's warehouse and riders that seemed to be looking for trouble rode through the busy streets of New Orleans with impunity. If they encountered any black militia they just left and sought out less guarded homes or farms. There were similar stories across the state as Army units moved north or just disbanded.

"Thaddeus," Sarah said as they sat together for their first dinner in over a month. "This letter came for you a week ago. It's from Amy. I didn't open it."

He looked at this woman he'd married and whom he loved. It was very different from the way he loved Amy. Both he and Sarah were aware of this perpetual unseen presence but they worked hard to make their life together a happy one. Thaddeus slowly opened the envelope as Sarah got up from her chair and began to leave the room.

"Please don't leave," he said. "There are no secrets between us." He scanned Amy's tiny handwriting. "See, it's to both of us," he began,

*'Dear Sarah and Thaddeus,*

*I hope this letter finds you both well. Bess and I were exhausted by the wagon trip. It just seemed to go on forever. The poor girl got a rash and diarrhea the second day. That and the heat made her terribly irritable and I wasn't certain she'd survive the journey. Thank goodness, she did. I guess she has his father's Michigan sturdiness.*

*John was so relieved to see us. Our baby daughter had grown inches since he'd seen her last. John found us a nice little house near*

*the Fort where he spends most of his days marching or parading or doing what soldiers seem to do when they don't have someone to fight. Fort Leavenworth is almost like a small town. They have almost everything but sometimes I feel a need to leave the fort and breathe open air. Then they assign two troopers to accompany me.*

*I have a sweet young Indian girl who helps me. I was told that she had been captured by the soldiers when her village had been raided. She wasn't much more than a baby then and both her parents had either been killed by the soldiers or they'd run away. No one quite remembers. Anyway, she's been raised at the fort. That was a long time ago. I think she is from a tribe of Indians called Pawnee. She says her name is Little Bird and we've become good friends. She adores Bess and Bess loves her. The other day she put a feather in Bess' hair and they both ran around the house making 'whoopee' noises.*

*John has been assigned to General Terry. They are supposed to go out and subdue some northern Cheyenne Indian tribes. John thinks they'll be gone nearly a month. I busy myself doing some nursing and some teaching. It isn't a life that I've ever known. This is truly a frontier but we are doing the best we can and I am trying to be a good Army wife.*

*Please give my love to Matthew and Sheila as well as Melanie and Rufus and everyone else I love and miss on a daily basis. And a special hug to Michelle and Stephen. Write and tell me all about everything you have been doing. I know it will be exciting and it will help me feel so much closer to you.*

*All my love,*
*Amy*

Thaddeus sat quietly staring at the letter. Sarah rose, touched his shoulder tenderly, and left the room. This time he didn't ask her to stay.

By the time Thaddeus put out the candles and readied himself for bed, Sarah was already asleep, her head turned away.

"Sarah, I love you," he said softly, not sure whether she was really asleep or just feigning. "What I had with Amy was the past, a young boy's past. What I have with you is the present and the future, our future. Please don't let a ghost from that past upset what we have."

Slowly she turned and faced him; his blue eyes expressed his love better than any words. He kissed her and they embraced. Slowly she slid her nightgown off her shoulders and let it gather at the bottom of the bed. Thaddeus' fingers drew a gentle line from his wife's lips, gathering her breasts in his hands and leaning to drink from their essence. He could feel Sarah undulate beneath him as he grew erect and her fingers sought him out, caressing and then guiding. As he entered, she gasped. He kissed her more deeply, his tongue reaching, searching, sharing. When he climaxed she followed an instant later. They fell asleep continuing to cling to one another until the morning.

"Sarah, I want us to move to Washington," he said over a breakfast of eggs and grits. They were both starved from the evening's physical and emotional drain.

"I've been offered an opportunity to work at Howard University and continue my education at the same time."

"Leave Louisiana? I'd be leaving my parents, my father's church, my mother, my brother, Jesse. I'd be so frightened," she said, as she sat and sagged in her chair.

"We'd be close to Sheila and Matthew and we can come back often to visit your parents," he said. "We can never find an opportunity like this here. With the troops gone, this state could well end up being in the middle of a civil war between blacks and whites."

"Thaddeus, I hadn't said anything yet because I'm not really sure but I may be pregnant and, if I am, I want to remain here at least until the child is born. I know it isn't what you want, but if you'll let me do that, the baby and I will join you in Washington."

"Pregnant? A child of our own? Sarah, that's so wonderful. I do love you so much. Of course you can remain here until the baby is born. I'll see if the University will allow me to postpone starting my classes until after the baby is born."

"No, I want you to go and begin your work. It will be exciting for you. We'll only be apart for a few months. Perhaps I'll just settle in with my parents. Since we'll be moving so far away, it will give me extra time with them. I'm sure they'll be thrilled. It will go quickly, you'll see," she said tearfully, but with a determined hope in her eyes.

Given everything Sarah had accepted in marrying Thaddeus, he couldn't do anything but acquiesce. He stayed another two weeks until they were certain that Sarah was pregnant but he had already sent a telegram to President Smith accepting his offer.

Since he would be gone for awhile, he made certain that they found time to visit all the friends who had been so wonderful to them and were practically family.

Thaddeus enjoyed a dinner alone with his old friend and mentor, James Longstreet and his business associate, Julius Freyhan. They were back at their sawdust-floored shrimp café at the harbor.

"Still eating 'traif' I see," smiled Thaddeus.

"You have a good memory for Yiddish. If you want to convert I can see if Eli Fineman would like to sponsor you. I'll even buy you your first 'tallis'."

"I've got enough problems being an irreligious Methodist from my father-in-law, Reverend Dinsmore. I'd better leave well enough alone," he smiled, pulling the red tail from a huge gulf prawn.

"I'm glad you'll be working with President Smith. Establishing Howard was one of the only productive things that came out of Grant's second term. And you'll love Washington. General Lee and I came awfully close to taking control of that city," Longstreet reminisced. "Might have changed the outcome of the war."

"What will happen around here now that the troops have gone?" Thaddeus asked.

"It won't be good," Julius said. "White hoodlums will mass into larger groups and prey on blacks and coloreds. They'll probably prey on Jews also. They like to lump us into the same slime of their ignorance. We aren't like them so we don't belong."

"Whites that tried to make a difference are leaving as well. Blacks that can arm themselves are forming militias but they're going to find themselves badly outnumbered. And, as the balance of power shifts we may find ourselves with some of the same segregation laws they've already begun to pass in Mississippi," Longstreet added.

"Meanwhile, enjoy the time with your wife and begin your new life. If anyone can help stem this tide it just might be you and it will certainly need to be done in Washington, not in any state."

Thaddeus and Sarah's trip to visit Rufus and Melanie was no longer as difficult as it had been a few years earlier. The Army had improved the roads between New Orleans and Baton Rouge and the rains had not yet arrived to make the trip slow and muddy. Sarah was beginning to get occasional morning sickness and Thaddeus needed to stop frequently to let her stomach resettle.

Carmody House looked even lovelier than Thaddeus remembered from their wedding day. Flowers, cotton blossoms and other landscaping now displayed a panoply of color that surrounded the house.

Rufus, Melanie and a noisy Michelle, greeted them even before Thaddeus and Sarah had climbed down from their buggy. Michelle had grown into a smiling walking toddler who stood, holding tight to her daddy's leg. Stephen yelped from the other room, eager to see more visitors.

"Before you say anything about me getting fat," Melanie said, "which I am, we're also expecting again. Melanie and Stephen will have a little brother or sister in the late fall."

"Us, too," Sarah and Thaddeus chimed at the same time as they all hugged one another.

So much had happened in the few months since the wedding. Amy, John and baby Bess were gone and their absence left a gaping hole in them all. Thaddeus told them about Matthew and Sheila. They were so proud that he would be working as an aide to a senator. His brother's first child was due soon and their life seemed to be filled with shiny opportunity.

Thaddeus told of the offer he had received from Howard University and their reluctant decision to move to Washington. Melanie and Sarah looked at one another and silently shared their awareness that when you love your husband, you follow wherever he leads.

"You have funny eyes," Stephen said, climbing on Thaddeus' lap.

"They're blue. What color are yours?"

"Mommy, what color are my eyes?"

"They're more blue-green."

"Does everyone have different color eyes?"

"No," said Thaddeus. "Some people have brown eyes."

"OK, do you want to play?" he said with the typical attention span of a young boy.

"Let me show you around. We've just about completed what we set as our goal for the house," Rufus said. "C'mon, Stephen, you can come with us and show Thaddeus around. We'll leave the women here to chat."

"OK, we'll leave Mommy and Melanie and Aunt Sheila here to chat 'cause they're girls."

"Has there been much violence hereabouts?" Thaddeus asked as he and Rufus walked through the maple and oak trees that were now beginning to shade the property.

"There's been some and we expect a lot more. We moved Melanie's mother to Carmody House along with Able and Benny.

"We had to bring them in and give up their farm," Rufus said. "Too many night-riders! Likely they'd be killed if they stayed. That farm was too remote to be properly protected and there's plenty of work and plenty of land here. Able has a good business head and he's pretty much running the Carmody & Williams Feed store."

"We should talk about that, Rufus. It's pretty much been your business these past years. Maybe it's time to remove the Williams name."

"If you let me pay you for your share we can talk about it, but the name stays. We started that business together and it's been pretty lucky for us."

"I truly don't expect anything, Rufus. I owe you so much in my life."

"We owe one another. We're family. I'll work out something fair," he said. "There are two more things we need to discuss, Amy and Josiah! First, we received a letter from Amy. I know she'd written you but I think this letter was written a few weeks later."

Thaddeus took the letter, sat and propped his back against a tree. For a few moments he just held the envelope, understanding this was as close as he was likely to get to Amy in this lifetime. Rufus sat quietly.

*Dearest Melanie and Rufus,*

*I hope this letter finds you in good health. I'm sure Michelle is getting to be a big girl now. I do miss her and Stephen so much every day but I am evermore grateful for the love you have given him. I dearly wish that they and Bess could grow up knowing one another. I know they would all be the best of friends. I am terribly nervous and alone as I write this. I had mentioned that John had gone with General Terry to subdue some Indian uprisings in the north. These things seem to happen more often lately. Little Bird, my Indian girl, says the tribes are all angry. Settlers keep coming onto land that was supposed to be set aside for them. Their people are starving.*

*I did learn that John had been attached as liaison to General George Custer's unit. General Terry had ordered Custer's regiment up somewhere near the Montana border. We don't know exactly what happened but the news that has drifted back isn't good. It seems that thousands of Indians under a chief named Sitting Bull confronted seven hundred of Custer's Union Cavalry, surrounded*

*them, and killed every one of our brave soldiers. I don't know if John*
*was with them but I lay awake at night with a dreadful emptiness*
*in the pit of my stomach. If he has been killed I have no idea what*
*Bess and I shall do.*

*Please keep us all in your prayers,*

*Amy*

"Oh, my God," Thaddeus said, nearly crumpling the letter nervously. "Is there anything we can do?"

"We haven't been able to think of a thing. It took more than a week for the letter to reach us. We wrote her back immediately suggesting that she return here if she finds herself alone."

"The moment I return to Washington, I'll ask Senator Bruce to make inquiries. He knows people in the War Department. This is so terrible for her."

"After that, I hate to mention the second item. It seems Henry enrolled Josiah in a school in Baton Rouge. Josiah had run away over something. Melanie found out on one of her trips into Baton Rouge. They'd had a tutor at Moss Grove but he'd been killed over some supposed tryst with a sharecropper's son. That plantation is beginning to feel as if it's cursed."

With all these new considerations they cut their visit short. The separation turned out to be more difficult than any of them would have anticipated. Their lives were taking very separate paths.

Thaddeus decided to stop and see Josiah. He was still uncomfortable with this miniature version of his biological father, replete with long blonde hair, and a body structure that was sure to develop like Henrys. Thaddeus felt a close kinship to Matthew but this sibling relationship was very different, especially given that Josiah wasn't even aware he had a half-brother.

Thaddeus and Sarah arrived at the school and introduced themselves to Mrs. Noresby. It was embarrassing trying to explain his relationship to the young blonde boy who never had visitors. She had become the boy's surrogate mother and was very protective of his well-being. Here was a colored couple claiming to be relatives. It took nearly an hour to explain the shared history that had brought them to her school.

Josiah smiled when he saw them. He remembered the wedding and the cake and taking a long walk with Thaddeus while Whisper ran through the woods. His face lit up as they laughed together.

Josiah had now been in school nearly three months. In all that time he hadn't heard from his father. Mrs. Noresby had written Henry every week describing how hard his son was working to earn the promised reward of getting his dog. She never received a reply and no matter how well he did, Whisper never came. The boy had retreated into his old solitary habits and neither Mrs. Noresby nor his few new friends could raise his spirits.

Thaddeus listened to the boy and heard the loneliness and disappointment. With Mrs. Noresby's permission they took the wagon into town for an extra surprise treat.

"No, I won't tell you what the treat is," Thaddeus smiled as Josiah sat next to Sarah.

"Do you know what it is?" he asked her.

"I don't. Shall we guess?"

They guessed candy. They guessed different types of toys. But to each guess Thaddeus just shook his head and smiled.

By the time he and Sarah returned Josiah to the school the boy was laughing, smiling, and hugging a jiggling hound dog puppy that pulled on its rope and tangled itself on everything.

"Mrs. Noresby, look what I've got. I have a dog just like Whisper when he was a puppy. I think I'll call him Whisperette. Isn't he beautiful?"

"He's very beautiful," she agreed as she wiped a tear from her cheek and thanked Josiah's two visitors.

By the time Thaddeus and Sarah's baby was born and Baptized, civil unrest in New Orleans was becoming a daily occurrence. Thaddeus had returned in time for the birth but he was now anxious to leave the racial vitriol he found all around him and settle with his family in Washington.

The new baby boy, born without a single hair on its head, was christened Noah. Thaddeus wanted to name the boy Jedidiah, explaining the affection he'd had for the white patriarch of Moss Grove who had saved him from a life of working as a slave in the cotton fields. That wonderful soft spoken man and his wife had broken laws by teaching him how to read. Naming his first son after him was the only sign of respect he could pay. But Reverend Dinsmore had convinced him that Noah, like his namesake, offered a new beginning, and Noah he became.

A month later Thaddeus and Sarah said their goodbyes, packed their belongings and, holding tight to their new son, boarded the train to

Washington. As Thaddeus settled in his seat, he unfolded the newspaper he had purchased at the depot. The news was disheartening but no different from what they'd witnessed the past month. The Picayune reported more and more killings. Blacks were beginning to give up and move north where they hoped for an easier life.

Thaddeus and Sarah settled close to Matthew and Sheila in a tiny Georgetown flat. With young babies to care for, Sheila and Sarah could alternate watching the children when the other had a work or school assignment.

Senator Bruce was unable to get conclusive information on whether Colonel John Shipley was alive or, like the rest of Custer's command, his bones had already bleached in the hot sun of the Black Mountains. The only reply they received was that the Army was still working on it.

Thaddeus was asked by Senator Bruce to give testimony to a Senate Investigating Committee looking into the increasing 'Exodus' of blacks out of the south. Minnesota's Senator Windom had proposed the government establish separate areas for blacks in the west. Sheila had gone to work for him as an enthusiastic supporter. It was becoming clear to many in the Federal government that this hasty withdrawal of Federal troops from the southern states was not working as it was intended. More than a decade of federal support for racial equality was being eroded daily. Establishing black enclaves in New Mexico, Nevada, and Arizona were all being considered.

> On the floor of the Senate, Windom asserted that the Southern white will 'tolerate no conditions but those of domination on one side and subservience on the other.' He had already formed the National Emigrant Aid Society to regulate the movement of blacks from the south to the west.
>
> The committee also heard from a colored politician from Kansas, Edwin McCabe. He urged the Senate to establish black enclaves within the Oklahoma Indian Territory. He, too, was unsuccessful. But the exodus was beginning to create a shortage of workers across the southern states as fewer black men were willing to share crop or labor in the fields. It seemed that none of the southern states wanted large numbers of blacks leaving. It denied them the cheap labor they needed to produce their crops. Meanwhile none of the northern

states was prepared for a large influx of migrant workers. They were already absorbing the Irish, Germans and Eastern Europeans coming into the United States. Settling them in the west seemed an obvious compromise, but that, too, was blocked by political pressures.

The unauthorized resolution was a blockade of major crossing points along the Mississippi River. General James Chalmers, ex-Confederate officer and Mississippi Congressman, directed a mob of armed whites. They sunk boats and threatened any person of color trying to relocate to the western side of the 'Ol Miss. More than fifteen hundred black souls were stranded as Chalmers wrote to President Hayes, "Every river landing is blockaded by white enemies of the colored exodus, some of whom are mounted and armed, as if we are at war."

# Chapter Thirty-Three

The Knights of the White Camellia preferred to make their forays in the early morning hours when it was more likely there would be no militia patrolling the streets. Most people would be asleep. Henry Rogers had begun riding with them as the pace of harassment directed at all people of color and their supporters increased. His life at Moss Grove continued to be lonely and sullen. Elizabeth was gone and Josiah was away. These white men had become his only companions. He and Alfred de Pue would often ride together.

This particular evening, with only the sliver of a moon to mark their way, they were joined by two dozen men led by Colonel Alcibiades De Blanc. Even Philip Lunstrum was with them. De Blanc's group had started out north from New Orleans just after sunset. No one was sure where they were headed or what target they'd selected. Secrecy was crucial. There was always fear that a 'jack' traitor might warn the black militias or the few remaining Union troops.

The two groups met at a prearranged crossroads just outside Baton Rouge. They all headed out again with De Blanc in the lead. But they weren't heading out of town this time. Their targets were on the outskirts of town.

"You men go around the back and flank those stores and small houses," De Blanc ordered, as the men began to array themselves in military fashion. None of these men wore masks but most wore some accoutrement of their former Confederate uniforms. De Pue and Lunstrum led the men around the rear while Henry and De Blanc divided the remaining men and moved to the front.

The rear contingent lit bundles of straw that would be used to ignite the barn, the stables and the rear of the feed store. No sooner had the first bundles been lit then a din rose inside as everyone was awakened by the light and the crackling sound of the dry wood. As the few people asleep inside rushed out they were confronted by a group of armed white men on horseback.

As the fire lit up the dark sky, Henry began to laugh. It wasn't a soft snickering laugh, but was a raucous gale. They were going to burn Carmody & Williams. What retribution! How appropriate!

"You find this very funny, Captain Rogers?" De Blanc asked. "We are here on God's mission."

"Of course, Colonel! Of course! But you see, I know the niggers that own this business. They used to be Moss Grove slave property and destroying it gives me an extra sense of pleasure."

"Well, keep your pleasure under control," he said sternly as he rode his horse closer to the house.

Seven blacks stood in front of them in their nightshirts. There were four men and three women, including Able and Benny who were now both living in the house and managing the feed store and stable.

"I knows you, Mister Henry Rogers. I recognize you with that one arm," Able said. "Why you do this to us? We ain't done no harm to you."

"'You haven't done any harm' is the correct way to speak, you ignorant nigger. And who are you? Doesn't Rufus Carmody still run this shit hole?"

"He our brother-in-law. Leave us be. Please," Benny said, pleading.

"Do you scum have a last name?" Henry persisted.

"Chartier!" Abner answered.

"Let's forget the family history, Captain. We need to finish this and move on before someone who sees the fires alerts the militia."

"One more question," Henry said, getting an uneasy feeling. "Is your sister, Melanie, a New Orleans slut who worked in gentlemen's clubs?"

"Our sister Melanie is a beautiful and wonderful woman. She marry Mr. Rufus Carmody."

"How delicious," Henry said as he grabbed his pistol and put one bullet each into the two brothers. In the quiet of the early morning as the burning buildings began to turn from bright red to grey ash, the sound of the pistols ringing out sent the birds scurrying from their havens in the tree branches.

"What the fuck are you doing, you crazy bastard?" Alcibiades asked, reining in his horse, frightened by the sudden burst of gunfire. "We aren't here to murder these people. We just want them out of business."

"Fuck you, too, Colonel. I owe them. No one takes advantage of Henry Rogers. They got what they deserved." Henry's eyes flashed like blue ice, reflecting off the burning embers.

"What you've done was not part of the plan, you crazy fool. This matter is not over," DeBlanc shouted as he mounted his horse. "Let's get out of here, now," he ordered.

The survivors stood there, frightened and crying, their friends dead and their lives destroyed.

The dark of the night raid was not finished as they rode off. De Pue looked at his friend, Henry, a little differently. He knew the man had a rapier-like temper but killing two unarmed men in cold blood made him nervous.

Henry rode alone as the rest of group clustered together and rode west. What that crazy bastard had done could bring them problems they hadn't anticipated.

The riders approached the recently built home from the back, failing to notice the carefully carved plaque at the front of a tree-lined lane that bore the name 'Carmody House'.

Once again they used the same tactics, lighting fires on one side of the house and forcing the inhabitants out the other side. This time, however, shots from within rang out and two of the riders fell from their horses, dead. The rest of the men took cover as the fire grew in intensity. Minutes later twelve men, women, and children stood in front of their adversaries.

"You killed two of my men," the Colonel said angrily. "We want you out of here, all of you. Niggers will not own property like white men, not in these parts."

Henry spied Melanie standing next to her husband, holding her daughter. Stephen stood off to the side, his grandmother unwilling to let him go. It was clear his onetime escapade was pregnant with another child. The bitch, he thought. And that's Rufus, next to her. Henry hadn't seen the man since that day at Moss Grove when he'd marched off with those nigger brats, Matthew and Thaddeus, following him. So that's Rufus Carmody. What a small world!

As Henry was staring at Melanie, she turned instinctively, feeling the intensity of his fury. There he was, one arm, blonde hair protruding from under his hat, trying to look regal. She walked toward the riders.

"Get back with the others," De Pue ordered.

She ignored him, pushed aside one horse blocking her way and stopped, staring up at this arrogant white bully who had affected her life in too many ways.

"Henry Rogers," she said, icy hatred in her voice. "How nice to see you again!"

"You know this woman, Captain?" Alcibiades asked.

"I do. She used to be a prostitute in New Orleans. I had the pleasure of fucking her. How are you, Melanie?"

"I'm fine, Henry. Just fine! I was sorry to hear your wife died. I met your son, Josiah, at Amy's wedding. He looks just like you, although he has not, fortunately, acquired your temperament," she taunted.

"Don't talk about my son or my family, you bitch," he seethed.

"We want all of you packed and out of this area within forty-eight hours or you'll find yourself dead," the Colonel interjected.

"Blacks and coloreds are not wanted in this parish, but you," he said, pointing toward Rufus. "You killed two of my men."

"They deserved it. You and your men attacked us. We are only defending our home," Rufus said, pushing his family behind him. Michelle cowered in her mother's dress.

"Nigger," DeBlanc spat as he raised his saber and spurred his horse forward.

"Run, hide," Marie whispered to Stephen. "The root cellar! Don't come out."

Rufus saw DeBlanc coming, dropped to one knee, aimed his pistol and let his last shot go. It caught the White Camellia leader in the upper torso as the raised saber came down, slicing Rufus across the neck. Both men died instantly, lying one atop the other, their limbs splayed, as everyone watched, frozen in place.

Melanie was the first to scream as she ran toward her husband. She pushed the white man off and cradled her husband in her arms. Her cries were screams of anguish as she rocked back and forth; trying to will him back to life.

"You killed him, you bastards," she wailed. "How can you hate colored folk and have one hidden among you?"

Henry blanched and an icy blast moved through his entire body.

Does she mean me? She can't know. Who would have revealed this past blasphemy? His mind raced, Elizabeth, Sarah? How had this colored trollop found out? He saw his life as a plantation owner ending.

"Shut up, you bitch," he said, as he pulled his pistol from his belt. He needed her dead, now. But as he pulled the trigger, Lunstrom's horse pushed against his and the shot went wide.

"What are you talking about?" Philip Lunstrum insisted. "He and I went to college together. What does she mean, Henry?"

"Ignore her," Henry demanded. "I'm in command now and I want all these people dead."

"Not until we learn what she means," several of the men who had ridden up with the Colonel shouted. "We aren't ready to take orders from you, Rogers."

"This man, Henry Rogers, has nigger blood in him, same as us," she screamed. "He ain't the pure white man he pretends to be."

"Henry Rogers? You're crazy," Alfred dePue responded. "Lying won't save your miserable colored ass, lady."

"I ain't lying. He had a nigger baby five years ago. Seems his mother, Ruby, was a Creole with black blood," Melanie sobbed, still writhing on the ground, Michelle frightened and crying, sharing her mother's grief.

"Amy, his sister-in-law, was told the whole story on her sister's death bed. Baby, named, Clara, was sent away, and died in a fire at an orphan's home in New Orleans."

"I remember that fire," one rider recalled.

"What do you say to that, Henry?" Lunstrum asked to the stares of every white rider. "You got nigger blood in you? 'Cause even you got one drop, you ain't white. That's the law."

"This bitch is lying. She hates me."

"We don't think so," another Camellia said. "People always speak the truth on their death bed. They don't want to go to God with a lie on their lips."

"Give me your gun, Henry," Alfred said.

"I will not surrender my gun," he said, the fury in his voice ricocheting off the crackling wood still burning. Henry raised his pistol and pointed it toward the man he had thought was his friend. From the other side Philip Lunstrum raised his pistol and pulled the trigger.

"We don't appreciate coloreds hiding the truth, pretending to be something they ain't," the man said softly as Henry Rogers seemed to rise in his saddle before falling dead, dangling from his shoulder harness connected to the pommel. He leaned but would not fall, suspended in an eerie pose until someone cut the strap and he fell.

"Kill them all," Lunstrum ordered. "We want no survivors to this mess." Screams and gunfire filled the air. Melanie covered her daughter but bullets took them both. Sabers struck and at the end only the dead lay as testimony to the horror. It was over as quickly as it began.

The news of the massacre reached them in Washington two days later. Stephen was the only survivor, hiding in a nearby root cellar until the remaining men of the White Camellias had ridden off. The marauders hadn't bothered to stay and look for others.

"Everyone is dead except Melanie and Rufus' young son, Stephen," Thaddeus cried. "All those people that we loved are dead. This is insanity. What could have happened?"

Matthew had brought the news home from the Capitol. A man in the office of a Louisiana Congressman, who he'd befriended, brought him the long dispatch. Sarah and Sheila had joined them as they stared at one another in complete disbelief.

"By the time the militia got there it was mid-morning. Everything had been burned to the ground. Two young black boys, sleeping near the stable, watched Melanie's brothers killed by a white, tall, one-armed rider. They ran to warn Rufus but they didn't get there on time. All they could do was watch. They weren't too clear on everything being said but they're pretty sure Melanie screamed out that Henry had colored blood in him after they'd already killed Rufus. Then everything went crazy. Later they found young Stephen hiding. I can only assume the riders were afraid to stay around any longer."

"My God! I've got to go there," Thaddeus cried out. "I'm going to wire General Longstreet to help me. He still has some influence."

It took nearly a week for Thaddeus to reach New Orleans and his friend's office.

"This massacre has the entire state in an uproar" Longstreet said, shaking his head.

"It's complete madness. One of the men killed was Colonel Alcibiades De Blanc, the founder and head of the White Camellia Society. Another was Henry Rogers, owner of Moss Grove, a large plantation north of Baton Rouge. There were a few other whites killed and a whole lot of blacks including your friend, Rufus Carmody, his wife Melanie, and everyone of her family except for a young son his father had sent into hiding when the violence began. Melanie was also several months pregnant with another child. What started as a raid to frighten blacks into subservience became a killing field."

"Henry Rogers was my natural father," Thaddeus said as he struggled with what he was being told. "He raped one of his young Moss Grove field slaves when he was in his teens and I popped out nine months later."

"Holy mother Jesus," Longstreet swore. Until now he had never made the connection.

"I am so sorry, Thaddeus. I knew you and Rufus were close and that you had ties to Moss Grove but I didn't know anything about your birth. There was so much that was evil about slavery and such mistreatment was one of them."

The two men sat silently, each in their own thoughts, each viewing the events from the lens of their own past.

"I assume that makes you the surviving owner of Moss Grove," James Longstreet said. "It could be a heavy responsibility."

"Henry had a son, Josiah, with his wife, Elizabeth. She was Amy's older sister but she died a few years ago. In her final minutes of life she confided to Amy that Henry's mother had black blood in her. That blood produced a colored daughter that Henry couldn't stomach. He sent the baby away and she later died in that Catholic orphan fire."

"I remember. So, when Melanie accused Henry of having black blood, she was telling the truth."

"Yes. I'm sure it tore Henry's insides apart. Anyway, Josiah is still young. He attends a boarding school in Baton Rouge. Sarah and I visited with him the last time I was in Baton Rouge. Moss Grove should be his."

"In that case it rightfully belongs to you both."

"I don't want it. I could never live there. I have a good life now in Washington. Before I return I hope you can help me organize ownership on behalf of Josiah."

As Thaddeus rode toward Baton Rouge he dreaded facing what he might find. Brenda, Amy's friend, was with him. She, too, was stunned by the loss and unwilling to allow Thaddeus to face these events by himself. There would be ghosts everywhere.

"Thaddeus, I have a letter for you from Amy. She enclosed it in a letter she sent to me. I didn't open yours but you should know it isn't good. I don't mean to heap more distressing news on you but I'm afraid it's unavoidable."

Thaddeus stopped the wagon and they climbed down, sitting on a fallen log near the side of the road. His hands shook as he tore open the envelope.

> *Dear Thaddeus,*
>
> *John is dead. It has taken more than a month for the Army to gather and identify what bodies they found. Of the seven hundred men killed, they were only able to find enough remains to identify less than two hundred. John was among them. Our Army has gone on an angry assault to hunt down and kill any Indian they find, even if those tribes had already been pacified. I am too drained to care. Everything John wanted for us is gone. I have carefully weighed Melanie's offer for Bess and I to return to Louisiana, but I worried that being close to you again was something that would not bode well for either of us. And, I adore Sarah. By now you will have a new baby to take care of and none of you needs the presence of your past returning.*
>
> *I will be leaving Fort Leavenworth in a few weeks. There are frequent wagon trains heading to California. Bess and I will join one of them. All the trains are protected by military escort so we should be quite safe. I have continued to look at the sky each night, knowing it will always connect us although our stars have not yet aligned.*
>
> *I will write everyone when I get settled but I needed to write this letter just to you. You are ever in my heart.*
>
> *Love,*
> *Amy*

Exhausted from its contents and overwhelmed by the cumulative emotion of the pain he felt, tears welled up and he sobbed. Brenda put his arm around him but there were no words that could ease the pain of what he was feeling. He handed the letter to Brenda.

"It's OK," he said. "You have been Amy's closest friend. I'm sure you know how we have always felt about one another. John is dead."

"I know. All the people we've known are dying from terrible violence."

she said, reading the letter, her pain for her friend increasing with every sentence.

"We need to help her. She's so alone. Thaddeus, think of something."

"I'll try but right now we need to deal with the tragedy ahead of us."

They rode silently the remainder of the trip. My dear God, he thought. I've lost my best friend and his wife. Now Amy lost her husband. So much damnable sorrow! How different might it all have been if we lived in a country that would have allowed us to love as we had wanted? He understood now that they would never see one another again. It made his entire being feel empty. Despite how much he loved Sarah and Noah, and he did, Amy had always been part of his very soul. Now, that, like so much else in his life, was closed and could only be remembered by risking even more emotional upheaval.

Before continuing on to Carmody house they decided to stop at the Freedman's Clinic and rest. First they made a brief stop at the Telegraph office and sent a wire to Matthew:

> *John Shipley dead. Stop! Amy on her way to California…Stop. Get word to her immediately to return to Baton Rouge…Stop. Henry dead. Rufus and Melanie's son, Stephen, alive.*
>
> *Thaddeus*

Brenda and Thaddeus rested only briefly at the Clinic before heading directly to the West Baton Rouge English & French Academy in search of Josiah. They met Mrs. Noresby and explained why they were there. She sat rapt, struck by the horrific nature of what she was being told. She had taken a special interest in this boy who was so alone, so forgotten. The boy hadn't made many friends nor had he received many visitors since he arrived. Instead he lavished all his attention on his dog, Whisperette, an odd name, but a substitute for the affections that would have otherwise gone unreturned.

Thaddeus rose as the boy entered and the two smiled at one another.

"Do you remember me, Josiah?" Thaddeus asked.

"Yes sir. You got me my dog. She isn't Whisper but she's good company. We also went for a walk when we were at Aunt Amy's wedding."

"That's right, Josiah. I'm a good friend of Aunt Amy and I knew your father. Would it be OK if you and I had a sort of man-to-man talk?"

The boy nodded seriously as Brenda and Sylvia Noresby made a quiet exit. Even at his age he could feel the gravity of the emotions that pervaded the room.

"I need to talk to you about something very sad. Do you think you're up to hearing some difficult adult news?"

"Yes sir. I think so," the boy said without any confidence in this voice.

"Your father was killed last week," Thaddeus said, sitting next to Josiah so that their eyes connected.

"Was it in a duel?" the young boy asked.

"No, why do you ask that?"

"My father had a duel with a man last year. It happened at Moss Grove and my father killed the man. After that he had a fight with Big George, our overseer, and killed him although Big George almost killed my father. I thought it might be something like that."

"No," Thaddeus said, searching for some way to make this easy. "I think it was a fight but I don't know the details."

"My father never came to visit me," he sighed, a tear drifting down his cheek. "I don't think my father loved me, not really. He promised he'd bring my dog, Whisper, but he never did. I think he changed when my mother died," Josiah said as random thoughts tried to bring meaning to what he was being told.

The two half-brothers sat silently side by side as each lost himself in thought.

"I'm sure your father loved you in his own way, Josiah. Sometimes it is hard for a man to know what to do with a child when he's lost his wife."

"Maybe," the young boy conceded. "I know my mother loved me. What happens to me now? Do I have to leave the school?"

"We're trying to get your Aunt Amy back to take care of you but until she returns you can stay in the school and I will let Mrs. Noresby know how to reach me if you need me for anything."

"Are we related, Thaddeus?" the boy asked with an insightfulness beyond his age.

"Yes. Yes, we are," he answered softly. "When you are a little older I'll explain everything."

They sat together a while longer. Thaddeus wondered whether the boy would ever have to confront the fact that he had a small amount of black blood coursing through his veins. The way things have gone that fact can tarnish his entire life. It ended up killing his father. He's too young to know the truth now, but someday…someday. Thaddeus tried to turn the conversation to what the boy was learning and whether he'd made any friends.

"Josiah," Mrs. Noresby said, when she and Brenda returned. "If you want to stay in my room for a short while, that would be fine."

"No, I'll be fine. I have my dog." He left them, shoulders bent as if he was bearing the weight of the world.

Thaddeus and Brenda continued on to Carmody House. It took them less than an hour. As their buggy pulled up they were stopped by a black militiaman, who insisted on them identifying themselves before allowing them entry.

A dozen blacks, most in uniform, milled around the area. The smell of ash and decayed bodies sickened their senses. One man was clearly in charge. He eyed the new arrivals uneasily. In all his years he had never confronted a massacre of such magnitude.

"My name is Captain Jefferson, Louisiana Militia, 4th Company. And you are?" he asked.

"My name is Thaddeus Williams. I was Rufus' friend and partner. We served in the Army together."

"Which Army?" Jefferson interrupted.

"Both of them!"

The comment elicited a wry knowing smile.

"This is a friend of mine and of those who died, Miss Brenda Summers. How could something this terrible happen?"

"I'm so sorry for your loss. It was a heinous atrocity and we are just beginning to learn the details. There were two witnesses hiding in the brush who survived. It seems they would normally just have burned everyone out but this man, Rufus, came out shooting once the fire was going. He killed two of the white riders so in retribution they killed him. With his last effort he killed the white bastard leading the raid, a Colonel de Blanc. Their young son is the only survivor of the raid on the house. The bastards came here after the attack on the stable and feed store. We don't know if were even aware the same family owned them both.

"Seems the man's wife knew one of the riders, a blonde man with one arm. She accused him of having colored blood in him. Then everyone who had a weapon started using it. Nearly twenty people dead for no sane reason!"

"Where is Stephen?" Thaddeus asked.

"He's with one of the womenfolk from the doll factory that got burned out."

"Hi, Stephen!" Thaddeus asked.

The young toddler was snuggled in the lap of one of the women Rose had trained to sew raggedy dolls.

"Uncle Thaddeus!" he cried as he rushed into familiar arms.

"They told me my mommy and daddy are gone and I won't see them again. Why would they go without me?"

"I'll explain it to you but not now. Just know you aren't alone. There are a lot of people who love you. We'll make certain you are taken care of."

"I was so scared. The fire! The guns! My father and grandma Marie telling me to run and hide."

"You're safe now...you're safe."

The funeral was simple, the sadness overpowering. Melanie, Rufus, and the others were laid to rest. Melanie's mother and her two brothers were buried nearby. Henry's body would be returned to Moss Grove for burial in the Roger's family plot.

Thaddeus sat by himself at the graveside after the service and wept openly. Brenda had held Stephen.

Rufus had been his brother, his uncle, and his surrogate father. They had fought together, walked the length of the country side by side and laughed. They'd seen the best the country had to offer and its worst. Rufus had so much life ahead of him that has been stolen. He and Melanie, her family and their unborn child, all taken from us.

The hole they leave in my heart, Thaddeus thought, will never be fully closed.

The telegram from Matthew reached Amy two days out of Fort Leavenworth. She blanched as the rider explained in further detail the news of the multiple killings that had occurred.

Stephen was still alive. He survived the massacre, thank God. What would happen now? Maybe it was time to acknowledge she was his mother. But what would that do to Thaddeus? She understood immediately that she and Bess couldn't continue on to California. She was happy to be heading home but she was filled with trepidation at the tragedy she knew awaited her. Whatever happened, at least she'd see Thaddeus again. Were there stars finally going to align? The ugly twists of fate had, perhaps, conspired to give them another chance.

Thaddeus and Brenda woke Stephen early and drove to the school to pick up Josiah. The young boy was still nervous and frightened. He clung to Thaddeus, his memories of losing his parents too fresh.

Together they all settled in rooms at the Freedman's Clinic until they figure out how to proceed. Once they learned that Amy and Bess would be returning everything became clearer.

"Thaddeus," Brenda said, as they readied the children for bed. "Have you ever taken a close look at Stephen?"

"I thought I had. He has a light complexion but so did Rufus and Melanie. They were mulatto."

"You both have a lot of the same features, the chin, and the forehead. He's also lighter than either of his parents. And, what color were their eyes?"

"I'm not sure but I think they were brown."

"I know Melanie's eyes were brown. She used to describe what she did to accent them with the right color makeup."

"OK, let's say that she and Rufus both had brown eyes."

"Stephen's aren't."

"Maybe his eye color came from his grandparents."

"Maybe!"

Neither felt comfortable carrying the subject further. The possibilities were understood, the ramifications dramatic.

It took nearly a month for Amy and her daughter to find an adequate military escort heading back east toward Baton Rouge that they could join and make the trip. Thaddeus wrote to both Matthew and Sarah explaining his need to stay until Amy arrived so that decisions regarding the future of Carmody and Williams as well as Moss Grove could be made. He tried to make the letters objective in their explanation but inside he knew that confronting Amy again would rekindle all the love he had worked so hard to contain.

With the help of Eli Fineman, James Longstreet and others, a crew was brought in to rebuild the stables and feed store. They were pleasantly surprised when Sven Diedenbach and his workers joined them.

"This was a terrible thing they did," Diedenbach said in his heavy accent. "You people were always fair and even brought me business when I started. Helping now is the least I can do."

Two of the men Rufus trained arranged to buy the business and pay for it from future profits. The doll business would be run by the women and directed by John Stokes. The name Carmody and Williams would remain. All the money would be set aside for Stephen. No one disagreed with that.

Amy's arrival should have been a happy reunion but there had been too much tragedy and when she and Thaddeus embraced it was to remember the terrible loss of so many loved ones in such a short time. Both their tears flowed freely. No words needed to be spoken.

Amy searched out Stephen first. He was excited to see her but his usual childhood resilience was missing.

"Aunt Amy, my parents are gone...Michelle is gone," Stephen cried. "Who is going to take care of me? Even Grandma Marie and our Uncles are gone. Everyone was killed by bad people."

Now that someone he knew was here, he let it all out and they both sobbed, their emotions no longer in control.

"We'll all be fine. I won't leave you. I lost your Uncle John. We've all lost someone we loved very much so we're going to need to hold one another very tightly for a long time. Now let's get Bess and go find Josiah. He lost someone also."

"Josiah, it is so nice to see you again," she said, as they greeted one another.

"Aunt Amy, Thaddeus said you'd come." In a surprise to them all, he rushed to her and put his arms around her neck as she knelt. All the emotion he had welled up inside suddenly burst and she could feel his small body shake. Stephen and Bess soon began crying with them, wrenching tears, so much grief.

"Shhh, it'll be alright. We'll all get through this together. None of you will be alone. I promise."

Thaddeus and Amy sat on the swings once the children had been put to bed.

"I didn't think you and I would ever see one another again," he said sadly.

"I wish it was under happier circumstances. I feel so raw, so naked of all emotion. I've lost so many loved ones these past months. All of the plans John and I had, everything Rufus and Melanie had built. And the children, what do we do with the children?"

"I don't have an answer. Sarah and Noah are waiting for me in Washington. At least they have Matthew and Sheila with them. You know, Moss Grove now belongs to Josiah. He's Henry's rightful heir."

Amy wanted desperately to explain that young Stephen was his son, their son, but the words stuck in her throat once he mentioned that his wife and child were waiting for him in Washington. What would he do if he knew? It would tear him apart. No, this was something she couldn't share, not now.

"I wonder if Moss Grove can ever be made happy again," Thaddeus said, shaking her from her reverie.

"It was happy before Henry took it over. It wasn't Moss Grove that lost its essence. Maybe the spirits of Jedidiah and Ruby are still strong enough to renew it."

The wagon moved slowly up the road toward Moss Grove. Henry was going home for his final journey. Ahead of them Thaddeus, Amy, Josiah, and Stephen sat in one buggy while Eli and Ruth Fineman followed in another joined by Bess and their two children.

Josiah and Stephen were clearly enjoying one another's company. Josiah delighted in playing the older brother showing the younger boy first one trick, then another, while Whisperette yipped along beside them.

They knew they were getting closer to Moss Grove as an older dark hound dog scampered up to them.

"Whisper, I'm back," Josiah laughed happily as he jumped from the slow moving buggy. They rolled in the dirt in a heap, the two dogs and the boy who loved them. Soon Stephen and Stuart Fineman joined them, three boys, legs tangled, laughing as the two dogs pounced happily over and around them. It wasn't necessary to introduce the two dogs to one another. They had an immediate kinship, licking Josiah's face, smelling one another and running to and fro, their tails wagging. Even in this time of tragedy, the adults were forced to smile.

The house staff came out and greeted Amy warmly. Chloe's smile was the broadest. She understood she was supposed to have been in charge but with no one around to direct everyone's chores, the entire staff moved slowly as if in a dream state. And, with the death of Big George, no one seemed to be supervising the field hands or overseeing the share croppers. There was going to be a great deal of work to do. Food supplies were running low and several families were preparing to leave Moss Grove. They had grown superstitious from so many people dying.

"Chloe, please let everyone know there will be a meeting on the back veranda tomorrow morning, and ask the kitchen staff to prepare extra food for everyone," Amy ordered.

With a new sense of direction, the staff began to move cheerfully through the house, preparing food and getting the rooms clean for the new arrivals. The young boys continued to play while the dogs scampered, tails wagging.

Thaddeus left Amy to get herself organized while he wandered the rooms in which he'd grown up. It was easy to remember his small room next to Jesse and Sarah and how angry they'd gotten at him for spending time with Amy. If they hadn't been so upset he imagined his life would have moved in a completely different direction. He wouldn't have run off. He would never have met Rufus, and along with Matthew, they would never have traveled the country.

"I'm sorry, Chloe. You and your staff are so busy, please just ignore me," he said as he wandered the kitchen and dining room. "There are just so many memories."

"We know who you are, Mr. Thaddeus. People here still talk about you. You the man that brought Massa' Henry back from the war when you was just a boy. You wander wherever you like."

As night descended and the stars came out, Thaddeus and Amy sat together on the veranda where tomorrow's meeting would be held. Ruth and Eli Fineman had taken control of all the children after dinner, gotten them bathed, and into bed. Everyone was exhausted. All the emotions surrounding the massacre and their return to Moss Grove had finally caught up with them.

The cicadas chirped, the only sound in the quiet evening. They could both recall the blissful memories they shared a lifetime ago.

"It feels so strange to be back here, doesn't it? Especially with Henry and Elizabeth gone," Thaddeus said.

"What am I going to do, Thaddeus?"

"You're all that Josiah has. You're his only blood kin. He belongs at Moss Grove. With John gone you and Bess could make a life for yourself here. You are also the obvious person to care for Stephen. They have no one else and Moss Grove is large enough to provide for all of you."

"It would be easier if you were here to help me but I know that isn't possible."

Thaddeus knew how easy it would be to stay. He could imagine the two of them, he and Amy, running this plantation that they both knew so well. He also knew it couldn't be. It was a dream…maybe it had always been a dream. Sarah and Noah were waiting for him. He loved them. He had responsibilities. No, the stars had not aligned but he knew in his heart that they were no less dim.

They sat quietly. A little while later Eli and Ruth Fineman joined them. The house was quiet, even the dogs rested quietly from a day of play. Together the four of them sipped drinks that Chloe had brought them. No one spoke.

"Amy, Ruth and I have been talking," Eli said, finally breaking the silence.

"I have little experience growing cotton but I have become quite skilled at selling it. If you would like us to stay here with you, until things are on a stable footing, we're happy to do so."

Amy smiled. "That would be such a relief. Not just to have you here but to have the children have one another, would be wonderful. Imagine, your Rachel and Stuart, Josiah, Stephen and Bess all being able to learn together…that would be so special. I accept your offer, and quickly, before either of you have a chance to change your mind."

It would be a new beginning for Moss Grove. The next day as the sharecroppers and house staff began to gather for a meeting, it was clear that each of them was nervous and curious to know what was to become of this plantation to which they had connected themselves.

"Thank you all for coming," Amy said in her loudest voice as she stood atop a small buggy that would enable her to see everyone and allow them to see her.

It was late morning and a brief funeral had been conducted interring Henry in the Rogers family crypt. Now nearly fifty people gathered around this woman with the green eyes and bright red hair, anxious to know whether they would need to stay or go. Thaddeus and the Finemans stood off to the side. This would be Amy's meeting.

"Mister Henry is dead along with several others who were my dearest friends. For those of you who don't know me or don't remember me, I am Amy Shipley. I am Elizabeth's sister, Mister Henry's wife, who died here. I spent a lot of my young years here as Amy Williams along with my parents during the war.

"The little blonde boy you see running around is Josiah. He is Henry and Elizabeth's son. He is now the owner of Moss Grove although if you told him that he'd be too young to understand.

"Moss Grove was always a good plantation, and everyone who lived here shared in the good years and shared in the bad ones. I want it to be that type of place again and I want your help to make it that way. If you'll stay, there will be a lot of work but we'll all share. No one will be cheated. Will you give me a chance?"

"What about all the money Massa' Henry say we owe to the commissary store?" one man asked.

"No one owes anything. We'll all start fresh."

"What about Big George's missus and little 'uns? Massa' Henry say they gotta leave."

"I'd love to have them stay. We're going to have some young children here who need schooling. We'll hire someone who'll teach all the children, black and white."

To that there were smiles and nods. They didn't know any plantations that were offering schooling to the children of share croppers.

"This is Eli Fineman, he's a good friend and he's going to help us. He and his wife, Ruth, and their two children, will also be living here. We need to find a good overseer and if any of you men think you can handle the job, please see one of us when we're through. Finally, if something isn't right I expect you to tell Mr. Fineman or me so we can try and fix it. Now, let's all eat, I'm famished."


"Did you tell him?" Ruth said obliquely, as they finished bathing the children.

"Tell him what?" Amy asked, nervously.

"That Stephen is his son," she said softly, not wanting any of the children to hear.

Amy turned pale.

"How did you know?" she sat on the bed as tears began to form.

"Eli and I have known from the beginning, Amy. We never said anything to anyone. We understood the reasons."

"Oh, Ruth, it's all such a conundrum. It happened one time when Thaddeus and I spent a few days with Rufus and Melanie."

"Amy, I knew you were pregnant and then you just disappeared for several months. There wasn't any other explanation. And look at the boy. If ever a child was a handsome combination of his parents, it is Stephen."

"I couldn't ask Thaddeus to give up the life he was building for himself, and Melanie knew a white girl couldn't raise a mixed child. They were so wonderful about it. They convinced me it was the only solution and, at least, I knew he'd get all the love in the world. Now things have changed again."

"Perhaps, but you have a similar situation with Josiah. Eli and I are with you. We love you and this way, here at Moss Grove, we can keep all the children together and, maybe, protect them from some of the hatred of the outside world."

That night they all shared dinner in the dining room served by Chloe and the staff. It would be their last evening together. Thaddeus would be leaving in the morning.

Eli and Ruth excused themselves early, not wanting to intrude on the feelings of these two people they admired. Thaddeus and Amy walked outside and instinctively headed toward their 'spot' under the tree by the river. It was a warm evening and the cicadas were harmonizing with the sounds of the river. Stars were beginning to appear against a blackening sky.

"I'll continue to look up at the night sky and see if our stars have aligned.

"And I'll do the same," Thaddeus responded, knowing that their hope of such an alignment had waned a long time ago. After that neither of them spoke. They just sat and held one another.

Thaddeus was back in Washington. It had taken the entire train ride to get his emotions into check and recognize the happiness of his life with Sarah and his young son, Noah. He was glad to be home. That evening after the children were put to bed, he sat with Sarah, Matthew and Sheila, trying to bring them up to date on the horrors surrounding the massacre that had taken Rufus, Melanie and her family. They talked about Moss Grove and Thaddeus struggled to avoid the questions in Sarah's searching eyes. That night he reassured her of his fidelity and love.

He went back to work the next day trying to get his head around the changes taking place.

"When we first left Louisiana to come to Washington, we had such high hopes," Thaddeus mused, as he stared into a glass of red wine that evening. He and Matthew were sitting in the small backyard of their Georgetown flats while the children were asleep and Sarah and Sheila were busy inside.

"Blacks were being elected to state offices; black-owned businesses were operating, and succeeding. And children, black and colored children, were finally being educated in decent schools."

"It may be the same across the entire south but it feels particularly bad when you hear about problems in your own state," Matthew added. "The election of P.B. Pinchback to Congress was overruled by the Democrats. He'd left politics to set up a black university in New Orleans.

"Louis Roundanez's New Orleans newspaper has been forced to stop publication and it was the state's only black newspaper. It was a combination of things. Whites were harassing his printing plant, breaking things and stopping deliveries. It was also a new desire of blacks, coloreds, and Creoles to read papers that appealed to more than the 'black experience'. He fought a good battle all these years that we've known him but it must have finally sapped his energy."

"Even our friend, Longstreet, who had been so vilely denounced as a scalawag, finally left New Orleans.

"Whites were furious that he had actually led black troops to quell disturbances in the city. He wrote me a letter telling me he has returned to his native Georgia where he hopes to spend the rest of his life in more peaceful solitude."

"Only Julius Freyhan is still there. He's now a success, producing sour mash whiskey and sporting a thick heavy brush mustache. But you know Julius. His family and his involvement in the city's small Jewish community are still his primary focus. I asked him if he was still eating 'traif' and he laughed. 'Of course', he told me."

"The racial problems in the country are becoming more severe," Matthew said. "Everyone I talk to in the halls of Congress is seeing the trend. All these recent decisions by the federal courts are continuing to embolden state governments to act as they choose and President Hayes is doing nothing to slow the trend. It isn't even clear that he cares.

"Remember the Civil Rights Act of 1875 we worked so hard to get passed?" Matthew continued. "From the time our friends proposed it in 1870; we worked our tails off cajoling whoever would listen.

"We were so thrilled when President Grant signed it. We'd finally have equal rights in all public places. Coloreds and Blacks would be able to serve on juries. It would be ingrained into the law. You and most of the others at Howard helped us. Most of the Republican Congressmen supported it although those segregationist Democrats from the south never did. Last week the Supreme Court said it was invalid and they nullified it."

"Why?" Thaddeus asked. "That was a good law. We needed that law."

"Remember, it isn't a Republican controlled court anymore. They decided the law protected social rather than political rights. They also said the 14th Amendment we were so happy with, only prohibits the states from depriving civil rights. It doesn't protect anyone against abuse by individuals. In other words, Louisiana can't abuse Blacks but every white man in the state can."

"That is unmitigated bull shit!" Thaddeus said angrily. "We helped fight a war. We've proven we deserve to be treated equally."

"At least Louisiana hasn't yet resorted to passing laws against blacks and coloreds as strict as states like Mississippi. They already have laws prohibiting marriage between whites and blacks. A man could go to prison for life," Matthew said.

They sat without speaking, knowing that had Thaddeus and Amy married, they could have been victimized by such a law.

"They've also passed laws prohibiting blacks from riding in white rail cars or being jurors or even voting. That's damn near a return to slavery."

"Except for the buying and selling part," Sheila said softly, reminding everyone that even with these new events, they'd all come a long way. She and Sarah had come outside but just smiled as their husbands railed at all the new injustices.

# Chapter Thirty-Four

Matthew finished his education and continued to work for the few black Congressmen still able to hold office. With increasing certainty none of these were elected from the south. A few of the northern states might still elect a Negro but garnering enough support to pass laws that would stem the increasing racial abuse within a state was impossible. The country had moved on to other priorities.

Rose, their daughter, had ceased being a toddler quite early, having discovered that she was a girl who adored clothes and makeup. She delighted her parents with her laughter as she dressed in her mother's clothes and jewelry.

Matthew and Sheila had their second child, a boy they both agreed they would name Rufus. The baby had his parent's dark skin but in his father's mind the child was the reincarnation of his close friend.

A year later, pregnant again, Sheila died from complications of child birth. The infant, a daughter, hovered between life and death for nearly two weeks before finally succumbing. Sheila and Matthew had decided that if the child was born a girl, to name her Tamara. In their mind it meant a hope for tomorrow. Matthew struggled with the loss. Sheila had brought such joy and balance to his life and now, she, too, was gone. He would have to be mother and father to both his children.

He tried to continue his work with the same intensity he'd always shown but the spirit and combativeness of his younger days were gone. He'd sit, every evening, reading to his children and holding them close. It was almost as if he worried he could lose them also.

Thaddeus and Sarah tried to shake him from his doldrums but to no avail.

"I'm going back to Louisiana," Matthew said to them one day. They were all in the park on a spring day, watching the children play. "I can't live like this. I've decided to return home. Sheila's parents, John and Penelope, are getting older. The doll business John and I had is struggling. I'll go back and try to salvage the business. Mostly, though, I want Rose and Rufus to be closer to their grandparents. I'll miss you both but when Sheila died, it drained every ambition in my soul. I'm tired, I'm despondent and I just want to be a parent for awhile."

The train pulled slowly out of the Baltimore station. Matthew had sold most of the furniture and household goods that Thaddeus and Sarah hadn't wanted. Anything he wanted to keep would have had to travel nearly one thousand miles by wagon and neither he nor the children seemed interested in such a tiresome journey. This way the children would be able to move around a little and sleep and the five day trip was certainly better than one which might take as much as two weeks.

The train snaked west slowly, crossing Virginia's Blue Mountains before moving past the Carolinas and into Alabama. They often stopped for a meal at the small railroad stations along the way. Everything was calm and the children were enjoying the adventure until they reached Mississippi. They passed into the state in the middle of the night and arrived in Hattiesburg for a breakfast stop and to allow the train enough time to pick up water and wood.

As they finished their meal and prepared to reboard the train they found all their belongings thrown onto the platform. Two angry looking white men were picking through their satchels.

"What are you men doing?" Matthew shouted as he hurried forward.

"This your stuff, nigger?" the bigger of the two man asked while the other continued, bent over, to search through the clothes.

"It's mine and my children's. What is it doing off the train? We have tickets all the way through to New Orleans."

"That's a car for white folks, nigger. You darker skin monkeys can ride two cars back. This is Mississippi. Blacks ain't allowed to sit with white folks in this state. Now pick up your shit and move to the back of the train before I put your ass in jail."

An elderly black woman came up to a nervous Rose and Rufus and took them by the hand. She could see that they were frightened watching the two angry looking men shouting at their father and they were both whimpering as they tried to hold back their tears.

Matthew reached down to grab his suitcases. As he shoved the clothes back in, the tall man hit him on the back of his head with the butt of a pistol.

"You show respect in this state, nigger. I don't know where you and your brats are coming from but here blacks don't grab things. Now get up."

Matthew raised himself on one knee, trying to clear his head. He stood slowly, aware that his children were watching. He faced the taller man.

"I'm the law in Hattiesburg, you hear. Now, you getting into the back of this train or am I taking you to jail?" he asked, spitting on Matthew's shoes.

Matthew hesitated. If he was alone he might have fought. If he backed off, however, what would his children think?

"I'll go to the back of the train," he said, mustering all the control he had, unwilling to leave his children untended. "Now, may I please have my satchel?"

"Give the nigger his clothes, Henry. He needs to take a short walk down the platform. You enjoy your ride, you hear!" he laughed.

Matthew grabbed his cases and followed the helpful woman back along the platform wondering if every white cracker that hated blacks was named Henry.

As they settled on the train the woman introduced herself.

"My name is Felicity Walters. I live in Houma, near New Orleans. I'm going home. I was visiting my mother. Here, let me tend to that bump where that Sheriff hit you."

As she cleaned the wound and removed the blood drying in his scalp, she said, "You obviously haven't been around these parts for awhile."

"Is Louisiana like this?" he asked, wincing at the pain in his head.

"Thank God, no, at least not yet. We need to pray that this sort of thing never comes to pass in our state," she said somberly.

"I worry that it will take a good deal more than prayer."

# Chapter Thirty-Five

Moss Grove once again achieved eminence among its parish neighbors. It was Eli Fineman's guidance and business acumen that was responsible for its resurgence. He quickly learned the most efficient and profitable way to grow cotton and other crops, including some sugar cane.

Twenty sharecropper families now worked the fields and while none of them earned much, the ugliness of their existence was gone. There was a new, larger church that was built for weekly Gospel meetings. During the week it was used as a school, complete with books, lessons, and a teacher. Josiah, Stephen, Bess, the Fineman children and the children of the share cropper families sat side by side without incident, immune to the conflicts of segregation in the greater world around them. When it was hot the children met outside under a tree where drinks and cookies were available.

A doctor visited them twice monthly. In between, Amy and Ruth were always available for any nursing that was needed. There were always cuts and scrapes to tend, and tears to wipe.

Never far from Amy's mind, however, was the knowledge that neither Stephen nor Josiah could permanently remain in Louisiana where someone might remember Henry and rekindle the bigotry that could destroy the boy's future.

Long after Amy arrived, she happened to notice some mail that had been sitting on the table, unopened. One of the letters was addressed to *'Henry Rogers – Important.'* She walked over to where Eli was sitting, working on the plantation's books.

"Can I interrupt you?" she asked. "You always seem to be adding or subtracting something."

He stopped, put down his pencil, and smiled.

"I think this plantation is like a finely made watch. If you wind a watch too tightly, the spring will break. If you don't wind it enough, it won't give you the right time. At Moss Grove, if we plant too much, we'll waste seed and time and we won't be able to harvest it all. If we plant too little, we won't get all the income that's possible. I just try to keep it in balance."

"Well, you're doing a wonderful job and I'm so grateful that you and Ruth are here. I don't think I'd ever have been able to manage. But I didn't come here to extend a compliment, however much deserved. Did you see this letter addressed to Henry?"

"Yes, but I didn't open it. It can't have anything to do with Moss Grove though. The attorney did a proper job of transferring the title to Josiah. Go ahead, open it."

"The letter is from the 1st National Bank in Chicago," she said as she unfolded the letter. "It seems they're concerned that there has been no activity on a rather large account in Henry's name. It goes on to say that this dormant account was uncovered during an annual audit and they are writing to make certain everything is still fine," she read.

"Do they say how much is in the account?"

"Am I reading this right?" she asked. "It says the balance is just over $40,000."

She handed the letter to Eli, who took the time to slowly reread the letter.

"That's what it says," Eli grinned. "It seems old Henry was hiding more than his parentage. I wonder how long he was also hiding money. The letter says the account is nearly thirty years old. That means it had would have originally been opened by Henry's father, Jedidiah."

"It might have been a hedge against the Confederacy," Amy mused. "My father lost everything when Rebel money became so much waste paper. My goodness, $40,000! It's like manna from heaven."

"I'll get the lawyer to transfer the account into Josiah's name with you as Trustee."

"Eli, the arrival of this letter solves a problem that has been plaguing me for quite a while. This money will allow me to leave Moss Grove and take the children to California. Moss Grove has become your home and you and Ruth deserve to own it outright. We both knew I'd have to leave eventually. This can't be where either Josiah or Stephen grows up. I just didn't know when it would be but I think finding this money is an omen telling me that now is the time."

Amy sat down, once again holding the letter in her lap. She retied the green satin bow in her hair, her hands trembling slightly as she considered the life-changing decisions she was contemplating. Her thoughts went to Thaddeus, as they often did. She missed him so but finally being able to raise their son at least allowed her to shower her love. She'd had two wonderful loves in her life and supposed that was more than most women are given. Eli's voice shook her from her reverie.

"Ruth and I have always understood your desire to protect Josiah's background, Amy," he said. "And we've always respected your secret regarding Stephen. We hoped that keeping Moss Grove isolated would postpone your need to make a decision for awhile. We've all been happy here and you've never made us feel anything but at home. Rachel and Stuart will definitely miss their playmates.

"I will be happy to pay you a fair price for Moss Grove and with this new found small treasure, you should have more than enough to provide you a comfortable living wherever you settle. Do either Thaddeus or Matthew know?"

"No. When Matthew was here with the children last year we didn't discuss it. I certainly want to see him and his children before I leave. I'm sure they'll come up from New Orleans to say goodbye. Thaddeus and I refrain from writing one another out of respect for his love for Sarah. My feelings for him have never changed and I sense that his haven't changed either. We don't need words on paper to reaffirm our love and I know that if I saw him I wouldn't have enough courage to leave."

Matthew arrived by buggy with his children. They no sooner arrived than the younger ones were off with their cousins, Stuart, Rachel and two dogs scampering away. Rose no longer played where she might get her dress dirty. It didn't trouble her at all to sit demurely with the adults.

Amy ran out to greet them. They hugged and kissed and made a huge fuss over the children.

"Matthew, dear Matthew, thank you for coming," Amy smiled.

"We're family, always have been."

"How're you managing?" she asked.

"I'm still not over losing Sheila. I don't think I ever will be. I knew she was the woman I wanted to spend my life with from the time I saw her working as a nurse at the children's center, her hat all askew. One smile was all I needed. Anyway, I think the kids are doing better. They get a lot of attention from Sheila's parents who are getting older but there is something about the relationship of grandparents and children that is very special. "

Amy waited until that evening after dinner to discuss her decision to leave Louisiana and Moss Grove. Chloe had prepared a special dinner of fresh catfish and greens. Since it was Friday, Ruth and Rachel lit the Sabbath candles and said a prayer over the bread before they ate.

"I need to leave here before Josiah is old enough to attend a school away from Moss Grove," Amy said as she and Matthew sat alone on a porch swing. "Someone will inevitably make the connection to Henry's blood line. When he's older, and somewhere where it might not be as volatile an issue, I'll explain it."

"Is it shame that he has some black blood in him?" Matthew asked, treading carefully on a sensitive subject.

"You know me better than that. In a different time and place I would have been proud to be your sister-in-law. But this is a child and this is a new south, filled with hate and fear. I don't want to expose him to that until he's old enough."

"And you never told Thaddeus that you and he have a son?

Amy stared, tears filling her eyes.

"How long have you known?

"I never really knew. I just sort of always suspected. It was Sheila, really, who noticed Stephen's resemblance to you both. We talked about it and decided that you had your reasons."

"I was afraid. Thaddeus had met Sarah. Melanie suggested they raise our son to keep him safe in a dangerous world. Then look what happened to them."

"Is there anything you'd like me to tell Thaddeus?"

"No," she sighed. "I just wish I could see and hold him one more time," she sobbed and crumbled into Matthew's arms.

# Chapter Thirty-Six

Sarah and Thaddeus had a second son, Robert. Noah now had a younger brother. Sarah had been forced to endure complete bed rest for the last half of her pregnancy. The birth, as the doctors feared, was a difficult one. The umbilical cord was twisted, and had she not been in a good hospital, it was likely neither she nor the baby would have survived. Robert was just over five pounds when he came into the world but more than half that weight had to be a set of lungs that produced cries that could be heard all the way to the Potomac River and beyond. It was an exhausting, but happy, reunion when they were all able to settle back into the safety and comfort of their own home.

Thaddeus graduated with a Law Degree from Howard University. Having to work and study had been a long and grueling process. But, oh, the sweet satisfaction when his name was called, and he stood, and walked across the stage to receive his diploma to the shouts of Noah and Sarah.

Finally, with school over, he could divide his time between raising money to support and expand Howard University and his work with Congress. Once she'd regained her health, Sarah resumed work part-time as a nurse and teacher and full-time as a wife and mother devoted to her family.

Thaddeus was particularly active as the election of 1880 neared. After Matthew had returned to Louisiana, Thaddeus began working with Senator Blanche Bruce, the single remaining black Senator. There was a small hope that the senator might be able to garner the nomination for Vice-President and no one worked harder to help achieve that goal than Thaddeus.

We can win some of the southern states if you put a Negro on the ballot, he and others pleaded. Most of Congress, however, was interested in who would succeed the President. Rutherford B. Hayes had announced early on that he would not stand for another term. He had been permanently tarnished by the rumors that he had bought the Presidency by agreeing to withdraw all Federal troops from the Southern states.

James Garfield, the affable Governor of Ohio, was nominated by the Republicans. For the first time in history, however, a Black, Senator Bruce, was successfully nominated by a major party and received seven votes. Success, Thaddeus was told, comes in small steps and hard work.

> *The November election of 1880 was close, a difference of only 2,000 votes nationally separated the candidates. Without exception every southern state and a number of western states voted solidly for the now united Democratic candidate, Civil War General Winfield Scott. The Republicans eked out a win in the electoral vote and with it, the Presidency.*
>
> *Four months later, the newly elected Garfield was shot by a mentally unbalanced man, crazed for not having received a political office he perceived to have earned. The nation was stunned by another Presidential assassination. It hadn't been that many years since Lincoln had been killed.*
>
> *Vice-President Chester Alan Arthur became President. A dapper dresser, bearing fashionable mutton-chop side burns and beard, his entire administration was spent trying to clean up political corruption within the Federal Government. Reconstruction efforts and racial problems were relegated to the past.*

Thaddeus spent most of Arthur's administration at Howard, teaching law to large classes of undergraduates. An increasing number of his graduating seniors were now able to qualify for government jobs, thanks, in part, to the new President's aggressive program of awarding civil service jobs on merit rather than patronage. These sorts of political plums had never been available to blacks.

Thaddeus was disappointed when the President announced he would not run for reelection. He had kept the fact that he had serious kidney disease hidden the entire time he was in office.

> *The Democrats returned to power dramatically in 1884. Grover*

*Cleveland, former New York Governor, succeeded in shifting that state away from the Republican column, and with that shift, and the consolidation in the south, the Democrats now controlled both the White House and the House of Representatives.*

Senator Bruce had aged. He no longer sought elective office but he remained influential with both Democrats and Republicans. This gave Thaddeus more free time to spend with his family. Caring for newborns and infants was now in the past. He and Sarah could finally enjoy pursuits that had never been available to a child growing up on a plantation.

Noah, his eldest son, was tall and light-complexioned like his father. The same intense blue eyes he had inherited had now been carried forward to his son's generation as well.

Robert was more like his mother, darker-skinned, wide dark eyes, and a little shorter. From infancy he demanded a pencil in his hand to draw pictures. His slight build made him look as if he was perpetually on the verge of a serious illness but, in fact, he never got sick.

The brothers were close and cared deeply for one another. Robert respected his brother's easy athletic talents without a hint of jealousy, while Noah encouraged his younger brother's artistic talents.

The family prospered and was held in high esteem while around them the Georgetown neighborhood, the Capitol, and the country continued to bleed varying degrees of racism.

Each southern state, now unfettered by Federal authorities, seemed to pass more egregious segregation legislation relating to schools, voting, elective office and personal relationships each year. Contracts kept sharecroppers attached with economic chains no less binding than those in place when slavery was legal.

Time after time Thaddeus wrote briefs on behalf of defendants seeking redress in Federal courts. He was rarely victorious. His blue eyes were still able to penetrate an adversary's weaker arguments in a court room but legal precedents were no longer on his side.

A telegram arrived signed from Rose and Rufus advising Thaddeus that their father, Matthew, had been killed in an accident. The police said that he had been elbowed off a sidewalk as he was on his way to a meeting and pushed into the path of an oncoming wagon. He was trapped under the wheel after being stepped on by the lead horse. Witnesses said he'd been pushed by an angry boisterous white man who was heard to shout that 'niggers' need to get out of the way of whites. No one was being held responsible.

Sarah couldn't make the trip so Thaddeus traveled to New Orleans accompanied by his son, Noah. The funeral had already been held by the time they'd arrived. New Orleans summer heat and humidity made it necessary to inter bodies quickly. Matthew and Sheila's children, now grown, met them at the train and accompanied their uncle to the cemetery.

He asked them how much they knew about the early years when he and Matthew were growing up at Moss Grove.

"Quite a bit," Rufus said. "Dad would make us laugh telling us stories about both of you and Uncle Rufus and even Aunt Amy."

"We especially liked the story about him wetting his pants in front of you and Aunt Amy. Somehow it was always difficult to imagine our grown father, a banker and a politician, wetting his pants," Rose laughed.

The years melted as they chatted. He was glad that Noah had come along to get to know his cousins. It had been way too long since they'd been together. It was clear to Thaddeus that Sheila and Matthew's children were growing up with the same drive and intelligence as their parents. He definitely wanted them to get to know his two sons before too much more time passed.

Thaddeus knew that Amy had been gone nearly two years already as he and Noah rode out to Moss Grove. It was his first trip back in decades and he had no idea what to expect. He knew the Finemans now owned and operated the plantation and that he'd be welcome.

It was more than a welcome. The Finemans had traveled to New Orleans for Matthew's funeral and had left instructions with Rose that Uncle Thaddeus was not allowed to return to Washington without coming to Moss Grove.

As he rode up the long plantation entrance, oak trees, even taller now, guided and shaded his path. He sensed the calm and beauty of his earliest home. Flowers bloomed and the share cropper cabins were larger and better kept than the old slave cabins. It was as he remembered it in its better days.

"Thaddeus, get down from that horse," Eli Fineman smiled, rushing to greet his friend. "And this must be Noah. Hi, Noah," Eli said, extending his hand.

"Mr. Fineman is a very old friend, Noah. He and his wife Ruth now own Moss Grove and you'll meet her along with their two children, Rachel and Stuart. They must be quite grown up by now," he said turning back to a smiling Eli.

"I see the blue eyes have carried over to another generation."

It was a warm visit. None of the house staff Thaddeus remembered as a young boy were still there and it was melancholy to visit the rooms he'd shared with Daddy Jesse and Mama Sarah. So much to remember, so long ago. Eli and Ruth gave him time to himself and he walked the paths and thought of Mama Rose, Massa' Jed, and Miss Ruby.

"It's almost eerie," he admitted as he joined his hosts on the veranda. "There are so many ghosts walking these hallways. Every turn brings forth another memory. It's a lot to confront at this point in my life."

"You haven't asked about Amy," Ruth said softly.

"I've been afraid to," he said.

"She left a letter for you. She wrote it just before she and the children left for San Francisco. I was told that I was to put it away for you if you ever returned here. It was not to be mailed. He took it and held it tenderly before opening it.

*Dear Thaddeus,*

*I'm writing this, not knowing if you will ever read it. Josiah, Bess, Stephen and I will be leaving for California in a few days and I will be leaving behind so many memories of the tumultuous life I've led. I just had to tell you one more time that what I will be taking with me is our love. It has never stopped burning inside me and each night I would look up at our night sky to see if somehow our stars had aligned. We shall likely never see one another again but it will never keep me from loving you forever and always.*

*Your Amy*

His eyes burned as he folded the letter and put it in his pocket.

Thaddeus returned to Washington and the life he had built for himself. He kept promising that he and the family would take a trip back to visit Matthew's children and show them Moss Grove but he didn't get back that year, or the next, or the one after that. Somewhere along the line there was another class to teach or an event the boys couldn't miss.

He considered retiring, but didn't. Then his beloved Sarah died of pneumonia and it made him all too aware of his own mortality. Her death opened a huge chasm in his life. He thought about traveling all the way to California and finally seeing Amy but the trip and the explanation to his sons that he had loved another woman at the same time he loved their mother was something he had no idea how to do. It would have to remain unspoken and in the past.

The election of 1888 came and went. Thaddeus was still teaching a few law classes but he had retired from political activism. It was another strange election. President Cleveland won the popular vote but lost the Presidency to Republican Benjamin Harrison. Thaddeus knew that it would make little difference these days whether a Republican or Democrat sat in the White House. As long as the Southern states wielded such a large bloc of votes, racism would not be dealt with at the Federal level. The country had moved on.

The following spring he received a long letter from Eli Fineman. He hadn't spoken to Eli since his visit following Matthew's funeral. They had exchanged a few letters but the most recent had been more than a year ago. He found his hands shaking as he sat and slit open the envelope.

*Dear Thaddeus,*

*It is with a terrible sadness that I write this letter. Amy is dead. Our Amy is gone. I received a letter a month ago from her daughter, Bess. It seems there was an outbreak of Smallpox in San Francisco and the doctor believes she contracted it while nursing at the local hospital. Before she died she told her daughter that she wanted to be buried at Moss Grove under a particular magnolia tree near the river where she'd had her happiest memories. She described the tree as if she were standing in front of it. Bess, Stephen, and Josiah are due here with the body sometime in the next two weeks and I thought you would want to know.*

*With deepest regrets,*
*Eli Fineman*

Thaddeus sat, almost catatonic, for an unknowing amount of time. The room got darker as night arrived, but he remained, unable to will his body to move, his mind tracing their times together and what might have been.

"Are you alright, father?" Robert asked, entering the dark room. "May I light some candles?"

"Of course! I forgot what time it is. Is it late?"

"Yes. I was out with friends and I think I hear Noah just returning as well."

As his older son entered the room, Thaddeus said, "We are leaving in the morning for Baton Rouge, the three of us. Aunt Amy has died and we need to get to Moss Grove as quickly as possible."

They departed on the morning train and while the three of them traveled together Thaddeus was with them but he was alone. He was silent and withdrawn even as they shared their meals.


"I'm so glad you're here, Thaddeus. It has been far too many years. You must be Noah and Robert. My name is Eli Fineman and this is my wife, Ruth. I wish we could have all met under happier circumstances. Rachel and Stuart have been away at school but they will be back tomorrow in time for the service."

He saw Bess first. It was impossible to miss the statuesque young red haired woman she'd become. She didn't have her mother's green eyes but she had tied her long hair with the same style her mother had used decades earlier. Even the freckles danced on high cheek bones.

"Uncle Thaddeus. I wouldn't have recognized you except for the wonderful stories my mother used to tell me." Her arms wrapped themselves around him. He closed his eyes and imagined they were Amy's arms embracing him.

Josiah and Stephen stood side by side smiling at Bess' display of affection.

Josiah had grown to his full height. He wore his blond hair short. His blue eyes smiled as he shook the hand of his half-brother. Thaddeus could feel Henry's presence in the man, but none of the evil or arrogance.

"Josiah, that's a powerful grip. You look good. I am sorry it has taken so long to reconnect."

"You were there for me when I needed support, Thaddeus. I was blessed to have both you and Aunt Amy in my life. Do you remember Stephen?"

"Not as a young man. You were quite young the last time we saw one another."

Each of the children, now grown, had heard the stories of how close their fathers were and it was easy for them to share a bond forged by their parent's love for one another.

Stephen waited until Thaddeus was alone. He was sitting in the library, a single candle lighting the room, deep in thought.

"I hope I'm not disturbing you."

"Stephen, no, please join me."

The two of them sat quietly for a long while.

"You probably don't remember much about your parents. They were wonderful people and your father was my closest friend."

"Yes, my mother told me everything before she died."

A look of confusion crossed Thaddeus' face.

"It's true," Stephen paused, uncertain how to continue. "Amy was my mother and you are my father. You were never told and I didn't know until a few years ago."

Thaddeus stared, looking at Stephen differently, unable to hold back his tears.

"She said she didn't want your life burdened with raising a mixed child when you had found a new love and a new life. The Carmody's agreed to raise me as their own. Then they were killed and it gave my mother a new opportunity to raise me along with Bess and Josiah."

"Did it upset you to know you had mixed parentage?"

"At first it did. I grew up in a white world. Even in San Francisco that meant extra privilege. Then I was told that Josiah had been told about his situation two years earlier. We were able to deal with it together."

"We still think of ourselves as white but we do what we can to bring more tolerance into the world. And, we both realize that before we marry that we'll have the problem of explaining the uncertainty of having children. I hope that explanation doesn't upset you. I wish you'd been able to be there more when I was growing up."

Father and son embraced, their mutual love for Amy connecting them.

The next day the service was held. Reverend Dinsmore had died several years earlier but his son, Jesse, had followed his father into the ministry and had traveled with his children to perform the ceremony. Brenda, now married, with her family, was also there. Some of the staff from the

Freedman's Medical Clinic and School had come and brought Sylvia Noresby with them. She and Josiah hadn't seen one another in years and their reunion of smiles and tears typified the sadness of the day. There was so much emotion. Amy had touched them all.

It was late in the day when they all gathered near the water's edge for Amy's final burial. Thaddeus had no difficulty remembering why she had chosen it. It was where they'd first met and she'd slid into the water, laughing at her own misfortune, when Henry and the others arrived. I think they'd both known then that they would love one another forever.

With the end of the ceremony everyone drifted back to the house.

"C'mon father, let's go back to the house," Noah said, touching Thaddeus' arm gently.

"I'll be along shortly. I want to remain here for awhile."

Thaddeus sat down under the tree where he'd rested nearly fifty years earlier after doing his morning chores. He remembered how Amy looked, a tomboy with freckles, and what she said. The moon rose over the river and sent its reflection onto her small headstone.

In the morning he was still there, his head tilted slightly, as if he was asleep. He had passed quietly during the night; next to the woman he'd loved so deeply his entire life. A love they hadn't been permitted to share. Perhaps where they'd both now gone to, they would be able to share what this lifetime hadn't permitted. Perhaps their stars were finally aligned.

# Historical Note

This is a work of fiction embedded in historic fact. Many of the characters in the book lived and had a significant role in American history. Neither Thaddeus, Amy, Henry, nor Moss Grove existed, but the characters they portrayed were spread across the Confederate landscape.

The battles at Fort Jackson, Port Hudson, and Vicksburg, framed the Civil War in and around Louisiana. Many slaves chose to fight, some for the Confederacy, others for the Union forces. The rise and fall of the price of cotton often controlled both the stability of employment and the degree of racial tolerance as well.

Readers will recognize Stephen A. Douglas, an Illinois Senator, famous for the Lincoln-Douglas debates. General James Longstreet and General Philip Sheridan were larger than life Civil War participants. Other characters and groups were also real and actively engaged in the good and evil of Reconstruction. These included Louis Roundanez, P.B. Pinchback, Colonel Alcibiedes de Blanc and his White Camellias. Senator Blanch Bruce, Congressman Charles Nash and Howard University's Edward Smith were all leading black post-Civil War statesmen.

The election of Rutherford B. Hayes as a result of the Compromise of 1877 is a tragic, but well-documented, event of American history. It reversed the Negro's economic and social progress of the previous decade and gave rise to a century of civil-rights abuses.

# About the Author

Carole Eglash-Kosoff lives and writes in Valley Village, California. She graduated from UCLA and spent her career in business, teaching, and traveling. She has visited more than seventy countries. An avid student of history, she researched the decades preceding and following the Civil War for nearly two years, including time in Louisiana, the setting for When Stars Align. It is a story of bi-racial love set against war, reconstruction, and racism. Most of all it is a story of hope.

This is her second book. In 2006, following the death of her husband, she volunteered to teach in South Africa. Her first book, **The Human Spirit – Apartheid's Unheralded Heroes,** relates the stories of an amazing array of men and women she worked with, people who have devoted their lives during the worst years of apartheid to help the children, the elderly, and the disabled of the townships. These people cared when no one else did and their efforts continue to this day.

Her third book, Winds of Change, is due to be released Summer 2011 and follows the characters of When Stars Align into the decades that closed out one century and led us into the next. These decades saw the advent of the automobile, the airplane, the telephone, electric lights and movies. They also saw the bloodshed of Spanish-American War and World War I.

# Acknowledgments

I am fortunate to have a wonderful cadre of professionals and friends who have taken the time to read and comment on this book. I want to thank Maureen Bacon, New York Editor, and Robert Thixton of Pinder-Lee Literary Agency, my agent, for his efforts and encouragement. My special thanks goes to Barbara Kosoff for her cover design, Jon Jackson  for his computer magic and Barbara Arsenault, Arleen Tisherman, Lauren Silinsky and Victoria Dahan for their keen eye in reviewing the manuscript.

*Carole Eglash-Kosoff*
*ceglash@aol.com*
*www.whenstarsalign-thebook.com*

# Winds of Change

*Follow the characters you've come to know in* **When Stars Align** *in the sequel,* **Winds of Change**, *to be released Summer 2011.*

*Read on for a preview*

*The Civil War had ended and 'the war to end all wars,' World War I, would not be fought for another half-century. A dark ages in American history, rarely studied in schools, seemed to exist.*

*In fact, it was a time of great changes in America. It was the time of Andrew Carnegie, John D. Rockefeller, William Randolph Hearst, Thomas Edison and the Wright Brothers. It was the time of Emily Dickenson, Scott Joplin and nickelodeons. It was the time of one of the worst economic depressions in the country's history.*

*But, in shame that would not be recognized for a century, thousands of Blacks were beaten or lynched without trials and the states that had formed the old Confederacy successfully deprived Negros of their civil rights with Jim Crow laws, Ku Klux Klan raids and facilities that were always separate but never equal.*

# Prologue

There is a dance that accompanies the rhythm of our lives. It has a logic...a pattern...a beat. Different sections of the orchestra blending into a single melody that defines who we are. I'm a man; you're a woman. I'm white. I'm tall. I'm a Christian. And then...wait a minute. It seems I'm not white. I have some Negro blood coursing through my veins that I'd never known about. The beat of the music suddenly changes as one section, maybe the woodwinds, puts their instruments away. The new rhythm is discordant...a rhythm with which I'm unfamiliar. It's a different tune, a genre I don't know how to play. I've lost the beat. The other orchestra members are staring at me in a different way.

I'm not sure what it all means. This isn't the South. It's already 1883. Slavery's been gone for nearly twenty years and the country has moved forward. I had a baby sister who had been born colored. I'd never known and it's interesting but it happened too long ago for me to feel sad. She died, my parents are both dead, and I'm still me. But that's the problem. In my head I suddenly feel like a different me.

My name is Josiah Rogers. My father and two generations before him grew cotton and got quite wealthy off the back-breaking work of the slaves they owned. Apparently my grandmother, my father's mother, had a black parent and no one knew it until a sister of mine who I'd never been told about was born chocolate brown. Amy, my aunt, and the woman who raised me after my parents died, understood that I could spawn such a child and I deserved to know that I had black blood in me. I had so many questions that evening she told me and yet there was nothing I could ask. I kissed her on the cheek, grabbed my jacket and my trumpet, and walked out of the apartment. Nothing was very clear those next hours. I remember sitting on the wharf and watching the last of the sun fall into the Pacific and a few remaining fishing boats pull into San Francisco's harbor. I remember walking through a cloak of evening fog, seeing buildings and people come into view like unearthly spirits and vanish again. I found an array of tiny North Beach bars, picked one at random and took a seat with a few tired musicians still blowing their horns. I pulled out my trumpet. I have no idea what I played or where I was.

We were a family of four. Amy held us together. Her daughter, Bess, was a few years younger than me. She had her mother's beautiful red hair and a face full of freckles set atop two deep dimples. Bess' father had been a career Union Army officer until he was killed in some battle with rebellious Indians. She had her father's height and gentle nature, which was good because Amy was definitely not a laid back soul.

Last was Stephen, my sort-of brother. He was the son of Amy's closest friends, the Carmodys, from when she lived near Baton Rouge. They had been slaughtered in the same racial riot that killed my father. He and I are the same age. Stephen is colored…really light-skinned, handsome, with blue-green eyes that always sparkled, but definitely colored. Girls, white and black, hover around him like lemmings. His color never made any difference to us but he occasionally felt the sting of some ignorant bigot and I know their remarks hurt him. He and Bess were in love. We all knew it. Amy knew it as well and while she never spoke against it, it was clear that their relationship made her very nervous. She did everything reasonable, and sometimes unreasonable, to keep them apart. Her efforts only succeeded in bringing them closer together. Their young raging hormones had not only connected, they had intertwined.

We received a phone call from San Francisco General, the hospital where Amy worked as a nurse. She was dead. She had caught an infection from one of her patients and before anyone even knew she was ill, she was gone.
Our anchor, the glue that held us together, had died.

## Also by Carole Eglash-Kosoff:

### THE HUMAN SPIRIT – Apartheid's Unheralded Heroes

Apartheid in South Africa has now been gone more than fifteen years but the heroes of their struggle to achieve a Black majority-run democracy are still being revealed. Some individuals toiled publicly, but most worked tirelessly in the shadows to improve the welfare of the Black and Coloured populations that had been so neglected. Nelson Mandela was still in prison; clean water and sanitation barely existed; AIDS was beginning to orphan an entire generation.

Meanwhile a white, Jewish, middle class woman, joined with Tutu, Millie, Ivy, Zora and other concerned Black women, respectfully called Mamas, to help those most in need, often being beaten and arrested by white security police.

This book tells the story of these women and others who have spent their adult lives making South Africa a better place for those who were the country's most disadvantaged.

Reader Comments about The Human Spirit:

The more I read, the more I enjoyed it. Helen Lieberman is truly a credit to humanity--if the world had more like her, what a wonderful world it would be! I am now looking forward to reading about the Hayes-Tilden times. Merci pour tout.

Dennis Hill, attorney, Encino, California

Dearest Friend...came home last night after a trying trip to Cape Town and to my surprise I saw a package on our dining room table ...from the USA and hastily I opened and WOW!!!!! your book and the cherry on the top is that I am featured in your book ....I am stunned and have no words to express my appreciation and gratitude towards you ...i started early morning to read and I am really fascinated by your amazing work... you have outdone yourself and did an absolute great work...i enjoy the book tremendously this far and cannot wait to start read and learn about this amazing people you write about. Thabiso is in Heaven and cannot stop talking about your magnificent writing skill and great humanitarian works…

From your St. Helena Bay Family
Johan and Team

More information is available on the website:
www.thehumanspirit-thebook.com